EMERALD NIGHTS

VIRGINIA BROWN

ZEBRA BOOKS
KENSINGTON PUBLISHING CORP.

Dedicated to my sister, Brenda Kay Albright.
Your laughter and love have made our lives brighter.

ZEBRA BOOKS

are published by

Kensington Publishing Corp.
475 Park Avenue South
New York, NY 10016

First printing: August, 1991

Printed in the United States of America

The shining splendor of our Zebra Lovegram logo on the cover of this book reflects the glittering excellence of the story inside. Look for the Zebra Lovegram whenever you buy a historical romance. It's a trademark that guarantees the very best in quality and reading entertainment.

A BOLD BEGINNING

When Bethany sank to the worn seat of the stone bench, she suddenly realized she wasn't alone, and turned with a muffled gasp.

Trace Taylor leaned against a wall, and when he saw she had noticed him, gave a lazy laugh. "Slumming, princess?"

She stiffened. "I don't know what you mean."

"Out here in the night all alone, with ancient gods and dangers. And dressed—or maybe I should say *un*-dressed—like a virgin sacrifice."

"Really, Mr. Taylor!" she began with a gasp of outrage, and he laughed softly, huskily.

He stepped closer to her, and she could almost feel the heat from his body.

"Ah, but you never know. Peru is a land of surprises. Could be one nearby, then what would you do?"

"Mr. Taylor . . ."

"Trace." His dark head lowered as he drew her closely to him. Bethany felt the heated thrumming of her heart, the surge of her pulses, and then he kissed her, his mouth warm and firm . . .

Chapter One

San Diego, California—October 1889

"Bethany!" Professor Horatio T. Brasfield turned with an excited expression, and called again. "Bethany! Come here—splendid news!" His hands trembled, and his thin face was creased into furrows of delight as his daughter appeared in the doorway of his study. She paused, surveying the litter of manuscripts and thick books on her father's desk, and shook her head with wry bemusement.

"You're quite untidy, you know," Bethany observed as she gingerly entered the book-lined room and her skirt caught on a jumble of artifacts. Grumbling, "How can you find anything in all this clutter?" she disentangled the folds of material from a barbed spearpoint adorned with ratty feathers, then stepped cautiously around a grimacing statue of a South American fertility god.

"I have a method," Brasfield replied vaguely, and turned to lift the crackling folds of a thick bark-page book arranged in accordion pleats.

A fond smile curved Bethany's mouth as she approached her father without further mishap, and her heavy-lashed violet eyes deepened with affection.

Rimless spectacles balanced precariously on the tip of Brasfield's nose, and his blue eyes were sparkling with glee as he tapped a forefinger on the pleated pages on his desk. Reaching out, Bethany smoothed back the thinning brown hair that straggled onto his forehead. "Papa, you really must take better care of yourself," she scolded, but there was no real censure in her tone. "You've been poring over those manuscripts for weeks, not getting enough to eat, or enough rest, and your eyes—you must rest them before . . ."

Waving an impatient hand, Brasfield cut off her rambling scold. "None of that matters! Look here at these figures in this ancient Spanish manuscript. Do you see?"

Peering over his shoulder, Bethany gazed at the colorful rows of figures postured in various poses. The professor had painstakingly removed centuries of grime to reveal bright colors beneath the layers of dirt, and she could barely make out what appeared to be a man in a feathered headdress holding a shield in one hand and arrows in another.

"Do you think . . ."

Brasfield interrupted excitedly, "I *know!* My interpretation *must* be correct! Bethany, I believe that there truly is a lost city in Peru—the legendary Vilcapampa where the Inca warlords fled from the Spanish conquistadores!" He lifted the fragile bark pages almost reverently. "If my deductions are accurate, this indicates that the last refuge of Manco Inca—a powerful ruler—is in the ancient province of Vilcabamba, just northwest of the city of Cuzco in Peru."

Bethany's delicate brows arched in faint surprise. "But I thought an expedition could find no trace of such a city. Didn't the university send out men with native guides a few years ago, and those fortunate enough to return reported no finds?"

"True, but they didn't allow *me* to spearhead the expedition, either," Brasfield said with grim firmness. "I informed Arthur Morton of his mistake but, of course, as head of the university, he was not amenable to my comments as to his ineptitude."

Bethany's voice was dry. "I should think not. Papa, you must practice tact on occasion if you expect to receive financial support from the university."

"I don't need them now." Brasfield lifted the thin bark pages from his desk. "Bentworth has enlisted the aid of a guide for me, and is providing the funds for an expedition. Private funds are much more lenient than those entrusted by the university."

A slight frown puckered Bethany's clear brow, and her small, straight nose wrinkled with distaste. "Spencer Bentworth? Mr. Morton claims he is unscrupulous when it comes to the acquisition of artifacts. Dare you risk your spotless reputation with a man such as he?"

"There's a lot more at risk than a mere reputation, dear child," Brasfield murmured, sliding his rimless spectacles back up his nose and peering closely at the scroll. "History is to be made, and I intend for my name to be inscribed as the man responsible for bringing back to light the magnificence of the Incas! Yes, the discovery of the lost city of Vilcapampa will ensure my place in the annals of history—here, read Bentworth's letter and you will understand."

"Papa," Bethany began, but her father was bent over his desk again, absorbed in the unraveling of the scroll's mysteries. Sighing, she took the crumpled sheet of paper he'd shoved in her direction, smoothed out the creases, and read Bentworth's terse message. Her father was right. Bentworth unreservedly granted him the funds for an expedition, and had even provided the name of a guide. Trace Taylor was said to have stumbled across the ruins of an ancient city on one of his forays into the jungles of Peru, and he now resided in the city of Lima. Bethany frowned. Did her father really intend to pursue this? It seemed unlikely that he would be able to realize his dream, but then, he had been studying the Incan civilization for as long as she could remember.

Another sigh slipped from between her lips, and Bethany replaced the letter on her father's desk, smiled slightly when he didn't even notice her, then left the study. She closed the door behind her, and returned to the small tiled veranda where she had been doing research of her own.

A stack of books stood beside the lounge on which she had been reclining, and she retrieved the top volume as she sank back onto the cushions. Somehow, though, her attention could not be trained on the words she had found interesting before her father's excited call. Travel to Peru? An extended exploration of dense jungles and mountainous terrain? Horatio T. Brasfield was not physically up to it, she feared. After all, her father was in his late fifties, and was more accustomed to poring over illegible tablets brought back by the more intrepid than he was actually doing the field work himself.

Oh, it *wasn't* that he hadn't wanted to go out into the field; on the contrary, he had pleaded with university officials for many years to allow him to do so. No, it was his erratic health that held him back, and Bethany feared that his determination to do so now might cause him harm.

"Foolish old goat," she murmured fondly. Her violet eyes softened, and she pushed back an errant strand of soft brown hair from her forehead. Sometimes she felt more like a caretaker than a daughter. After his wife's death ten years before, Professor

Brasfield was prone to forget about food or time when he was working, and if she didn't take him a tray of nourishing food, or insist that he rest, he might have perished from starvation long ago. Bethany was the only person he would allow to bully him into resting for any length of time, and knowing this, she decided that if her father was so determined to follow his dream of discovering the lost city of the Incas, she would have to go with him.

Smoothing folds of material over her knees, Bethany closed the book she had been reading on great artists, and gazed across the veranda at the slopes leading seaward. Their house was small—as befitted a professor whose concerns lay more with scholarly pursuits than fame and fortune—perched on a California hillside overlooking the hills and ocean. Seawinds brushed over Bethany, lifting her hair, ruffling the lacy collar of her blouse. It was autumn, and the air was brisk.

Stretching luxuriously, Bethany tried not to think of anything, no worries of past, present, or future, nothing but an idle enjoyment of the moment. She closed her eyes against the bright press of sunlight, breathed deeply of the rich fragrance of fall flowers on the hills, felt the silken touch of the wind across her bare arms and face. It was almost as comforting as a caress, she thought before she could stop herself, then her eyes snapped open and she sat upright.

There was no point in even contemplating such things. She'd had enough of that, hadn't she? After all, Stephen had proven to her how faithless a man's touch could be, how utterly casual and deceitful. And Stephen was gone now, had never really been hers in the first place. No, it was not meant for her to love. Her lot in life was to assist her father, to delve into history and leave lasting monuments of their work.

Why else would she have willingly given up what one professor at the university had called her "exquisite talent with a paintbrush and chalks" to help her father? After all, what was her small amount of talent compared to the mark her father would leave on history? And he'd always said she was the only assistant he'd ever had who possessed such a light touch with ancient artifacts. She could clean dirt-encrusted pottery without leaving so much as a mark on them, while others often shattered fragile pieces.

Sighing, Bethany tried not to recall how desperately she had once wanted to become an artist. That had passed, of course, with time. Now she was content being her father's assistant. And he depended upon her to get things done, take care of matters that he could not do when he was so involved in such time-consuming research and study. All his colleagues said that she was an excellent, capable worker, and how lucky Brasfield was to have her!

Bethany's delicate brows knit into a faint frown, but her lips were thinned into a determined line. Whatever was she doing relaxing on the veranda when there was so much to do? So many arrangements to make—passage on a steamer to Peru, supplies for an extended expedition, bearers to carry the supplies, and, of course, a guide. What was his name? Taylor. Yes, that was it, Trace Taylor. He'd better be good, Bethany thought firmly, and rose from the comfortable lounge to begin preparations for a wonderful adventure.

Chapter Two

Lima, Peru—October 1889

"Get up!" There was a fierce pounding on the door, and the words filtered through the solid oak again. "Get up! I have to talk to you!"

Inside the cluttered office that doubled as a lodging, a man and woman were entwined on a narrow bed, both naked. The man recognized the voice at the door, but pulled a fat pillow over his head and swore softly. It sounded as if all the mission bells were ringing at once, and every time the pounding on the door resumed, he muttered a more colorful phrase than the last. Noise reverberated inside his skull, bounced back and forth with a boom reminiscent of thunder. Just when it seemed as if it would never stop, at last came a sweet, blessed silence, and he closed red-rimmed, swollen lids and smiled.

His pleasure was short-lived. The thunder was replaced by an earthquake; actually, he was being shaken by his shoulder, and reacted without thinking.

Sitting up and reaching at the same time, he faced his tormentor with a lethal weapon in his hand, a .45 pistol pointed with a remarkably steady grip considering his badly inebriated state.

Gil Fortune took an involuntary step backward, his fair hair falling into his eyes as he moved quickly. All the blood drained from his face to leave it ashen. "So, Taylor, you've taken to savagery as well as drink?" he managed to say in a shaky voice. His gaze flicked to the woman, who sat up with a quick start of fear and muffled cry.

Trace Taylor glared at him with bleary eyes, then put the pistol down on the bed. "I've always been savage. You just never noticed before," he said through clenched teeth.

"The hell I didn't. And speaking of hell—you look like it."

"What does that matter?"

"To most people, nothing. To me—or your prospective client—a great deal."

Stretching out beside the woman and flicking the edge of the sheet back over them, Trace slid the .45 back under the mattress and closed his eyes again. "I don't have any prospective clients. Remember?"

Gil pulled a straight-backed chair close to the bed and slid his slender frame into it before replying. "You do now. I just got the mail packet. It's late, but there's a letter for you stating that a Professor Brasfield will be in Callao on the 15th of October, and as you were referred to him, he expects you to meet him at the boat."

There was no reply for a moment, then Trace opened one eye. "What's today?"

"October 14th," was the prompt answer. Trace groaned, and Gil smiled slightly. "There was a storm and the mail was delayed, but at least it arrived, which is better than we can expect, really." Leaning forward, Gil fixed his friend with a critical eye. "Trace, you've got to forget what happened a while back. Your services are being hired for Brasfield. It pays well. You need the money. I'll make some coffee while you clean up, then we'll talk."

Trace made a rude comment about what Gil could do with his coffee *and* Professor Brasfield, but was ignored. When it seemed definite that Gil intended to clatter pots and pans, he swung long legs over the edge of the cot and stood up. The woman stirred, sulkily holding the sheets up over her bare breasts as she demanded to know if Trace intended to allow that man to stay. He slung his gaze toward her and cocked a dark brow.

"That's my business. But you need to go now anyway."

With an indignant toss of her long, dark hair, the woman slid from the bed, and heedless of her nudity in front of Gil, shrugged into her clothes muttering under her breath. She stormed from the small room without glancing at Trace again, and slammed the door behind her so hard that he winced with real pain.

Stumbling as the room seemed to pitch and sway, Trace grabbed the edge of the table to steady himself and glared at Gil. "You can get out of here, too!"

Gil kept his back to Trace and continued making coffee on the small, pot-bellied stove that served as heat in the winter. "Not until you're sober."

"You won't live long enough for that to happen," Trace growled when Gil lit the stove. "And I don't need coffee. I need something stronger."

"Believe me, this will be strong enough to put hair on your chest," Gil shot back, turning and gazing at Trace. "Or maybe I should say *more* hair on your chest," he amended when his gaze flicked over Taylor's darkly furred torso.

"Maybe you should just get out of here," Trace said, raking a hand through his thick, dark hair, then wincing at the pain that brought. He reached for the pants lying across the back of a chair, and stepped into them, pulling them up around his lean waist and buttoning them.

"I probably should, especially as how you are the most ungrateful friend a man could have. But strangely enough, I had the thought you might appreciate a friend right now."

Meeting Gil's steady gaze, Trace had the unwelcome suspicion that he might be right. He shrugged. "Yeah, I probably do. I suppose you've elected yourself for that?"

"Do you see anyone else pounding on your door?" Gil asked with a wry smile.

"No, and it's damn lucky for them that I don't. I'm still thinking about shooting *you*."

"What a lucky bastard I am." Gil rattled the battered tin coffeepot. "Everyone in South America should have friends like you. Now have a cup of coffee and sit down and listen for a few minutes. You might find this next trip interesting."

"I doubt it," Trace muttered, but he sat down at the table and took the chipped, cracked mug of steaming coffee Gil shoved toward him a few minutes later. He grimaced at the bitter brew, but drank it all down. When he'd finished the second cup, he crossed his arms on the table and looked at Gil. "All right—what?"

"You've been referred as a guide for Professor Horatio Brasfield. He's searching for Vilcapampa."

It took a moment for this to filter through the clouds in Trace's mind, then a caustic smile curled his mouth. "By whom, may I ask?"

"What do you mean?"

"I mean," Trace ground out, "*who* referred me?"

Gil frowned. "What does that matter?"

Trace's laugh was harsh. "Think about it! Seven months ago, I led an expedition into the Andes, and I'm the only one who makes it back. Normally, that's enough to ruin any guide. Call it curiosity, but I'd like to know who recommended me to this professor and why."

"Bentworth," was the reluctant reply, and Trace's "Ah!" contained a wealth of implications. "Look," Gil added in an urgent tone, "you need the work, Trace! If you ever expect to guide another expedition, you've got to prove to everyone—including yourself—that the last time was fate and not a reflection on your ability. Everyone in Peru knows that you're the best damned guide around."

Trace gave him a faintly amused glance. "If they do, they sure aren't admitting it lately. I haven't been able to get a job leading little old ladies across the street, much less anyone into the jungle or mountains. No, Gil, I think Bentworth has something up his sleeve. After all, it was his money that funded the last expedition, and he said then he'd see to it that I never worked again. He did."

"Obviously, Bentworth has had time to reflect, and has realized that there were circumstances beyond your control. And besides, you did your best to talk those fools into coming back, didn't you?"

"That's what I told the magistrates—look, they're dead, and sometimes the dead speak more loudly than the living." Trace shook his head. "It's not worth it."

Standing abruptly, Gil's voice was angry. "I've never thought of you as a coward, Trace Taylor! Look at you—you sit in this cheap room most of the time, only going out to buy whiskey or find a woman. What are you going to do when the last of your money is gone—rob banks?"

Surging to his feet, Trace faced Gil with a harsh glitter in his dark eyes, his big hands curled into tight fists at his sides. A tiny muscle leaped in his jaw as he glared at his friend without speaking for a long moment. As Gil gazed steadily back at him without flinching from the fury in Trace's eyes, some of his tension eased. Slowly uncurling his fists, Trace sat back down. His voice was thoughtful.

"You may be right. Do you have the letter with you? It won't hurt to meet this Brasfield, and maybe find out his connection with Bentworth." Rubbing a hand over his beard-stubbled jaw, Trace added, "But I have no intentions of taking anyone into the Andes again. Not looking for Vilcapampa, anyway. That place is cursed."

Laughing, Gil said, "Don't tell me you believe those old myths!"

There was an odd note in his voice when Trace said, "I never did before, but the last time—" He paused, then said more softly, "The last time, it seemed as if everything we did was jinxed. I've never seen anything like it. Ropes that were fine the day before, were suddenly rotten. Food that was sealed tightly in tins was opened and found to be filled with snakes." He shook his head. "No, I don't intend to guide another expedition to Vilcapampa, not for all the gold in Peru!"

Chapter Three

Pacing the steamer's deck with impatient steps, Professor Brasfield almost danced with glee as the vessel neared shore. "We're almost there, Bethany!" he shouted over the noise. His eyes behind the thick spectacles were bright and sharp, and his mouth curved into an excited smile that made his daughter smile back.

"I must admit, I thought we would never arrive," she said, bracing herself as the steamer rolled with a swell. By now, she could remain upright during even the heaviest seas. They were south of the equator, and it had grown warm again. In California, it was winter. Here, it was foggy and warm. Her brown hair lay in damp strands against her neck, and Bethany grimly decided that keeping it in a tight knot atop her head would be the coolest way to deal with it. For convenience' sake, she also wore trousers instead of a skirt, and her blouse was short sleeved and made of thin cotton.

At first, Professor Brasfield had been slightly shocked by Bethany's decision to abandon her skirts, but as she explained to him the practicality of wearing trousers, he had to agree. His only doubt was that they fit her long, slender legs a bit too well.

"Makes you look . . . well . . . look *female,*" he muttered in an unhappy tone that made Bethany laugh.

"I am female, Papa!"

"Must you advertise it?" Brasfield ran a hand through the few remaining strands of his hair and gave her a lopsided smile. "I don't want some handsome adventurer taking one look at you and sweeping you away from me," he added in what was meant to be a teasing tone, but it somehow fell flat. There was an awkward pause, and he flinched at the sudden flash of pain in his daughter's eyes. "I'm sorry, Bethany. I always seem to say the wrong thing. . . ."

"It's not you, Papa. It's me." She smiled and shrugged. "I shouldn't let what Stephen did affect me. After all, he was one rotten apple in an entire barrelful of people. I don't intend to live the rest of my life as an emotional cripple."

But that was easier said than done, she reflected later when her father had gone below to see to the last of the packing and she was left leaning on the rail and watching the coastline grow close. Stephen Averill had wooed, won, and abandoned her two years before, and the memory was still as sharp as the Amazonian spearpoints her father had collected. Why? Why couldn't she forget him? Forget the pain he had caused, and the humiliation of being left at the altar? Perhaps not literally, but close enough. Well, she had at least learned not to take seriously handsome men with glib tongues and an eye for the ladies. Stephen had done her a favor by admitting that he could not bear to be tied down to one woman. If he had only said that before she'd fallen in love . . .

Tearing her thoughts away from Stephen, Bethany turned as her father approached, a bright smile on her face to cover her pain. "It's about time! We're almost at the dock. I thought you were going to stay in your cabin forever."

Professor Brasfield gave her a distracted smile as he fished through the pockets of his short-sleeved jacket. The jacket had been especially made for him and bore no less than eight pockets sewn down the front and on the sides. It was to carry his wealth of notes and writing utensils, plus maps, small tools to dig with should he stumble across any interesting archaeological spot, several handkerchiefs, his pipe, matches, tobacco, and whatever else he decided was vital.

"The porter is to bring our baggage to the hotel, but I cannot remember the name of it, Bethany," he said in a helpless tone. "And I know we're to meet someone—our guide that Bentworth hired for us—but I don't know who. How do we recognize him, or . . ."

"Papa, we are to go to the Royal Arms hotel, and our guide's name is Trace Taylor. I have the information written down up here," she said, tapping a finger against her temple. "If we miss Taylor at the docks, I'm certain he will be able to find us at the hotel. Now, why don't you point out our porter, and I'll see to the baggage."

"Yes, yes, excellent idea!" Brasfield beamed. "He's the tall man, with a bald head and white uniform jacket."

Bethany surveyed the crowded steamer. There were a great many tall men with bald heads and white uniform jackets, and she sighed. "I'll find him. If we become separated in this crush, you go ahead to the Royal Arms Hotel and I'll find you. I'll be fine," she added when it looked as if he would protest. "I'm quite capable of taking care of myself."

It was true. During the years, Bethany had grown quite proficient at caring for her father and herself.

She was accustomed to his rather haphazard manner of dealing with the outside world. His element was archaeological finds and old, musty tablets and pottery shards. Point out a modern building to him, and he could not tell you what it was or when it had been built. But only show him a small chunk of stone, and it wouldn't be long before he could identify it as a piece of a pre-Colombian or Aztec temple. No, her father lived in an entirely different world.

Turning to the rail again, Bethany eyed the teeming harbor with growing excitement. How exotically wonderful! Endless miles of high sand dunes rimmed the coastline to the north, barren desert reaches that stretched almost to the harbor. Behind the Callao harbor lay Lima, and behind the city bristling with cathedral spires, lay the more impressive high ridges of the Andes. The fog-shrouded peaks ran like the tail of a dragon, distant and mysterious, hiding ancient mysteries, and she shivered at the thought. This promised to be very exciting, and she was glad she had come with her father.

By the time Bethany found the porter with their baggage and had arranged for it to be delivered to the right hotel, she had misplaced her father. More correctly, the professor had absentmindedly climbed aboard the wrong cart, and was taken from hotel to hotel before the frazzled donkey driver found the Royal Arms and his daughter.

"I should have known," Bethany murmured as she pressed a generous tip into the annoyed donkey-driver's hand. "Papa, didn't you remember the Royal Arms?" she began, but saw that her father wasn't listening. He had spied a familiar face across the crowded lobby, and was waving.

"Hola! Bentworth! Here!"

Bethany gave an inward groan as she turned. She

immediately recognized the tall, spare Englishman, with his distinguished gray hair and natty garments. He always wore a cap, a jaunty tweed headpiece with a half bill that he apparently thought made him look sporting, and carried a carved pipe with a lion's head bowl and sharply curved stem. She stifled her distaste. Why was Spencer Bentworth here in Callao? How unfortunate! She didn't like the man, and didn't trust him. There was something about him that seemed a bit too . . . smooth. Yes, that was it. He was another one of those glib men with an answer for everything, a soothing comment to brush away every worry. It was only later that one discovered the carefully arranged fictions.

Spencer Bentworth walked toward them with a welcoming smile that gave her a shiver. "Dreadfully good of you to meet me here, old chap," he greeted Brasfield. "I know how anxious you must be to get on with the expedition, what-ho? Right, heh? Ah, and the very lovely Miss Brasfield! My, you do look rather fetching in those trousers, m'dear. Had no notion that you wore glasses, however. Nearsighted?"

His effusive pleasantries grated on Bethany's nerves, but she managed to greet him cordially enough. "Thank you for such kind words, Mr. Bentworth, and I wear my glasses whenever I feel the need."

She gave a defiant push at the thick-framed lens perched on the bridge of her nose. Actually, she didn't need them at all. In a way, they had become sort of a protection, an armor against intrusion. She'd discovered quite by accident that certain people were put off by those who wore spectacles, and deferred to the individual an intelligence and astuteness that ofttimes was undeserved. It was one of the more interesting quirks of human nature that she used to her advantage. Yet Bentworth was immune to the ploy, it seemed. Bethany straightened her shoulders and met his faintly amused gaze calmly.

"Sorry. Didn't mean to pry, Miss Brasfield. Simply surprised to see you, I s'pose. Hadn't thought you would come with the professor."

"Why wouldn't I? I've been known to be a great help to my father in his work." Bethany's chin tilted slightly. Did he think her a moron, or an incompetent simply because she was a woman?

"Yes, of course you would, Miss Brasfield," Bentworth said in such a patronizing tone that she flushed. "Being the daughter of such an estimable man, you must have learned a great deal simply by default, heh?"

"No, Mr. Bentworth. I've learned a great deal by study and hard work, like anyone else would do."

"Ah, just so, I'm sure." Bentworth turned back to the professor. "I've made the necessary arrangements for you to meet with your guide in the morning. Suggest an early start, what? I know how you must be looking forward to getting on with it, so I've taken the liberty of paying the man a retainer fee to get him started."

"Yes, yes! Now, you say the man has actually seen this lost city for himself?" Brasfield asked, impatiently waving aside the details. "That is where the artifact you sent me was located, am I correct?"

"Somewhat. It was discovered on a lower slope leading up to what appeared to be ancient ruins." Bentworth paused, gazing shrewdly at the professor. "There is an element of danger, you must know, in such an undertaking. It is my understanding that the expedition ended rather—shall we say—unfortunately. Of course, that was due to the carelessness of the members, not the guide, but . . ."

"Wait a minute." Bethany fixed Bentworth with a sharp gaze. "Am I to understand that this guide, this Taylor, has been responsible for a disastrous expedition?"

"Hardly, m'dear," Bentworth returned coolly, and took his pipe from his mouth to smile at her. "It was more of, shall we say, a misunderstanding between Taylor and the leader of the expedition."

"Explain that, please," Bethany demanded crisply when it seemed as if Bentworth meant to placate her with lies. "I would like to know just exactly what is meant by an *unfortunate* expedition."

Clearing his throat, Bentworth motioned to a table nearby and suggested they take a seat and order cool drinks before he gave them all the details. "It's the weather here, what?" he murmured with another smile.

When they were seated, Bentworth addressed his remarks to the professor instead of Bethany, and his voice was cool and casual. "It seems that there was a disagreement about whether or not the party should push on, and whether or not Taylor knew their exact location. Of course, you have to understand that Gibbs was not the most tractable of fellows and had a remarkable affinity for provoking the most mellow of individuals. Taylor is not, to say the least, mellow. He objected to Gibbs's insinuations that he did not know where he was, and thus the party was divided. Some wished to go with Taylor, others with Gibbs. In the end, however, Gibbs prevailed, according to Taylor." There was a long pause before he finished, "Gibbs and his party did not survive. Neither did Taylor's party, though Taylor himself managed to return."

"We have no one else's word for what occurred?" Bethany broke in. "Were there any survivors to corroborate this Taylor's story?"

"Unfortunately, no," Bentworth said after a moment. "He has worked for me before, however, and I have a great deal of faith in his judgment."

"How comforting!" Bethany snapped. "I note that *you* are not a member of our expedition—can Taylor's incompetence be a factor?"

"Ah, Miss Brasfield, Miss Brasfield," Bentworth said soothingly. "You are overreacting a bit, what? The fate of that expedition had nothing whatsoever to do with Taylor's competence. The journals he brought back with him are a vivid testimony to his innocence. In fact, at the trial . . ."

"Trial?" Bethany was livid with anger. "You have hired a man to be our guide who has been on *trial?"* Her voice had risen several levels, drawing curious glances in their direction.

Professor Brasfield fidgeted nervously, and leaned forward to put a comforting hand on his daughter's arm. "Now, Bethany, allow Bentworth to finish his explanation. It is only fair."

Her head whipped around to stare at her father, and she saw in his placating smile his eagerness to continue the expedition in spite of any odds. Wavering between distrust for Bentworth and the impulse to please her father, Bethany settled for a cold, "I'll listen, but that's all!"

A smug smile curled Bentworth's mouth as he lit his pipe and continued, "There is always an investigation in these things when it concerns the Crown, you must know that. Of course, Taylor was thoroughly quizzed, and was proven to be innocent of any wrongdoing."

"Now, see here, Bentworth," Brasfield began, and Bethany had a moment's relief that perhaps her father had begun to see the light. That relief was shattered when he scooted forward on his seat and said, "You do realize that the credit for any finds must go to the university with which I am affiliated. I know that as a man of the Crown, you may wish to claim artifacts, but I must be given precedence!"

"My dear professor!" Bentworth exclaimed with uplifted brows, "Of course, you shall! I would never ask you to conduct this expedition if I did not intend for you to take the honors for discovering the greatest find of the decade—no, century!"

Sitting back, Brasfield smiled with relief, not noticing his daughter's angry glare. "Really, Papa! Is that all you can think about? What about the dangers?"

"Tut, tut! No danger is too great if it means success, my dear." Flushed with victory, Brasfield gave her a fond smile. "And Mr. Bentworth has very graciously conceded that the discoveries shall remain mine and the university's in spite of his financial aid. Quite generous of him, don't you think?"

Bethany didn't think it was at all generous. She thought that there must be an ulterior motive behind Bentworth's "generosity." Of course, once the discovery of an ancient city was made, the world would know it was her father who had made it. Still, there was something about the entire matter she didn't like.

"Why Taylor?" she demanded abruptly. "Why not another guide—one who has not been the sole survivor of a disaster that claimed his companions, perhaps?"

"Oh, there is quite a simple reply for that, m'dear. Taylor is the only man alive who knows how to get there. The only white man, that is. I'm certain there are natives who know the way—if you can get them to tell you."

Her lips thinned as she met Bentworth's smoothly smiling face, but she only asked, "How many expeditions has this Taylor led since the . . . fatal . . . journey?"

"None."

"None?" she echoed, flicking a glance toward her father. The professor seemed singularly disinterested in the direction of the conversation, and Bethany fumed with frustration. "May I ask why?"

Bentworth seemed to take a malicious delight in saying, "Because after the unfortunate expedition and subsequent trial, he took rather heavily to drink, I'm afraid. Poor chap was quite distraught over events."

"Oh, that is perfect!" Bethany stood up, her body rigid with anger. "Papa, I suggest we leave on the next steamer back to California. It is quite obvious to me that Mr. Bentworth has no consideration for our safety at all. And I cannot imagine why he thinks we would . . ."

Bentworth cut in coolly. "My dear Miss Brasfield, the simple reason I have retained Mr. Taylor's services, is as I have stated—there is no other white man alive who knows how to locate the ruins. Or one who is capable of coming out alive from what is quite dangerous territory. Taylor himself, you see, is dangerous—necessarily dangerous. A less dangerous man would not survive. But, if you are reluctant to go"—he rose from his chair—"I will be most happy to fund Professor Moriarty. Splendid chap, Moriarty. Not as knowledgeable about the Incas as Brasfield here, but . . ."

"No!" Brasfield leaped up, his face distraught. "She did not mean to distress you, Bentworth. Bethany just worries too much, like her mother used to do. Of course we don't mind Taylor! And what's an expedition without a little danger to keep you sharp?" His fingers curled tightly around Bethany's wrist when she would have spoken, and he shook his head. "We'll be ready at first light in the morning."

Grimly, Bethany nodded at Bentworth's inquiring

gaze. It did not appear as if she had many choices. But she did not have to be happy about it, in spite of her father's apparent satisfaction with the situation.

The rest of the day was spent exploring Lima and waiting for their guide to appear. Bethany had her reservations, of course, but was willing to give the man a chance since her father was so determined. With that thought in mind, she allowed herself to be taken to the impressive ancient cathedrals, the Historical Museum, and the Museum of Anthropology and Archeology.

Lima itself was impressive, she thought, though a bit shabby and dirty. The city whirled around plazas wheeling out in a pattern laid out in 1535 when Pizarro founded the capital. Carved baroque balconies hung over streets so narrow it was impossible for two mule carts to pass at the same time. Stoic Indians drove llamas and vicuñas down the choked streets, their beasts of burden and suppliers of wool for thousands of years, and she could almost imagine how it had been in the days after the Spanish had come. Of course, the Spanish influence was very evident in the architecture, buildings that had been built atop Inca foundations.

By the time they reached their hotel again that evening Bethany felt as if she could give a lecture on the Incas herself. Professor Brasfield was elated by portions of an old manuscript he had been allowed to copy, and insisted that it provided detailed directions on reaching the lost city.

"I intend to go to my room and study it closely," he said when Bethany asked if he would join her for dinner. "You go ahead, dear. Have dinner with Bentworth. He seems good company."

"Really, Papa," Bethany murmured with a twinge of dismay. "Perhaps I'll just have dinner in my room."

"Do that, dear, do that," he said distractedly, pushing at his glasses and peering down at the manuscript he held as carefully as if it had been carved from gold. "And have a good time."

"Yes, Papa," she said with a faintly amused smile. "I'm quite used to entertaining myself."

But alone in her room and gazing out the window at the dark, serpentine shape of the mountains looming on the horizon, Bethany couldn't help but wonder if the rest of her life would be spent on the fringe of her father's attention. There were times she felt the sharp pangs of loneliness, and thought that even the pain she'd felt with Stephen was better than the emptiness and desolation of her existence.

"How ridiculous!" she scolded herself. "I have the best of my father's world, don't I? And I will be with him when he discovers a lost city, an opportunity few people have!"

As she undressed and slid into bed, Bethany hoped that their guide would prove all her reservations to be unsound. It was one thing to go off on an expedition in a foreign country, and it was quite another to risk one's life in the mountains with a treacherous guide. No, she would hope for the best. This Trace Taylor was probably an excellent guide and when she met him, she would feel much better.

Blowing out the bedside lamp, Bethany snuggled beneath the sheets of her bed and stared at the ceiling for a long time before she fell asleep. And when she did sleep, dreams of being lost in the mountains disturbed her rest.

Chapter Four

Bethany's first introduction to Trace Taylor did not go well at all. Instead of meeting them at the docks or even the Royal Arms, Taylor went to the warehouse where Bentworth had gathered the necessary supplies. When she and her father arrived, their guide was nowhere in sight.

"Ah," Bentworth soothed Bethany when she demanded to know if Taylor was avoiding them, "I believe he's carefully checking over the bundles of items such as ropes, food tins, and digging utensils. A cautious man, is our Mr. Taylor."

"Cautious, or suspicious?" Bethany inquired coldly. "Doesn't he think we just might know what is needed for a lengthy expedition?"

"Now, now, Miss Brasfield, I'm certain Taylor is only being careful," Bentworth said with an amused smile. "It's just that there are a great many supplies, and some of them may not be suitable for the mountain heights. He's a man of experience with the area where you are going, and it is expected that he ensure everything is proper. Supplies, mules, bearers, that sort of thing."

"We will have Indian bearers, I suppose?" Bethany asked more calmly, and Bentworth nodded.

"Or *mestizos*. As many as you need, though it will cost a pretty penny. They are quite reluctant, you understand, and my men have had to resort to a certain amount of trickery in order to gather enough of them."

"Trickery?" Bethany echoed. "What sort of trickery?"

"Nothing too demonic, I assure you," Bentworth replied with another fatuous smile. "Actually, it's rather simple if one plays upon the customs of the people. You see, if a man is paid for a service, he *must* perform it. That is a strict law. So, either Brody or Reagan will walk up to a strong-looking Indian or *mestizo* and hold out his hand as if to shake the man's. When they take it, they find a coin pressed into the palm, thus payment has been accepted and the man forced to accompany my employee and become one of our bearers. See how simple things can be if one only knows the customs of the people?"

"Or the fears—how terrible, Mr. Bentworth! Why are the men so afraid? Is this trip that dangerous?"

"Ah, the Indians are a superstitious lot, you know, and don't like being away from their homes for very long. They are basically farmers, though their Incan ancestors were reputed to be fairly warlike." Bentworth lit his pipe and smiled at her. "Can't tell it by the docile Quechuas! They are very placid by nature. Must be due to generations of slavery and the chewing of coca leaves."

Bethany felt a wave of reluctant relief. She should be more sympathetic, she supposed, but for a moment, she had envisioned fierce, rebellious Indians with bows and arrows and spears barring mountain roads.

"I see," she said. "Our main obstacles will be the terrain, I presume."

"That, and attracting too much attention."

Professor Brasfield turned from his inspection of an archaeological digging utensil. "Heh? What's this? What does that mean, Bentworth?"

Shrugging, Bentworth slid his hands into the pockets of his light jacket. "There is always the possibility of rival expeditions, Brasfield. Surely, you realize that."

"Of course, but I had no idea we were competing with a rival at this time!"

"Not quite, old chap, don't carry on so. I've only heard rumors that there may be others interested in this Vilcapampa—the lost city of gold!"

Straightening his narrow shoulders, Brasfield said, "As you must be aware, I am interested in only the historical finds as they relate to plotting the lives of the Incas. They were a mighty people in their day, and until the Spanish wiped them out, they were a proud people."

"So I hear," Bentworth said so casually that the professor frowned. "A pity that these wretched Indians did not retain some of their characteristics, don't you think?"

"Yes, I suppose." Brasfield smiled uncertainly. "It is certainly a pity that they no longer make such lovely pottery or artifacts as they once did."

Bentworth's eyes gleamed as he said, "If they did, we would all be wealthy men, I assure you! Their reputed access to mountains of gold—enough gold to gild entire cities—has been hidden by the centuries. . . ."

Professor Brasfield seemed surprised by Bentworth's response, and his voice was alarmed. "I have assumed that you felt the same reverence for the Incas, Bentworth, and are not just interested in the monetary value of our finds. That is true, isn't it?"

Bentworth's brows lifted. "My dear Professor! How could you think otherwise? Would I finance an expedition of this sort if my interest was only greed? Please, old chap, give me credit for a certain archaeological respect!"

His brow cleared, and Brasfield nodded. "Sorry. Didn't mean to imply otherwise, but I just wanted to be certain of your real interests."

"I could answer that for you, Professor," a deep voice drawled from behind Bethany, and she turned to see a tall man striding toward them. "But I won't," he added softly when he reached them, and she saw Bentworth's mouth tighten into an exasperated line.

For some reason, Bethany instantly thought of a Western gunman as the man approached with a fluid, careless stride. It could have been because he wore a holster and gun slung low on his hip, or because of the snug-fitting cords and knee-high boots he wore. Or, it could have been because he had the same arrogant air of danger about him as the men who made their living with fast draws and blazing guns. Her eyes widened slightly when he stopped beside her, his gaze still riveted on Bentworth with an expression of dislike carved into his coldly handsome features.

"I presume you are still irritated about certain statements I made in the past, Taylor," Bentworth said in a calm voice. "You can surely understand my distress at that time. Let bygones be bygones, I say. After all, I'm showing my trust for your judgment by hiring you for this expedition, aren't I?"

Shrugging, Taylor flicked a cold glance toward the professor and his daughter. "Could be because you know I'm the only white man who knows how to get there," was the laconic reply as his gaze lingered skeptically on Bethany.

She flushed at his close stare, at the way his dark

eyes swept over her from head to toe, lingering where her breasts pushed against the thin cotton of her blouse, then shifting to her face. Her chin lifted in an unconsciously defiant gesture, and she met his gaze coolly when his eyes lifted to her face.

"Is something wrong, Mr. Taylor?" she inquired icily.

"Not from where I stand," he replied. "And not unless you think you're going along on the expedition."

"I most certainly intend to do so."

Taylor shook his head. "Not with me as your guide. I don't take women along."

"Now see here," Bethany began hotly. How dare he refuse to take her? It should be *she* who was refusing to be guided by a man such as he!

"Taylor, Taylor," Bentworth broke in, "why start a squabble over such minor details? You seem quite out of sorts this morning. Perhaps it's best if we had a private talk before going on, what?"

"Look, Bentworth," Trace said in a hard, flat tone, "I don't have many conditions, but I do draw the line at taking along a woman."

Bentworth's mouth curved into what might have passed for a smile if it were not for the animosity in his eyes. "I say, old chap, you do not seem to understand. The professor and his daughter are the heads of this expedition while you are just the guide. If . . ."

"Then let the professor and his daughter get there the best way they know how," Taylor interrupted. "I have no intention of trying to navigate dangerous terrain with a complaining, whining woman at my back. The Urubamba River valley is no pleasant stroll, and there are enough dangers out there to make a strong man quake, much less a woman."

"Mr. Taylor," Bethany said coldly, "I am quite capable of withstanding discomfort and danger as well as any man. In fact, history can bear out the fact that women endure hardships much better than their male counterparts." Her violet eyes had deepened to a stormy purple as she glared at Taylor, but he didn't seem a bit put out by her anger.

"Is that so?" he drawled, raking her with an insolent stare that made her even more furious. "Well, this male *counterpart* has no intention of enduring so much as an hour with you, Miss Brasfield, so I suggest that you go home and tat some lace, or something more appropriate to your gender than traipsing down sheer mountain cliffs and risking snake bite in the jungle."

The thought of sheer mountain cliffs and snake bites were admittedly daunting, but Bethany would not have said so to Trace Taylor for all the gold in Peru. Crossing her arms over her chest, she rapped out, "Perhaps you should go back to your cave and discover fire or the wheel, something more appropriate to your intellect, Mr. Taylor!"

A hint of a smile tugged at one corner of his mouth, and Trace shifted slightly so that he was facing her, one leg relaxed, a fist resting on his hip. "I thought vipers were sharp-tongued, Miss Brasfield, but I do believe you could match even a fer-de-lance for deadliness."

"Do you? Considering that the fer-de-lance is known as the deadliest snake in the world, I will accept that as a compliment, Mr. Taylor."

He actually grinned. "You do that. And while you're at it, accept some advice—this is too dangerous a trek for you. Stay here."

"Not on your life!"

His face darkened slightly, and his brow lifted. "Not on my life? Fine. What about yours? That's what it boils down to, Miss Brasfield."

Bethany bit back the harsh retort that sprang to her lips and said, "I appreciate your advice. Please appreciate my right to make my own decisions."

Shrugging broad shoulders, Trace turned away. "I won't accept the responsibility for you. If Bentworth or your father takes you along, that's up to them. I'll give you a try—but only until we reach Cuzco. Don't expect luxuries, or even special treatment from anyone. If you can't take care of yourself, you'll be left behind at the first delay."

Angrily staring after Taylor as he strode away, Bethany flashed a glance toward her father. The professor made himself conspicuously busy, rummaging through canvas sacks and wooden crates. Only Bentworth would meet her gaze, and his expression was faintly amused.

"Don't judge him too harshly, Miss Brasfield. I'm sure that Taylor doesn't think you capable of endurance because you seem so soft and feminine. Now, if you appeared to be of sturdy pioneer stock with a broad back and arms as stout as trees, he would have probably assigned you a pack to shoulder."

"I suppose you think this is all quite amusing?" Bethany snapped at him. "It might have helped if *you* had pointed out some of my capabilities, Mr. Bentworth!"

"Ah, but Miss Brasfield, I'm not at all certain I have explored your, ah . . . capabilities. Perhaps we should have dinner this evening, so that I might become more familiar with your—talents, shall we say?"

Bethany felt her cheeks grow warm at his implications, but she managed to say quite steadily, "I do believe that you are every bit as crude and uncouth as the guide you have hired, Mr. Bentworth."

"Ah, you wound me to the quick, Miss Brasfield!"

His lips twitched with amusement. "You must not be so thin-skinned if you insist upon traveling in a man's world. Most men do not recognize that a woman can be as versatile as you have proven to be."

"Is that supposed to make me feel better?"

"Not really. It's just supposed to explain the reaction you will receive from men in this profession. I am surprised your father has not better prepared you for this sort of thing."

Bethany's smile was wry. "My father's interests, as you may have noticed, are focused upon archaeological discovery and the interpretation of such finds. He does not seem to care for the opinions of others, except as it relates to his work."

"I did notice, I confess," Bentworth replied. His eyes lingered on Bethany for a moment, as if assessing her. "You know," he said softly, "it might not be a bad idea if you were to wait in Cuzco for the expedition to return. I do hate to think of the risks you will face, and the possible fate."

Lifting her brows, Bethany wondered if he was trying to frighten her. "Is that a gloomy prophecy, Mr. Bentworth?"

"Not at all, not at all. Let's just say"—he hesitated before continuing—"a warning of what might occur should the worst happen. I strongly urge you to heed my advice, my dear."

Thoroughly exasperated, Bethany said, "I do wish that you would stop using the tactics of a bogeyman to try and scare me, Mr. Bentworth! I am not a child to be frightened away by possible danger. I am fully aware of the risks in climbing high mountain trails and pushing through dense jungle! It is not as if I am naive."

"No, I suppose not," Bentworth said, and there was a note of regret in his voice. "Well, you are not as fainthearted as I, I freely admit! And I admire your courage, if not your wisdom, Miss Brasfield."

"Thank you!" she snapped irritably.

His smile was genuine. "You're quite welcome. Now, if you would care to go over the list of supplies, I am sure that Taylor will oblige you. If there are any questions you may have, please feel free to ask me."

Bethany took the printed list he handed her, then fumbled in her jacket pocket for her glasses. Sliding them up her nose, she briefly scanned the list, then looked up at Bentworth.

"Why are we supplying the entire expedition here, instead of some of it in Cuzco?"

"That is simple enough—supplies are cheaper here than there. It may be a bit inconvenient to have to carry them three hundred miles, but then, it would be dreadfully inconvenient to need them and not have them. And besides, Taylor insisted upon it."

Bethany sliced a glance toward Trace Taylor, who stood with his back to her, talking with what looked to be an Indian bearer. For a brief instant, she spared a moment's self-admonition. She shouldn't allow him to frighten her with his harsh demeanor. He was only a man, and a hireling. She knew how to handle hired help, didn't she? Then she would be able to handle this Trace Taylor. She just needed a different approach.

As if he knew she was thinking about him, he half turned and looked toward her, then turned back to the Indian at his side. Bethany stiffened, and wished she could better hear what he was saying. She could not understand the dialect, and assumed it must be one of the obscure languages she'd heard the natives used.

"Quechua," Bentworth explained, correctly reading her puzzled expression. "Most of the Indians speak their own dialects."

"But I thought Spanish was the predominant language here!" Bethany exclaimed in surprise. "I spent the entire journey from California brushing up on my vocabulary."

Bentworth shook his head. "The Spanish left many legacies behind, including architecture and language, but the Incas were stubborn people. The Indians preferred—and still do—their own language. Even with the Spanish subjugation of them, they felt free to do as they pleased in some matters. Taylor understands Quechua and Aymara, too."

"I see." Bethany glanced toward Trace Taylor again, and felt a moment's frustration that he would be so invaluable. She would have much preferred having a guide with the same qualities, but a more careful reputation. Taylor seemed too brash, too arrogant. Had he really left an expedition to the mercies of the elements or other dangers? Or had it been, as Bentworth assured them, a dreadful misunderstanding and accident? She doubted she'd ever know the truth, but it was certainly disturbing to think that a man who might have murdered an entire expedition was now going to be responsible for her life as well.

Self-consciously smoothing back strands of light brown hair from her eyes, Bethany decided to approach Taylor and try making a better acquaintance with him. After all, if they were going to be thrown together for the next few weeks, she needed to be able to at least converse with him without degenerating into a fit of anger.

She stilled the fluttering in her stomach, and the slight tightening of her throat, and walked toward him with grim determination. "Mr. Taylor," she said when the Indian had turned and left, "may I speak with you a moment?" She pushed nervously at her glasses and cleared her throat.

Taylor turned, a dark brow lifting, and his eyes immediately narrowed at her. "That depends on what you want to talk about, Miss Brasfield."

"Compromise," she said promptly. "I am fully aware of your reluctance in allowing a . . . woman . . . to accompany this expedition, and I only want to assure you that I will not be one of those *complaining, whining females* you seem to despise so heartily. I am quite capable of bearing my own weight."

He seemed amused, and his mouth briefly slanted in what might have been called a smile. "I believe you already stated your determination and grit, Miss Brasfield, and I have given in to your demands. What else do you want from me?"

Stilling the spasm of irritation she felt, Bethany said as politely as possible, "Nothing, Mr. Taylor. I merely wished to clear the air between us. I do not relish the idea of going off for several hundred miles with a man who is waiting for me to fall on my face."

"Ah, but you can't really do anything about that." Trace motioned for one of the Indian bearers to come to him and said before he approached, "I appreciate your effort at *clearing the air,* but I've stated my dislike of the situation. Bentworth has made it clear that you are to go, and you're his responsibility, so you can go. Just don't expect me to make it easy for you."

"I hardly expect you to do anything decent!" Bethany snapped. "And I don't need for you to make it easy, Mr. Taylor, so you can ease your mind on that score! I'm an independent woman. I can take care of myself without your help!"

"Thank you," Trace said, then laughed softly when she wheeled away from him and immediately tripped over a canvas bag on the warehouse floor. She almost went sprawling, but managed to grab hold of a wooden post to stop her fall. Her glasses flew from her nose and crashed to the floor, sliding to a halt at Taylor's feet.

Bending, he picked them up and held them out, staring down at her floundering form as she tried to regain her balance. His voice was mild when he asked, "Does your independence mean I shouldn't try to help you up now, too?"

"Go to the devil!" Bethany snarled, her cheeks hot as she snatched her glasses from him. She regained her balance but not her composure, and walked away with as much dignity as she could muster. It was embarrassing that he had seen her stumble right after her lofty statement that she could take care of herself.

"I detest that man," she told her father when she joined him, but Professor Brasfield was so busy examining the new digging utensils—small spades and shovels, and the measuring instruments needed to properly divide the site into squares for digging—that he just murmured, "Umm hmm," in a vacant tone, and didn't even look up at her when she spoke to him again. Bethany sighed. "Not that anyone cares," she said quietly, "but I think I'm going to join an Amazonian tribe of women and go bare-breasted in the jungle and carry a sword and enslave every man I see."

"Umm hmmm," her father murmured again. "That's nice."

"And then," Bethany ground out, wondering if anyone at all cared how she felt, "I intend to melt down every golden artifact you find, and form it into gold bricks and sell them to the highest bidder. There will be nothing—*nothing* left of the Incas when I get through!"

"Eh? What's that you say?" Professor Brasfield asked, jerking his head up to peer at her with a squint. "What was that about the Incas and golden artifacts?"

Bethany restrained the urge to stomp her foot with exasperation, knowing that would only make her look foolish and childish. "Nothing, Papa," she said with another sigh. "I only hope we can find enough artifacts to make this expedition worthwhile."

"My dear child," Brasfield said with a smile, "*one* genuine artifact will be enough to make it worthwhile! My entire life has been spent in seeking more knowledge of the past, and now—now, I get to experience firsthand the actual discovery of ancient peoples. Oh, yes, Bethany, any find at all will make it worthwhile as far as I'm concerned."

Bethany's irritation with Trace Taylor faded as she looked at her father's earnest face. Yes, she supposed that it would be worth anything to her father to find an actual lost city. It was an archaeologist's dream, and he was embarking on it with high hopes and enthusiasm. She could not let Trace Taylor tarnish this expedition with his surly attitude and arrogance. No, she would just have to endure him as best she could. It was the least she could do for the man who had so patiently reared a motherless daughter with as much love and devotion as he could give her. And if at times she wished for more attention from him, she was only being ungrateful for all he had done. After all, he did the best he could, and it was difficult for a man alone to raise a daughter. She would just have to try to involve herself more fully in his interests.

"We leave first thing in the morning, I believe," she said, and her father nodded eagerly.

"From here through Lima, then up an ancient Inca highway to Cuzco! Just think, Bethany, we will be traveling the same roads the kings of old traveled, the actual Incas! I can almost picture them striding regally along, or being borne aloft by their servants in golden chairs draped in alpaca and llama wool blankets—ah, it stirs the imagination, doesn't it? Just picture it!"

"If I had my paints or chalks, I could paint a record of the journey, but I suppose the photographic equipment you brought will be more dependable," Bethany said, and her father smiled distractedly.

"Of course, dear. That would have been nice. The Incas left no written record of their lives, only scenes on pottery, or works of art." He sighed. "Too bad they did not, or did not leave a history. Now we must rely on what we can put together about the Inca and his people!"

"I assume you are using the term Inca in its real sense instead of applying it to the entire race of people," Bethany observed with a fond smile.

"Yes, yes, of course! The Incas—kings—were the true rulers of the nation, considered as both a god and a king, or emperor, of the empire. Of course, his chosen nobles came to be known as Incas, too, but the man with the real power—the only power, was *the Inca.* His people were there merely to serve this direct descendant of the sun. If only the Incas had been wise enough to allow a more democratic form of government, perhaps the Spanish would not have been able to so thoroughly exterminate them."

"Perhaps," Bethany agreed, "but then, the Spanish were rulers of the world in the 1500s, and masters of sea and land. It would have been difficult for any people without extensive knowledge of their brand of modern warfare to resist them for long. . . ."

"Just so, just so!" Brasfield said, nodding. This was his favorite subject, and Bethany had read enough on the primitive civilizations to be able to keep up with him, though when he began going into details about the various civilizations and their customs, and what was known and only guessed at, she had trouble keeping up.

As he launched into an analysis of ruins found in Mexico, and the Aztec and Mayan people, and how they were similar in certain cases to the Incas, Bethany let her attention wander back to Trace Taylor.

He was talking with the Quechua again, a short, dark man with a wide-brimmed hat and a multicolored cape over his shoulders. Trace towered over him, his broad frame almost dwarfing the Indian, but there was only an open friendliness in his attitude.

Bethany had the thought that Taylor showed none of the animosity and arrogance he had shown to her and her father, and she wondered why. What had they done to incur his enmity? Or was he only angry because she insisted upon being included in the expedition?

Straightening her shoulders, Bethany's chin lifted in a gesture of defiance. Well, if he thought she would yield to his arrogant comments or Bentworth's veiled warnings, he was quite, quite wrong. She would show them all how women could endure!

Chapter Five

If Trace Taylor had specifically created the terrain to intimidate and frighten Bethany, he could not have done better than what nature had provided. The journey had begun quietly enough, weaving through the dirty, narrow streets of Lima and the adobe and straw slums that were dotted here and there with bright geraniums or hollyhocks. The road ran along the banks of the Rimac, the river for which the city had been named. Somehow, the Quechua name of Rimac—meaning "He who speaks"—had degenerated into *Lima*. Bentworth—a mine of information, Bethany was discovering—told them how Pizarro had laid out the city in 1533 after conquering and taking as prisoner Manco Inca, the king.

"It is Manco Inca's lost city that you now seek, the last citadel of the last king," Bentworth said as they rode along the narrow track that wound from the city to rise higher and higher in elevation. "He is said to have gone there to escape the Spanish and protect his rule."

"Not quite the last king," Brasfield corrected, his voice floating eerily through the fog. "There were a few others after him, but I do believe that Manco Inca was the last truly effective Inca."

"Yes, yes, of course. That's what I meant, Brasfield." Bentworth sounded testy, and no one said anything for a few moments. Only the echoing sounds of the mule's hooves on the cobbled stones broke the silence as they wound through the tight, narrow streets and past the Plaza de Armas, and then the *barriadas,* or slums by the river.

In the gradually lightening day, Bethany could hear the ring of hammers against stone, and the *thunk* of shovels into dirt. She peered through the foggy mist at the forms of workmen.

"A railroad," Bentworth explained with a wave of one arm.

"How convenient, Bentworth!" the professor exclaimed. "When will it be finished?"

Laughing, Bentworth observed that the railroad had been begun in 1879, and if they expected to have it completed before the turn of the century, he considered them dreamers. "When we get farther on, you'll see why I say that, Professor," he predicted.

Bethany eyed the Chinese coolies laboring on a bed for the railroad, and had the thought that it certainly would have been easier if it was already completed. She wasn't at all sure she could become accustomed to the gait of a mule.

Day broke in gray shadows, light filtering down through the clouds in a haze as they rode along the rocky road. Bethany found it hard to pay attention; her gaze kept straying to the increasingly higher rock walls. The sky, as it had been since their arrival in Peru, was a slate gray. It hung low, the clouds seeming to press down on them as if filled with rain, but none fell. Bentworth had also said that it rarely rained in this part of the country.

"Cursed place," he said cheerfully. "Gray skies for six months of winter, and then unrelenting sun for the six months of summer. No compromise, what-ho?"

Nodding weakly, Bethany found it difficult to speak. She was finding it hard to breathe easily, and her head began to swim.

"Breathe slowly and deeply," Trace advised when he saw her white face. "And if you feel sick, don't try to be brave about it—tell somebody!"

"Why couldn't we just take boats down the river instead of ride mules?" Bethany asked feebly, turning her head away at the sight of the climbing trail and steep drop only a few feet away.

Trace gave a derisive snort. "You won't ask that question when you see the river a few miles up, I'll bet!"

And when they had ridden further, Bethany saw why. The river tumbled furiously in places, swallowing tree limbs in a frenzy of brownish froth, then hurtling on its way. No one could have traversed that boiling water in a boat, she realized with a sinking feeling.

Glancing down at her white knuckles, and feeling the betraying moisture of perspiration beneath her light clothes, Bethany swallowed hard. She had never realized that she was afraid of heights. Perhaps she had never known it because she had never been introduced to such perilous heights as those she was now experiencing.

To her surprise, Trace rode up beside her, positioning his mule between her and the edge of the road. "It's not so bad once you get used to it," he said, flicking her a curious glance. "Everyone has the same reaction their first time."

"Not you, I'll bet," she muttered resentfully, hating his half-condescending attitude and the way he sat his mule so easily and comfortably.

"Yeah, even me." At her disbelieving glance, he

shrugged. "I came from flat, barren land, and the first time I rode up these mountains, I wondered if I'd have enough courage to ride back down them."

"I notice that you did, though." After a brief pause, and not because she was really curious but only being polite, she asked, "Where are you from, Mr. Taylor?"

"Texas. Southwest Texas, where the land is *really* flat, and the biggest hills are made by prairie dogs." His dark gaze drifted to her face, and the suggestion of a smile teased the corners of his hard mouth.

Bethany couldn't help wondering what it would be like to kiss that hard, unsmiling mouth, then flushed at the direction of her thoughts. It must be the high mountain air that was making her so lightheaded!

"Somehow, I knew you were from the West," she said in a desperate attempt to cover up her mental lapse. "Only, I thought maybe Arizona or New Mexico."

His dark eyes met hers, and he lifted a brow. "Oh? Why did you come to that conclusion?"

"First, your drawl. Then your gun, and the way you wear it. You know, like a gunman from Tombstone."

"Well," he said in his soft, husky drawl, "I admit to having visited Arizona a time or two."

She wished she hadn't said it as soon as it was out, and knew from the sudden glacial look in his eyes that she had gravely erred, but Bethany could not stop the next question. "Are you running from the law, Mr. Taylor? Are you an outlaw, perhaps?"

"It looks more like I'm a victim of your overactive imagination," he said in a mocking tone, but in the next moment he was pulling his mule back and dropping away, leaving her to her own thoughts.

She stared after him a minute. He hadn't answered her question, but then, it had been a little rude. If he was an outlaw—where had that notion come from?—

he certainly would not appreciate her curiosity, and if he was not an outlaw, he certainly wouldn't appreciate her presumption. For all his cool courtesy one moment and his infuriating arrogance the next, Trace Taylor remained an enigma. Even Bentworth had not unraveled any of the mystery about his past, except to say that the last expedition had been an unfortunate incident that should not be discussed.

There were times the two men circled one another as warily as two strange dogs, but she had the unmistakable impression that Bentworth was cautious around Trace. Why? Did he think Taylor might be more dangerous than he'd admit? It was not a comfortable feeling, knowing that their guide was a possible murderer.

Bethany fastened her gaze on her father's back as he rode just ahead of her, and kept it trained there. If she just didn't look over the edge, didn't see the steep, rocky slopes that cut cleanly to the center of the earth, it seemed, then she wouldn't be frightened. She was supposed to *endure,* right?

But endurance was a word much more easily spoken than lived, Bethany decided as they passed through barren mountain reaches where there was nothing but cactus, then rode through villages cultivating violets and carnations.

Women sold fruit to them in one of the villages, attractive women that Trace said were called *cholos,* people with less than half-white blood. The social classes were fairly strict, ranging from Peruvian-born Spaniards known as *criollos,* to *mestizos,* or mixed bloods, to the Indians.

The fruit bought from the *cholos* was all Bethany was able to eat that day. Soon after leaving the first village where they bought fruit, the trail narrowed considerably, dropping perpendicularly for a thousand feet. Her appetite vanished, and was replaced by a rising sense of nausea.

They passed dry arroyos and green terraces, and crossed a stone bridge that spanned a deep crevasse. It began to grow dark early, as the high mountain peaks cast long shadows. They had left Lima before first light, and were not even halfway to Huancayo by the time they stopped for the night. Grateful for the dusk, Bethany hung weakly over her mule's neck when they stopped in a small village. She felt frozen to the back of her mule, and only at her father's coaxing, could she relinquish her death grip on the animal's saddle.

"Dear me," Professor Brasfield lamented anxiously, "I wonder if Mr. Taylor is right about your not accompanying us on this—"

"Don't say it!" Bethany gasped out as she sagged in her father's arms. "Just don't say it—not after what I've been through today!"

Lowering her to the ground, Brasfield glanced up at Trace with a worried frown. "What should I do for her?"

He shrugged. "Let her rest. I'm more worried about her mule than I am her. She'll be fine, but the mule looks a little ragged around the edges."

Bethany glared up at his unsympathetic face through her lashes. Her hair had come loose from the neat braid she'd wound around her head that morning, and now hung lankly in her eyes, partially obscuring her vision. She brushed it aside so that she could glare at Trace more clearly.

"Don't worry so, Mr. Taylor, I'm fine, really I am!"

"I had no doubts about that, Miss Brasfield," he replied in an amused tone. "You seem sturdy enough."

For some reason, that term stung. Sturdy was a word that should be applied to chairs and tables, or perhaps to young men, but never *never* to a young woman! But, of course, she could not deny the term, or he might point out to her that a fragile woman had no place on such an arduous trip.

So Bethany forced a smile at him, and gritted, "Thank you," in a voice that sounded singularly unthankful.

With the sun down behind high, jagged peaks, the air was much cooler. Though it certainly had not offered much in the way of light, Bethany realized that it had provided a great deal of warmth. She shivered, and dug into her pack for a thick sweater and several blankets.

"You won't really need those, Miss Brasfield," Trace said to her. He swept one arm toward the collection of mud and straw huts. "The villagers here are quite friendly, and know how to keep their homes warm. They've shared their *chuño* with us, a welcoming gesture since their supply has dwindled by this time of year."

"Chuño?" Bethany echoed uncertainly. "What is that?"

"An Andean food staple—potatoes with the moisture squeezed out," he replied. "Their word for potato is *papa,* the same as the Incas used. It tastes quite good," he assured her when she gazed at him skeptically. "Don't insult them by refusing their hospitality, please."

"I wouldn't dream of it!" she snapped, but couldn't help a shudder when he gave her a small, flat potato and told her to eat it. It wasn't bad, but she much preferred the food they had brought with them, and told him so.

"Then I suppose you won't want to get in out of the cold tonight?" he mocked lightly. "It's much warmer in the huts than out here on the cold ground."

"Do you mean we are to actually stay in one of

those huts?" She looked at the squat structures uncertainly. They didn't seem at all inviting.

"Not we. You."

"By myself?" she squeaked in alarm.

"No. Usually the family offers a clean pallet and a meal for a price, but space is limited here. You can stay inside, and we will remain outside."

"But . . ."

"Being difficult, Miss Brasfield?" Trace asked coolly. "I thought you intended to be no trouble."

Clamping her lips tightly together, Bethany grimly decided to accept fate. If she was to be murdered in an Indian hut in Peru, then it was meant to be.

In spite of her brave acceptance, Bethany found it hard to sleep that night. Every time one of the other occupants rolled over or made a noise, she felt the hair lift on the back of her neck and her skin prickle. By the time morning came in another gray haze, she was sleepy and grouchy and glad to be out of the hut.

Then she was half ashamed when one of the children shyly pressed a fresh bouquet of violets into her hand before she left. She smiled back at the child.

"Not exactly headhunters, are they?" Trace murmured as he passed her, leading a mule.

Bethany shot him an annoyed glance, then sighed. "No," she replied, adding, "but I'm not so sure about you!" She had the dubious reward of hearing him laugh softly as he swung into his saddle and nudged his mule closer. Her chin lifted, and her eyes narrowed warily. She supposed she had been rather foolish about staying in the hut, but how was she to have known?

"You look better without those godawful glasses you wear," Trace said so bluntly and unexpectedly that she gave a start.

"Excuse me?"

"Those eyeglasses. You know the huge, owl-eyed things that cover most of your face and hide your eyes. You look better without them."

Flushing, Bethany shot him a quick glance and tightened her hands on the reins of her mule. "Am I supposed to say thank you?"

"I don't really care. It wasn't a compliment. It was an observation."

"Really! You are the rudest man I believe I've ever met in my life, Mr. Taylor!"

"Am I? You've led a sheltered existence if that's so, Miss Brasfield." There was a thread of amusement in his voice as he stared at her from under the brim of his battered brown fedora.

"Not so sheltered that I haven't had experience with arrogant, brash men like yourself," Bethany returned as she met his steady gaze. "Are you determined to punish me with rudeness because I dared to come along when you made it plain you didn't want me to do so, Mr. Taylor? If that is the case, let me add childish and immature to my opinion of you."

To her surprise, he laughed. "If words were weapons, I would be mortally wounded right now. Who taught you to fight so furiously, Miss Brasfield?"

"I . . . I don't know what you mean!" she said uncertainly. "I just dislike being treated with rudeness or contempt."

"Truce?"

"What?"

"Truce—you know, a cease-fire of hostilities. Until something else comes up, anyway."

Bethany had the thought that when Trace Taylor smiled, he was quite devastatingly handsome. There was a rugged appeal to his features that she supposed some women found irresistible. Of course, she was immune to the physical attractions between male and female. Stephen Averill had shown her the folly in such a course only too well!

"Perhaps," she relented when he prompted her again. "But I reserve the right to resume hostilities at the first sign of attack, Mr. Taylor!"

"Ah, trustful, aren't you?" Trace said. "Not that I really blame you."

She half turned in her saddle and met his darkly amused gaze. "May I ask why this effort at being polite? It seems rather forced."

"It is. But I have the same aversion to traveling with a surly companion as you do. And besides, if you don't trust me now, you may not trust my decisions once we're in the mountains. That could be deadly."

"Mountains?" Bethany echoed. "What do you call these cliffs we've already climbed? Does it get worse than this?"

Trace shrugged. "You'll find out soon enough, if you insist upon staying with the expedition when it gets really rough."

"You seem pretty certain that I'll be too weak to keep up with the rest of you, Mr. Taylor."

Trace tugged at the brim of his fedora and gestured to the Indian bearers carrying their supplies. "Even the Quechuas find it difficult at times, Miss Brasfield. Why should I expect you to be any different?"

"But you are different? Is that what you're telling me? That you and my father are able to carry on when I—a mere female—cannot?"

"Look," he said with a snap, "I'm used to it, your father would kill himself just to see a few ancient rocks, and the Quechua will simply disappear when it gets too rough. You, however, will try to push yourself beyond what you can do just to make a point. I know your type."

"Do you? Then you must know that nothing you

say—ever how nicely you say it—will make me turn back." Bethany met his smoldering gaze steadily, and wasn't surprised when he kicked his mule into a trot and rode away without replying. She hadn't really expected him to answer her. He'd only chosen another form of manipulation with his smiling effort to coax her into staying behind. So much for the truce.

Gazing after him, Bethany had the thought that he was not a man to take "no" for an answer. He undoubtedly thought she would eventually stay behind, and had no scruples about using whatever method possible to ensure that she would. If it hadn't made her so angry, she would have found the situation amusing. But it did make her angry that he would stoop to using what he obviously considered his "male charm" to coax her into a truce he had no intention of keeping. Did she seem to be that desperate for a man to notice her? To pay her backhanded compliments? She seethed with anger as she watched Trace ride ahead of the small caravan. It may kill her, but she would never give him the satisfaction of seeing her surrender!

As they climbed higher the air was even thinner. Bethany could hardly breathe, and gasped for breath, bending over her saddle horn and wheezing. Her head ached, and the world reeled with dizzying speed around her.

She hadn't even realized her mule had stopped until Trace was beside her, pulling her from the saddle and setting her on the ground, his hands quick and efficient.

"Here," he said, and pressed something to her quivering lips. Bethany tried to turn her head away but he persisted, forcing her mouth open as he poured in a warm liquid that tasted faintly bitter, but smelled sweetly pungent.

"Aargh, what is that?" she muttered when he took away the gourd and wiped her dripping chin.

Sitting back on his heels, Trace peered at her with an amused smile. "Tea made with coca leaves," he replied, and grinned when her eyebrows flew up.

"Coca leaves? Are you sure? But why—?"

"Don't ask so many questions. It should help your blood adjust to the change in altitude, but it will adjust soon anyway." He flicked a glance toward the professor, who was kneeling close by and gazing anxiously at his daughter. "*Soroche*—altitude sickness," Trace said, rising to his feet. "It's a frequent malady up this high. You need to watch for the symptoms yourself, Professor. We'll give her a half hour to recuperate, then push on."

"A half hour?" Bethany echoed in a sort of moan. "How kind!"

"Are you sure you'll be all right, my dear?" Brasfield asked. His brows were knit into a frown, and his glasses had slid to the end of his nose as he gazed at her.

Bethany managed a reassuring smile, though she felt anything but reassured. "I will be fine, Papa, really I will! I'll get over this in a few minutes, and we can go on."

It took longer than a few minutes, but they were soon on their way again. Bethany did feel better, but she still clung precariously to the back of her mule, and was grateful when they reached a mining town at the juncture of two rivers. They stopped to eat, a meal of hot tea, beer, and bread, and oddly enough, she found it delicious.

"I see you've recovered," Trace said as she finished the last of her lunch, and she nodded.

"I think so. I hope so." Shrugging, she tilted back her head and met his gaze. "But I will go on, Mr.

Taylor, whether I feel well or not."

"Do you know, Miss Brasfield, I had this feeling you might," he said with a lifted brow and polite smile. His eyes narrowed slightly as he looked at her, noting the way her face flushed slightly and her violet eyes darkened with uncertainty. It was becoming easier to predict her reaction to his comments, he thought. All he had to do was wait her out, and he'd be able to leave her behind in Cuzco.

Tugging at the brim of his fedora, Trace moved past her to the mules where he was joined by one of Bentworth's men. "We'll be in Huancayo by nightfall," Brody said, and Trace turned to look at him.

"Yeah. Got plans?"

Brody nodded. "Bentworth said me and Reagan could have the night to ourselves. You got any problem with that?"

Trace shook his head. "Brody, like I told you a few years back, I don't give a damn what you do so long as it doesn't interfere with me."

"You still holding that against me, Taylor?"

Turning back to the mule, Trace didn't answer and Brody shifted nervously. He was a slender man of medium height, with fair hair and the annoying habit of tugging at his earlobe whenever he felt uncomfortable. He tugged at it now, jerking until the lobe was red and there was a faint popping of cartilage.

"Bentworth said there was no hard feelings," Brody said after a moment, and Trace shrugged.

"Forget it, Brody. Just try to stay out of my way, and we'll get along fine."

"I don't want no trouble . . ."

"Then don't make any!" Trace snapped in irritation. "We have a long way to travel, and there will be enough problems on the trip without you or Reagan causing any more of them. I won't say anything about what happened a few years ago, and you just do what you're told to do. Got it?"

"Yeah," Brody muttered, backing away. "I got it."

Gazing after him with narrowed eyes, Trace wondered why Bentworth had chosen Brody and Reagan for this trip. Of all the drifters in Lima, he had picked the two who had been partially responsible for the death of a very good friend ten years before. And if he ever found out that they could have done better than to leave Rick Scanlon to the not so tender mercies of the Apaches that long-ago day, he'd even up the score.

"What a group," Trace muttered to himself as he rubbed down his mule and checked the packs. Two worthless drifters, an English pirate, a self-absorbed professor, his stubborn daughter, and a score of sullen Quechua bearers, all being led by a man accused of murdering an entire expedition. If he hadn't been so determined to clear his name, he might have laughed about the situation. As it was, he had no sense of humor.

Chapter Six

Bethany thought wearily that they would never reach Huancayo, that it was just a myth made up to frustrate her. Frustrating, too, was the memory of her assumption that she would have no trouble keeping up with the others. It was a lot more difficult than she'd thought it would be. Her back and thighs ached miserably, and the high altitude left her constantly struggling for air. She felt light-headed and dizzy at times, but would not mention it for fear Trace would insist she be left behind at the next village. She longed desperately for a rest in something besides a crude, thatched hut.

Even worse was the increasingly bumpy gait of her mule.

Not one to swear, Bethany found herself forming words of abuse for the plodding animal she rode. It stumbled, it slid on the steeply descending trail, it terrified her. Was there a worse way to get down the mountain? she wondered, and then, as they rounded a sharp curve and she had a dizzying view of debris at the bottom of a sheer cliff, she knew that there was at lcast one . . .

"Thinking of jumping over the side, Miss Brasfield?"

She didn't have to turn to know it was Trace Taylor

beside her, and Bethany shook her head. "Thinking of getting down in one piece," she muttered, and he laughed.

"We'll be in Huancayo soon."

"I think that's a fairy tale made up to soothe foolish travelers," she shot back. "I'm beginning to think that all of Peru is made up of barren rock and Spanish needles."

"Spanish . . . ? Oh, you mean maguey. It does look like the plants you see in Arizona, I guess. Part of the same plant family, I think."

"Fascinating," Bethany murmured as she saw the hairpin bend of the trail just ahead of them and tightened her grip on her mule. "Mr. Taylor, I don't believe there is room enough for both of us to negotiate the turn just ahead," she said when it looked as if he intended to ride beside her.

"There isn't," he agreed affably, but made no effort to drop back or move ahead.

Bethany slanted him a frightened glance. High rock walls rose on one side, and the trail dropped off into a sheer fall only a few feet away on the other. "Then, I suggest you allow me some room!" she snapped.

"We've got time before we get there. Look, Miss Brasfield, I think you should know that this trail is the safest on the entire journey. If you're having problems with the height and altitude now, think of what is ahead of you."

Gritting her teeth, Bethany shook her head. "Now is not the time to discuss anything like that, Mr. Taylor! *Now* is the time for you to move . . ."

But Trace waited until the last possible moment to drop back, and could see from the drawn expression on her face that Bethany was terrified. He hadn't done it on purpose, but he knew she wouldn't believe that. He'd just wanted to point out to her how ridiculous it was for her to continue the journey when everything about it scared her. Was she that stupid, or that courageous to force herself into going on when it so obviously frightened her? He wondered if she knew the answer herself.

Clinging fiercely to her mule, Bethany was only aware of a sweeping sense of relief as the caravan passed neatly planted garden plots and villages with trees and tiled roofs instead of straw. Civilization of a kind, she thought hazily as she spied women in bright pink skirts and fringed scarves. Eucalyptus trees blended the skyline, and terraced crops burgeoned with new life. Springtime in the Andes.

By the time they reached Huancayo it was nearly dark, and thin edges of sunlight fringed the gray clouds in places. "The sun will shine tomorrow," Bentworth predicted. "It's the beginning of summer."

Sliding from her mule, Bethany leaned against its damp sides wearily. She welcomed the thought of sunshine, but was too tired to comment. Right now, all she wanted was a decent bed and good food and a respite from the terrifying heights. Who would have ever thought she would be so scared of thousand-foot drops? she wondered with wry mockery.

Trace and Bentworth's hired men saw to the settling of the mules and supplies, while Brasfield and Bentworth secured rooms in a small but nice hotel. To Bethany, it was pure, unadulterated luxury.

Cotton sheets were stretched over her straw-stuffed mattress, and blankets woven of vicuña wool were neatly folded over the end. Each room was tiny but clean, with a washstand and pitcher with which to wash, and a balcony overlooking the street and a panoramic view of snow-capped mountain peaks. Bethany's room was in the angle of another wing, but she still had an excellent view.

"Was heaven ever so appreciated?" she murmured gratefully as she sank to the comfort of the bed and sighed. A fire burned in a small, tiled stove, emanating enough heat so that she was able to remove her thick sweater.

Though a bath would have been wonderful, Bethany settled for the washbasin and pitcher of tepid water, just glad she did not have to sleep in a mean hovel. Perhaps she wasn't as hardy as she'd thought she was, she mused as she shrugged into a high-collared silk blouse with leg-of-mutton sleeves, and a long, tailored skirt and belt. Her clothes were a bit wrinkled from being packed in her bags, but serviceable, nonetheless, and she realized she'd actually missed wearing skirts. Maybe it was being released from the bondage of straddling a mule for hours at a time that prompted her sudden desire to wear a skirt instead of trousers.

Or maybe it was just because she wanted to feel feminine again. After all, she didn't want to forget who she was on this journey where she was surrounded by men.

Humming a light song—grateful for the brief respite they would enjoy in Huancayo—Bethany paused in front of the mirror and gazed critically at her reflection. Her pale hair hung lifelessly around her face, brushing her shoulders, and she frowned. She looked so—plain. Maybe she should do something different with her hair, make it more flattering. Not that it really mattered, of course, but it would make her feel better to look her best. On impulse, she removed her glasses and put them away. She wouldn't admit, even to herself, that she'd heeded Trace Taylor's comments, but she did admit that she looked better without them.

Bethany brushed her hair until it shone, then

plaited it in a loose braid from the top of her head to her nape, before tucking the secured ends into a lace bow on her neck. A few stray tendrils of light brown hair escaped her efforts to smooth it back, and dangled in front of her ears. As she attempted to tuck them back into the coils of hair, a light knock sounded on her door.

"Bethany," her father called through the door, "do come down and join us for the evening meal."

Smiling, she crossed to the door and opened it, laughing when her father's eyes widened.

"My, my!" he exclaimed. "Don't you look lovely!"

"Let's not exaggerate, but I certainly do look better than I did awhile ago," Bethany teased as she joined him. Her eyes sparkled with laughter, and her cheeks flushed as her father shook his head and said, no, he was quite certain she was the most lovely woman he had ever seen.

"And if you don't believe me, just ask any of the men at our dining table," he added as he escorted her to the dining hall.

For some reason, Bethany's gaze sought and found Trace Taylor as her father pulled out her chair for her. He had stood politely upon her entrance, and as he seated himself again in the opposite chair, his eyes met hers. A faint smile crooked his mouth, and Trace let his gaze linger on her flushed face until her eyes dropped.

Irritated at herself for allowing Trace to make her uncomfortable, Bethany turned her attention to Bentworth on her right. "This hotel is such a wonderful surprise! I had no idea such comfort could exist so high up in a remote area."

"Ah, it's amazing what can exist where one least expects it," Bentworth replied with a smile. "It is said that civilization is where one makes it, and I suppose that is true."

"Quite so, Bentworth," Professor Brasfield said, "quite so! Have you considered, for instance, how the Quechua Indians have managed to haul heavy objects up the mountain much in the same way as their ancestors must have done hundreds of years ago?"

"Yes, astounding, isn't it?" Bentworth responded. "It still surprises me."

Shaking her head, Bethany muttered, "I find it unbelievable after having traversed the same roads they must use."

"But most of the Indians have grown up in the Andes, Miss Brasfield, and think nothing of scampering along ridges that obviously terrify you," Trace put in, his dark gaze still resting on her face.

Bethany flashed him an annoyed glance. "Really, I admit to finding it a bit difficult to adjust, but I am certain I will soon feel more comfortable. My mule *could* be a bit more tractable, you know."

Trace seemed amused. "Tractable? I think your mule is half dead! He's so tame, I'm surprised he hasn't been eating out of your hand."

"More like eating my hand, you mean! I could hardly keep him on the trail today."

"Keep in mind, Miss Brasfield," Trace said seriously, "that mules are surefooted animals, and if your mule stops or hesitates, pay attention."

"In the middle of the trail?"

"Wherever." Trace shrugged lightly and took a sip of his wine. "A mule could save your life someday."

Bethany laughed. "That is certainly something I'll have to think about for a while."

Bentworth began to tell stories he'd heard about men being saved by clairvoyant mules, and teetering on the edge of disaster only to be brought back by courageous animals, and Bethany let her attention drift to Trace. He sat drinking his wine and ignoring the meal of rice and chicken and vegetables the proprietors had brought, and she had the thought that he seemed restless.

Once again the mental comparison to a hard-eyed gunman sprang to mind, and Bethany couldn't help but wonder about Trace. He looked almost dangerous as he leaned back in his chair, one hand cupping his almost-empty glass of wine, his eyes remote and distant as he listened to Bentworth's rambling dialogue. It occurred to her that she may have been right about him. He could very well be one of those quick-tempered quick draws, and she made a silent note to ask Bentworth more about him. Shouldn't she know important details about the man who was their guide, who held their fates in his hands?

But in a moment of rare self-examination, Bethany also realized that she wanted to know more about him simply because he intrigued her. There was something behind his caustic words and brief flashes of kindness, something that lurked behind his deep brown eyes that drew her to him, and she didn't know what it could be. He was admittedly good-looking; she'd already conceded that. But Stephen had been good-looking, too, and he'd been a bounder.

Bethany's hand tightened around her glass, and she dragged her attention from Trace Taylor back to the voluble Englishman and his meandering conversation. Bentworth had progressed from tales of miracle mules to the great artists of Peru, and she brightened immediately.

"Oh," Bethany broke in, "I am extremely interested in learning about Peru's artists. I studied briefly at the university in San Diego, and my professor was only beginning his lectures on Peruvian artists when I stopped."

"You studied art, m'dear?" Bentworth asked with a lifted brow and polite smile. "I had no idea."

Half embarrassed, Bethany said, "Well, only for a short time. I don't have much talent, you see, only a great interest, and so I thought it best to stay home and help Papa with some of his projects."

"Yes," Professor Brasfield said, "I believe I was working on the Mayan tiles at the time, wasn't I? And I had to have someone competent enough to help me without shattering those fragile pieces of clay." He shook his head ruefully. "Bethany is the only one I've ever trained."

Trace looked at Bethany with narrowed eyes for a moment. "How fortunate that she has such limited talent," he said softly, adding, "Otherwise, she might have pursued a career in art and you would have been without an assistant."

Professor Brasfield gazed at him with a slight frown. "Yes, I suppose that's true," he said slowly. "It does sound rather awkward when you put it like that though, Mr. Taylor."

"Does it? Sorry."

Bethany had the thought that he didn't sound the least bit sorry, and shifted uneasily in her chair. "Well, at any rate," she said quickly, "I still dabble with my paints or chalk now and then. I've wished I had brought them with me. I could have sketched spectacular views of the mountains from my window."

"Ah, isn't that the way it always goes?" Bentworth said with a shrug. "One goes off and thinks one has remembered everything, then *voilà!* One discovers that one has left behind something quite useful."

As Bentworth began to relate stories of journeys long past, Bethany tried to avoid Trace's considering gaze. His dark eyes returned to her again and again as she ate her rice and chicken, and made her wish the meal was over.

"There's dancing in the central plaza," Bentworth said when they had finished their meal and were drinking cups of *cortado,* a sweet espresso topped with frothy mounds of cream. "Shall we go and watch?"

"Dancing?" Bethany asked. "Is this a nightly event?"

"No, just on Saturday nights. Tomorrow is market day, one of the most famous in South America," Bentworth said. "I believe we intend to stay until Monday, do we not, Taylor?"

Shrugging, Trace replied, "That was yours and the professor's decision, Bentworth. I'm just the guide. Remember?"

There was a veiled mockery in his words, but his eyes revealed nothing when he met Bentworth's sharp glance.

"Yes, Taylor, that's right," Bentworth said, and rose from his chair to extend a hand to Bethany. "Come, m'dear. Allow me to be your escort. I've always wanted to escort a ravishingly beautiful woman to a dance."

Slightly embarrassed by his effusive words, Bethany could feel Trace's amused gaze on her and felt even more uncomfortable. How could the man make her feel so uneasy by just a glance? she wondered irritably. Well, she had no intention of allowing Trace Taylor to spoil her evening! A dance was a dance, and it had been two years since she had last been to a festival or party of any kind. That had been with Stephen, and since then, she had not been interested in those things. Now it seemed like an excellent idca!

"Spencer, do go on without me," the professor said as they left the dining room. "I am beginning to feel some of what Bethany felt earlier today, and I prefer resting in my room tonight so I will feel like going to the market tomorrow. You will look after her for me?"

"Papa, I'll stay with you," Bethany began, but her father shook his head.

"No, no, please go without me. I would feel better if you did, and I only intend to rest." He smiled at her. "I have some reading in my new chronicle that I want to do. Father Calanacha wrote detailed reports from the missionaries who once lived in the lands controlled by Manca Two, you know, and there may be some helpful information in his work. He mentions a city by the name of Vitcos, and I'm trying to see if he somehow confused it with Vilcapampa. It's in the same area, in the Urubamba river valley, and—ah, but this is interesting only to me." He leaned forward to press a kiss on Bethany's forehead. "Go and enjoy, dear. I will be quite entertained, I assure you."

When Bethany turned to invite Trace to go with her and Bentworth, he had already gone. There was no sign of him, and she felt oddly abandoned. Turning to the Englishman, she smiled brightly and said, "Let me fetch a wrap, and I will be delighted to go with you, Mr. Bentworth!"

The night air was crisp and cool, chilly enough for her thick sweater, and Bethany pulled it snugly around her as she walked beside Bentworth. Torchlights and lamps lit the plaza, and doors had been flung open to allow in laughing patrons. Many of the people were Indians, and quite a few of them looked to be American.

"Bolivian or Chilean," Bentworth said when she asked. "Huancayo is a famous marketplace, and people come from far and wide to attend. The Indian art, you understand."

"I see. It seems rather a remote spot to come for a

market'," Bethany said, and Bentworth shrugged.

"In Incan times, Huancayo was a principal city on the road from Quito to Cuzco. The Calle Reál is still the main street, as it was several hundred years ago. Huancayo has been the capital of Peru three times, and in 1854 Castilla signed a decree abolishing slavery here."

"I had no idea it was such an historical town," Bethany murmured, thinking that it seemed so primitive to be so well-known. "How exciting to be here!"

"Right now, Miss Brasfield, Huancayo is simply a waystop on our road to fame and fortune," Bentworth said as he maneuvered her into a tightly packed cantina, one arm over her shoulders. "Soon, we shall look back on all this as merely a precedent to the greatness we are about to achieve!"

He had to shout to be heard over the noise of music provided by blind musicians who had no other way to make a living. Stringless guitars called *charangos* throbbed loudly and were joined by *cerpas,* massive wooden harps. The blind musicians wore brightly striped ponchos and knitted woolen caps with ear flaps and tassels on the pointed crowns.

In the din of music and talk and laughter by the other patrons, Bethany had to lean closer to Bentworth to hear what he was saying. As she did, she happened to look up and see Trace Taylor leaning against a wall several feet away. He was looking directly at her, a glass in his hand, a mocking smile curling his lips, and for some reason she felt guilty.

Then she was angry at herself for feeling that way. He had not expressed a desire to come with them, had he? Why should she feel badly about being with Bentworth?

"I believe I see a vacant table!" Bentworth shouted into her ear, and steered her away from the door to a far corner. Bethany sank into the rickety chair he pulled out for her, and flashed him a smile as he sat down beside her.

"This is quite unique, Mr. Bentworth."

"Please," he said loudly, "call me Spencer. I believe we can dispense with the formalities now, don't you?"

"Well, yes, perhaps so," she agreed slowly. He was smiling at her so warmly, his pale blue eyes resting on her features so closely, that she began to fidget. "Though we don't really know one another that well," she said, "I do appreciate the fact that you have been kind enough to give my father the money for this expedition. He has wanted it so badly for years, and now you've made it possible for him to be here, Mr. Bent—"

"Ah, ah—Spencer," he corrected, and she smiled weakly. "You know, Miss Brasfield," he leaned close to say, "I find you to be quite refreshingly lovely."

Slightly startled, she managed to say "Thank you," then asked if he would order her some coffee. "It's quite chilly in here in spite of the crowd," she explained, "and I could use a warm drink."

"At your service, m'dear," Bentworth said smoothly, and rose. He hesitated a moment, then leaned down and said, "I apologize if I have made you uncomfortable, but I could not resist speaking the truth."

A smile flickered on her mouth, and she nodded, but could not dispel the uneasy feeling it gave her when he paid her compliments. For some reason, she felt they were insincere, too smooth, too practiced. She would have felt more comfortable with Trace Taylor's barbed insults than she did Bentworth's sweet words.

Watching as Bentworth pushed his way through the crowd toward the long bar stretching across one end of the cantina, Bethany felt oddly out of place among the gaily dressed people. The women wore brightly colored skirts and blouses, with striped shawls and flat-crowned hats, and the men wore loose trousers and brilliantly hued ponchos. It was an exotic mix of people.

She was actually enjoying listening to the languages flow around her, some of which she understood but most she didn't, so was faintly startled when a deep voice drawled in a familiar language.

"It will take him a long time to get back to you, so I decided to keep you company," Trace said, sliding into the chair Bentworth had vacated.

"I don't recall inviting you to sit down," Bethany shot at him, but he just shrugged.

"I didn't realize you and Bentworth were so close," he said as if she had not spoken. "Is this something new, or have you been seeing each other for some time?"

"Mr. Taylor, not that it is any of your business, but Spencer Bentworth is an associate of my father's, as you well know, and that is all!" Violet eyes flashed at him, and her mouth tightened angrily when Trace lifted his brows and murmured, "Is that so?" so softly she knew he didn't believe a word she said. "Yes!" Bethany snapped, "that is so!"

"How cozy."

"How rude you are!"

"Look," Trace said, leaning close so he didn't have to shout, "I just like to know the situation when I'm involved. It saves a lot of trouble later."

"I can't imagine what situation you might mean!"

Trace's dark eyes narrowed slightly, and one corner of his mouth lifted in a faint smile. "Is that so? I think you do."

Her heart began to pound furiously, and her throat

grew tight as she stared back at him. He was watching her so intently that she felt suddenly awkward and uncertain. What was he talking about? What situation?

"Do you know," Trace said when she remained silent, "I wonder just how far Bentworth would go with this."

Finding her voice, she said shakily, hating the way her voice trembled, "Go with what?"

Trace reached out and took her hand in his, ignoring her feeble efforts to draw away, letting his fingers stroke her palm with light, tickling motions. His hand was warm and firm, and Bethany couldn't help noticing how strong his clasp was as he held her wrist. When he let his fingertips range from her wrist up under the lacy cuff of her sleeve, massaging the soft flesh in circular movements, she found the strength to pull away, meeting his speculative gaze with a bright glare.

"Mr. Taylor, I don't appreciate being fondled!" she began, but when he grinned at her she grew furious. "If you are trying to compete with Mr. Bentworth, I find you quite ridiculous!"

"Compete with Bentworth?" Trace shook his head. "I don't know whether to be amused or insulted. Actually, I was just trying to see if you had any female reactions beneath that suit of armor you wear so badly."

When she gasped with anger, Trace stood and said, "Here comes your admirer, so I'll leave you to him." He leaned down close to her and said so softly she wasn't certain she heard him correctly, "Guard your heart, Miss Brasfield."

The nerve of the man! Bethany thought as she watched Trace walk away, threading his way through the crowd and disappearing out the front door of the cantina. Guard her heart? What on earth could he mean by that? Surely, he did not think that she and Bentworth . . . that she had any interest whatsoever in . . . oh, it was just too ludicrous to be considered!

But the seeds of doubt that Trace had planted grew quickly, much to Bethany's dismay. Now, she read different meanings into every comment Bentworth made to her, read hidden motives into his actions. She hadn't needed Trace to make her wonder about Bentworth's sincerity, but now she was doubly suspicious.

It didn't make it any easier for her to sleep that night. She tossed and turned, and wondered if it was the high altitude that made her so restless, or her tormented thoughts. A window had been left cracked to allow in fresh air, and she could still hear sounds of revelry in the streets below. Sleep seemed impossible.

Finally, rising from her bed, she stuffed her feet into warm slippers and thrust her arms into a thin robe. Perhaps if she stood outside on the tiny balcony, she would be able to clear her head of the disturbing thoughts that kept her awake. It was worth a try, and she certainly wasn't getting any rest anyway.

The balcony door opened with a high-pitched creak, and she edged out. A wrought-iron railing edged the small space in fancy curls and designs, and a pot of flowers dipped in the wind. Bethany put her hands on the railing and leaned forward to stare down into the streets. They were almost deserted below her room; most of the light and laughter came from the square where she had gone with Bentworth. It was such an exotic town, a mixture of old and new, and she wondered if all Peru was like what she had seen so far. It was a land of vast contrasts and mystery.

Time passed, and Bethany finally began to grow sleepy. She started back into her room when a sound caught her attention. It was a drawling, familiar voice, thick with laughter. She leaned back over the balcony, and saw a light shining brightly in a room opposite hers, on the hotel wing that angled sharply right. With the light inside the room and the curtains open, she realized immediately that she could clearly see the occupants, and drew back. Then something—she wasn't certain what—made her lean forward again, her heart racketing against her rib cage.

That voice—it was Trace's. And he had a companion with him in the room—a dark-haired woman. Though she knew she shouldn't watch, that it was snooping at its worst, Bethany could not tear her gaze away. Her throat closed, and she wordlessly lifted one hand to her mouth to stifle a cry. The room was too well lit for it not to be obvious what they were doing.

She could see perfectly, almost as if they were in her room, they were so close. Her legs were as stiff as if frozen, and there was a huge lump in her throat as Bethany watched.

The woman was naked, with large breasts and generous hips. Her eyes were large and dark, and her lips curved into a wide red smile as she stood looking up at Trace, winding her arms around his neck and rubbing her body against him. He laughed again, softly, and with an undercurrent that Bethany was beginning to understand.

Bethany's fingers closed around the railing in a convulsive movement.

Trace wore unbuttoned cord pants, and though he had his back half turned to her, Bethany could see his muscles flex as he lifted the woman. She could see the woman's face more clearly than Trace's, and saw her small tongue dart out to wet her lips, saw her eyes half close as she slowly slid down his body, pulling his pants with her, her mouth trailing kisses over his bare skin.

Catching her lower lip tightly between her teeth to keep from crying out at the sudden sharp pain that sliced through her, Bethany tried to look away but couldn't. She'd never dreamed that sex would be so primitive—had never thought too much about the actual act itself, as it was still more a mystery than anything else. Who would have explained anything to her? Horatio Brasfield would have been horrified at the very notion, should she have been foolish enough to ask. The nuns at the convent where she had taken classes would have given her a severe penance for being interested in carnal matters. With no mother to tell her anything, Bethany had been left to imagine how it would be.

Her imagination, she saw, had not come close to reality.

As Bethany watched, Trace pushed the woman back on his bed and mounted her, wedging between her legs. She clung to him, her hands clutching at his broad shoulders, her head tilted back and soft cries coming from her mouth. Lifting her legs, she bent them over his back as they moved together in a fierce, rocking motion that grew faster and faster.

Hot tears blurred Bethany's eyes as she stood in stony silence, wishing she had not seen them, wishing she dared move. She could hear the soft animal sounds coming from them: the pants and gasps for breath, and a high, hot flush stained her cheeks as she squeezed her eyes tightly shut. No more. She just could not watch any more, and she didn't know why she was so upset.

When the noises finally stopped and she opened her eyes again, Bethany saw that they had stopped moving so wildly. Trace still lay atop her, a sweaty sheen glistening on his powerful muscles as he raised to his elbows.

It was so close a scene, so intimate, that Bethany could not stop the sudden sob that tore from her throat. To her horror, Trace's head whipped around, and he stared out his unshuttered doors straight at her. Did he see her?

Standing in the shadows, Bethany held her breath, but she saw from the sudden narrowing of his eyes and the twist of his lips that he'd seen her. Unable to stand there another moment, she threw dignity to the winds and whirled around, flinging open the balcony door and into her room. It shut with a firm click behind her.

Trace was furious. More with himself than circumstances. He'd had too much to drink, and had let himself bring a nameless, meaningless woman back to his room with him. Now that he knew Bethany had seen them—God, seen them like this!—he only wanted to be rid of the woman as quickly as possible. Maybe that wasn't fair to her; after all, she was not a whore, but a comely woman who'd been attracted to him when they'd met earlier. The sex didn't mean anything to either of them. It had been a temporary solution to being alone and in need. And for some reason, he felt a vague sense of regret that Bethany had seen them together.

Now that Bethany *had* seen them coupling like wild animals, she'd be too shocked to allow him close to her again. Not that he *should* get close to her, he thought ruefully as he rose from the bed and stepped back into his pants. The woman looked up at him lazily, a faint curiosity in her dark eyes. He shrugged.

"It's late, and I've got to get up early tomorrow."

"You don't want me to stay?" she murmured in surprise.

"No."

A sultry pout thrust out her bottom lip as she rose

from the bed in a sinuous twist of supple flesh, and giving Trace another long look from under lowered lashes, she began to dress. Before she left, he gave her a swift, hard kiss and a vague promise that he might see her again one day if he came back to Huancayo. When the door shut behind her, Trace muttered a soft curse.

Matters were even more complicated than he'd thought in his worst moments of pessimism.

Chapter Seven

Bethany, lying shivering in her bed, could not get the picture of Trace Taylor and the woman out of her mind. If it had been someone else, perhaps the shocking reality of what was happening between them would have been lessened. As it was, her attraction to Trace made her feel foolish and ashamed. Why did she even think about him? And why did she feel so fiercely jealous when she thought of him with that woman?

Rolling over, she gave her pillow a vicious punch with her balled-up hand. Every time she closed her eyes, she saw Trace Taylor's hard-muscled body, his rocking thrusts atop a dark-haired woman, and it made her moan with shame. More shameful was the knowledge that she was still undeniably attracted to him. . . .

The next morning, when she met her father to go to the market at the central plaza, Bethany wore her eyeglasses again, and had pulled her hair back into a tight, unflattering knot on the nape of her neck. She stayed by her father's side as he exclaimed over the Indian folk art displayed in long stalls on both sides of the central plaza. Herb vendors hawked a wide variety of folk cures for impotence, hexes, fever, and other ills, along with burlap bags filled with sea stars to be used against heart disease.

All of the Indian people wore hats, some with the crown designating their birthplace, as once required by Inca law. Many of the women wore white straw panama hats with black bands around the crown, while sunshades covered some of them. Bethany thought the bright sunlight a welcome change from the clouds that covered the lower slopes of the mountains.

Rows of carts bearing fruit, vegetables, meat, coca leaves, ponchos, blouses, hats, rugs, and heaps of worked jewelry lined the plaza. *Mates* spread out on a woven blanket captured her father's attention immediately, and he smiled with pleasure as he held up one of the uniquely worked gourds.

"Look at this exquisite workmanship!" he exclaimed, and turned it in the light so that Bethany could see the small figures and floral design that circled the gourd. The pattern had been burned into the long-handled squash shape with a *quinál,* or white-hot instrument of fire-resistant wood, then burnished to a high sheen. "They remind me of Greek vases," Brasfield commented as he purchased several of them.

At one stall, Bethany couldn't resist buying a colorful blouse and matching skirt of loosely woven cotton, with intricately embroidered designs on the skirt hem and blouse cuffs. As the merchant was folding her purchase and wrapping it in a large square of paper for her, Bethany looked up to see Trace.

"You paid too much for it," he said, and when she glared at him he added, "but it's worth it. You'll be very pretty in those bright colors."

Bethany hesitated, uncertain whether he was mocking her or was serious, and decided to make a prudent reply. "Bright colors flatter almost anyone, Mr. Taylor."

"Some more than others, I think." The corners of

his mouth flicked up in a slight smile, and his cold black eyes beneath the brim of his hat were glittering as if he knew how cautious she was being. "Come with me. There's something I want to say to you—and to show you."

"No, thank you," she said in a short voice. She glanced at her father and Bentworth, who were dickering enthusiastically with a merchant over the price of a *mate*. "I prefer staying here where it's safe . . ."

"Come on," Trace said, reaching to take her paper-wrapped package from the giggling Indian woman with one hand, and tucking her hand into the crook of his elbow and arm with the other. "It's not far, and I'll protect you."

"Have you stopped to think it might be *you* I need protection from?" she demanded tartly, but he only laughed softly as he pulled her along with him.

"Why are you doing this'?" she hissed as soon as they were out of her father's earshot. "Is it because of . . . of something you think I saw?"

His lips curled in amusement, but his voice was low and hard. "I know what you saw, Miss Brasfield. And I don't intend to talk about it here."

He took her to the edge of the plaza, then down a narrow street filled with people. The sun was bright and the sky a searing blue, and when he led her up a series of stone steps cut into what appeared to be the very mountain, she saw at the top of a flat building a glistening granite spire. It gleamed in the light as if aflame, glowing white and seeming to shimmer.

"What is it?" she murmured when they paused in the shadow of a wall. "A temple of some sort?"

"No, just a nameless monument." His eyes lingered on her face until she turned away from his gaze. He shrugged. "It's solid granite, and there's no indication of how the builder got it up here or carved it from one solid block." Trace was quiet for a moment, squinting at her from beneath his hat brim. He silently damned himself for being weak enough to allow a woman—any woman—to get under his skin. This one had. He didn't know why; he only knew that he wanted her.

It had been a long time since he'd thought of more than a few minutes of intimacy with a woman. Maybe his way of life had a lot to do with it, the running that had ended in Peru, his job as a guide into remote jungle and mountains. Always restless, always running, he'd never known any other kind of life. Lima had seemed as good a place as any to end up, and he liked it. Or he had until the fateful expedition. Now he wanted vindication. And Bethany Brasfield.

Leaning back against the shadowed wall, Bethany gazed at Trace for a long moment. He stood with his face shadowed by his hat brim, his eyes distant. She had the disturbing thought that he was a very handsome, very intriguing man, and she wondered why he persisted in being so hateful to her at times. Did it really matter that much to him if she was along on the expedition? It hardly seemed worth the fuss and trouble that had already been made about her going along.

"I didn't really bring you here to talk about this damn monument, and you know that," Trace said abruptly.

"Do I?"

"You should. Have you ever been with a man?" he asked her so unexpectedly that she was momentarily shocked into silence. "Have you?" he prompted when she just stared at him with wide eyes the color of dainty spring violets.

"Really!" she snapped furiously. "That's none of your business!"

"I'm making it my business." Ignoring her gasp of anger, he curled his hands around her upper arms and drew her close against his hard body. She could feel the metallic press of his belt buckle cutting into her stomach, and the nudge of his gun holster against her thigh. "Have you?" he asked again.

"No!" she blurted out, then was furious with herself for deigning to respond. Her head tilted back defiantly. "I was once engaged to be married, if that's what you're asking, Mr. Taylor, but somehow, I have the feeling that's not what you want to know."

His mouth twisted. "You're right. Has a man been inside you? Like what you saw last night?"

Her hand flashed up to strike him, but he was too quick for her. He caught her wrist in a painless grip and held her tight.

"Let go of me!" she raged at him.

"This isn't your style, Miss Brasfield." A faint sheen of laughter made his eyes glow, but his mouth was a harsh slash in his grim face. "I have a reason for asking."

"Meddling? Nosiness?"

"Let's just say—curiosity."

Her cheeks flamed. "I told you—no," she said stiffly.

His hands shifted subtly from her wrists to slide up her arms to her elbows, and cupping them, he pulled her even closer into his embrace. "I was afraid you'd say that. It makes everything worse."

Comprehension flooded her, and her hands curled into fists, her nails digging into her palms. "How dare you even think that . . . that I might . . . that you could . . . how dare you!"

"I'd dare a lot more than that if . . . aw, hell, never mind. I'll just show you."

Before she could guess his intentions, Trace reached out and removed her glasses, then pulled out the pins binding her hair with deft movements. He caught her when she tried to twist away, gripping her chin in his large palm. His dark head bent swiftly and his mouth captured her startled lips, his tongue sliding between them in a smooth, hot movement that made her breath catch in her throat. A wave of panic swept through her at his harsh embrace, the steel coil of his arms holding her so that she couldn't move away from him, and when her head fell back, she shut her eyes against his intrusion.

What was happening to her? Why wasn't she screaming, pulling her head away, forcing him from her with any means she could use? Instead, she stood meekly while he plundered her open mouth with his, making her senses spin out of control. It was insanity, but she felt the beginning of a response, and moaned softly.

Hearing her moan, Trace leaned into her, pressing her back against the stone wall with his body, his fingers caressing the nape of her neck and tangling in the still-coiled ropes of her hair. The heavy lengths of soft brown hair cascaded over her shoulders in a cape, and he crushed it in one hand, his other moving to tilt her chin back as his mouth continued to move on her lips.

"No," Bethany was finally able to gasp as sanity began to return in a heated rush. "Stop it!"

"Are you sure?" Trace murmured against her ear, and she shivered as she nodded.

"Quite . . . quite s-s-sure," she stammered breathlessly.

To Bethany, this kiss was as inexplicable as it was unexpected. A swift thrumming in her head made her feel dizzy, and she thought she could actually hear the humming of blood flowing through her veins.

When he moved back, Bethany opened her eyes to meet his quizzical gaze, and could not think of anything to say that would not sound foolish or immature.

He smiled, and she noticed how his face seemed softer somehow, not as harsh and unyielding as it usually did.

"Why did you do that?" she asked impulsively, then flushed. She had said something foolish after all.

"I wanted to," Trace said with a shrug. "Or maybe it's just that you were staring at me so intently, with eyes like pretty flowers and your mouth soft and open, that I couldn't help myself."

"I'm inclined to believe the former, Mr. Taylor!" she said sharply, and he laughed as he bent and picked up her paper-wrapped bundle.

"That's probably wise. And it's easier to explain." He handed her the package. "I wish you would take my advice and remain in Cuzco, Miss Brasfield. I have this feeling that if you go along on the expedition, I won't be able to stop what happens between us."

"Good God!" Bethany glared at him angrily. "Of all the ridiculous things to say! If you're still trying to frighten me away, Trace Taylor, I must say you chose a fate much worse than headhunters or vipers! In spite of your vile threat, however, I think I will manage to have enough self-control for both of us!"

He laughed softly. "Don't be too sure of that, Miss Brasfield."

Somehow, Bethany thought disgruntledly, she had never considered having to endure the jolting gait of a mule when she had so blithely announced to Trace Taylor and Bentworth how well she could endure. The balky beast jerked and plodded, stopped when she wanted it to go, went when she wanted it to stop, and pierced the air with incessant brays of protest. The mule she had ridden into Huancayo had been left behind, due to one of those strange diseases animals were prone to get, and Trace had given her this new mule.

Mutiny, she thought grimly, was just ahead. This mule was decidedly *not* tractable, and now she understood why Trace had said her first mule was tame. Even its face bore a—well, *mulish* expression, Bethany thought as she nudged the beast's sides with her heels.

The mule chose that moment to squat down on its haunches and offer a loud protest that sounded to Bethany like the squeal of an unoiled door hinge. Flailing for balance as the beast rocked wildly, its long ears laid back and its head lifted, Bethany found herself in the ignoble position of being flung forward to keep from sliding completely off the animal and to the ground. She grasped its neck and hung on, while trying to disentangle her feet from the stirrups that were now dragging the ground.

"How goes it?" Trace rode up beside her to ask, his voice pleasant, his dark eyes alight with laughter. Bethany chose not to answer, and he shook his head as he rode past her.

Glaring after him, Bethany managed to dismount and tug at her mule's reins. Still braying, the beast was finally persuaded to rise and plod along the dusty track that Trace claimed was a highway from Huancayo to Cuzco. It hardly seemed like a highway to Bethany. It was rutted and hard as brick, and miserable.

"If you can't manage now, Miss Brasfield, you can stay in Cuzco when we get there," Trace had told her in a hard, unsympathetic voice that had only made her mad.

Guessing that he would have even more to say about her inability to manage her mule, she was determined to force the stubborn beast to follow her directions. Still, she straggled behind a few yards, and a patient Quechua who had obviously learned about recalcitrant mules, came back to cut a switch and hand it to her.

"Strike the mule back here," he instructed her in rough Spanish, and pointed to the animal's haunches. "It takes a switch, sometimes, to point a mule in the right direction."

To Bethany's surprise, the mule plodded along quite briskly after a few desultory whacks with the thin switch, and she was able to catch up with the rest of them. Trace slid her an amused glance, but her father was so busy rhapsodizing about the remnants of Incan ruins on the slopes they were passing, that he appeared not to even notice Bethany's flushed cheeks or angrily sparkling eyes.

"Do you see those?" Brasfield was exclaiming, waving an excited arm toward the brush studded hills rising above the road. "Terraces! Evidence of how the Incans were able to raise food crops almost anywhere! See? Do you see the stone walls dug into the slopes? They must have planted beans, maize, potatoes, tomatoes, and other food crops there—and here, beneath the very hooves of our mules, still lie the stones ancient Inca hands placed on the roadway hundreds of years ago!"

"Does he always carry on so?" Bentworth nudged his mule close to Bethany to ask. "He seems quite carried away by a few moldy stones and crumbling walls."

Slanting him a curious glance, Bethany nodded. "Yes, he does become excited over such things. Tell me, Mr. Bentworth, don't—"

"Spencer, remember?" he prompted, and she managed a smile.

"Spencer, then. Don't you ever become excited about your finds? Pardon me if I'm wrong, but I sense a great deal of—shall we say—detached—interest, instead of a genuine excitement about archaeological discoveries. I would have thought that a true explorer would understand my father's pleasure at seeing these things."

"Forgive me if I seem rather blasé about these old walls and stairways, m'dear," Bentworth replied, "but I am quite accustomed to seeing them, you understand. I've passed this way many times before, and therefore I know that there is much more to be seen, things that will make these ancient stones pale by comparison. Do you understand what I mean?"

"Yes," Bethany said slowly, "I suppose I do. It's just that I would have thought you would be more understanding."

"Miss Brasfield—may I call you Bethany?—I know that these vegetation-covered ruins are of vast interest to him now, but I also know that when he sees what lies ahead—ah, he will never look upon these ordinary walls as spectacular again!"

"I'm sure you' re right," Bethany agreed after a moment. But when Bentworth had ridden ahead to join her father and point out other interests to him, she couldn't help but think about him. He seemed so casual about things that she had always considered of great interest, and Bethany remembered her doubts of the night before, the doubts that Trace had only magnified with his barbed comments about Bentworth's sincerity.

Was he interested in the value of the finds as monetary rather than historical? Even the men he'd hired to go along with them seemed more mercenary than archaeological, rough men who couldn't look directly at her, but looked away whenever she was near. Brody and Reagan were supposed to help her father with the heavy work of excavation when—and if—they found the lost city. Bethany doubted they would be of much use, however, as menial laborers.

She was still pondering her doubts when Trace Taylor dropped back to talk to her, his dark eyes skimming over her in a slow, knowing way that made Bethany uncomfortable.

"Artega was able to give you a few pointers about your new mule, I see," he said, and Bethany glared at him.

"You could have done the same, I'm sure!"

"Ah, but you told me—let me think of your exact words—'I can take care of myself without your help!'—So I didn't want to interfere with your right to do so."

"That's very kind of you, Mr. Taylor. I'll remember that in the future." She sat stiffly, aware that his gaze was lingering on her face, and wondered why she felt that odd, nervous fluttering in her stomach every time he was near. It had been that way even before she'd seen him and that woman, even before his insolent question and stirring embrace the day before.

She remembered too vividly the kiss he had given her in the shadow of that ancient wall, and felt a shiver ripple down her spine as he nudged his mule even closer.

"When are you going to admit that this is much harder than you'd thought, Miss Brasfield?" he inquired in so pleasant a voice that it was as if he was just remarking upon the weather.

"Are we back to that again?" Bethany shrugged. "I would have thought you'd be smart enough to see that none of your obvious ploys are going to work, Mr. Taylor. I fully intend to go the entire distance. It has been voted upon by my father and Mr. Bentworth, and we outnumber you."

"You've no true idea of what lies ahead of us. The high mountains are just a minor inconvenience compared to some of the dangers." Trace leaned closer to her, so close she could see the tiny scar at the bottom corner of his right eyebrow, a scar she had not noticed until now. His dark brown eyes were glittering, and his mouth had tightened with annoyance. "Don't be a suffragist, Miss Brasfield. You have no vote in this particular expedition."

"Don't I?" Bethany quivered with anger, and glared up at Trace. "Don't be too certain of that, Mr. Taylor!"

He let his dark gaze skim her face, noting the violet sparks in her eyes, the furious tightening of her lips, and the angry flash of the single dimple in her cheek. Bethany Brasfield was definitely a determined woman, he mused, and none of his efforts were working. Perhaps he was working on the wrong person.

Tugging at the brim of his hat, Trace nodded at her silently and nudged his mule into a trot, leaving her glaring after him. He'd have to see what he could do with Bentworth. Once the expedition left Cuzco, it would be too late for Bethany to turn back, and he doubted she'd survive the trip. It occurred to him to wonder why he felt so keenly about her survival, but he shrugged it away.

Trace waited until they had taken shelter in a *poste* that night before he approached Bentworth. The rough mud and thatched hut where they were lodging belonged to gentle farmers, and offered barely enough room for the family, much less visitors. Bethany was to stay inside as she had once before, while the men slept outside under a lean-to of sorts.

"Look, Bentworth," Trace said after she had gone into the hut, "I don't like this. I thought you told me she would change her mind about going along once she had a taste of it. She hasn't."

Firelight from a low fire flickered over Bentworth's face with wavering shadows. "Now see here, old chap, I hardly need you to point that out to me," he said with an amused lift of one gray eyebrow. "She's a rather sturdy girl, it seems, and apparently quite determined."

"Apparently."

"Perhaps if you wouldn't get her back up, she might see the sense of remaining in Cuzco," Bentworth suggested. "If you continue to use your unflattering methods of persuasion on her, she might just end up going the entire way."

"When I took this job, there was no mention of a woman. If there had been, I wouldn't have taken it!"

Bentworth took a step back and looked up at Trace's angry face. "Do I detect something more than a profound dislike of endangering the gentler sex, Taylor?"

"Yes, you do," Trace said bluntly. "If she goes along, I don't guarantee her safety. She's too damn good-looking."

"My, my!" Bentworth said with some amusement. "So, you are not immune to the fair Miss Brasfield, after all!"

"I wasn't talking about me. You know there will be other men on this expedition." A small muscle leaped in his jaw as Trace glared at Bentworth.

"I think that her father's close proximity will provide a perfect deterrant to any male urges, Taylor," Bentworth said so primly that Trace wanted to hit him.

"Do you? How naive."

Shaking his head, Bentworth said, "Surely, you can't mean that you would—"

"Look," Trace cut in harshly, "the professor wouldn't notice his daughter if she paraded naked in front of him! Unless she was holding an Incan statue or piece of pottery in her hands, that is. Do you seriously think he'd pay any attention to what is going on around him? I've seen too many dedicated men like him, and so have you."

"I find it ludicrous for you to stand here and suggest that you won't be able to control yourself around a woman. Are you so callow a youth?"

"We aren't talking about me, remember?"

"Ah, that's right—we're talking about the other men on the expedition." Bentworth's smile was nasty. "I suppose you are claiming to be immune to feminine appeal?"

"No, just realistic. Women are trouble on an expedition like this, Bentworth. And I've had to break up fights over a woman before. I'm quite sure I can control myself. It's *your* men I'm not so sure about."

"Ah, I suppose you mean Brody and Reagan."

"You suppose right." Trace shook his head, narrowing his eyes at Bentworth. "I've had trouble with those two before, if you'll recall, and I'd just as soon they stay in Cuzco."

"You don't wish to be responsible for Miss Brasfield, remember? And I must be represented." Bentworth added smoothly, "It's not that I think Professor Brasfield would be dishonest, it's just that I know how the archaeological mind works. He will want to record every tiny detail, and want the pieces he finds to go to some museum before I have the opportunity to claim my share." Shaking his head, he added, "No, my men must go along."

"As long as they understand they follow my orders or be sent back, fine. If not, you can hire them to lead the expedition because I won't."

"My, what a touchy chap you are, Taylor! Don't worry. Brody and Reagan have their instructions. They'll follow orders to the letter."

"*My* orders, Bentworth—not yours."

An amused smile curled his thin lips as Bentworth gave a slow nod of his head. "You've learned a bit since the last time I hired you, Taylor. All right—*your* or-

ders."
"And the woman?"
"I can't do anything if she insists upon going along. I am afraid that her father would balk if she were to be left behind unwillingly. And to be quite frank, I need Brasfield and his expertise."
"You need me, too, remember?"
"That, my dear chap, is the only reason you are here," Bentworth responded coldly.
Trace took a step closer, and felt a moment's satisfaction at the flare of uneasiness in Bentworth's eyes. "No, the only reason I am here," he said softly, "is because I need to prove something. And if you try and mess it up for me, I don't make any promises about finding this city you seem to want so badly. I might just forget how to get there."
Clearing his throat, Bentworth took a step back and blustered, "Now see here, Taylor! Is that a threat?"
"A promise. I'm still not certain you didn't have something to do with the fate of the last expedition I led."
"Of all the ridiculous—! I was in Valparaiso at the time of that expedition, as you well know. . . ."
"That's not what I meant. I don't think you want to climb mountains and commit sabotage. But I do think you had an interest in the failure of it."
"If you will recall, I am the one who lost money on that risky venture, as well as a very close friend!"
"Did you? I had the idea that Reynolds wasn't that close a friend." Trace shrugged, and gazed narrowly at Bentworth's face in the dim light of the fire. "Or maybe he didn't know that."
"I'm beginning," Bentworth said tightly, "to regret hiring you!"
"Then fire me." When Bentworth remained silent, Trace laughed softly. "Right now we need each other.

Remember that."

After Trace pivoted on his heel and strode away into the shadows, Bentworth remained gazing after him for some time, his brow furrowed in thought. "Cocky bastard," he murmured finally, and motioned for Brody to join him in front of the lean-to.

Glancing over his shoulder, Trace saw Brody join his employer, and saw them confer in hushed tones. He smiled to himself. He had to be crazy to continue! It would have been obvious to the dullest wit that Spencer Bentworth had every intention of cheating Brasfield out of any artifacts he found. If the professor hadn't been so focused on just his work, he might have noticed it himself. He was surprised that Brasfield's daughter hadn't noticed it—or maybe she had. She wasn't stupid, and she certainly wasn't unobservant.

In the next moment, he reminded himself that the fate of this expedition's finds didn't matter to him—only the outcome. If Brasfield and his daughter weren't smart enough to keep from being cheated, that was their problem. He had nothing to do with that portion of the expedition. His reputation as a guide rested solely on getting them to and from their destination safely. And that was all he intended to worry about.

Chapter Eight

Bethany wore her glasses again. Actually, it was more an act of defense against Trace Taylor than it was against unwelcome attention from anyone else. Not that she had too much to worry about on that score. Bentworth seemed preoccupied, Brody and Reagan seemed to prefer keeping their distance from her, and Trace had not spoken more than a handful of words to her since their last quarrel.

There were moments, Bethany thought ruefully, when she wished her father were not so single-minded. Right now she could have used some fatherly advice.

She pushed at the heavy eyeglasses on the bridge of her nose and glanced up from the book she was reading by the fire. There was no *poste* to seek refuge in this night, only the hard ground and wild terrain around them. She could hear vague rustlings in the thick underbrush, and the distant scream of a wild animal that made her shudder.

"Cold?" Bentworth asked solicitously, and Bethany shook her head.

"No, not really. Though the wind is brisk and the air cool when the sun goes down."

"It's the altitude. Here, take my poncho. It's quite

warm." He handed a brightly colored woven garment to her, and Bethany shrugged into it with a smile of thanks. "You know, we'll be in Cuzco in a few days," Bentworth said. "After a day's rest, you will continue on your adventure, and I will go on to La Paz in Bolivia for a time. They have recently finished construction on a railroad there, and perhaps travel will be more—convenient—than by mule."

Laughing at his wry expression, Bethany sympathized, "I find it difficult to adjust to mules myself! At least they seem to be surefooted on some of the worst part of the road."

"They're good animals for mountain trails, less skittish than horses, I understand." After a pause, Bentworth said, "I hope you don't think I'm prying, m'dear, but is there some personal reason for your insistence upon continuing the journey with your father? I would greatly enjoy your lovely company in Cuzco—chaperoned, of course—and you would like La Paz very much. I understand that the ruins at Tiahuanaco are quite easy to reach, and provide an excellent opportunity to view ancient temples. . . ."

"Spencer," Bethany interrupted, "I appreciate the offer, but I am persuaded that my place is with my father. After listening to him describe the Incas for so long, I am as excited as he about the prospect of a lost city high in the clouds. I want to be with him when he realizes his dream. Surely you understand."

Sighing, Bentworth smiled at her. "Yes, I do understand your motives, if not your perseverance in the face of grim dangers."

"Grim dangers?" Bethany echoed. "How melodramatic! Are they as bad as all that?"

"Let me answer that," Trace Taylor said, coming up beside them with a loose, easy stride, then crouching down just beyond the fire. Light played over his face as he caught Bethany's startled gaze, and his voice was flat. "I have already mentioned snakes, Miss Brasfield, and there are plenty in the jungles. There are also dangerous animals—jaguars, pumas, lethal insects whose bite can kill a man within seconds, and . . ."

"All right, Mr. Taylor," Bethany cut in icily, "I can see where this is leading. Pray, don't go on."

"Ah, but I shall. There are high mountain tracks that are not even two feet wide, and we'll be riding mules over them. A misstep will plunge you and mule over the side of a sheer cliff that drops maybe a thousand feet before you'd hit jagged rocks that can cut a mule in two as cleanly as a knife. And as if that weren't enough to make most men stay behind, there are Indians out there who aren't too fond of other Indians, much less white men. They dip their arrows and spears in a deadly poison before using them, so that just in case the arrow misses a vital organ, the poison will do the trick. And if they happen to capture someone alive, why then the fun has just begun." His voice lowered to a husky growl that sent shivers down her spine. "Sometimes, Miss Brasfield, they keep their victims alive for days before being merciful enough to kill them. Quite inventive are these primitive tribes. Shall I describe one of their favorite methods of torture? They . . ."

"Stop!" Bethany stood up and put her hands over her ears, glaring at Trace. "You know very well that you're just exaggerating things so that I won't go along! Well, it won't work! In fact, I'm more determined now than ever!"

Wheeling around, she saw Trace's mouth quirk in a mocking smile that made her palm itch to slap him.

Insolent beast! He was only trying to frighten her with scary tales like a young boy would use! – wasn't he? She tried to ignore the tiny warning voice inside her that warned he might not be exaggerating. After all, his dark gaze had not left her face, and no one had contradicted him . . . but that was truly ridiculous! He was lying. He had to be.

As she stormed away from the campfire, Trace shrugged. He slid a glance around the men sitting by the fire. "It was worth a try. And if you had any sense, Bentworth, you would make it a condition of your financing terms that she stay behind."

"Just so you won't be tempted, old chap? How unique! I had no idea you were so weak willed when it came to women. Of course, I should have guessed, after your fling last year with Sylvia Whit–"

Surging to his feet, Trace's eyes narrowed dangerously as he cut in softly, "I wouldn't finish that sentence if I were you, Bentworth."

Silence fell over those grouped around the fire, and it wasn't until Trace had wheeled and walked away that Spencer Bentworth found the courage to murmur, "Well, it seems that not all the wild animals are confined to the four-legged variety!"

"No, I daresay not," Professor Brasfield said with a frown. He looked from Bentworth to Taylor's retreating form and then back. "Are you certain this man is suitable for my expedition? There has been a great deal of friction, I've noticed, and Taylor seems to be one of the major causes."

"So, you do notice things besides stones and pottery shards," Bentworth observed. "I was beginning to wonder."

"While I admit to being quite absorbed in my work at times, I am not unaware of all that goes on around me, Mr. Bentworth! My daughter is very capable of defending herself against most things, though I believe everyone has been a bit of a nuisance about her going along on the expedition. If I see no problem with it, I cannot imagine why anyone else would concern themselves with her presence." His tone was faintly accusing, and Bentworth inclined his head in Brasfield's direction.

"Touché, Professor! There will be no more said about your lovely daughter going along on the expedition. I do hope you know what you're about, however. It is quite an arduous trek for even a seasoned expert like yourself."

"I'm well aware of that. I have every confidence in her ability to endure. She is an exceptional young lady," the professor said firmly, and there was no argument.

Not from anyone still around the campfire. Trace Taylor, however, was not thinking very kindly of Bethany at the moment. *Stubborn, hardheaded female* was the kindest thing he could think of to apply to her, and there were a few other appellations he chose not to use. Did she think that she was immortal? he wondered. Did she think she was so strong and impervious to danger that nothing could harm her? He felt like shaking some sense into her at the moment and had to restrain himself from going after her.

The least of the problems he could foresee was her looks. The worst was her lack of strength and endurance despite her insistence that she could endure anything. He'd been the trail; he knew how rough it was; she could only guess.

Swearing under his breath, Trace stood in the dark and listened to the night sounds and knew he'd done all he could. And he intended to remind her of it when the time came. . . .

For a time, Bethany began to see the most breathtaking scenery she had ever dreamed existed. Quaint villages gave way to vast reaches of barren rock and cloud wisps, the road winding through deserted areas where only silent terraces and stone walls lay in abandon. No inhabitants tilled the once-fertile terraces, nor lived in the shadow of huge shoulders of granite.

A small lonely but promised only a brief respite from the hard road as a bed at night, and once more Bethany was given limited space in a hut. She was not, however, very grateful.

"They keep pigs in the house," she muttered, and Trace shook his head.

"Guinea pigs. They're small, and don't take up much room. Besides, they're cute and furry, aren't they?"

"They'd be cute and furry if they didn't try to sleep with me," she shot back, remembering how she'd struggled against the last host family's collection of guinea pigs. "If I have to sleep with one more of those fat little rats," she warned Trace, "I swear I'll throw it in a cooking pot!"

He grinned. "Go ahead. Why do you think they raise them, anyway—as pets?"

That made her nauseous when she recalled how she had accepted her host's offer of stew. Clapping one hand over her mouth, she fled to the roadside. Sleep that night was not easy, even without guinea pigs under her blanket.

It was almost a relief to reach a village of some size again. When they arrived in Ayacucho, she saw the tall, slender spires of a cathedral thrusting from the valley floor. Professor Brasfield was delighted to learn that among the structures in Ayacucho was the oldest colonial building in Peru, the convent of La Merced. La Merced and the San Francisco de Asis and Santa Clara churches were all built in the middle of the sixteenth century, and were unique in their adobe-cane construction.

"Only a forerunner of what is to come, however," Bentworth said as they rode down steep, narrow streets to an inn. "Just rank newcomers compared to the Incan ruins."

"I find myself growing impatient with the journey," Brasfield said, "and wish we were already in Cuzco. From there it is not far to our destination."

"Yes, so Mr. Taylor has said. I regret that I will not be going on with you, but duty calls me elsewhere, I'm afraid," Bentworth said with a smile toward Bethany.

Aching from the terrifying journey over dizzying roads and bridges barely wide enough for a mule to cross, she could only manage a brief smile in return. She could feel Trace's gaze on her, and kept her back straight with an effort. The altitude sickness she had suffered had not returned as severely, but she still didn't feel well enough to go on without rest. Would they stop longer than a night here in Ayacucho? She hoped so. She could use a decent bed and food. And rest.

But sleep would not come. She was restless, just as she had been in Huancayo, and got up from her narrow, hard bed to look out the window. Though this room was not nearly as comfortable as the last, it had a certain charm. In the courtyard a stone fountain tinkled musically, and a profusion of early flowers brightened the stone tiles in places. Moonlight streamed down through a break in the cloud bank, shimmering in the deserted courtyard. Bethany pulled a robe around her shoulders and stepped outside.

A brisk wind curled her hair back from her face and tugged at the loose edges of her robe, and she held it around her with one hand. Her footsteps echoed loudly on tiles worn smooth by centuries of sandaled feet, and she crossed to look at the interesting figures gracing the fountain. Carved stone animals and gods grimaced from the tall spire, and water poured from the mouth of a llama into the shallow basin beneath.

Bethany skimmed her fingers over the cold stone. It gave her an odd feeling to be here in a land where time had changed so many things, yet left them the same. It was vaguely comforting to know that she would be a part of the effort to unravel some of the time-locked mysteries.

When she sank to the worn seat of a stone bench, she suddenly realized she wasn't alone, and turned with a muffled gasp.

Trace Taylor leaned against a wall, and when he saw she had noticed him, pushed away with a lazy laugh. "Slumming, princess?"

She stiffened. "I don't know what you mean."

He waved a hand to encompass the courtyard and the dark looming mountains over the city. "Out here in the night all alone, with ancient gods and dangers. And dressed—or maybe I should say *un*dressed—like a virgin sacrifice."

"Really, Mr. Taylor!" she began with a gasp of outrage, and he laughed again, softly, huskily.

"Don't worry, Miss Brasfield. They stopped that sort of thing awhile back. Damn shame, I think, though I would have to disagree with their method of sacrificing the virgins."

The conversation was getting entirely out of hand. She could see from the slight glitter in his eyes that he was well aware of how nervous he made her, and Bethany debated on trying to flee back to her room or brazen it out.

"This is hardly a subject for us to be discussing," she managed to say so primly that her cheeks flamed when he laughed at her again.

"I thought you were an avid student of the Incan lore. Surely, you know about their habits of sacrifice?"

"Llamas, Mr. Taylor, llamas!"

He stepped closer to her, and she could almost feel the heat from his body. Bethany shivered in spite of herself, and wondered desperately when she would have enough sense to remain in her room at night. Midnight prowlings seemed to end disastrously in this country—and where Trace Taylor was concerned.

"Llamas, children, healthy young men. Beautiful virgins. You'd qualify for the last, I think."

"Enough!" Her eyes sparkled with embarrassment and anger, and she glared up at his amused face. "This is not a fit subject to be discussing with you when I'm out here in my nightclothes."

"And alone."

Her throat closed suddenly. "Yes," she managed to say around the thick lump, "and alone."

"You know," Trace said conversationally, "if I were a young virgin and a high priest told me I was going to be sacrificed, I might have to do something about that."

"I don't think you have anything to worry about, Mr. Taylor!" Bethany shot at him, and rose to her feet. "Now, if you are through being ridiculous for a while, I'm going back to my room."

His hand flashed out to grasp her wrist, not harshly, but firmly, his warm fingers curling around the delicate bones and holding her. "What if there are still some Incan priests running around looking for suitable sacrifices?" he asked lightly, drawing her toward him in spite of her firm resistance.

"I hardly think—!"

"Ah, but you never know. Peru is a land of surprises. Could be one nearby, then what would you do?"

"Mr. Taylor . . ."

"Trace." His dark head lowered as he drew her closely to him. Bethany felt the heated thrumming of her heart, the surge of her pulses, and then he kissed her, his mouth as warm and firm as she remembered it. When she would have twisted away, he put up a hand to cradle the back of her head, his fingers tunneling into the heavy mane of her hair to hold her still, while his other arm curved around her back to pull her even more closely against him.

Bethany moaned, wondering why she was allowing him such liberties, then knew that she could have stopped rain from falling more easily than she could have stopped Trace Taylor from kissing her. He was a determined man, and he seemed determined to wrest some sort of response from her poor quaking body. How could she be hot and cold at the same time? Shivering and yet flushed with heat?

And—appallingly—she knew she liked the feel of his lips on her mouth, felt her reluctant response to him. He felt it, too, and smiled against her smooth skin. His mouth drifted in a searing path up the line of her jaw to her ear, then down the smooth column of her throat. Her eyes closed to blot out the sight of him, his heavy brows and thick-lashed dark eyes that seemed to see right past her pathetic resistance to the longing beneath. What was he doing to her?

When Trace's hands moved to cup her hips and bring her body up hard against him, Bethany felt the rigid thrust of his male body against her stomach. It shocked her. It frightened her. She didn't know quite what had happened, but she knew there had been a drastic change. His lips were more insistent, his hands more daring, and there *was* that, the nudging prod of him against her in a way that was vaguely arousing.

Wrenching her mouth from his, Bethany sucked in a deep, steadying breath. "Please! I . . . I need to go inside now."

Trace allowed her to step back from him, but his eyes were knowing and mocking. "No, I don't think that's what you need. I don't think that's even what you want. If the evidence of my damn male urges upset you, maybe you should think about why." His voice lowered to a rough, husky timbre that sent shivers down her spine. "There are a lot of different ways to sacrifice a virgin, Bethany Brasfield. I'd like to show you my favorite."

"Stop it!" Her hands shook as she pulled the edges of her robe more tightly around her aching body. "I know what you're trying to do, and it won't work. . . ."

"Won't it? Are you sure you want to go the rest of the way through the Andes with a man like me, Miss Brasfield? Maybe you can pretend to everyone else that you despise me, but you and I know better."

"I do despise you!"

He grinned, and ran a finger across his lips. "If this was evidence of your hatred, I think I could get real fond of it."

Spinning around, Bethany did not deign to answer.

She didn't feel safe until she was back in her room with the door slammed shut and the lock thrown. And even then, she didn't feel safe. No, there was something between them that left her feeling more unsafe than she'd ever felt.

The feeling lingered the next morning, and she would not even glance in Trace's direction as they started out. The rising of the sun found them up and on their mules again, pushing on toward Cuzco. The jolting gait of the animal made Bethany groan, and she cast a regretful glance back at the village of adobe and stone sprawling below.

They passed an endless parade of tiny villages, some no more than two or three huts, and when they'd left behind a fairly large village called Abancay, Trace informed them they were almost to Cuzco.

"By tomorrow evening, we'll be there," he said, and slanted Bethany a frown when she moaned audibly.

"Tomorrow? I feel as if I've ridden across the entire continent!"

"Not even a major portion, Miss Brasfield," he said. "But the mountains should be picturesque enough for you now."

Peering at the barren slopes fringed with green terraces still being farmed, she shrugged, still not forgiving him for his brazen actions the night before. "A decent hotel would be even more so. And I can't be the only one who feels that way!" she defended herself.

To her surprise, Trace grinned. "We all feel that way. It's been a good trip though. No losses, and plenty of fodder for the mules."

"No losses?" Professor Brasfield echoed. "How about that crate of photographic equipment that slid down the mountain before we reached Abancay? That was a tremendous loss!"

"It can be replaced in Cuzco," Trace replied coolly. "I meant no loss of life, Professor. And if the crate had been tied on correctly, it . . ."

"I know, I know," Brasfield hastened to say. "It was my fault, so I shouldn't complain. I've just never been very good with knots."

"What's that noise?" Bethany interrupted, half standing in her stirrups to peer ahead of the little caravan. "I hear something that sounds like . . . like a train coming!"

"It isn't," Trace said. "Not up here. That's what the Indians call the Great Speaker." He pulled his mule to a halt a few moments later.

"Great Speaker?" Bethany asked. "What is that?"

"The Apurímac River." Trace dismounted from his mule and walked to the edge of the rock-strewn road. He waved an arm toward the gorge below.

The road ended abruptly at the high, stark edge of a river. A sloping bank dropped three hundred feet to end in a swollen, rushing current. As she drew closer to the edge Bethany shuddered, feeling the wet air sent up by the river. A low, distant growling signaled the existence of rapids just around a rocky corner, and the water boiled past in ever-rushing fury. The caravan stood on the upper banks, pausing in awe at the grand spectacle below.

"Marvelous!" Brasfield exclaimed. "Majestic!"

"Bloody hindrance," Bentworth muttered with a sigh.

Bethany felt neither emotion. "How are we supposed to get across?" she finally asked, dreading the answer.

"Keshwa chaca," Trace replied, then shrugged when she stared at him blankly. "That rope bridge."

Unwillingly, Bethany turned slowly to gaze in the direction he was pointing. Her heart plummeted, and her throat closed. Braided ropes were suspended above the river with twigs laced together for the footing. The bridge swung slowly at the gusts of air being forced up by the river's raging current.

Bethany shook her head in disbelief. "You can't possibly mean that we are to cross on that spindly little grass bridge?" Her gaze shifted from Trace to the yellow braids looping sixty feet above the boiling brown ribbon of water. Looking from the rope bridge back to Trace, she shook her head. "I won't do it."

"You've crossed rope bridges before," Trace pointed out. "Why not this one?"

"That bridge looks too dangerous."

Impatiently, Trace said, "It's been used for hundreds of years, and can surely last one more day."

"This very bridge?" she echoed, her voice rising. "It looks as if it's about to disintegrate at any moment!"

"M'dear," Bentworth spoke up, "I know how dreadfully scary it seems, but those bridges are actually quite strong. Indian *chaca camayocs,* or keepers of the bridge, are responsible for building new ones every year or two. From *coyo,* I believe, an extremely strong grass. As this is one of the few crossings on the road to Cuzco, I am quite certain that this bridge is sound."

"Look," Trace broke in, irritation creasing his face, "I see no reason for lengthy explanations when we still have a ways to go. Now, Miss Brasfield, if you want to go with us, you'll have to get you and your mule across the river. If you don't—stay here. Or go back to Abancay. It's not that far back. Meet new friends. Make a new life for yourself. I assure you that no one will miss you."

Gritting her teeth, Bethany flashed a look toward her father, but he had descended to the bridge and was busily inspecting the horizontal stone bollards that were anchored in bedrock and securing the rope cables. Turning back to Trace's mocking face, she said tartly, "If you make it across, I'll go. But you go first."

He shrugged. "If the bridge is weak, Miss Brasfield, it may hold up for one or two to cross and then—the frayed ends will unravel, and down it will go. Have you thought of that?"

"Obviously not." Her gaze was drawn back to the river again, then to the fragile-looking rope bridge that swung with the wind. "But if I go first," she murmured softly, "I might fall—"

"Enough conjecture," Trace cut in, turning to rap out orders to the Quechua bearers. They obediently made their way down the rocky slopes, picking careful paths to keep from slipping, and began to cross the bridge.

Bethany held her breath. The rope creaked and moaned, and swung from side to side as the men walked across in apparent unconcern for the steep cliffs and deadly drop. Moss-hung stones seeped water from lichened cracks, and grass sprouted in erratic clumps on the cliffs overlooking the river, and sixty feet beneath the sandaled feet of the Indians, the raging water roared past.

"Now the mules," Trace said when the Indians stood on the opposite bank, and he turned to Bethany. "Do you want to go first?"

She gulped. Her palms were suddenly wet, and the blood roared in her ears as loudly as the rapids churning beyond a dark defile. "N-n-o," she stammered, then bit her lower lip to keep it from quivering. "Give me a minute—do I have to lead my own mule?"

"You can take care of yourself, remember?" Trace mocked lightly. His expression subtly altered as she gulped and nodded, and he added in a kinder tone, "But if you think your mule might give you too much trouble, I'll get one of—"

"No!" She shook her head. "No, I'll do it."

"All right, Miss Brasfield, whatever you say." Trace turned to the others, and in a few minutes Bentworth, Brody, and Reagan were on the other side. Only the professor, Bethany, and Trace remained. "Who's next?" Trace asked mildly, looking from Bethany to her father.

"I will go," Brasfield said, then offered, "and I will come back and lead your mule over for you, Bethany. No, I insist. It's the least I can do."

"Papa, really," she protested, "I will do it! It's only that the bridge sways so, and my mule is so contrary. I said that I could manage things—as Mr. Taylor so kindly just reminded me—and I will. Go ahead. I'm right behind you."

"That's a good idea," Trace said. "Professor, you go first, then your daughter, and I'll bring up the rear. If her mule acts up, one of us can help."

"Why is it only *my* mule that seems so ornery?" she muttered resentfully. "I do believe you gave me a mean mule as retaliation, Mr. Taylor."

Grinning, he said, "No, I didn't, but only because I didn't think of it." He gestured to the narrow path. "Well? Shall we go?"

Sucking in a deep breath, Bethany followed her father down the close path hewn into the rocks, and when they reached the bridge she closed her eyes for a brief moment. It felt like the icy breath of death was rising up to envelope her, the gusts ruffling her hair and dampening her clothes. Her mule snorted nervously at the roar of the river, and her grip tightened on its bridle.

Behind her, Trace prompted, "Your turn, Miss Brasfield," and her stomach lurched.

Taking a step forward, she felt the bridge sway, and tried not to scream. Her palms were wet, and she had to retighten her hands on the mule's bridle as she tugged firmly. A shudder seemed to ripple through the bridge, and she dared a glance up to see her father not far ahead, his mule plodding behind him with ears pricked forward.

"Don't look," she grated out to her mule when it began to snort nervously again. "Just don't look down!"

The animal was trembling with each step, and Bethany held the mule with one hand and the rope bridge with the other, trying not to look where she was placing each foot. She could hear Trace behind her, could feel the vibration beneath her, and quivered from head to toe.

"Keep going," came Trace's steady voice from behind her, muffled by the river's roar as she paused in the middle, unable to keep her gaze from dropping to the swiftly rushing torrent so far below. It boiled ominously, the madly churning water carrying along whatever was in its path, and she could see an entire tree disappear in the boiling swells, then reappear briefly before being dragged under.

Frozen with fear, Bethany could not force her feet to move as the bridge swayed ominously. Her mule began to paw at the twig footing, and the movement made the bridge sway even more.

"Keep moving!" Trace shouted again, and Bethany flung him a half-desperate glance over her shoulder.

"I can't . . . I can't!"

"You've got to!" he said, and stepped toward her. The bridge swung dangerously, and Bethany could hear the ropes groaning.

"No! Don't come any closer—we'll fall!" She took a step forward, then another, and her mule balked. Damp strands of hair hung in her eyes as she glanced up to see that her father had reached the opposite side and was gesturing encouragement to her. She couldn't hear what he was saying, only saw his mouth opening; fear and the roar of the river drowned out everything else.

Vaguely aware that Trace was beside her, that he had his hand beneath her elbow and was reaching for her mule's bridle, Bethany tried to tell him that she could manage. The words would not come.

One glance at Bethany's wide, terrified violet gaze and her pale, pinched face convinced Trace that he'd have to take control. Her mule was growing restive, and if it grew panicky, they were all in danger of being tilted over the high rope handrail. He stretched for the mule.

For some reason known only to the mule, it chose that moment to bolt. Long ears laid back, and the beast lunged forward, dragging Bethany alongside in the narrow confines of the rope bridge. She tried desperately to untangle her fingers from the mule's bridle, but as it pulled forward, she could not get loose. She was forced to race beside the snorting animal just to keep from being dragged. There was no time to shout; there was no time to call for help; she could only try to keep her footing as the rope handrail burned past in the headlong rush to the opposite bank.

Her legs churned madly, trying to keep pace with the wild-eyed mule snorting and puffing over the twig footing of the bridge, and several times she stumbled and almost fell before desperately regaining her feet.

Behind her, Bethany could hear Trace shouting, but his words were lost in the roar of the river and the blood pounding through her ears. There was only the survival instinct that drove her, the instinct to keep upright and make it to the rocky bank only a few feet ahead now.

As the mule scrambled up the granite path to steady footing, Bethany was panting with exertion and fear. Her eyes were huge and dilated, her hair hanging in her eyes, and somehow her blouse had become torn in the flight over the gorge. She didn't care. She was on solid ground in spite of her mule and her fear, and legs that were shaking so badly she felt as if she was about to collapse. She looked up at her staring father with a tremulous smile.

"I made it."

"Yes, you did," he agreed with a worried frown, "but why did you have to run? That was a dangerous thing to do, Bethany."

She couldn't speak. She just stared at him for a long moment. Run? As if it had been her choice? A sudden urge to laugh welled up, and she quickly stifled it. He might think her hysterical if she began laughing, and she wasn't sure she'd be able to stop if she began. Leaning against her mule, Bethany just shook her head.

She wasn't prepared for the hard hand that grabbed her arm and spun her around, or the bright anger that glittered in Trace Taylor's eyes.

"What in the devil did you think you were doing? What were you trying to prove by that run across the bridge?" He gave her a rough shake as she opened her mouth to protest. "I ought to shake some sense into you!" he growled angrily, and flashed Brasfield a hard stare when the professor spoke up.

"Now, see here, Taylor! That's my daughter you're talking to like that. You shouldn't . . ."

"Then you do it!" Trace spun her around again and gave her a shove toward her father. "If she pulls another stunt like that, I'll quit the expedition and you can get another guide."

As he stormed off up the slope toward Bentworth and the others, Bethany just turned and looked at her father. She had not said a word, not offered the first protest, and now she just shrugged. Nothing mattered but that she was safely across that bridge.

They made camp that night on a rocky shelf beside the road. As her first relieved reaction to be on solid ground wore off, Bethany grew angry at Trace for his rough treatment and high-handed attitude. She went to look for him with grim determination, and found him near the tethered mules.

"You had no right to do that!" she stormed, grabbing him by the arm in much the same manner as he'd grabbed her, and turning him to face her. "And for your information, Mr. Taylor, I did not run across that bridge on purpose!"

"No?" A dark brow lifted mockingly. "Sure looked like it to me."

"Appearances can be deceiving!"

"So I've heard." Raking a hand through his dark hair, Trace stared down at her for a moment, his eyes skimming over her furious face. Then a faint smile curled his mouth and he shook his head. "All right. So you didn't run across the bridge on purpose. I believe you. Feel better now?"

"Not much," she said.

"And what will it take to make you feel better?" he

asked in such a soft, silky tone that for a moment Bethany felt as if they were all alone in the world, as if no one sat around the low fire pretending not to listen to them.

"I don't know what you mean," she said with a glance over her shoulder. A campfire burned only a short distance away, and the hired men, Brody and Reagan, were crouched by the flames.

"Sure you do. You're angry at me. We talked about a truce once before. Maybe we should again."

A slight shiver rippled down her spine, and she pulled her Indian shawl more tightly around her. "I want you to give me credit for having some common sense, Mr. Taylor," she said quietly. "I fully realize that having a woman along inconveniences you, but I would appreciate your giving me credit for not being as difficult as you thought I'd be."

"I would if that were true, but as it is—"

"You know I haven't been any trouble!" Bethany snapped with a stomp of her foot on the ground. "Except for that altitude sickness, and I wasn't the only one to suffer from it."

"No, you weren't," he agreed. Tugging his fedora back on his head, he watched her from beneath the brim, watched the play of firelight on her sculptured features, and the range of emotions that flickered like shadows. "You know," he said after a moment, "you're really a very unselfish woman, Bethany Brasfield."

Taken aback, she stared at him. "What? What does that mean?"

Shrugging, he said, "Just what it sounds like. I don't know many women who would give up their lives for a parent, but you have. Not only have you given up what you really want to do, but you've enslaved yourself to a man who is so engrossed in himself and what he wants that he doesn't even care."

"Really, Mr. Taylor, I don't think this is any of your business! You're overstepping your boundaries, and I refuse to listen to—"

"It's true and you know it." Trace grabbed her wrist when she tried to wheel away, pulling her back around. "I'm only telling you this because—as a friend."

"Friend?" Hot tears stung her eyes. "I don't think you know the meaning of that word!"

Pulling her with him deeper into the shadow of a high boulder and away from the others, Trace ignored her protest as he said, "Think about it. Would your father know if you have other needs? Would he care? All he cares about is an able assistant. Isn't that what he said at dinner that night in Huancayo?"

She tried to wrest away but he held her fast, his fingers digging in the tender flesh of her shoulders. "Oh no, Bethany, there are some things you can run away from," he murmured huskily, "and some things you can't. . . ."

Anger warred with a mounting anticipation as she saw his shadowed head bend, felt his warm breath across her cheek and knew he was going to kiss her. When she would have turned away he gripped her chin with one hand and held her. "Give me your mouth, Bethany," he murmured, and ignored her faint protest, his lips brushing lightly over her mouth at first, then more insistently. Her eyes closed instinctively, and she gave a convulsive shudder.

Bethany wanted to tell him to stop, but the words would not come. Her brain had ceased functioning, and her arms felt suddenly weighted. Her breath came in long, shuddering gasps for air when he briefly lifted his head, and she struggled to keep from yielding to the unexpected surge of response she felt at his touch. Why did he have the power to make her feel so breathless, so—alluring?

It came to her in a swift rush of comprehension that Trace Taylor's long, considering gazes and brief caresses had been a very potent form of seduction, and one which was working. She did respond to him, to the sweep of his hand across her arm, or the brush of his lips over hers. . . .

"Enough!" she choked out, turning her head and pulling back. Yet she could not move away.

Trace could feel her rapid pulse beneath his fingertips, the slight fluttering in the hollow of her throat as her head tilted back even further. Her eyes were closed, her lips half parted, and in spite of her plea, he knew she did not want him to stop.

"You don't mean that," he murmured, and she didn't deny it.

Dark shadows surrounded them, and the fire's glow did not reach where they stood beneath an overhang of rock. It was as if they were secluded from the world, and Trace could not keep from pulling Bethany even closer against his body, feeling her soft curves beneath his hands, and the swift thud of her heart against his chest. His hands dropped from the small of her back to her hips, molding her slender form against his hard angles and planes, feeling the sharp intake of her breath as he pressed against her.

Bethany was in an agony of confusion. She'd been expecting him to kiss her again, and had denied and dreaded her own reaction even while she anticipated it. Yet, somehow her arms were around his neck, her breasts crushed against his broad chest, and her lips were returning hot, searing kisses with a fervor she hadn't known she still possessed.

She was as surprised as Trace at her response, and when he pulled her even deeper into the shadows, Bethany went without question. She was trembling from head to toe, and had forgotten where she was and who she was and who he was. All she could think about was the raging inferno that made her body ache for Trace's touch, for his lips against hers, for his caress. She couldn't think beyond the moment; her senses were hazy with a surging emotion she hadn't felt since Stephen . . . no, she'd never felt these emotions, these driving urges that pounded through her now. Stephen had been too much aware of her upbringing to kiss her as Trace Taylor had done. His kisses had been light and sweet, his touch soft and tender. There had been no urgency, no fierce pleasure in his embraces as there were in Trace's.

For a brief instant, the memory of Trace and the woman in his hotel room in Huancayo flashed through her mind, then his hand moving along her collarbone and beneath the edges of her cotton blouse erased everything but the moment. A deeply primitive emotion took hold of her as his hand lightly cupped her breast, his hard palm grazing across her rapidly hardening nipple. Shock waves radiated through her at his intimate touch.

Gripping his arms with both hands, Bethany could feel the strength in him. His muscles were as hard as iron bands beneath her fingers, and she quivered as he ignored her feeble effort to push his hand away from her breast. He could do anything to her, and she would have no way to stop him. In spite of her strongest effort, he easily mastered her every attempt to squirm away from him.

"Trace, no," she whispered wildly when his thumb

and forefinger circled the hard peak of her breast and rolled it in a sensuous motion that made her ache heavily. Parts of her body burned where she hadn't realized she had parts, and she moaned softly.

"You know you don't want me to stop," he muttered in a husky voice that sent shivers down her spine.

"Yes! My father . . . the others . . . oh, God, what are you doing?"

His head had bent, his lips tracing the path his hands had taken, and she instinctively arched into him instead of away, her body reacting with shock. The movement brought her firmly against him, and she could feel the unyielding length of his body against her, nudging urgently into the soft round of her stomach. Reaching around her, Trace cupped his hands over her hips and brought her up and hard against him so that she was pressed even closer. His mouth covered hers again, his tongue sliding between her lips in deep thrusts as he ground his hips against her quaking body.

Bewildered by the change in his body—he didn't always have that hard ridge there, did he?—Bethany was even more bewildered by the hot curling fire deep inside her own body, low in the pit of her stomach, making even her thighs ache for him. It wasn't right! It wasn't normal! There had to be something inherently wrong with what they were doing, or it wouldn't feel so deliciously wicked.

Boldly, more boldly than she had ever thought she'd be, she fenced lightly with his tongue as he explored her open mouth with hot, steamy kisses. She felt him shudder at her timid response, and knew that she was affecting him. It was only fair, she reflected dimly; he was wreaking havoc with her nerves. Just the abrasive scrape of his bare hand over her naked breast made her body feel entirely boneless, and her knees buckle. Did he feel even a tenth of what he was making her feel with his kisses and caresses?

"Trace . . . I don't know what's happening to me," she managed to half sob, and felt his arms tighten briefly.

He didn't speak for a moment. He couldn't. All his male urges were too hot and high for him to risk saying anything to her until he regained control. Dammit, how did she do that to him so quickly? He'd thought the woman in Huancayo would give him some relief, at least for a while, but it hadn't seemed to work. Just a glance at Bethany, at her pale classic features and the thick sweep of light brown hair that gleamed like raw silk in the sunlight, made him forget anything but holding her close.

Breathing raggedly, he loosened his tight hold on her. His voice was low and taut as he said, "I know you don't. Not now. One day, when the time's right and you're ready, you'll know."

Stark white moonlight silvered the edges of the rocks above them, and in the shadows Bethany clung weakly to Trace. Her cheek lay against his chest, and she could feel the strong, steady beat of his heart.

"With you?" she couldn't help asking, though she wasn't at all certain she wanted to hear his answer. He didn't have marriage on his mind; she was certain of that. But if not, what?

Sensing that Bethany's train of thought was miles from his, Trace didn't have the heart to tell her the truth. And hell, he wasn't sure he knew it anyway. The entire situation was crazy, and he damned Bentworth as heartily as he damned himself for creating the tension. He should have had enough sense to quit immediately. But he hadn't, and unless he could persuade Bethany to remain behind in Cuzco, there was going to be trouble.

"Maybe," he compromised. "If you want it that way."

His reply was even more confusing than she'd thought it would be. If she wanted it that way? Did that mean that he didn't? Or simply that he didn't care one way or the other?

"What do *you* want?" she heard herself ask, and could tell by his sudden stiffening that he didn't like her question.

"I can't answer that."

"Can't, or won't?" she persisted. Why was she bothering to ask? she wondered with a rising sense of bitterness. He was rapidly making it apparent that he was uncomfortable with the direction of her questions.

"Let's just say, it's too soon for me to know exactly what it is I want." Trace slipped her arms from around his shoulders and held her hands in his. A crooked smile tugged at his mouth. He'd had a lot of experience with the same kind of questions Bethany was asking, worded differently, perhaps, but asking the same thing. He had no intention of allowing her to trap him into any kind of commitment.

He held her hands for a moment, staring down into her upturned face. "I can't let myself get too involved," he said as casually as if he was commenting on the weather. "It will only complicate things."

Bethany could feel a rush of heat stain her cheeks, and her eyes were bright with embarrassment as she took her hands from his grasp and nodded. "Of course. I feel the same way. I suppose I was just—curious."

An amused smile curved his mouth as he repeated, "Curious? Is that what this was—an exercise in curiosity?"

Feigning surprise, Bethany said, "Why, yes! Surely, you didn't think it was more!"

Trace murmured wryly, "When it comes to women, whatever a man thinks is usually wrong. No, sweet Bethany, I didn't attach any importance to a simple kiss, and I'm glad to see you didn't either."

Stepping back, Bethany managed a bright smile. "Now that we have that settled, I suppose I should be getting back to the fire. Papa will be wondering what we're doing out here."

"He's not the only one," Trace muttered as Bethany wheeled and walked away.

Chapter Nine

Wearily focusing on the road ahead of her, Bethany was barely aware of the sheep and llamas grazing side by side on the dirt road leading through the valley. An ancient church stood at the roadside, its twin towers reminding her of California missions. Behind the church, serrated mountain peaks still capped with shawls of snow gnawed at the bright blue sky.

"This is the sacred valley of the Incas," Bentworth said as they rode the last few miles down into Cuzco. "The heart of the lost empire!"

To Bethany, it didn't seem like much of an empire. She longed for a hot bath and civilized houses, not rude mud huts with straw roofs and guinea pigs kept inside. But when they rounded a curve in the road and came out of a wide saddle of rock, she gasped with delight.

Rising in the valley between crumpled mountain peaks, Cuzco sprawled beneath the shadow of a gigantic stone fortress high on a hill. Buildings crowded together in a seemingly haphazard shape. Cathedral spires thrust up from foundations that had once held the Inca's magnificent Temple of the Sun.

As they rode down into the city and across stone bridges spanning aqueducts and river, Bethany tried to imagine what it must have looked like in the days of the Incas, when there would have been nothing but straw-thatched roofs.

Would there have been sculptures of gold and silver? Would the royal warehouses have been filled with tribute for the current Inca? Llama, vicuña, and alpaca clothing would have been worn, along with magnificent capes of varicolored feathers. She could almost envision the pomp inside the curved walls of the Golden Enclosure of the Temple of the Sun. It was a wonderful fantasy.

Bethany wasn't prepared for the reality of Cuzco.

Cuzco was worse than any city she had ever seen. It was worse than anything she could have imagined, Bethany thought as she covered her nose with a scented handkerchief and tried not to choke at the stench. Open gutters ran with raw sewage. Dead animals lay rotting in the sun close to market stalls selling fruit and vegetables. Flies swarmed everywhere, buzzing from bloated decay to the shining, ripe melons piled high in woven baskets.

Stone-cobbled streets were slick with a malodorous slime that caused the mules to slip several times. The narrow streets zigzagged erratically between high buildings. Many of the structures had been built on Incan foundations of stone, but the whitewashed adobe had chipped away in places to leave evidence of the unpainted stonework of the Incas. Earthquakes frequently shook Cuzco, and only the Incan stone foundations remained relatively unharmed.

"Simply marvelous!" Professor Brasfield enthused as they passed a building where the Inca foundations showed through the adobe covering.

Bethany stifled a choking retch. Marvelous? Perhaps the architecture was grand, and the people interesting in their brightly colored ponchos, wide-brimmed panama hats and fringed pancake hats, but Cuzco was not what she'd thought it would be. And she certainly didn't think it was as marvelous as her father did!

Catching Trace Taylor's sardonic glance at her pale face, Bethany straightened her spine and managed to sit erect atop her plodding mule. How could she claim to endure hardship if she couldn't even bear the stench of refuse? But her hands felt clammy, and her palms slipped on the leather reins as she tried to guide her mule over pocked stone ruts. Fortunately, the narrow streets left little room for the beast to go astray.

Her attention was trained on keeping the mule in the middle of the stone-paved road, so that Trace's appearance near her side startled her.

"Oh!" she exclaimed, jerking hard on the reins. Her mule responded by digging its hind feet into the cobbled stones and sliding on its haunches, depositing Bethany on the street with a slamming *whump*. She still held the reins in one hand, and could vaguely hear Trace ordering her to let go over the frantic braying of her mule and the noise of its hooves scrabbling on stone as it tried to regain its balance.

"Dammit, let go!" Trace commanded again, and leaned forward to yank the reins she still held in one hand.

Bethany's mule chose that moment to rear straight up, and its head slammed into Trace's mule. An immediate frenzy erupted as the two mules lashed out with flying hooves in the narrow street, and scattered the rest of the caravan in different directions.

Over the tumult, Bethany could dimly hear her father's voice calling to her above Trace's curses, and could hear the faint echoes of laughter from someone else. Bentworth? It didn't matter. What mattered was not getting trampled by the mules flailing around on the slick streets.

Slipping on the slimy stones, Bethany found it almost impossible to get to her feet, or even to roll out of the way. She could feel the greenish muck penetrating the seat of her pants and smearing her legs, and her palms slid wetly over stone worn smooth by centuries of use. In the whirling kaleidoscope that passed in front of her eyes, she had a quick, hazy view of flashing hooves and flicking tails, and tucked her head into the cradle of her upflung arms.

Just when it seemed as if she would get a well-planted hoof in her head or chest, she felt someone grab the back of her shirt and yank her up from the street and backward. Her heels and bottom skidded across the stones, and she bumped along the street in a series of jerks and hops before stopping. Stumbling and slipping, she tried to stand up, but the hand holding her shirt only tightened.

"Keep still," Trace's voice growled in her ear. "You'll only fall down again if you keep struggling."

Though she realized he made sense, somehow just the notion that Trace Taylor had rescued her from being dragged through more muck made Bethany rebel. She tried to twist out of his grasp and lurch to her feet in spite of his warning.

Unfortunately, Trace was right. Her efforts to stand in the muck only made the slick soles of her boots slide from under her again, and when she successfully managed to wrest away from his grip at last, she immediately found herself sitting hard on the cobblestones at his feet. He gazed down at her with an uplifted brow and an expression of mild amusement on his face.

"Determined little thing, aren't you, Miss Brasfield? I suppose you're satisfied now."

Almost retching at the odorous sludge clinging to her clothes and hands, Bethany tried to capture the remnants of her dignity. "Actually, I am quite embarrassed, Mr. Taylor. And filthy. If you will be good enough to help me up, I promise not to resist this time."

A note of laughter edged his voice, but Trace nodded solemnly. "At your service, Miss Brasfield."

When Bethany once more stood on her feet, she cast the now sedate mule a murderous glance. "Wretched beast!" she muttered, rubbing her palms against her pants before she realized that her clothes were even more soiled than her hands. "Oooo!" she wailed with a grimace.

"Here," Trace said, whipping off the bandana from around his neck and handing it to her. "Use this. It will help until we can get you somewhere to clean up."

"Bethany," her father called as he wedged a path through the mules and crowded street. His face was anxious, and he gave one of the mules an impatient shove as he pushed by. "Are you all right, Bethany? Nothing is broken?"

"Only my pride is injured, Papa." She made a rueful face. "Don't come too close—I'm afraid that I smell rather bad at the moment."

Professor Brasfield's nose wrinkled with distaste, but he struggled bravely to come closer to his daughter. "That is quite all right—I can stand it."

Trace snorted at the expression on the professor's face, and shook his head. "Look," he said, "why don't I take Miss Brasfield with me since we are both a bit . . . offensive . . . at the moment? I know a gentleman who has an excellent Roman bath, and is also well acquainted with a lot of Incan lore. You and the others can meet us there after you clear things with the city officials."

"Well, I don't know," Brasfield began hesitantly, but Bentworth broke in.

"Signore Bertolli? Of course, Taylor, that's a marvelous notion! I was leaning toward suggesting Bertolli myself before this unfortunate occurrence." He turned to Brasfield with a wide smile. "Signore Bertolli is an Italian merchant who has lived in Cuzco for many years. He is a wealth of information, and extends superb hospitality. He would be much better than one of the hotels." Bentworth turned back to Trace, pressing a handkerchief tightly to his nose. "I'm certain you can smooth over a somewhat—shall we say, odorous—arrival? Brasfield and I will see to the official arrangements, then meet you at Bertolli's villa, what?"

The matter seemed settled without Bethany having been given the opportunity to comment, and she stiffened. When she turned to say that she had no intention of riding off alone with Trace Taylor, he leaned forward and said softly into her ear, "Are you afraid to be alone with me, Miss Brasfield? I promise not to lose control of myself and assault you—at least, not until you've bathed."

Flushing from anger and resentment, Bethany realized how ridiculous she would sound if she protested. Her chin lifted, and she met his mocking gaze with an expression of feigned surprise.

"Really, Mr. Taylor, I only object to arriving unannounced and grubby on the doorstep of a complete stranger!"

Trace shrugged. "Signore Bertolli is no stranger to me, Miss Brasfield." A wicked glint shimmered in his eyes and he grinned as he added, "I'll vouch for your presentability underneath all that muck, if you like. All you have to do is nod at the right times."

"How kind of you!" Bethany said with a snap. "I'll do my best not to embarrass you."

"Thanks. Now, just get back on your mule and we'll be on our way. . . ."

"I have absolutely no intention of getting back on that mule again today!"

"All right. We'll walk," Trace said promptly, and took the reins of both mules in one hand. "Follow me, Miss Brasfield, and you'll be much more comfortable in a very short time."

Following Trace's tall frame down the narrow, winding streets, Bethany had an excellent opportunity to see Cuzco close up. The uneven stones of the road were missing in places, and stuck up so high in others that she found it almost as difficult to walk as it had been to ride her mule down the streets. They pushed their way through the Plaza de Armas filled with burdened llamas and Indians, then down more narrow streets lined with Spanish-style houses built atop the fitted blocks of the Incas. Trace walked swiftly in spite of having to pull the mules with him, and Bethany had trouble keeping up with his long-legged stride. She was glad when they came out of the shadowed streets and into the open again, climbing a steep slope that led upward.

"That's it just ahead," Trace said in answer to her testy query as to when they were going to arrive at their destination, and he pointed.

She wasn't quite certain what she had expected, but Bethany had definitely not expected the sprawling mansion perched atop a hill overlooking the city, and she jerked to a stop at the end of the curved drive.

Standing almost in the shadow of what Trace said was one of the greatest citadels in the Americas, the Italian merchant's home rose in a gleaming mixture of marble and stone that blended in perfect harmony with its surroundings. Tall trees rose in the cultivated garden, and exotic plants flourished around tinkling fountains and stone masonry. Several archways of stone resembled the Incan architecture she had seen, and it was most impressive.

Glancing down in dismay at her muck-spattered garments and the crust of wet mud coating her shoes, Bethany gave a faint moan. Pushing at the tangled mat of light hair in her eyes, she looked up at Trace. He had only a small amount of muck on him, mostly what had come from trying to pull her up from the street, and he was looking back at her with a skeptical gaze.

"You can't take me up there looking like this!" Bethany said, appalled at the thought of arriving in her filthy state. "I'll be humiliated!"

"Bertolli won't care, trust me," Trace said with an edge of impatience from manhandling two fractious mules through the narrow streets. "Now come on."

"But . . . but this man must obviously be very important, and I look like a . . . a beggar!" Bethany protested. "He won't want to let us in the door!"

Trace flashed her an impudent grin. "I know Bertolli, and he's very open-minded. Besides, I can always sneak you in the back door. . . ."

"Trace Taylor, if you think I'm going to be treated like a second-rate . . ."

"Don't finish that," he cut in. "I can supply the rest of your sentence myself. Do you think you're the only person who has ever fallen off a mule? Give Bertolli a little credit for being able to see that you don't usually roll in street gutters, Miss Brasfield. Now, you can come with me, or you can wait here like a beggar at the end of his driveway for one of the servants to come out and run you off. Which will it be?"

Through clenched teeth, Bethany muttered, "I'll take my chances with you, I suppose."

Trace's smile was enigmatic as he said softly, "You might be taking a big chance, Bethany Brasfield, you just might at that!"

She had no opportunity to ask him what he meant by that remark, because he had started up the curved drive ahead of her, the two mules following obediently behind as if knowing they were close to food and rest. She lagged behind them, grumbling to herself, but noticeably quiet when Trace gave the mules into the keeping of a servant and ushered her into a marble entrance hall. They waited in silence for an Indian servant to fetch his master.

To her relief, Bethany discovered that Trace had not exaggerated. Signore Bertolli was the most sympathetic and gracious of hosts, and insisted that she avail herself of his Roman bath at her leisure.

"Buono! But of course!" the portly Italian merchant exclaimed when Trace asked if they might impose upon his generous hospitality for a night. "I insist that you stay, Taylor! You are always welcome in my home, as I have told you many times." He executed a half bow in Bethany's direction. "And your beautiful signorina complements my humble home with her presence." Clapping his hands sharply together, Bertolli summoned an Indian servant and spoke to her quickly, then turned to Bethany with a smile. "Martina will show you to the baths, and will fetch some clean clothes from your baggage for you. Please, make yourself at home."

Bethany flicked a hesitant glance toward Trace, and he grinned at her. "I'll wait here for you—unless you want me to scrub your back?"

"As kind as your offer may be, I think I'll be able to manage on my own," Bethany said with a forced smile and a warning glare.

Trace's expression was innocent as he shrugged. "If you are sure you don't . . ."

"Thank you, no!" Pivoting on her heel, Bethany followed the Indian servant from the room, fully aware of not only Trace's eyes on her, but Signore Bertolli's interested gaze. How dare Trace subject her to rude conjecture! she thought angrily. And how like him to try and embarrass her.

Bethany's irritation quickly disappeared when the shy Indian servant led her to the baths Signore Bertolli had built. Marbled steps led into a deep tub fed warm water by a series of conduits, and baskets of perfumed soaps lay near towels heated by steam vents. High walls surrounded the baths, and a profusion of greenery cascaded over the tiles and from wide planters, making the high-ceilinged room look as if it was in the open woods.

"How lovely!" Bethany breathed, and Martina smiled shyly and said something she couldn't understand. By broken words in Spanish and descriptive gestures, Martina was able to convey her desire that Bethany undress and allow her to wrap a thick cotton robe around her shoulders.

Once done, Martina disappeared with Bethany's dirty clothes, leaving her alone. Bethany walked to the edge of the tub and paused. Water frothed invitingly, and after a quick glance around, she shed the robe and stepped down into the tub, immersing herself up to her neck in steamy water. Bubbles of heated water frothed, and within reaching distance lay a basket of scented soaps.

Lying back and closing her eyes, Bethany gave a sigh of pure pleasure. The motion of heated water flowing into the huge tub had a therapeutic effect on her, and she smiled. Long wet ropes of her hair swirled around her shoulders in a silken cape, tickling her back and waist. Sliding beneath the surface, Bethany thoroughly wet her hair, then washed it with strong, vigorous strokes, using perfumed soap from the basket.

She lingered as long as she dared take advantage of the wonderful bath, and when she emerged, Martina appeared again to help wrap the thick robe around her and lead her to a small room not far from the bath. In a mixture of Spanish and Quechua, Martina made Bethany understand that she was to help her dress, and had brought her clothes from the baggage.

Instead of the trousers and shirt she had grown accustomed to wearing, Martina had brought Bethany the blouse and skirt she'd purchased in Huancayo.

"Oh, but—!" Bethany began, then stopped. Why not wear them? Isn't that why she'd bought them? And what better place to wear such lovely, bright garments than in an ancient city! Besides, it was a welcome change from the plain trousers, shirt, and jacket.

That change was reflected in her father's eyes when Bethany joined them in the main *sala* of the house, a huge room with a massive stone and marble fireplace and plush chairs scattered about.

"Bethany!" Brasfield said with a pleased smile when she paused in the doorway. "Why, you look quite lovely in those garments!"

She smiled self-consciously as she crossed to where

he stood by the fireplace, feeling several pairs of interested eyes on her. Trace stood next to Bentworth, and Signore Bertolli came forward to greet her.

"Ah, signorina! You found everything to your liking, I hope?"

"Yes, thank you, Signore Bertolli. Everything was very nice, and Martina most helpful."

Bethany could feel Trace's gaze on her, but didn't dare look in his direction. His smile would be mocking as usual, and she didn't want to ruin her evening. Martina had brushed her hair until it gleamed with pale highlights in the lamplight, then wound it atop her head in a very attractive style, using deft twists and several combs. It had been a long time since Bethany had felt pretty, but she did this evening. The soft fabric of her clothes moved with each step, clinging and whirling around her legs, and the peasant-style blouse left her shoulders bare to gleam with an ivory sheen. Yes, she felt lovely tonight, and didn't want anything to spoil it, especially Trace Taylor!

Signore Bertolli sat at the head of the long table in the dining room, with Bethany on his right and Trace on his left. Tall candelabras illuminated the table with flickering light, making the exquisite china and heavy silver gleam. An array of dishes—some familiar, some not—were served to the guests, and Bethany ate sparingly of all of them. A servant kept replenishing her glass with a light, dry wine that was cool and delicious, and as the meal continued, Bethany began to feel quite vivacious.

She thought that though older and a bit portly, Signore Bertolli was quite attractive in his way, with thick, black hair sparsely sprinkled with gray, and flashing white teeth beneath a neatly trimmed mustache. He obviously enjoyed her company, and laughed frequently at her comments about the trials she'd endured on the journey to Cuzco.

"So, signorina," he said with a wide white smile, "you found a way to cross the bridge quickly, heh?"

Nodding, Bethany said, "Yes, though it was my mule's idea, certainly not mine!" She slid a glance toward Trace, who was listening with a faint smile. "Not everyone believed that, however," she added with a lifted brow, and smiled at Trace when he looked up at her. "Isn't that right Mr. Taylor?"

"Not everyone is gullible, Miss Brasfield," Trace said with a slightly malicious grin. "But you are mistaken if you think *I* didn't believe you. If that mule hadn't dragged you across the bridge, I would have had to, I'm sure."

"We're not all as courageous as you," Bethany said over the rim of her glass, her eyes fastening on his face. She felt an odd surge of recklessness, a desire to prick Trace Taylor's smug male complacency, to provoke a reaction from him. She had no idea why; perhaps it was the wine that made her so reckless, and perhaps it was just Trace's mocking smile and nonchalant shrug that provoked her into it.

Taking another sip of wine, Bethany said softly, "You seem to be a man accustomed to danger and violence, Mr. Taylor. I mean, the way you're always wearing you're gun low on your hip, like a gunman would do. Are you absolutely certain you don't have wanted posters out on you in America? I'd almost bet on it."

Trace's expression didn't alter except for a slight narrowing of his eyes and tightening of his mouth, and his tone was pleasant and indulgent. "I'm not a betting man, Miss Brasfield, but if I were, I'd bet that you're not accustomed to drinking more than one glass of wine."

"While you consume your wine by the bottle?" she shot back with a laugh that sounded a bit too loud even to her own ears. Why was she doing this? Why didn't she stop now, instead of going on? She could feel her father's puzzled frown on her, could see from the corner of her eye Signore Bertolli's amused gaze, and heard Bentworth stifle a cough with his linen napkin. But she didn't stop. Leaning forward and smiling brightly, she ignored the warning glint in Trace's eyes. "I think there are all sorts of dark secrets in your life, Mr. Taylor. Am I right?"

Shrugging, he said, "Probably. But if I admitted to them, then they wouldn't be secrets anymore—would they?"

It wasn't the answer Bethany had wanted, though she wasn't quite sure what she had wanted. A confession, maybe? An admittance of past wrongs? Or had she merely wanted to see him uncomfortable, as embarrassed as he had made her earlier? Now she wasn't certain. All she was certain of, was that she had made everyone at the table uncomfortable but the one man she had desired to see squirm.

Fortunately, Signore Bertolli deftly changed the subject by asking Spencer Bentworth if he had heard of any more Inca ruins that the Indians preferred keeping secret. That immediately brought on a lively discussion of the rumored city of gold they were hunting, and Bethany pretended to listen while she kept an eye on Trace.

Her behavior was as inexplicable to her as she was sure it was to her father, but she did not intend to apologize. Why should she? Trace had never offered an apology for all the things he'd said, or the way he'd acted toward her. No, not one word, beyond his casual comment that he had no desire to become "involved," whatever that meant! Her face flamed slightly at the memory of how easily she had yielded to his embrace, and not only yielded—returned it. Did he know that her response had not been just curiosity, but an ardent desire to be held and kissed? She hoped not. She hoped that he believed she was only bored and curious. It would be too humiliating if he knew how attracted she was to him, especially after . . . after seeing him with that woman in Huancayo.

But when she looked up a few minutes later and met his dark, intent gaze, Bethany knew that she had not fooled him for a moment. Nor was she fooling herself when she tried to pretend she disliked him. She was unaccountably attracted to him.

With that thought, Bethany excused herself from the table. "I'll just leave you gentlemen to your cigars and brandy," she said as they all rose.

"If I may suggest, signorina, the terrace is lovely in the moonlight," Bertolli said slyly. "The ancient Incas even named a precious metal for the goddess of the moon. They called silver Tears of the Moon, because of the silvery light that floods the mountains."

Bethany managed a smile. "That is a lovely legend, signore. I'll think of it while I admire your garden."

But once out on the moonwashed terrace her mind wandered and she didn't think of the legend at all. Ambling slowly along the wide stone balustrade on the terrace overlooking the garden, Bethany thought instead of Stephen Averill.

She remembered his handsome face, his fair hair, and the boyish grin he'd always worn when he'd come to see her at night. It had taken days and weeks just to keep from looking at the clock at his usual time of arrival, and even now when it was seven-thirty she sometimes caught herself waiting for a knock on the door. Or she had, she amended, until she'd met Trace Taylor. Now, instead of Stephen's face clouding her dreams, it was Trace's. And that bothered her more than anything else. Why Trace Taylor? How had he supplanted Stephen?

Pacing the stone terrace, Bethany shivered at the cool wind. It was almost cold up in the higher elevation, though she had thought the mysterious city nestled in the broad valley would be warmer than the barren peaks they had traveled. Another shiver rippled down her spine and she hunched her shoulders against it, thinking that it was fiction that wine made one warmer. Although it did give her a vague, flushed feeling, it definitely did not warm her.

Bethany turned, intending to go back inside where it was warm, and saw Trace walking toward her. Even with the light behind him leaving his face shadowed, she knew it was him. She'd recognize his easy, almost lazy stride even in a crowd.

Heart pounding, she waited silently, wishing she had not had that last glass of wine, wishing she had not been moved to provoke him earlier. Her chin lifted, and she listened warily as he stopped only a hand-span from her.

"All alone in the moonlight, Miss Brasfield?" Trace asked softly. "But I'm sure you knew I'd come looking for you, didn't you."

"I assumed you wouldn't miss an opportunity to rake me over the coals for daring to say what was on my mind," Bethany shot back at him. "That is why you came out here, isn't it? Because I dared you to be honest?"

She'd moved away from him a little bit, backing closer to the balustrade as if afraid of being too close to him; but Bethany was well aware of Trace's proximity, of the soft, dangerous glints in his dark eyes, and she wondered why she didn't just go back inside as swiftly as she could. Maybe she was curious, more curious than afraid.

"What do you want?" she demanded bluntly, and his brow rose.

"Why do you think I want something?" he asked, moving toward her with a graceful, fluid step.

She had to force herself to meet his dark gaze, and bit back the hasty words that sprang to her lips. Instead, she said calmly, "You wouldn't be out here if you didn't."

"Ah, you're so right, Bethany Brasfield." He'd reached her now, and the light from a window played across his face and illuminated the taut line of his features. She gulped back the words she'd been about to say, and managed a smile.

"I'm cold. Why don't we continue this discussion inside where it's warmer?"

"Here's fine."

"But what if someone should overhear?" She gave a nervous start when he shifted to put a hand on the smooth stone balustrade, and recognized danger in his silky tone.

"I don't give a damn if they do."

"But I do. If you'll excuse me, I'm going inside."

Trace's hand closed around her wrist as she started to edge past him, and he brought her arm up and between them as he backed her against the wide stone balustrade.

"Oh no, Bethany Brasfield, you aren't going to get off that easily." He was angry. She could hear the taut fury in his voice, though he kept it low and soft. "You want honesty from me, is that it? Well, there *are* secrets in my past, and probably more in my future." He pressed her back further with his hard body against hers, until the edge of the balustrade pinched her back. "Who knows—maybe you're one of my future secrets," he muttered just before his lips descended upon her half-open mouth, crushing any protest she might have made.

With the stone balcony digging into her back and Trace's hard body against her front, Bethany was effectively pinned between them. She couldn't move, not even to avoid his punishing kiss. This was completely different from any other kiss she had ever experienced. This kiss was bruising and painful, overpowering her. Trace held her so tightly against him she could feel the thunder of his heart beating against her breasts, could almost feel the racing of the blood through his veins.

There was no tenderness in the kiss as there had been in the others, nothing gentle about it. Trace kissed her savagely, brutally, his tongue plundering her moist, open mouth with a thoroughness that left her weak and limp in his arms.

Forcing her head back with the pressure of one hand beneath her chin, Trace did not let her move away from him. He held her fast, his lips searing a hot path along the line of her jaw to her throat, then pausing before drifting lower. Bethany moaned softly.

The bright peasant blouse she wore low on her shoulders did not offer much protection against his searching lips or the chill night air, but now she was shivering more with reaction than the cool wind across her bare skin. She could feel Trace's lean thighs pressing into her stomach through the thin material of her skirt, could feel the corded muscles in his arms as he coiled them around her quivering body. His fingers sought and found the rapidly hardening peak of a breast, and she gasped. Inexperience with the reactions raging through her was confusing; instead of backing away as she should have done, her hips instinctively met his slow grinding, sending shock waves of sensation through her. Trace made a low, rough sound deep in his throat, and his mouth returned to capture her lips.

Bethany's body refused to cooperate with her brain; it simply refused to push him away, to protest his invasion of her. Instead in the pit of her stomach a fire coiled like a serpent, writhing upward, stealing through her body in a hot, fluid rush that left her weakly whimpering against his touch and not even knowing it. He nipped gently down the arch of her throat in stinging little bites. She felt his hands in her hair, removing the combs Martina had carefully placed there and tossing them aside. It fell down her back, a warm cape over her shoulders as Trace cradled the back of her head in his palm. His other hand pulled her harder against him, and Bethany barely realized what she was doing when her arms lifted to circle his neck and hold him, lifted her lips to his mouth again, longing for his kiss.

Arching against him, her slender curves aching for his touch, she blindly sought his mouth, found it and clung. He shuddered, his muscles contracting when she fit her body into the angle of his.

"Bethany," Trace muttered, his voice sounding like a groan of protest. "I don't think you know what you're doing to me."

She didn't. She wasn't certain of anything at the moment, except that Trace had ignited a fire in her, a deep coiling fire that raged through her and left all her good intentions in ashes. She was vaguely aware that he was shaking almost as badly as she was, and didn't know it was from the effort to hold back.

"This is crazy," Trace muttered softly. "I came out here to teach you a lesson, and I think I'm the one who's learned something."

For a moment, Bethany didn't say anything. She couldn't. All she could do was lean against him as he held her in a light embrace, listening to the rapid thud of his heart beneath her ear.

Then Trace put her away from him, and his voice was hard and flat from having to deal with his painful arousal. "This isn't going to work, Bethany. I knew it wouldn't when I first saw you. My advice is that you stay here in Cuzco, because I can't promise what will happen once we're on the trail."

When Bethany just stared up at him with heavy-lashed violet eyes, his fingers dug into her shoulders and his voice grew harsh. "Do you understand what I'm saying, Bethany? Dammit, you re too innocent to be off in the jungle with a man like me! You wanted honesty, right? Well, I'm being honest when I tell you that I want you, that I have from that first time I saw you back in Lima. And if *you* were going to be honest, you'd admit that you want me, too. I've seen it in your eyes when you didn't even know it was there, but I also know there's no place for it on a trip like this." His dark eyes were cold and bleak. "I don't have time or the patience for young women like you, Bethany, naive young women who need moonlight and stardust and romance. And if you're smart, you'll stay as far away from me as you can get."

"How can I be honest with you when I'm not certain what it is that I want?" Bethany flashed. "All I know is that it feels good when you kiss me and hold me, but I don't know if I'm in love with you. I only know that I'm missing something in my life, but I'm not at all sure that it's you or anyone like you!" Her voice quavered slightly, and she clenched her teeth together as she ground out, "But you don't need to worry that I might throw myself at you or be easy again! I assure you that I'll stay just as far from you as humanly possible!"

Whatever Trace might have said to that was lost, as Professor Brasfield and Signore Bertolli walked out onto the terrace to join them. As the Italian merchant pointed out the ruins of Sacsahuaman on the hill above Cuzco, Bethany tried to concentrate on what he was saying, but could only think of Trace Taylor and the wild emotions he'd sparked in her.

Nothing would ever be the same, she thought with an uneasy feeling, nothing. And she knew he felt the same way, knew from the frowning glances her father gave her, that he knew the reason for her disheveled appearance. No one was rude enough to say anything about it, but the avoidance was almost palpable.

Trace was right. The trip was going to be difficult enough without what was between them, but she had no intention of remaining behind. No, she'd go. She'd just stay as far away from him as possible.

Chapter Ten

That night, lying in a luxurious goose-feather bed on the second floor, Bethany tossed and turned for hours. She could not sleep, could not think of anything but what had happened on the terrace with Trace. He'd called her naive, and maybe she was, but she wasn't so naive that she could not see that he wanted her. He'd admitted it, too, said in a harsh, rough voice that he'd wanted her since the first time he'd seen her, and Bethany couldn't help but wonder if he meant it. But what did it matter? she wondered in the next breath. Why should it matter if he wanted her? It was only—only physical, a simple matter of attraction between two people, without emotion or attachment.

And she should know by now, she thought as she rolled over and gave her pillow a vicious punch, that mere attraction was never enough for one to base a relationship upon. Hadn't Stephen taught her that?

Yet Bethany found herself wondering what she would say or how he would act when she saw him again. Would Trace look at her from under his hat brim, his eyes narrowed and unreadable? Or would he look at her as he did sometimes, his gaze direct and open, hot and unflinching?

Shivering, Bethany pulled the tightly woven blanket up around her shoulders and shoved her face back into the pillow in a vain effort to sleep. But Trace's face kept haunting her, his dark liquid eyes and the high, stark line of his cheekbones, his sensual lips quirking in a mocking smile that could be as tempting as it was infuriating. And even worse—she could almost feel the taut fabric of his body beneath her hands, the hard band of muscles flexing as he pulled her close, his hand tangling in her hair.

Bethany sat bolt upright in bed. She'd never be able to sleep if she kept thinking about Trace! Why couldn't she just forget him? Forget the way he made her feel, all hot and funny and confused inside? She was a quivering mass of contradictions now, where not so long ago she had known—or thought she'd known—what she was going to do with her life. There were worse things than being her father's assistant, worse things than devoting one's life to the pursuit of knowledge, even the knowledge of ancient peoples and their history. She had reconciled herself to the fact that she would be alone. Until now. Until Trace Taylor had come into her life, Trace with his mocking dark eyes that made a lie out of everything she'd thought she wanted.

This strange, feverish emotion that swept through her—was it love or was it desire? She hadn't felt such intensity for Stephen, though she had loved him. Why not? Stephen had made her feel secure for a time, loved, but had never left her shivering with a heated longing like Trace did.

It was a long time before Bethany fell asleep, and when she did, her dreams were of Trace.

Her restless night did not leave her in the best of moods the following morning, and when she joined her father and the others at the table, she pointedly ignored Trace. She could feel his dark, amused gaze resting on her, and knew with a sudden flash of irritation that he was well aware of her efforts to ignore him. Did the man have to know everything? she wondered in annoyance.

"Good morning, everyone," she said with a forced smile as a servant pulled out her chair and she sat down. "I trust everyone slept as well as I did," she added, hoping Trace would think she had not lost a moment's sleep over him.

Professor Brasfield looked pleased. "It was a most restful night! I can hardly wait to begin on the final leg of our quest." Leaning forward, his pale eyes glittering behind his glasses, he added, "Signore Bertolli has been telling me the most interesting things, dear! And he, too, agrees with me about Worsaae's methods of excavation."

"Oh, you mean stratigraphic succession," Bethany said with an effort. How could she intelligently discuss methods of excavation when Trace Taylor was so disturbingly near?

"Yes, yes, the careful recovery of different layers of occupation, rather like a cake, as it were." Brasfield used his fork for emphasis as he began dividing his biscuit demonstrating how he intended to study Vilcapampa when they found it. "You see, we shall begin most meticulously, recording every bit of archaeological material. There are the natural accumulations of decayed vegetation and soil, and others that are the result of human occupation. The top layer is, of course, the newest, while the succeeding layers become progressively older." He tapped his biscuit with the fork, dividing it into layers. "It is done thusly. . . ."

"Did I tell you, Professor Brasfield," Bertolli said, "that I have met Giuseppe Fiorelli?"

Brasfield was immediately interested. "The Italian gentleman who is responsible for the excavation of Pompeii? I understand he has only recently developed a method of pouring plaster into cavities left by volcanic ash, thus recreating images of people, animals, and objects."

As the professor and Bertolli engaged in a lively discussion of different archaeologists and their methods, Bethany turned her attention to her breakfast, and the hot, sweet coffee that was served in thin china cups. Spencer Bentworth, seated on her right, leaned close.

"I believe your father is in his element here, don't you, m'dear?"

"If he gets started on grids and sections," she said ruefully, "I'm afraid we'll be here for some time."

"Ah yes, new things are popping up every day, it seems. And Brasfield is keenly interested by new techniques. I do hope he uses some of them to discover a vast array of gold and artifacts in Vilcapampa. It means a great deal to all of us."

Bethany frowned. "What exactly do you intend to do with your portion of the discovery, Spencer? Am I to understand that your interest is purely pecuniary, or are you also interested in preserving antiquities?"

Spencer smiled, and his blue eyes darkened slightly. "I fail to see why it must be one or the other, m'dear. Cannot a man serve both interests? Must I choose?"

Faintly startled, Bethany stared at him. "Well, I would think it would create conflicts of interest in how to dispose of an ancient artifact. There are unscrupulous collectors who pay a great deal for antiquities, with no plans to share them. Isn't that why

Peruvian officials have insisted upon sending along two of their own men?"

"Quite so, but that is just so they can claim their portion of the finds." Bentworth shrugged lightly. "There are corrupt officials as well as collectors, you know."

"So I hear," Bethany murmured.

"Tell me, Bentworth," Trace said, "how do Peruvian officials expect only two soldiers to make any difference?"

"Perhaps they know that two men are all that is needed to make a report, Taylor." Bentworth's smile did not reach his eyes. "Are you planning on doing away with them?"

"You're confused. I don't give a damn one way or the other about antiquities. My interests lie elsewhere."

"Ah yes, I recall! You're concerned with clearing your name, isn't that right? A successful expedition now should go a long way to doing that, Taylor."

Recognizing the slightly malicious edge to his tone, Bethany wondered about the enmity between Spencer Bentworth and Trace. It was as obvious now as it had been when they first started out. She looked from Bentworth's mildly inquiring expression to Trace, and her heart began to thud. His face was a polite mask; only his eyes showed any reaction, but he quickly shuttered them, and she thought she must have been mistaken.

For a moment, she had surprised a murderous fury in Trace's eyes, and it made her uneasy. Had he really looked so . . . savage . . . or was that only her imagination, her interpretation? Now there was nothing in his face or voice to indicate any such emotion.

Signore Bertolli was a man of many talents, one of

which was the capability of listening to two conversations at the same time. Though he heard everything Brasfield said and was able to respond intelligently, he was also very much aware of the conversation among Bentworth, Taylor, and Bethany. It interested him. Bertolli was a man who liked conflict and intrigue, and there were elements of both in this situation.

A faint smile curved the red lips beneath his thick mustache as he observed Bethany Brasfield's heightened color when she looked at Taylor, her air of flustered nonchalance that fooled no one. He wanted to tell her about Trace, warn her that she was treading dangerously. He knew Taylor, knew him well, and knew his reputation.

Trace Taylor had shown up in Peru ten years before, with the look of a man on the run. He wore his gun low, tied to his thigh, and Bertolli had seen him use it with an expertise that spoke eloquently of his background. Not many men dared cross Taylor, and he'd made a few enemies, as men like him were bound to do. Bertolli could have sworn that Bentworth was one of those enemies, which is why he was so surprised to see them together.

It was an incongruous collection of people, Bertolli mused, his gaze surreptitiously flicking from one to the other. It amused him to have them at his home where he could peruse them so extensively. The girl, now she was a different matter. Ah, *bella donna!* No wonder that Trace Taylor was attracted to her. It should make for a very interesting situation in the mountains, very interesting, indeed. Bertolli wondered rather maliciously if the eagle would find his wings clipped, or if the dove would yield. Perhaps he should warn Bethany Brasfield not to allow herself to become too intrigued.

Women had always liked Trace Taylor, perhaps because he was so elusive. But he used them; Bertolli had seen and heard enough to know that, yet as far as he knew, Trace had not been cold and calloused enough to pretend any emotion he hadn't felt. Somehow, he knew it would be different with this young woman. Behind her carefully erected barrier beat the soul of a sensual woman; unfortunately, she was also very vulnerable, and Bertolli wondered if she had enough sense not to get too involved with Trace. It was bound to end disastrously.

Bertolli would have been surprised to know that Bethany was thinking along those same lines herself. Any involvement with Trace was dangerous, she thought as she tried not to look in his direction, tried not to notice his gaze on her. In less than two weeks' time, he had managed to become the focus of her dreams at night, the direction of her thoughts during the day. A man like Taylor was dangerous to sheltered young women.

Turning her attention to Spencer Bentworth, Bethany tried to pretend interest in his tales about Bolivia, and the Mayan ruins he had seen in Mexico, but she felt only a sense of relief when the meal was ended. She'd intended to escape quickly, before Trace could speak to her, but to her irritation, he disappeared before she could. Did he think he could ignore her that easily? Kiss her in the moonlight, then pretend she didn't exist? Indignant at his defection, she didn't notice the perversity of her own thoughts.

It wasn't until later, when her father and Bentworth had gone with Signore Bertolli to view the ruins of the fortress above Cuzco, that she allowed herself to reflect upon her wildly ranging emotions. Bethany had begged off, citing a return of the *soroche* that had plagued her in the mountains, but she only wanted to be alone. Enduring an entire afternoon of crumbling ruins and her father's interminable archaeological observations suddenly seemed like more than she could bear.

So they left her behind, promising to return before dark so they could retire early. Tomorrow morning, Spencer assured her, they were to continue their journey. Bethany watched them leave, then spent a leisurely morning poring through Signore Bertolli's library. She found several volumes on Peruvian art that interested her, and curled up in a chair to read.

At noon, Martina served her lunch out on the terrace, and Bethany ate slowly, enjoying the warm sunshine and cool breezes sweeping over her. The solitude was welcome, much more welcome than the past weeks of enforced companionship with so many people. Tilting back her head, she closed her eyes against the prick of sunlight, letting her thoughts drift. The events of the night before seemed much more prosaic in the light of day, as did the city spread out below the hilltop mansion. She was only imagining things when she felt uneasy about Spencer Bentworth, she decided. After all, he was an Englishman, with the natural reticence and dry humor of the English. If she did not feel easy in his company, it was not because he was evil, only rather cold and standoffish.

Unlike Trace Taylor, she thought in the next breath. He was just the opposite of Bentworth, caustic and mocking, with an underlying streak of violence lurking just beneath his thin veneer of civility. Hadn't he proven it more than once with his quick, rough kisses and searing embrace? It was obvious he considered her available, and she had to admit it was because she yielded so easily to his touch. It was as annoying as it was frightening; how could she deny the surge of emotion she felt when he touched her? And why did she feel that way for him, of all people?

Shrugging away the uneasy direction of her thoughts, Bethany rose from her chair and ambled over to the wide balustrade to look out over the city. In the light of day, Cuzco seemed less mysterious and more mundane.

Propping her chin in her palm, Bethany's attention drifted to the massive stones of the ancient citadel where the others had gone. Sacsahuaman perched on a high hill over the city, easily visible from the terrace now that it was day. Sunlight gilded the huge, curved stones scalloping the hill, and drifts of fog shrouded the tall peaks of the mountains surrounding the city.

"Quite impressive, isn't it?"

Startled, Bethany turned, her heart fluttering as Trace strode toward her. He was bare-headed, and his thick black hair was wind-ruffled, giving him a devil-may-care look. She noticed that he wasn't wearing his gun as he usually did, and that the bright sunlight picked out certain details about him she'd forgotten; the way his dark eyes curved when he smiled, and deep grooves etched on each side of his mouth. Trace Taylor was far too handsome a man, she told herself, but managed a polite smile in spite of her fingers tangling in the folds of the cotton skirt she wore.

"Yes," she murmured, "very impressive."

"I wonder if the Spaniards found it impressive when they tore down the Temple of the Sun, or if they were just motivated by greed." Laying an arm on the balustrade beside hers, Trace met her quizzical gaze. "Greed is a powerful motivation, you know. Men have done murder for the love of gold."

"Are you trying to tell me something?" Bethany asked in a quavering voice, suddenly nervous at his proximity. "Or are you just making idle conversation?"

"Both." He shrugged, and turned to gaze out at the city below them. "Make what you want of it. You will anyway."

She pushed at a twist of hair that tickled her neck, self-consciously aware of her appearance and half angry at herself for caring. If it wouldn't be obvious that she was running from him, she would have fled into the safety of the house, but she would not give him the satisfaction of knowing how uneasy he made her.

"Why didn't you go with the others?" she asked after a moment, feeling safer with mundane topics.

"I've seen the ruins. Why didn't you go?"

Bethany smiled. "I wasn't certain I could stand hearing about the ruins, though I'm sure my father will be careful to give me detailed descriptions when he comes back."

"Is that how your life is going to be, Bethany?" he asked softly, and she was so startled at the question she didn't even notice that he'd spoken so familiarly. "Are you always going to live on the scraps of others' lives?"

"I don't know what you're talking about!" she began angrily, but he shook his head and took her hand between his.

"Yes, you do. You're letting your father live your life for you, doing what he wants to do, going where he wants to go, not thinking about yourself. Dammit," he said when she tried to pull away, "I can't figure out if you're being noble or just plain stupid!"

"It isn't your place to figure it out!" Bethany jerked her hand away and glared up at him, anger making her violet eyes darken to a stormy purple. "It isn't your life, and I don't see why you should care what I do or don't do!"

"I just hate to see waste, that's all." He was as angry as she, his mouth thinning to a tight line and his dark eyes narrowed.

"I suppose you think your life isn't being wasted?" she shot back at him. "Is what you're doing some marvelous feat that no one else can do?"

"Bethany, Bethany, can't you see beyond today? At least I'm doing what *I* want to do, not what someone else tells me I want to do." He grabbed her arm when she tried to walk away, turning her around to face him. "That's it—run away. Then you don't have to admit that I'm right."

"I can stand right here and not admit that you're right! I don't need to walk away. . . ." She choked on her words, and was just as furious at herself as at him. Why did he have to make such an ordeal over this? Then it occurred to her, that it was just another tactic to keep her from continuing on with the expedition.

"Oh, I see what you're trying to do, Trace Taylor! You don't really care if I have my own life, if I'm happy! All you care about is this stupid expedition, and leaving me behind because I'm too much trouble!"

Trace's hand dropped away from her arm, and he gave a shrug of his broad shoulders. "I see that we've degenerated into wild accusations again," he mocked. "Are you always so suspicious?"

"When it comes to you—yes!"

"I don't suppose Bentworth's idle gossip has anything at all to do with that, does it?"

She eyed him narrowly. "He did mention a few

things about you, yes," she admitted after a moment. "Are they true?" she blurted then, and didn't realize she was holding her breath until he grinned.

"Probably. That depends on how much he left out, I guess." Cocking his dark head to one side, Trace drawled, "It's common knowledge in Lima that I'm the only one to survive my last expedition. That usually ruins a guide in this country. People expect to come out of the mountains with as many as they went in with." His tone was still faintly mocking. "Sometimes, one or two people are foolish enough to get killed; never an entire expedition. It makes a man wonder about things."

"Such as?"

"Such as how supplies spoil overnight, or disappear completely when all precautions have been taken. And how natives who have always been friendly suddenly turn vicious. That sort of thing."

Bethany stared at him. "Are you saying . . ."

"I'm not saying anything," Trace cut in flatly. "I'm just wondering aloud."

"Well, I think you're just trying to frighten me into staying behind," Bethany said. "I hope you don't intend to keep this up once we're on our way tomorrow."

A faint smile slanted his mouth, and his eyes narrowed in amused appreciation of her tart reply. "I guess I won't have much choice, will I?"

"No, Mr. Taylor, you won't."

"Maybe I should give in gracefully."

She met his dark gaze steadily. "Maybe you should."

Trace took a step closer, until he was almost brushing up against her. "But then, I'm not used to giving up easily," he said in a soft voice.

The husky timbre of his tone alerted her to what he

was about to do, but she could not have moved to stop him even if she'd wanted to. She'd half expected this since he'd first come out onto the terrace to join her, and when he took her hands and pulled her into the angle of his body, she didn't resist.

"Every time we see each other," she murmured against the rough fabric of his shirt, "we argue. Can't we just have a normal conversation without . . . without kissing or fighting?"

"Depends on what you call normal," Trace said into the thick wealth of her hair. He breathed in the scented soap she had used to wash it, then lifted one hand to undo her braid.

Bethany felt it fall, felt his hands tunnel through her hair to hold the back of her head, cradling it in his palm as his other hand tilted up her chin for his kiss. She closed her eyes, her heart pounding and her breath coming so fast she was certain she sounded like a faulty bellows.

This kiss was much more gentle than the last had been, almost tender and searching instead of the harsh anger of the night before. She didn't pause to consider her motives for not protesting at this invasion, didn't pause to wonder why she yielded so eagerly to his embrace. It was enough for the moment that she was in his arms, that his mouth was touching her lips, her brow, the closed curve of her eyes, then tracing a moist path over her cheek to her ear. She shuddered slightly, and his arms tightened around her.

"You're dangerous, Bethany Brasfield," Trace muttered a moment later, and released her to stand back. He kept one hand on her shoulder, and it steadied her as she looked up at him with dark, shadowed eyes.

"What do you mean—dangerous?"

A slight smile tugged at his mouth. "I mean, you

make me forget all my good intentions."

Bethany knew how he felt, because he'd certainly made her forget hers. Just his touch seemed to chase away every vow she made when she was away from him, and she steeled her resolve again.

"I suppose this is where the saying 'Curiosity killed the cat' comes in," she said lightly, letting a teasing smile touch her lips. Let him think that she was only experimenting! It was much better than him knowing the truth, that she was more attracted to him than she had ever been to any man in her life.

To her surprise, Trace laughed. "Yes, I guess curiosity is one way to describe it," he drawled, but the glint in his dark eyes mocked her.

A slight flush stained her cheeks, but Bethany's voice was as remote and faintly amused as his. "Mr. Taylor, that is the *only* way to describe anything between you and me. Any other word would be inaccurate."

Grinning, Trace said, "I suppose you know the answer to that old cliché, don't you?"

"I'm not sure what you mean. . . ."

" 'Curiosity killed the cat, but satisfaction brought it back,' " he quoted softly.

"What makes you think I'm satisfied?" she blurted, then wished she hadn't.

"I know you're not—not yet," he said with a wicked grin. "But neither am I."

Stepping away, Bethany wondered wildly how the conversation had descended into such innuendoes and suggestive remarks, and saw from the look on Trace's face that he was enjoying himself far too much. Gathering as much dignity as she could muster under the circumstances—with Trace looking at her so knowingly and her pulses still hammering from his kiss—Bethany decided a rapid retreat was in order for the moment. Later she could regroup and think of something witty and cutting to say, but now her best option was strategic withdrawal.

"I think I'll go to my room now," she said calmly. "I will see you this evening, Mr. Taylor."

"Yes, you will," he acknowledged, and when—like Lot's wife she thought later—she looked back over her shoulder at him, he was gazing at her with a faintly mocking smile that made her shiver.

Trace had made it sound like a promise, and she wasn't at all certain why.

Chapter Eleven

When she returned to her room, Bethany found a large square package lying upon the bed. Curious, she perched on the edge of the mattress and picked it up. There was no card or note to indicate it was for her, and it wasn't until she looked closely that she saw her name scrawled atop the brown paper.

After shaking it briefly, as she had done as a child at Christmas and on her birthday, she tore off the wrappings. A delighted smile curved her mouth when she recognized the wooden box that held neat rows of different colored chalk.

"An artist's set!" she murmured, lifting out one of the sticks to make an experimental stroke across a torn piece of the wrapping paper. A brilliant crimson streak glimmered against the plain brown paper, and her smile grew wider. "What a wonderful surprise, but who—?"

Bethany let it slide slowly to the bed amid a crackling of the wrapping paper. Who would have given it to her? Her father had not yet returned, and everyone else had gone with him to the ruins except for . . . but no, that was impossible. And besides, it could have been on her bed since breakfast, so it must have been her father. Or perhaps Spencer Bentworth, or even

Signore Bertolli. Anyone could have left the set for her. After all, giving a young woman a set of paints or chalks was not an unusual gift. It was a common gift, such as those given by uncles, or old maid aunts.

Yet Bethany could not help but wonder why she would have received a gift like this from her father. Professor Brasfield was not prone to gift giving. In fact, if it did not pertain to archaeology or ancient pottery, he usually did not take notice of much of anything.

Well, Bethany decided as she clicked shut the lid to the wooden box of chalks, she would tell her father how much she appreciated his thoughtfulness when he returned from viewing the ruins with the others. It was so unlike him to think of such a gesture.

Somehow, she wasn't too surprised that evening to learn her father had no idea who had left her the set of artist's chalks.

"No, no, dear, it wasn't me," Brasfield protested with a slight frown. "But that certainly was kind of someone to buy them for you. I just can't imagine why you would need them out here."

"Don't you recall, Papa? I was wishing not so long ago that I had brought my paints with me so that I might sketch some of the—but, of course, you wouldn't remember that."

Looking faintly bemused, Brasfield shook his head. "No, I can't say that I do recall that conversation. But it is nice that someone remembered you liked to doodle with paint and, er, chalk. Quite nice. And since we lost the photography equipment, you could have sketched a likeness of those stone bollards at that bridge. . . ." He looked suddenly pleased. "Yes, that's it! It would be tremendously helpful if the new camera I purchased today becomes lost or in need of repair—you would be able to render a sketch that would help later. How fortunate."

"Yes," Bethany murmured, feeling somehow deflated, "that is very fortunate indeed."

When she glanced up, she met Trace's slightly mocking gaze and flushed angrily. Did he have to hear everything? But of course, they were all sitting in Signore Bertolli's main *sala*—except for Trace, who preferred standing—so it wasn't likely that he wouldn't have heard. Still, it was embarrassing for her father to provide proof that what Taylor had said was right. Did he have to be so wrapped up in himself? Why couldn't he prove Trace wrong?

Her chin lifted, and she managed to meet Trace's steady gaze with defiant eyes, daring him to say something. To her relief, he didn't, and for some reason he was especially polite to her, even when she made a few barbed comments about his ability to find this lost city of gold.

"I wonder, Mr. Taylor," she said tartly, "whether or not there truly is a lost city, or if it is just the product of a rather fevered imagination."

"You're not alone in that, Miss Brasfield," he replied politely. "However, I did actually see the ruins of Incan buildings, and before we were forced to retreat, Gibbs found a solid gold ceremonial mask."

"And did the mask make it back to civilization?" she asked shortly. "Or was it lost, too?"

"Ah, yes," Bentworth put in, his eyes glittering, "I saw that mask myself! We can only hope there are many more like it."

"As well as other indications of their daily lives," Brasfield said, his eyeglasses sliding down to the end of his nose as they did when he became excited or agitated. "I would prefer finding evidence of how they lived on a day-to-day basis, the foods they ate, what they wore, and how and why they built such magnificent temples. They were geniuses in architecture, it seems, constructing conduits to bring water to their cities, and so forth, and a true archaeologist much prefers finding such facts as well as the evidence of how they worshipped, their gods and sacrificial items, etcetera." Brasfield took a deep breath, removed his eyeglasses, and wiped them clean with his handkerchief. "I will be glad, however," he added with a faint smile, "to take whatever we find!"

Signore Bertolli leaned forward. "You do realize, don't you, Horatio, that there could be nothing in the city when and if you find it? Grave robbers are common here also, and you could find only empty caves or crumbled ruins."

"But even those yield plenty of information to a man willing to look for it, Carlo," Brasfield replied as he replaced his eyeglasses, and Bertolli sat back with a shrug.

"I do admire a dedicated man, Horatio, and I am pleased that you feel that way. The Incas' wealth and history should not be lost to mere collectors. It should be written in the books of the ages." Shaking his head, Bertolli said, "It pains me to see greedy men plunder that which should be preserved for antiquity." He stood up and surveyed them for a moment, his dark eyes faintly glittering. "I have a few objects I would like to show you now," he said abruptly. "I waited, you understand, until I was certain they would be properly appreciated. Please, gentlemen—and the lovely signorina—*venga con me*. Come with me."

Somewhat mystified by his secretive manner, they followed Signore Bertolli from the main *sala* down a wide hallway. He stopped and removed a key from his pocket, fit it into the door's lock, then turned it and swung open the door. *"Si fermi qui.* Wait here a moment, please," he said without turning to look at them, and disappeared into the dark room.

Puzzled, Bethany glanced up at Trace. He shrugged his broad shoulders without speaking, but a faint smile curved his mouth. It wasn't until Bertolli had lit some lamps and asked them to enter that she began to understand.

Stepping into the long, narrow room without windows, she could see rows of dully gleaming artifacts. Some were animal-shaped jugs and cups, some were masks and statues, and many of the pieces arranged on long tables and shelves were solid gold. Behind her, Bethany could hear Bentworth's amazed exclamation.

"Dear God! All of this is yours?"

"Somewhat," Bertolli replied. "I've been a collector for years. Some of the pieces are owned jointly with the government of Peru, if you will. They have a dislike of letting valuable antiquities escape their country without proper recompense." His mouth twisted, and he stroked his mustache with a finger as he added, "If one speaks to the proper official, one can do just about anything, however."

"Do you sell these?" Professor Brasfield asked anxiously. "Surely not!"

"Oh no. I am a firm believer in preserving the history and art of a country. I am Italian, Professor, and a true devotee of the arts, if you will!"

"Of course, of course," Brasfield said hastily. "I did not mean to insult you. It's just that one can learn so much—do you intend to create a public exhibition?"

"Some day, perhaps. Not now. Security is rather lax at this time, and I would not want these stolen." He picked up an ornate figure. "This, for instance, is dated back to the first century, A.D.—perhaps at the very beginning. It is a fine example of early life.

I believe it was during the Moche dynasty. Handle it carefully, please."

Brasfield took it gently, his eyes gleaming behind his glasses. "Look at the detail! How splendid!"

Bethany drew close to look. The figure was of an entwined couple, and their sexual posture was obvious, even to her inexperienced eyes. She was immediately reminded of Trace and the dark-haired woman in Huancayo. Her throat grew tight with embarrassment, and she felt her cheeks redden.

Signore Bertolli went on, his voice that of a benevolent lecturer. "Note, if you will, how many of the pieces of that period reflect their daily lives, not only a marked preoccupation with their carnal appetites, but other areas as well." He picked up another piece and handed it to Bethany.

She was relieved to note that it was of a man in regional dress. "This is ceremonial, I suppose?" she asked Bertolli, and he nodded.

"The Mochica society raised the first true cities, and were advanced for their time. They were pre-Inca, you see. If you examine the figure I now hold, you will see that it is a ceramic pot with an extremely lifelike blind drummer depicted. Then—as they do now—the blind frequently earn a living by making music. The Mochicas stressed reality, where the Inca artists were more austere in their decorations."

Bertolli showed them golden earplugs worn only by the nobility, and heavy pieces of gold in the shape of men and animals. There were also items of silver, and even caps for teeth made of silver.

"A fascinating collection, Carlo," Professor Brasfield murmured, closely examining a ceramic jug found on the coast of Peru.

"Worth a fortune, I should imagine," Bentworth added. He hefted a solid gold drinking cup in his palm, and slid his host a speculative glance. "It's no wonder you have kept your collection a secret."

Bertolli smiled. "It's well guarded. I have the only key, and there is only one entrance. If one does not know, an unsanctioned entry could be fatal."

"Oh?" Bentworth glanced around. "Whatever do you mean?"

"Simply that I have used ancient secrets learned from the Incas to guard my collection. Only I know the secret. If an intruder enters—he finds death."

"You mean it's booby-trapped?" Bethany blurted with a shiver. "That is why you had us wait outside?"

"That is correct, Signorina. It is for protection, you see. *Capisce?*"

"Yes, I understand." Bethany glanced up at Trace, who had lifted a long, slender rod fringed with dangling cords.

"A *quipu,* isn't it?" he asked Bertolli, and the Italian nodded.

"Yes, a method of accounting, much like an Oriental abacus. The *quipu camayoc,* or keeper of the *quipu,* did actual computations on an abacuslike counter then recorded the totals with knots in the cords of the *quipu*. A quite effective means of accounting, but, unfortunately, the Incas kept no written history. It was all done orally, and with the conquest and destruction by the Spaniards, we lost a wealth of information."

"I intend to do my best to retrieve as much as possible from the ruins we seek," Brasfield said as he replaced the object he held. "I must commend you, on recognizing and respecting the true value of your collection. You are a man after my own heart, Carlo."

"Which is why I have shown you my most prized pieces." Bertolli strode to a table and lifted a ceramic piece. "Examine this object, if you will," he said, tossing it to Bentworth with a careless flick of his wrist.

Bethany gasped, and her father blanched. "Carlo!" Brasfield exclaimed in shock. Bertolli laughed.

"It is a very clever fake, Horatio. Look at it closely, *prego*. It was crafted in Germany, then brought to Peru to sell to credulous collectors. I show it to you to warn you all to beware of such items."

Glancing at the ceramic figure, Bethany saw it was in the style of the Mochicas, with a man and woman posed in a lewd position. She quickly glanced away, and happened to meet Trace's amused gaze. She flushed then, remembering him with the woman in his room, and the heated coupling she had seen, the posture very much like the piece of pottery.

"Don't be embarrassed," he said softly. "It's only art."

"I'm not embarrassed!" she lied. "Just . . . uncomfortable. I mean, I do recognize that . . . that such pieces are valuable in detailing the lifestyles of the Incas, and appreciate them as such."

"But that is a clever fake, remember?"

"Yes, of course, but I was referring to the position—I mean, the style in which it was created—you know, using the same kind of postures that . . . of the Moche. . . ." Feeling as if she were only making an awkward situation worse, Bethany faltered and glanced helplessly toward her father.

Professor Brasfield was deeply involved in a discussion with Bertolli about the merits of the forgeries as opposed to allowing antiquities to leave Peru, however, and did not notice her glance. Sighing, she turned back to Trace.

Thankfully, he did not pursue the subject. Instead, he pointed out a large golden ceremonial mask and told briefly of how he had seen several like it in the city.

"Grave robbers must have missed those ruins," he added. "I'm not surprised. They're very difficult to reach."

"But not impossible," Bethany said pointedly, and he grinned.

"No, obviously not. Of course, you may wish for wings before we get there."

"I may. But I will go, no matter how difficult."

"Did I say differently, Miss Brasfield?" Trace asked with mock surprise. "It's understood that you intend to persevere to the bitter end."

"Good. Then I don't have to keep repeating it!" she said sharply.

Leaning back against one of the tables, Trace leveled his dark, mocking gaze on her flushed face. "Working up your courage?" he asked softly. "I think you're trying to convince yourself more than me."

"No one asked your opinion, Mr. Taylor. You are only supposed to guide us, not offer unwanted advice."

"Ah, so you've said. Several times. But I wonder if you would feel the same if it was someone else offering the same advice."

"What do you mean by that?" she demanded.

"Only that for some reason, you resent any advice I may give you. Even when it makes sense."

"We've been through this," Bethany began angrily, then noticed that they were receiving curious stares from the others. "And I refuse to discuss it again!" she ended.

Bethany turned to the door. "I am going to retire early so that I will be fresh in the morning," she said calmly. "If we're going to find this lost city, I prefer to be at my best."

Her father came to give her a swift peck on the cheek as he wished her a good night. "I will be up soon, myself," he assured her. "I believe that Mr. Taylor said we are to leave before daylight in the morning, isn't that correct, sir?"

Trace nodded. His arms were folded across his chest and he was leaning against the table with a sardonic smile. "That's correct, Professor. We need to be in the mountains as soon after day breaks as possible. I don't like to travel those mountain roads in the dark, and we need to make good time before night falls."

"They can't be any worse than those we've already ridden in the dark," Bethany muttered, and Trace shrugged.

"I'll let you revise your opinion later, Miss Brasfield. I'm sure you will." Levering his lean frame away from the table, Trace murmured a good night and left the room without another glance in Bethany's direction.

It was almost like a cold dismissal.

She felt faintly discouraged, but didn't know what she had expected from him. Some show of attention, perhaps? An acknowledgment of her? It must have been Trace who'd left her the chalks; no one else would have thought it important to her. And, for some reason, that was just as irritating as it was gratifying. If he'd bought the chalks for her, why not say so?

Trace gave her the opportunity to ask him that when he stopped her at the foot of the curved staircase leading to the second floor.

"Bethany," he said softly, his voice coming from the shadows and startling her into whirling around.

"Oh! What are you doing, lurking here in the dark like a thief!" she demanded crossly. "You frightened me."

"You're easily frightened." He stepped from the shadows beyond the pool of lamplight, one hand sliding along the smooth wood of the stair rail. The dim light made him look more intimidating, she thought uneasily, more—saturnine—than he usually seemed, and her voice was determinedly light to prove that she was *not* easily frightened.

"I suppose I have you to thank for the chalk set? I appreciate it very much, though I don't know why you didn't indicate that it was from you," she added when he smiled.

"And let everyone know how thoughtful and considerate I am?" he replied in such a mocking tone that she flushed.

"How is it you can make even a nice, kind gesture seem rude?" she snapped. "And here I was, beginning to think that perhaps you had some decency after all."

"Be careful of those kind of thoughts, Bethany Brasfield. Next thing you know, you'll be admitting that you want me as much as I want you."

Her mouth opened, then closed with a snap. "You are an insufferable beast!"

"Admitted. See? At least I'm honest. What about you? When are you going to be honest with yourself?"

"I don't have to listen to this," she began, turning to start up the stairs. Trace caught her hand, and his low tone was insistent.

"No, you don't have to, but remember—we'll be together for the next few weeks. If you can't face the truth now, what are you going to do tomorrow? Or the day after that?"

"Really, Mr. Taylor, you imagine things! I told you that I was just . . ."

"Curious," he finished for her. "I know." His mouth curled into a tight smile. "I didn't believe you then, and I don't believe you now."

"I really don't care if you believe me or not!" She glared at him angrily, unwilling to admit that he was right or even close to right. So she had wanted him to kiss her—and she had been curious about the nature of the feelings he aroused in her—but she had no intention of letting him know that. He was obviously too sure of himself as it was. And damn him for knowing how she felt when it had taken her so long to realize it herself!

"Good night, Mr. Taylor," she said frostily, pulling her hand from his grip. "I shall see you early in the morning."

"It's going to be a long trip, Bethany," he said softly. "I hope you know what you're doing."

She turned on the fourth step, staring down into his eyes. For some reason, her heart lurched as she met his gaze. Maybe it was because he wasn't mocking her now; his eyes were alight with a dark flame that seared into her soul.

"Maybe I don't," she said slowly, "but I'm not certain that you do, either. I suppose we'll both find out something about ourselves before this trip is over, don't you?"

"It looks like it. Are you ready?"

"Just as ready as you are, Mr. Taylor."

It wasn't until later, lying alone in her bed, that Bethany wondered if she was truly ready to find out how she felt about Trace. It had only been two years since Stephen, two long years that had left her painfully afraid of ever falling in love again. Could she dare? And why on earth, she wondered in the next instant, had she ever become attracted to a man like Trace Taylor? And damn him for knowing it! she thought crossly. It must be obvious to everyone. Everyone except her father, of course. Horatio Brasfield would not notice anything unless it was over a hundred years old.

Sleepily, Bethany reflected that she was still young,

young enough to fall in love even when her common sense told her to beware. She would simply have to be on her guard, that's all, and her eyes snapped open when she suddenly recalled Trace's mocking warning in Huancayo.

Guard your heart, he had said. She'd thought at the time he was talking about Spencer Bentworth. Had he been talking about himself, instead?

Chapter Twelve

Fortunately, the next morning brought so much activity Bethany had no time to think about Trace or the way he made her feel. It was still dark, and it was cold without the sun to warm the city lying in the broad saddle of the high mountain peaks. Shivering, she helped her father load his precious supplies atop the mules, and swung her own scant baggage to the back of her mule.

"I'm glad to see that you're a woman who knows how to travel light," Trace observed as he passed, and Bethany couldn't think of a thing to reply.

Her brain was still sleep-hazed, and her vision bleary from a night of tossing and turning in her comfortable bed. After saying good-bye to Spencer Bentworth who was departing for La Paz that morning, Bethany surveyed the caravan with heavy eyes. There were still quite a few of them, including the two Peruvian army officers who had been sent along to protect Peru's interests in any valuable finds. They didn't look at all happy with their assignment, but stood sleepily and sullenly with the Quechua bearers. A faint smile curved her lips. She understood that emotion all too well!

Bethany managed to bid Signore Bertolli a coherent farewell in spite of her frequent yawns, and it wasn't until they had ridden down the drive and out into the streets of Cuzco that she paused to consider the Italian merchant's parting words to her.

"Whatever did he mean by that?" she murmured as her mule trotted docilely behind the others. *"Watch where I walk?* Isn't that our guide's job, to find safe paths? And I still don't understand why Signore Bertolli said it so softly, as if afraid someone might overhear. . . ."

The morning chill and her mule's jogging step soon banished any thoughts from her mind but the numbing desire to be warm and comfortable, and Bethany concentrated on peering into the murky shadows ahead of them. In the still, quiet streets, hoofbeats echoed loudly, and she could hardly see through the early morning fog that drifted over them. Thank heavens Trace knew which way to go, she thought once, because she certainly would never be able to find her way out of the city alone.

By the time the sun rose and dissipated the mists hanging low over the city, they had ridden into the foothills of the towering Andes. Snowcapped peaks were still hidden by wispy shrouds, and the trail they rode seemed to climb straight up.

Bethany gasped once, quickly, when she happened to glance over the side to see a perpendicular wall dropping below. From then on, she vowed grimly, she would keep her gaze straight ahead. One more glance down the side of a mountain, and she was liable to freeze as she had done in the middle of the rope bridge just past Abancayo.

Rocks skittered from under the hooves of the mules, and the sun beat warmly on her back as she clung tightly to her saddle horn. Damp strands of hair clung to her neck and fell from the neat braid she had twisted early that morning and by the time they stopped for a rest at noon, Bethany felt as if she had been on the trail forever. She dismounted from her balky mule and sank gratefully to the hard comfort of a flat rock, resting her hands on her knees.

"Are we near yet?" she couldn't resist asking Trace when he passed by. "I mean, how much further before we reach the spot you spoke of, the place where we are to rest for the evening?"

"Ready to quit already?" Trace asked with an uplifted brow. "And I thought you said you were . . ."

"I only asked," she cut in sharply, "how much further before we reach the camp you told us about! I am not about to quit. I'm only curious. . . ." She stopped suddenly and flushed, wondering if that word brought to mind for Trace what it did for her. It obviously did, because his mouth squared into a grin, and his eyes flickered beneath the broad brim of his battered fedora.

"Ah yes, curiosity. You seem to have more than your share of it, Miss Brasfield."

"And you seem to have more than your share of insolence, Mr. Taylor!"

"What do you intend to do about it?" His voice was flat and amused, as if he knew she could do nothing.

Bethany's mouth tightened. "For one thing, I *don't* intend to sit here and allow you to speak to me like this. I'm going for a walk."

"You can't do that."

She shot up from the rock where she was sitting and gave a defiant toss of her head. "I beg your pardon! I am quite capable of taking a stroll without having to ask your permission!"

"This isn't a city park. Walk at your own risk." He met her angry gaze calmly, but she could see the spark of fury in the dark depths of his eyes. "I won't be responsible."

"*You* aren't responsible for me, remember?" she returned in a taunting tone that made his mouth tighten.

"I remember."

"Good!" Bethany felt a moment's triumph at her success. She had bested Trace Taylor in a battle of wills, and she basked in her momentary glory.

Trace saw it in her eyes, in the fine glow of satisfaction that glinted in the violet depths, and for a moment he was more amused than angry. So she thought she had won a battle, did she? Well, maybe she had. One battle did not win a war, however, and he knew that a lot better than she obviously did. He watched her walk away, her spine stiff and straight, the sunlight glinting from her fine-spun hair and making it shine with tawny lights. His gaze dropped to the swing of her legs as she crossed the grassy plain where the mules were grazing, and his eyes narrowed.

The cotton material of her trousers tightened invitingly around her hips with each step, and he couldn't be the only man there who noticed it. His hard gaze swung toward the other men, and he saw Brody and Reagan watching her with hot, intent eyes. They were the only ones who dared be so bold. The Quechua bearers, if they noticed her, would not have dared show interest.

Trace walked toward Brody and Reagan with a long, loose stride. "You boys see something that interests you?" he asked in the cold tone that usually made a man back off. His right hand swung idly by his side, just above the butt of his pistol, and his eyes were hard.

Reagan, shorter than the fair-haired Brody and dark, quickly shook his head. "Naw. Not me, Taylor. I'm jus' watchin' out for me."

When Trace's gaze swung to Brody, the man

laughed. "If I am noticin', that's my business, ain't it? The way I heard tell, you ain't got nothin' to do with the girl, only with Bentworth's interests." He stuck a long piece of grass between his teeth and grinned. "Only maybe, you forgot that you ain't s'posed to mess with the girl."

"And maybe you forgot that you aren't fast enough to be interested in my business, Brody." Trace shifted slightly so that his feet were slightly apart and his body relaxed, both hands hanging casually at his sides. "That's not real smart of you." For the first time in a long while, he felt a tingling anticipation at the thought of a fight. He needed a fight, needed something to take his mind off the girl, and so he didn't mind violating one of his own rules by allowing a man to bait him into reaction.

Bridling, Brody swung around to face Trace, and for a moment considered drawing on him. Then common sense returned in a rush and he shook his head. Taylor was fast. He'd seen him draw more than once, and the man was snake-quick and lethal.

"Bein' smart ain't got nothin' to do with whether you're pokin' the girl, Taylor," he said at last, and there was a sneer in his words. "If you ask me—and I know you didn't—that's not real smart either. We've still got a long way to go, and me and Reagan have a job to do, too. Bentworth pays us damn good to do what he says."

"Is sticking your nose in my business part of the job?" Trace's drawl was dangerous, and his eyes deadly, and Brody gave another shake of his head.

"You're lettin' what happened between us in Arizona get to you now, Taylor. That's best forgotten until this is over with. A man can't concentrate on two things at once without riskin' his neck."

"Advice, Brody? How thoughtful." Trace smiled,

the smile that wasn't really a smile but more of a threat. It grew quiet around them as the others slowly noticed the tension between the two men, and in the distance only the shrill calls of birds could be heard in the thick trees. "Now let me give you some advice—stay away from the girl."

Brody didn't answer, but when his gaze shifted away from Trace to his partner, it was answer enough.

Pivoting on his heel, Trace walked away, feeling their eyes on him, his muscles tense with expectation should Brody change his mind and draw. He headed toward the thick line of trees just ahead, following the grasses Bethany had parted on her walk.

Irritated that he'd let his taut nerves outweigh his better sense, Trace softly cursed Bethany Brasfield for having an effect on him. He should have kept his mouth shut and let Brody stare at her, if that was what the man wanted to do. It wouldn't hurt anything, as long as that was all he did, and God knew, he liked looking at her himself. A sharp stab of annoyance knifed through Trace, and he swore again, harsher this time, his growling voice cutting through the air. Where the hell was she?

Annoyed just as much at herself as she was at Trace, Bethany swung the slender switch she carried for her mule at the tall grasses as she ambled into the fringe of jungle beckoning with cool shadows and muted noises. Her short boots slid on her feet and rubbed against her legs, and she wished for a moment that she could remove them. It would be a relief to let her toes wiggle, and feel cool air over her hot, aching legs.

After only two days in Cuzco, her body had to get used to the gait of her mule all over again. Already, her thighs ached from riding, and her bottom felt as tough as the leather on which she rode. But, it was better than walking, she supposed, and her mule was surefooted.

In the dense foliage of the jungle, it was cooler, and Bethany paused just inside the trees to peer into the dark interior. Shadows flirted with sunlight that pierced the thick canopy overhead in gloomy shafts, and she could hear the muted mutter of birds and an occasional screech and flapping of wings. She glanced back over her shoulder to reassure herself that she hadn't gone too far, and could barely see the brown forms of the mules as they grazed, and the men milling about in the sun.

If she looked behind and up, she could see only the steep, towering peaks that slashed the sky with white-capped ridges above the jungle; if she looked straight ahead, she saw only a few feet into a tangled web of vines and ancient trees; if she turned a few yards in the other direction, she would be at the stark, bony edge of a rocky defile that led straight down into a canyon several hundred feet below. Behind them lay the soft, fertile plains of the valley below Cuzco, a paradise of flowers and fruit in the summer months. Tender green shoots greened the earth and attracted man and beast alike. From the cultivated valley, it had been only a short distance to the tortured, twisting trail through the Grand Canyon of the Urubamba River.

A shiver tickled down her spine as Bethany reflected that for the first time since the journey had begun, she truly felt like an explorer, an adventurer. She had come this far safely, hadn't she? And there had been moments when she'd been certain she would plunge down a steep slope to her death, yet she hadn't.

The cool air enveloped her as she went deeper into the thick jungle, and another shiver rippled down her spine. It was noticeably different here than it had been out in the open; the air was cooler, and smelled almost stagnant, as if decay lay just beneath the fallen leaves underfoot. But, of course, it would be that way, she told herself. Leaves fell, decayed, and the next year it happened again, until layers had been built up just like layers of the earth. Nothing unusual about that at all.

Damp patches of her shirt clung to her in spite of the chill in the air, and Bethany plucked at the material. A vague rustling in the underbrush made her pause, and she half turned. While she hesitated, a brightly plumaged bird rose from a clump of bushes and into the air in a whirr of beating scarlet wings. A sweep of relief made her smile, and she shook her head at her nervousness.

Still swinging her switch in a lazy half circle in front of her, Bethany advanced into the musty jungle until she came to a small stream that plunged over a ledge of rocks that were head-high. Fresh, clear water splashed into a small rock depression that formed a perfect pool, and she knelt beside it with delight.

It was the perfect opportunity to bathe her hot, tired feet, and she sat on the spongy bank and pulled off her boots. Gingerly sticking first her toes, then her entire foot in the water, she sucked in her breath sharply at the icy chill. With the thawing of snow atop the mountains, the streams were deeper than usual, and swift and cold. It felt delicious, and she shivered as she splashed her feet.

It was so quiet, with only the musical rush of the water and the muted murmurs of birds in the trees, that Bethany was quite enchanted. Cupping her hands, she dipped them beneath the clear, icy surface and brought them to her face in a swift movement to sip the water.

"Don't drink that!" a voice barked behind her, startling Bethany.

Half falling, she caught herself with an outflung hand, then whirled angrily to face Trace. Her heart dropped at his fierce expression, and she faltered briefly before gathering her courage. "I was only taking a drink of fresh water!" she spat at him, wiping at her wet face with one arm.

"And you would have been sorry quick enough," he shot back at her, stepping forward to seize her wrist and drag her to her feet. "That's ice-cold, and at this altitude, you would have been doubled over with cramps in a matter of minutes."

"I . . . I don't believe you," she stammered out. "It's just water!"

"What the hell do you think you're doing out here alone anyway?" he demanded harshly. "Don't you know you could find yourself in trouble with no one to help?"

"I'm only a few yards from everyone," she defended herself in a sulky tone, jerking her wrist away and rubbing at it. "You bruised me."

"You're lucky that's all," Trace said. He pushed the brim of his hat back and raked her flushed face, bare feet, and damp hair with an assessing gaze. When he tucked his thumbs into his gun belt, Bethany noticed the long, wicked knife he wore unsheathed, and her eyes widened as he ground out, "I should have let you stay out here until dark just to teach you a lesson."

"I told you . . ."

"I know what you told me. If we're so close to the others, why don't you just find our way back now?"

Bethany stared up at him uncertainly. He looked so angry, and she glanced over his shoulder. She'd come the same way he had, and straightening, she shot him a dark glance as she muttered, "All right, I will!"

Struggling clumsily back into her boots, she was aware of his impatient gaze on her, and it made her even more clumsy and slow. Finally, stomping her foot the last inch into her boot, she stood and met his cool gaze. "Follow me!" she rapped out, and started back up the path.

But it wasn't as easy or as evident as she'd thought it would be. She'd gone only a few feet when she realized that she wasn't certain which way was out. After a brief pause, she set off determinedly, and soon found herself in an impenetrable thicket. She floundered bravely, realized she had chosen the wrong path, and backed out, smacking directly against Trace's broad chest.

"I thought we were only a few feet from the others?" he mocked softly as his arms automatically closed around her, and she jerked away again.

"Give me a minute! I . . . you made me lose my bearings! If you'll just back up a bit, and let me start over, I know I can go back the way I came."

Bethany pushed at an untidy strand of hair in her eyes and turned to give Trace a defiant glare. He shrugged and took a step back. "Be my guest," he said in that faintly ironic tone that she hated.

Using the switch much as someone might use a divining rod, Bethany held it in front of her and walked back to the mountain pool. Trace followed her quietly, and she didn't have to turn around to know that he was probably grinning sardonically at her confusion. It had looked so easy earlier, but now—even if she went back the way she had come, she wasn't at all certain she was going in the right direction.

Pivoting, she met his brittle gaze with bright, angry eyes. "All right, you've made your point. I'm lost. But I don't think I would have had any trouble if you'd left me alone. You've just confused me, that's all."

"Right," Trace said in a tone that neatly conveyed his skepticism. "And now you're wet as well as lost."

Glancing down, Bethany noted the large wet patches on her shirt where she had splashed water. A surge of dismay swept through her as she saw how the damp material clung to the outline of her breasts, and that it was apparent to anyone who cared to look—like Trace—that she was chilled. Her nipples had hardened to rigid peaks that were quite evident beneath the wet cotton shirt. She crossed her arms over her chest and looked back up at Trace defiantly. "So? That's my problem, not yours. It'll dry."

Trace leaned back against the broad trunk of a tree and crossed his arms over his chest. A soft perfume filled the air, and Bethany noted distractedly that the tree trunk had a profusion of orchids blossoming over it. Trace's weight against the trunk crushed the fragile flowers and released their delicate scent into the air. Dragging her attention from the flowers to his face, she saw that he was staring at her intently, and her chin lifted even higher.

"May I ask why you are looking at me like that?"

"Does it bother you?"

"Yes!"

"Why?" His mouth quirked in a slight smile when she didn't answer and her cheeks grew pink. "I know why," he said softly, so softly she almost didn't hear him over the increasing chatter of birds overhead.

Bethany was only vaguely aware of the scarlet and green and yellow birds hopping about on thick tree branches and filling the air with noise. Her world had narrowed suddenly to Trace Taylor.

"It bothers you to have me look at you like that because you like it, don't you?" His mouth curled when she didn't answer him. "That's all right—I like it, too."

"I don't know what you're talking about!" she managed to croak, acutely aware of his hot, dark eyes resting on her.

"I think you do." Trace pushed away from the tree and she could almost feel his heat wafting across her, smell the distinct fragrance of tobacco and man. He was watching her closely as he reached out and pulled her slowly into his arms, saw her eyes widen and the pupils dilate to absorb light shining through the jungle canopy overhead. There was a world of light in her soft eyes, in the way she looked at him, and he felt his body's instant response to the soft curves beneath his hands.

"Trace," she murmured helplessly, knowing she should pull away but wanting somehow to feel his lips on hers again. The temptation to have him kiss her was too strong to deny, and she quivered with the force of it.

When he brushed his mouth lightly over her parted lips and she arched into him, Trace took advantage and cupped one hand over her breast. Gasping, Bethany tried to pull away but he wouldn't let her. His other arm coiled swiftly around her back to hold her next to him, holding her so close that she could feel the rigid imprint of his arousal against her stomach.

"Stop that!" she whispered, her body aflame with desire and shame at the same time. "You shouldn't . . . we shouldn't be doing this!"

"Why not?"

The simple question stopped her. Why not, indeed? It felt so right, but she knew—all her years of rules in a girls' school had taught her—that it was wrong. Ladies simply did not allow a man any liberties until they were married, and then it was a woman's duty to please her husband. But Trace wasn't her husband—had not even said the word marriage—and she had no idea if he loved her. She had no idea if what she felt for him was love, or only the unfamiliar yearnings of her body, yearnings that she hadn't known existed until he'd come into her life.

"Because," she said after a moment, "it just isn't the right thing for me to do."

He held her for a moment, and, oddly enough, saw the truth in her words. It wasn't the right thing for her to do. Not with him. She should have a man who would marry her and care for her, not just want her. Yet it was difficult to think of that now, when his arousal was almost painful and he wanted only to bury himself inside her sweet body.

Pushing her away with a supreme effort, Trace let his arms fall to his sides, and noted with grim satisfaction that she was breathing as raggedly as he.

"Maybe you're right," he said shortly. He leaned back against the tree trunk again to give himself time to ease the tightness in his groin, bringing one leg up so that the sole of his boot rested flat against the tree. "It should be interesting to see who gives in first, though."

Bethany was having her own troubles schooling her fast breathing and madly pumping blood into a more reasonable pace, and it took her a moment to reply to the last. When she did, her words were indignant.

"It's not exactly a matter of giving in!"

"Isn't it?" Trace shook his head. "Seems like it to me."

"That's your problem, Mr. Taylor!"

He grinned. "Just for now."

Levering his lean body away from the tree with a graceful push, he took a step closer to her, bringing one hand up to present her with an orchid. She looked at him suspiciously.

"Like the Greeks, you bear gifts, I presume?" she

asked tartly. "And what form of trickery will this gift take?"

"Why do you think I have ulterior motives? It's only a flower. They grow wild out here, as you may have noticed."

She took the flower from him, feeling suddenly rather foolish. How did he so easily confuse her? And he knew he did. That was probably why he did it. Attack and retreat, that seemed to be his favorite method.

"Thank you," she murmured, then tucked the orchid into the hair over her right ear.

"No," Trace said, "that's not right. Over the right ear means you're taken. Over the left ear means you're available."

"Available for what?" she couldn't help asking, and her breath caught when he smiled down into her eyes.

"Available for—whomever comes along," he said softly. He reached up and removed the flower, then tucked it gently behind her other ear, his fingers brushing against her cheek and sending shivers down her spine. For a moment she thought he would kiss her again, but he didn't. After securing the delicate blossom, he let his fingers trail in a feathery caress over the line of her cheek to her neck, then his hand dropped away and his voice was brisk. "All done. Shall we go back?"

Feeling flushed—almost as if they had done a lot more than kiss—Bethany managed a light shrug. "Of course. I'm sure everyone is wondering where we are."

"Oh, I can promise you that," Trace said. He paused as if about to say something else, then shrugged. "Follow me," was all he said, and Bethany trailed behind as he strode down the barely discernible path.

The change in temperature was immediate as they

walked from the jungle into the open again. Sunlight struck her like a fist, and Bethany's damp shirt dried before she reached her mule. Digging into her pack, she avoided the curious gazes in her direction as she found and tugged on a floppy-brimmed hat to shade her face. It also shielded her from prying eyes, and she felt a faint flush stain her face as she studiously rebuckled her pack.

Trace appeared at her elbow, his voice low and soft. "Do you get the feeling we're being stared at?"

Slanting him a quick glance, Bethany muttered, "I get that definite feeling!"

"Too bad we didn't do anything to deserve it," he said with a mocking laugh that grated on her nerves, and she jerked to glare at him.

Yanking on the strap to her pack, Bethany turned her back on him. He could fluster her with just a glance, or a few soft words, and he knew it. How much did he want from her? she wondered with mounting frustration. And how much did she want from him?

Trace was wondering that very thing himself as he strode to his pack mule and gave the signal for everyone to remount and ride. He tugged his hat brim lower over his eyes. His mouth twisted. Bethany Brasfield would not like the direction of his thoughts most of the time since he'd met her. Even when he told himself he wouldn't think about her anymore—at least not in that way—he ended up doing that very thing. It was as maddening as it was frustrating. At night when he should be sleeping, he found himself thinking about her, remembering the soft feel of her hair beneath his hands, or the touch of her velvety skin, or the ripe, luscious taste of her lips and the sweet flash of her dimple—then he'd damn both her and himself. It was crazy. This was a job. He knew better than to let himself get involved with a woman, especially a woman like Bethany. She was trouble, with her long-lashed violet eyes and air of innocence. And trouble would come quickly enough without his inviting it.

Nudging his mule with his heels, Trace rode ahead of the others, picking his way carefully along a trail only two feet wide. He'd better concentrate on the terrain instead of Bethany, or he'd make a mistake he couldn't afford to make.

Chapter Thirteen

Shivering uncontrollably, Bethany squeezed her eyes shut. It was almost dusk, and vague shadows thrown by the jagged mountains darkened the trail ahead. It was just as well. If she could plainly see the crumbling road, she would probably sit down and refuse to move. How could they navigate such terrain safely?

Even Trace looked grim. The narrow ribbon of road wound around the mountain in a corkscrew, each sharp turn abruptly dropping off in a sheer fall into the canyon. One false step, and animal and rider would plunge over the side into eternity. The normally placid faces of the Quechua bearers bore expressions of stolid suffering, and the two Peruvian officers alternately swore and prayed in low moans.

"Isn't there another way to get there?" Professor Brasfield asked through tight, white lips. "I fail to see how the Incas could have carved out any homes of substance at these heights. Dragging up huge stones as large as some monoliths . . . Bethany, are you all right?" he ended anxiously as she swayed atop her mule.

"I'm fine, Papa," she lied bravely, struggling to keep her tight grip on the saddle horn and not look to the side. Her stomach lurched as her mule stumbled, trembled, then regained its footing on the narrow trail. Gasping with fright, she managed to keep her seat in the saddle, but the terrified glance she flung toward Trace made him pause on the trail.

"It's only a few yards further, then we'll come to the end," he reassured both the professor and Bethany. His eyes rested on Bethany, and he smiled at her. "You can make it. Keep going."

"I don't have much of a choice," she muttered, but managed to smile back at him.

A low rumbling grew louder as they wound their way down the mountain, until it drowned out all other noise. It was the raging Apurimac, boiling through rock channels in a frenzy of melting snows and rushing water that swept along anything in its path. The tremendous amount of water being forced through a narrow gorge created the loud roar that could be heard for miles.

By the time they reached the end of the narrow trail that slithered around the mountain, Bethany was weak with relief. She slid from her mule in the gathering shadows, and looked back up at the trail they had just ridden. Her eyes widened. It looked impossible; it looked as if birds would not dare traverse it, a slender ribbon of rock that curled around the sheer granite face in a steep spiral.

Collapsing in a heap on the ground, Bethany hugged her knees to her chest, barely paying attention when her father pointed out the stone terraces cut into the hillsides.

"Doesn't it make you wonder how the Incas did it?" the professor was marveling. "In places where most people would find it impossible to exist, they thrived! And people refer to the ancients as primitive. . . ." He shook his head as he strode a few yards down the incline and perched atop a wide shelf of rock not far from the river's edge.

"I wouldn't sit too close to the river, if I were you, Professor," Trace called loudly, his voice barely carrying over the noise of the pounding water. "This time of year, it's unpredictable, and a sudden surge might come over the edge."

Brasfield immediately rose and walked back up the hill to join the others on the strip of grass and rock. Bethany had not moved from where she'd collapsed near her mule, and glanced up when Trace paused beside her. He hunkered down, a faint smile curling his mouth.

"Well, that's not the worst of it, you know," he said, and she shuddered.

"If you're trying to make me feel better, it's not working!"

He slanted a glance back at the mountain they had just come down. "It's not as high as it looks from here. I'd say it wasn't over six thousand feet. . . ."

"Good heavens!" She stared at him with wide, frightened eyes. "Six thousand feet sounds high enough for me!"

"Look, I tried to tell you about this. Some of the way, we're going to have to abandon the mules and walk, because it will be too steep for them. The trail gives out, and in places we'll be doing good to crawl on our hands and knees. I know you thought I was only trying to keep you from coming along, but I knew this would frighten you."

"I am frightened," she admitted frankly, "but I have no intention of turning back or not going on. And I would have come no matter what you said."

"How did I know that?" he said lightly. "Like I said once before, you're a sensible, determined woman, Bethany Brasfield."

She met his dark gaze for a moment, and oddly

enough, there was no mockery in his eyes. "You're right, Trace Taylor," she said softly, her mouth curving into a smile. "I am a very determined woman. And I'm determined to finish this journey with the rest of you. I don't want to hear about the ruins, I want to see them for myself."

"I hope it's worth it to you." Trace glanced over at her father. "I know it's worth it to him. He'll be pleased if we don't find anything but a few broken pieces of tablet or pottery, but you – somehow, I think you're expecting more than there's going to be."

She frowned. "What do you mean by that?"

"Just that there may not be any gold left like Bentworth expects there to be. Like the Peruvian government hopes there is, and like those two mercenaries of Bentworth's have been told there is. There may be nothing more than ancient stones and ghosts."

Bethany shrugged. "That's enough to satisfy my father."

"But it's not enough for everyone else." Trace looked down at his hands for a moment, then back up at her, and his voice was soft. "I'm beginning to think this might be a dangerous trip for all of us, Bethany. And I'd rather you'd stay behind."

A sudden flash of anger ripped through her. Just when she'd thought he was trying to talk sensibly, he had to go and spoil it all!

"I see," she bit off, her eyes narrowing at him. "I see that you are still not content to cease your efforts at leaving me behind." She rose abruptly, her chin tilting when he rose, too, his large frame towering over her. "I will not be left! You can give up now, because I'm here and I'm not going back!"

"I take back the part I said about your being sensible," Trace said evenly. "And I'm changing determined back to stubborn. You're as ornery as your mule."

"And you're as low as . . . as a snake!" Bethany shot back at him. "Why can't you just leave me alone? I don't hear you trying to convince my father to stay behind!"

"All right!" Trace said shortly. "I give up. This was your last chance to stay safely behind. You can take what's out there just like the rest of us. Once we leave here in the morning, there won't be another chance. You'll have to go on no matter what."

Bethany was only slightly mollified. "I suppose you are concerned about my safety and I appreciate that, but I really want to finish what I started."

"So you've said." Trace tucked his thumbs into his gun belt and eyed her flushed face for a long moment. She looked so damned defiant, he mused, and as if she expected him to argue some more. Mentally shrugging, he said aloud, "If I didn't care what happened to you, I wouldn't bother saying anything. I guess you know that."

Startled, she shook her head. "No. I didn't know that."

"Now you do."

"Yes," she said softly, "now I do." When he turned and walked away, she stared after him for a long time.

The river was a constant sound now. As they sat huddled by a low fire, eating boiled sweet potatoes and drinking hot tea, Bethany tried to remember what silence was like. It was faintly unnerving to hear the incessant, vaguely ominous roar of the river, and she wondered more than once if it would rise over its banks and flood the canyon.

"We're far enough up not to worry too much," Trace had said in reply to her father's query. "Just don't go down too close, and you'll be all right."

Had it been only that day she'd been congratulating herself for being an intrepid adventurer? Bethany wondered with a shiver of apprehension. Maybe she should have listened to Trace. Maybe she should stay behind when they pushed on at first light the next morning. After all, if it was going to be worse than what she'd already endured, she might very well be too frightened to continue.

Sucking in a deep breath to steady her frayed nerves, Bethany glanced up and across the low-burning fire. Trace sat across from her, talking in low tones she couldn't hear to one of the Peruvian officers. Munching on her meal of boiled sweet potatoes, Bethany watched him curiously. He was deep in conversation, his dark head bent, the firelight playing across his stark, rugged features. Her throat grew tight, and she felt an odd ache in her chest.

Just when she'd thought he felt nothing for her other than obligation or mere responsibility, he had shown her another facet of his feelings. But what did it matter, she thought in the next weary breath, when she wasn't certain how she felt about him? One moment she was positive she was attracted to him, and in the next she was furious and wishing he was a hundred miles away.

But now, with Trace sitting across from her and not paying any attention to her, she had time to reflect on how she really felt about him. His rare moments of kindness—the artist's chalks he'd bought and his sympathy at unexpected times—could be counted on one hand. He was gruff and mocking, and bluntly hateful most of the time. It seemed that he took great pleasure in embarrassing her at times, and at other times—oh, those other times, when he held her in his arms and kissed her as if he really meant it—those were the times that most confused her. Did he mean it? How could he hold her and kiss her if he didn't mean it? But, of course, she told herself in the next moment, hadn't

Stephen done the same thing? He'd held her in his embrace, kissed her, even asked her to marry him, and yet, he'd decided that he could not be faithful to one woman. It had embittered her, almost ruined her life, but now—now, she was too cautious to be caught like that again. Oh no, she wasn't about to let Trace Taylor get away with sweet words he didn't mean!

Stiffening her resolve and her spine at the same time, she tore her gaze away from Trace and concentrated on what was left of her sweet potatoes. They were cold. Food at high altitudes chilled quickly. She should have remembered that, she thought with a sigh. Instead, she had been thinking of Trace, and the strange way he made her feel, the way he made her *want* him to touch her intimately. . . .

Bethany looked over at her father. Professor Brasfield seemed not to need food, or rest. He was reading by the light of the fire and a small lantern, his legs scrunched up beneath him and his copy of Father Calanacha's book on his knees. She sighed again. How could she compete with the history of the Incas?

She couldn't. Her problems would seem petty to her father, and if she thought about it, maybe they were. What did it matter if Trace Taylor was truly attracted to her? The world would go on whether he was or not. It had gone on after Stephen had left her, and it would go on if she never saw Trace again.

But later, lying wrapped up in her blankets with the roar of the river in her ears, Bethany could not stop thinking of Trace and how he made her feel. He'd said earlier he cared about her—how much? Or did he only mean as a person, any person, not someone special?

Rolling over and sighing, Bethany stared into the dark, wavering shadows beyond the fire. The flames had burned into embers, gray ashes winking with flickers of orange and red, sullenly smoldering and providing scant warmth and light. A faint, pearly light from the moon flirted with clouds scudding across the silvery surface, making wavy patterns over the camp. Bethany closed her eyes, but it was no use. A thousand different images seemed to be battling for her attention, and she groaned. She couldn't sleep. She could not even think of sleep. Every time she closed her eyes, she saw Trace's face and it snapped her awake. Damn him! Why did he have to haunt her so? And where was he? she wondered in the next instant. He had left camp earlier, walking off into the dark and disappearing without any explanation.

Suddenly restless, she decided to read herself to sleep. She'd brought only two books with her, one a volume on ancient Greek art and the other a romantic tale of star-crossed love by an English author named Brontë.

"In my state of mind," Bethany muttered ruefully, "I'd best settle for the book on Greek vases."

Wrapped in her thick shawl and shivering, she quietly probed her leather pack for the book, then fumbled with her lantern. It took her a moment to light it, and she glanced up as the wick caught. No one seemed to notice her. The others were all asleep, pinwheeled around the fire with their blankets over their heads, soft snores mingling with the roar of the river.

Settling back with the pack behind her for a pillow, Bethany tried to concentrate on the printed pages. The words didn't make sense. The drawings of the vases wavered in the poor lantern light, and she sighed. After several minutes she snapped the book shut and blew out her lantern. It was no use. Concentration was impossible when she felt this strange yearning, this puzzling disquiet that made her almost ache inside.

Another sigh escaped. It was crazy to feel the way she felt, crazy to want a man who was so obviously unsuited to her. What made her want anything to do with him? Sometimes, when he looked at her with his hot, dark eyes slightly narrowed and glittering with a knowing light, she had this strange, aching need deep inside. And the times when he said, bluntly, that he wanted her, she wanted him, too. Bethany shuddered, more with reaction to her thoughts than the night chill.

"Cold?" a voice asked behind her, and her head whipped around, her muscles tensing when she saw Trace.

"A little," Bethany admitted. Her heart was pumping furiously, and her breath was annoyingly short as she met his dark eyes. "Aren't you cold?" she managed to ask in a steady voice as he knelt on the ground beside her blankets.

Trace shrugged. "A little."

Bethany's breath caught in her throat as he reached out a warm hand to cup her chin in his palm. His thumb stroked lightly over the line of her jaw, and his fingers cradled the madly beating pulse in her throat. His eyebrows rose.

"Are you frightened of me?" he asked softly, and she shook her head.

"No," she whispered. "I'm frightened of myself."

"Ah," was all he said, but there was a wealth of understanding in the short syllable.

Bending forward, Trace brushed her parted lips with his mouth and she shuddered, closing her eyes. The roaring of the river seemed to grow louder, and she had the sensation of falling, as if she was tumbling off a rocky ledge into space and time. Was this what it was like? Was this falling in love? She couldn't remember. Surely, she hadn't felt this way with Stephen. She remembered only the pain, not the breathless feeling that enveloped her now as he sat back and stared at her in the faint moonlight.

"Come with me," Trace said, and Bethany did not reply as she pulled on her short boots and stood to go with him.

A thousand different emotions were raging through her, and she knew if she stopped to consider just one of them, she would pull away. Purposefully, daring more than she had ever dared before, Bethany threw all caution to the winds and put her trembling hand into his outstretched palm. For one brief moment, their eyes met and held, and then she was walking into the shadows beyond camp with him.

"Where are we going?" she summoned up the nerve to ask when the moonlight flickered briefly over rocks and brush.

"I know a secluded spot just ahead that I think you'll like." He squeezed her hand as if to give her courage, and Bethany shivered.

Had she gone mad? What was she doing? She must know better than to go off into the dark with Trace Taylor, yet here she was—blithely skipping along beside him as if he was the most trustworthy man in the world!

"Trace," she murmured once, pulling slightly away, but when he turned to look at her, her protests died unuttered.

"There's a place just ahead, Bethany," he said. "I found it a few years ago, and have never shown it to anyone else. The ancients obviously knew about it; they probably came here often. When you see it, you'll know why."

Faintly puzzled, Bethany followed with mounting anticipation and curiosity. The roaring of the river grew louder, then faded as they walked along rocky ledges and beyond crumbling stone terraces. Small, timeworn stones paved the ground in a rambling pattern, making a smooth walkway as Trace led her under what looked to be a stone arch almost hidden by clumps of brush and tangled vines.

Just when she was about to say that they had gone too far from camp for her comfort, Trace paused, swung aside a leafy branch, and led her under a low doorway. Bethany felt her way along, her palms sliding over damp stone as she stepped cautiously through and out onto a wide ledge. Her eyes grew wide as she paused on the top step of shallow stairs cut into a cleft of the mountainside.

"Trace! What—this is beautiful!"

"I know." He said it softly, as if he felt the same sense of awe and beauty. His arm tightened around her spare waist, and his hand slid to her hip as he pulled her forward.

"The Incas must have spent a lot of time here," Bethany breathed as her eyes became accustomed to the dim, hazy light. "Trace! See that low rock over there? It's actually a seat, carved and polished smooth. And see here, where the water in this natural stone tub is bubbling? That's heated underground. The Incas must have chosen this spot for the hot springs, and probably came here winter and summer."

Moonlight splintered the gurgling waters of the roughly shaped pool, shimmering like patches of silver on the surface, reflecting the light so it seemed even brighter than it was. Bethany gazed at the profusion of exotic plants spilling over rock and ledge. It made her think of how the Garden of Eden must have looked to Adam and Eve. She felt a sudden lurch in her stomach. Why had Trace brought her here? Her gaze sought and found him a few feet away.

There was a brief, hot spurt of flame as Trace struck a match against a stone block. Watching as he lit a small oil lamp that looked as if it had been there since the Incas, Bethany saw his face in the dimly flickering glow, and caught her breath at the sudden intensity in his eyes. There was a guarded expression behind the wanting in his face, and she suddenly knew just why he had brought her there. To hide her confusion, she began to chatter nervously, and to her chagrin, felt his amused gaze rest knowingly on her as she rambled.

"You haven't shown this to anyone else? Why not? It's such a lovely place and"—she gulped—"and I would think you'd want others to know about it," she ended lamely.

He shrugged. "Some people have a way of exploiting the beautiful. I never wanted this ruined, or made into a spot where bored heirs and heiresses would want to come. Besides, if the Incan people haven't revealed this secret in all these centuries, why would I assume that right?"

Bethany tried to still the nervous quivering of her hands as she moved to sit beside him on the smooth stone seat carved into the wall. "But you're willing to lead my father to a lost city of gold. Isn't that the same thing?"

"It could be viewed that way, I guess." Trace frowned, and the lamplight made his face seem less rugged and harsh. "Once I met your father, however, I knew that he wasn't the kind of man to allow mercenary exploitation to happen. If it had been just Bentworth . . ."

His voice faded and Bethany asked, "You dislike Spencer Bentworth very much, don't you?"

"Very much," Trace agreed, and once more there was that mocking, sardonic twist of his mouth that annoyed Bethany. "But you don't have to feel that way just because I do," he added when she stared at him. "My grudge with Bentworth is my own."

After a moment, Bethany said slowly, "I was well aware of that, but I wasn't certain you were. At least you now acknowledge that I have my own opinions and feelings."

"Oh, Bethany Brasfield, I've never doubted for one moment that you have your own opinions," Trace said with an amused smile. "Just your tendency to express them when it's obvious to everyone around you that you're wrong."

"What do you mean by that?" she snapped.

"Nothing. I don't want to argue with you. That's not why I brought you out here tonight."

"Why did you bring me here?" she couldn't help asking.

Rising to his feet, he began to unbutton his shirt. "I didn't bring you here just to look at the pool," he said when she stared at him with wide eyes. "It's time for a swim. Do you dare?"

The last was said teasingly, in the form of a challenge, and Bethany glared at him indignantly.

"Don't think I'm going to fall for that worn-out old hat trick, Trace Taylor! Do you think all you have to do is dare me and I'll be fool enough to . . . what are you doing?" she ended on a gasp.

"Undressing so I won't get my clothes wet." His eyes were hot and narrow. "And unless you want to go back with wet clothes, you'll do the same." The shirt peeled away and left bare his broad chest, thickly furred with a dark pelt of hair that dipped to the waist of his cord pants. His muscles flexed smoothly as his hands moved to unbuckle his gun belt. It dropped to the ground on top of his discarded shirt and the boots he'd kicked off, then his fingers moved to the buttons of his pants.

"Stop that!" she exclaimed in horror, but he ignored her. His fingers moved deftly, and when she saw that he had no intention of stopping, she made a strangled sound in her throat and hastily turned away. Her face felt hot, and her breath was coming in short, rapid pants for air.

She didn't know where to flee, and when she heard him step into the pool and his voice, warmly inviting, tell her the water was fine, she shuddered.

"I didn't come here to be humiliated," she said in a tight voice over one shoulder, and heard Trace move through the water toward the rocky edge of the shallow pool.

"I didn't bring you here to humiliate you, Bethany," he said quietly. "You have to know why I brought you—for the same reason you came without asking. We're a long way from camp, and you can't deny that you want the same thing—I've held you too many times for you to try. Are you coming in? Or do you want me to come and get you?"

"What if I don't want to swim?"

"That wasn't one of your choices."

She shook her head, and dared a glance in his direction. With the moon and a shallow oil lamp for the only light, Trace was well hidden in the dark waters of the pool. She could see his wetly gleaming chest and slicked back hair, but nothing else as the water lapped about his upper body. All her years of training—the lessons she had learned about a woman's modesty and dignity—were in jeopardy. Should she yield to the emotions tumbling through her? Or to the heavy ache inside that urged her toward him? She carefully averted her gaze when he moved closer and the light shone on his face.

Trace waited for a moment, and when Bethany heard the splashing of water as he heaved himself out of the pool, she decided that surrender was inevitable. "All right!" she said hastily. "I'll swim, and that's all! But . . . but I want to undress myself. And I want you to turn around."

"I don't want to turn around."

"Trace—please." She hated to sound frightened, but the dark glitter in his eyes was almost terrifying, and the thought of undressing while he watched was overwhelming. If he forced her, she would never forgive him.

After a brief pause, he said, "All right. I'll wait."

Hurriedly, before she lost her nerve, Bethany shed her trousers, boots, and shirt, except for her underwear as she slipped hastily into the water.

"All right," she said after a moment, clearing her throat when her voice broke on *right,* "You can turn around now."

Chapter Fourteen

Bethany lifted her gaze when the silence dragged on too long, and saw Trace staring at her in the wash of moonlight over them. He was in the pool again, the water reaching to his waist. A tiny muscle leaped in his jaw, and his eyes were fathomless as he gazed at her without speaking for a moment.

The heated water made her flush—or was it Trace's dark eyes on her that caused that reaction? she wondered in the next instant. Whatever it was, she suddenly felt as if she had stepped into a volcano of molten lava.

"Now, this isn't so bad, is it?" Trace finally said, and she shook her head.

"Not yet."

"Have you always been so trusting?"

"Have you?" she countered, and saw his smile.

"Truce, princess." His words were soft, but his smile—oh, his smile! It reminded her of a predator, hungry and waiting.

"Truce?" She managed a steady smile in spite of her shaking knees. "I didn't know we were having a war."

"Didn't you?" Trace moved catlike through the water, his strides long and graceful. His fingers were warm when he lightly gripped her wrist in one hand. His other hand came up to brush gently against her cheek, the backs of his fingers wet yet stingingly warm against her cool skin. When his hand dropped from her cheek to the lacy fringe of her chemise, Bethany gave a violent start.

"What . . . what are you doing?"

Trace didn't answer. A faint smile tugged at the sensual line of his mouth, and his dark eyes were glowing with a light Bethany recognized. But this time, instead of frightening her with his intensity, she felt a heated flush of response move sluggishly through her veins. Everything seemed to slow in motion; she could hear the erratic rasp of her breath, almost feel the slowing surge of blood through her veins, the *pop-pop-pop* of her heartbeat sounding much too loud in her own ears. Could he hear it, too?

But Trace could hear nothing but his own ragged breathing and the silent voice of his need. He hadn't thought that the sight of Bethany's thin, wet undergarments straining over her ripe curves would provoke him into behaving rashly instead of taking his time, but it had. She obviously didn't even realize it as she stood looking at him so warily, her eyes as huge and luminous as woodland pools. Her hair, hanging loose and flowing over her slender shoulders, floated lightly on the surface of the water, moving silkily with her every motion. The thin muslin of her chemise, held up by ribboned straps, clung damply to her skin, and his imagination quickly provided the few details the material hid from his narrowed gaze.

"Trace! I . . . I . . . perhaps we should . . ." she began, but he pulled her through the heated water, his splayed palms on her shoulders and the small of her back as he held her against his hard frame. She could feel his body tremble with something—emotion? The effort to hold back? And she trembled, too.

Trace wore nothing but moonlight and the satiny press of warm water, and Bethany quickly realized matters had gone too far to hesitate now. The thought came unbidden that she did not want to prevent what was about to happen. Hadn't she come out here with him willingly, knowing in the back of her mind what would happen? Of course, she had. And she'd gone too far to back down now.

Dimly realizing that she had been waiting for this moment since first meeting him, Bethany closed her eyes as his lips seared across her mouth in a kiss as hot and bold as the man who held her. Whatever came after, she would know what it meant to love a man completely. . . .

Sliding his hands down over the arched curve of her back to her slim hips, Trace held her hard against him, his tongue exploring the warm, moist interior of her mouth, his heartbeat matching the quickening staccato of hers. The soft, wet thrust of her firm breasts against his bare chest made him almost groan, and he had to remind himself to go slow. He didn't want to frighten her; he could sense her inexperience and wariness, and was surprised at his fierce need for her to enjoy his taking of her.

Bringing one hand up to cradle the back of her head in his palm, Trace very gently, very slowly, slipped one of the ribboned straps of her chemise down over her shoulder. Still kissing her, muffling her soft moans with his mouth, he caressed her bare skin with tenderly searching fingers. When he felt her response, the slight pressing of her body against his, he moved to lower the other strap.

Shuddering as his fingers trailed wetly over her slick skin, Bethany wondered wildly what she should do next—was it normal to want his caress so badly, to circle his lean body with her arms? Was this the way things were done? She had no previous experience to judge by, only instincts that seemed as confused and hazy as her thought process. Nothing had ever prepared her for the intensity of her response to him, the hot, aching void inside her that longed for Trace and an unknown ending.

Blindly, not yet brave enough to open her eyes and see his dark, handsome face so near hers, Bethany kept her face upturned, letting his kisses warm her trembling lips. As some of the heat from his mouth and the bubbling water warmed her shivering body, Bethany began to kiss him back.

While they kissed, Trace gently untied all the laces of her chemise to pull it down around her waist, freeing her breasts to his touch. His mouth trailed from her parted lips to her ear, his breath husking over her skin and making her quiver. When he shifted slightly to bury his face in her damply curling hair, she could feel his lean, hard body pressing urgent and hot against her, and was suddenly afraid. She hadn't been prepared for the taut insistence of a man, the rigid prodding against her woman's mound with his body. It was vaguely terrifying, and in spite of the gush of heated response she felt, the desire to cling to him, she tried to back away.

He held her fast; his grip was not rough, just firm. He could sense her withdrawal and sudden fear, but they'd gone too far now to stop. When his mouth moved from her throat to cover her lips again, it was too late for her to offer a protest.

Trace's hands skimmed over her pale breasts, then down the length of her curves, exploring the velvet hollows with his fingertips, pausing to tease a response from her. With her mouth still captured by his lips, Bethany shivered as a hot, coiling fire burned deep within her. She wasn't surprised by the bubbling of the water around her; her body heat alone should have made it boil.

Nothing she'd ever imagined had prepared her for the sweep of urgent desire that coursed through her in a raging tide. The reality of what was happening to her, her abandoned response to Trace's exploring hands, seemed quite different from any vague imaginings of the past.

Softly murmuring her name, Trace eased Bethany's arms from around his lean waist, and she shivered again as she felt him curl his fingers in the wet material of her chemise to slide it from her body. Before seeing Trace with the woman in Huancayo, it had not occurred to her in any of her hazy imaginings that she would be completely nude. Ridiculous, of course, that she had not applied that scene to one in which she was a principal player . . . she clenched her teeth together to keep them from chattering with nervous reaction at his intimacy.

Why did the hot, hard press of his bare male body against hers make her vibrate with longing for him when she should still react with shock? Had she become inured to the most intimate of acts? She must have, yet she could not imagine an ending to this searing need. The silky lapping of heated water around her only heightened the need she felt instead of quenching it, and Trace's lingering kiss and caresses coaxed soft moans from her. Bethany's instinctive modesty made her clench her teeth to keep from leaping away. Trace was, thankfully, gentle and patient with her, and his light touch gently erased her worst fears.

His dark, wet head moved from her mouth to the creamy swell of her breasts, and Bethany arched against him with a soft cry. Teasing a taut pink rosette with his tongue, Trace heard her moan at his hot mouth on her damp flesh. The bud tightened more at his expert flicks of the tongue, and she clutched him fiercely when he took the entire nipple into his mouth.

It was almost more than she could stand. The sharp contrast of his scalding mouth and the lap of bubbling water on her body made her shudder with a heavy, throbbing ache. A strange breathless longing built up slowly inside her, and her hips began to grind against his body in the ancient rhythm of love. He felt her move, and lifted his head to gaze down at her face. Her eyes were closed, long lashes lying like tiny wings on her cheeks, and her lips were parted as if for his kiss.

There was something so enticing, so erotic about the heated water and Trace's hands and lips, that Bethany forgot about modesty, or why she had come, or what she was doing. She thought only of the moment, only of Trace, and how to please him as he was pleasing her.

When her shy, inexperienced hand trailed over his chest to the hard, flat bands of muscle on his stomach, he half groaned, and caught her wrist when she would have jerked away in sudden embarrassment.

"No, love, don't be shy," he muttered against the wet skin of her breast. "I like for you to touch me . . . I like touching you . . . does this feel good? And this?"

Bethany's senses whirled rapidly out of control as his hand grazed between her quivering thighs in gentle strokes. His mouth on her breasts, teasing her nipples with his lips and tongue, made her shiver, and her head fell back as he moved upward, her fingers clenching his broad shoulders as he trailed hot kisses over the line of her throat to her lips, then to her ear. He kissed her mouth with increasing urgency, then her breasts again, until Bethany was flushed and shaking. Her emotions swept over her in an overwhelming tide that threatened to render her incoherent, and she could barely understand his muttered words, love words that heightened the feelings of desire.

"Ah, love, you feel so ready," he was murmuring thickly against her damp skin, his hands gliding over her in silky motions. "I'm ready for you . . . can you feel how ready I am?"

His hand curled around hers and guided it to his belly and then lower, and Bethany thought at first she would die with embarrassment when he put her fingers around him. "No, don't take your hand away," he said softly against her ear when she tried to jerk away. "I want you to touch me there, to make me feel as good as I want to make you feel. . . ."

"But Trace, I . . . I don't know how," she moaned with acute embarrassment.

"I'll show you." His hand taught her the motion, and she felt his leaping response beneath her untutored hands, and to her astonishment, felt a sense of power that she was able to prompt such shivering reaction from him. "That's right, love, that's right," he muttered hoarsely, and then he took her hand away before he lost his tenuous grip on his self-control.

When he did the same to her, when his hands moved to stroke between her thighs with lingering motions that made her writhe, Bethany could not stop her cries. Her soft cries only spurred Trace to greater effort, and when she convulsed, her body arching against the arm he had behind her back, he smothered the cries with his mouth.

Somewhere in the rapid vortex of emotions that spun inside her, Bethany found the strength to resist fainting. Odd, she had never been a woman prone to fainting, but now she had to hold tightly to her consciousness to keep from swooning in Trace's arms.

"Hold on to me, love," she heard him whisper, and her arms automatically closed around his waist. "No. I mean like this," he said, moving her arms to his neck.

A feeling of weightlessness swept over her as she briefly floated, then Trace's arms were under her, his hands bracing her in the water. Lifting her until she was above him, his muscles tightening with the movement, Trace slowly slid her down, his tongue tracing hot, searing patterns over her wet body and making her cry out. Her hands were on his shoulders, her fingers tangling in the thick, dark strands of hair lying wetly on his neck.

"Trace! No! I don't . . . we shouldn't . . . oh, I don't

know what to say . . ." she whimpered as he slowly eased her down, her thighs rubbing against his chest, then the flat, taut band of muscle on his lean stomach. Bethany could feel the heat of him against her, prodding insistently into her soft, yielding flesh. "Oh!" she gasped, half frightened by the increasing pressure of him against her. "This is . . . is not what I expected. . . ."

He laughed. "Can't you offer better compliments than that, love? Not what you expected?" His mouth found the wildly fluttering pulse at the base of her throat before he added in a soft murmur, "With your imagination, I'm not sure I want to know what you expected."

Faintly, her voice came to him through the thick waves of her hair sweeping across her face. "I guess I'm a bit embarrassed by all this . . . the intimacy, I mean."

Trace's hands caressed her back and the curve of her waist. "Don't be embarrassed, love. Not with me. Not ever with me. I wouldn't hurt you for anything. Now hold me. With your arms around my neck. Close, like you did before. Now wrap your legs around my waist and lean back so I can see your beautiful face and eyes. . . ."

Shyly, trying not to look as clumsy as she felt, Bethany let him curve her legs around him so that she was gazing into his dark eyes. Lightly at first, she trailed her fingertips over his shoulders, exploring the taut muscles in his chest and upper arms, the faint ridges of old scars that suddenly made her remember how dangerous a life he'd led, then the angle of his jaw with its light burr of beard. His intense concentration, the hot lights in his eyes, and the faint leap of a muscle in his jaw made her uneasy, and Bethany looked away, catching her lower lip between her teeth.

"Still afraid, love?" he asked, and she shook her head.

"No, just . . . I can't stop shaking."

Bethany moaned as he pulled her even closer and buried his face in the curve of her breasts. Then she gasped as his lips closed around a taut, aching peak again, sucking gently.

Her fingers curled around his neck as she arched into him, and his hands caught her in the bend of her knees to hold her afloat. It was the oddest, most exciting sensation she'd ever known, with Trace's mouth scorching across her wet skin and the water lapping around her, and exotic birds echoing in the towering jungle behind walls built hundreds of years before by a civilization now extinct.

Walking slowly through the water, Trace held Bethany close as he sank to the wide, shallow ledge of a series of steps cut into the stone walls of the pool. She sat facing him, her legs around his waist, the water lapping about her shoulders and his face buried in her wet hair, his breath warming her cheek as he whispered to her.

"God, you're so beautiful . . . I've wanted to hold you like this since the first moment I saw you . . . don't be afraid . . . I'd never hurt you. Here, don't you want to touch me, too?"

Emboldened by his hoarse mutters in his ear, Bethany began to caress him again, tentatively at first, then more boldly, hearing his quickly drawn breath and muffled groan before his kisses changed from soft and gentle to hard and urgent. Just when she thought she would explode with pent-up tension, Trace lifted her slightly away from him, his eyes burning into hers.

"Are you ready for me, sweetheart?"

Bethany hesitated, then nodded, not quite certain what he meant but knowing she had to have an ending to this aching need inside. Sliding her up over his outstretched legs, Trace cupped her hips with his hands, his mouth finding hers as he rested her against him for an instant. Then, with a swift movement, he pressed into her, his lips stifling the soft cry she gave at the sudden thrust of his body. Pain knifed through her, and he held her fast as she tried to wriggle away, his hands hard on her waist to keep her still.

"It's all right," he muttered thickly in her ear, "it won't hurt again."

He held her still, not moving, but waiting until she stopped shaking before he began to lift her, rocking her atop him in gentle thrusts. As the pain of his penetration lessened, Bethany began to match his quickening rhythm. He was right. It didn't hurt badly now. Instead, she began to feel a return of the earlier tension, the aching need that built swiftly into a rising urgency and when it crescendoed into a hot, searing release, she cried out against him. An endless wave of rolling contractions closed her velvet heat around him, and she could feel his body's explosion.

Half sobbing, she clung weakly to him as tide after tide of quivering warmth pulsed through her, and barely heard his voice in her ear, calling her love, kissing her softly. Sliding her fingertips from his back up to the nape of his neck, feeling the wet, silky strands of his hair slide through her fingers, Bethany wondered hazily why she had not known how wonderful it could be to love a man. This was different from anything she had imagined; this was more intimate—more soul-searing—than she had ever dreamed.

Weakly, she felt the cadence of his breathing slow, and offered no protest when he rose and led her from the water to a shadowy alcove with strange, painted figures on the stone walls. He'd brought towels, and as he tenderly, gently dragged a soft towel over her wet, quaking body, Bethany met his dark gaze.

"I didn't know," she said simply, and he looked at her. "I hope you aren't disappointed."

She shook her head, dropping her gaze shyly as he drew the towel over her back to her breasts, rubbing the water away with gentle, abrasive strokes.

"No, I'm not disappointed. Surprised, maybe."

Trace brought the towel up her throat, then down over her shoulder to her arm. He was still wet, and drops of water fell onto her where he had just dried her as he knelt in front of her. Bethany took the towel from him and began to draw it over his body, over his broad chest and muscled arms, down to the flat, taut muscles of his belly and his lean thighs. She could feel his intent gaze on her, heard the quick drawing in of his breath as she stroked lightly with the towel.

"Pleasantly surprised, I hope," Trace said in a tight voice, and Bethany glanced up at him quizzically. "You said you were surprised," he reminded, and when she smiled, her dimple flashed enchantingly.

"Yes. I didn't know there could be such . . . intensity . . . I guess." Her cheeks warmed as he put out his hands to touch her, one finger tracing the dent of her dimple. Bethany found it hard to meet his searching gaze.

"I didn't know it either," he said so softly she leaned closer to him. His hand drew along the line of her cheek to her trembling lips. "Not until a few minutes ago."

Feeling suddenly awkward and embarrassed, she quipped with an attempt at humor, "I suppose this is not how the Incan High Priests sacrificed virgins."

Trace laughed, softly, and drew her into the damp embrace of his arms. A thread of laughter still edged his voice when he murmured, "Maybe not, but it's certainly my favorite method."

Scraping her fingertips over the square angle of his jaw, Bethany kissed him, her eyes closing as his arms wrapped around her to jerk her closer. When she drew away, she saw familiar flames dancing in his eyes. A faint smile curved her lips as she murmured, "There's a lot to be said for your method."

"I think so, too," Trace agreed just before his mouth

came down over hers in a hungry kiss. "I think so, too. . . ."

Pushing her gently back on the stone floor, Trace molded his hard body against her with a swift urgency. She felt his hands on her breasts, touching her lightly, teasing a response from her, and suddenly her body was moving to accept his, matching his rhythm with a fevered anticipation. There was only Trace, and the hot, hard ache within her that he knew how to ease.

The stone floor beneath her was heated by the hot springs bubbling below ground, and it scrubbed against her shoulder blades as she arched toward Trace. Nothing else mattered, she thought hazily, nothing but the man above her.

Bethany didn't want to think about anything but the moment, about Trace and the fact that he wanted her, had to love her, or he wouldn't be holding her this way, wouldn't be muttering her name over and over. He'd made it so wonderful, and she felt a soaring emotion fill her as he rocked against her, his lips and his hands wresting a sweet response from her eager body.

Her hands slipped up the smooth muscles of his back, and she felt his pace gradually grow faster, until she could think of nothing at all, could do nothing but move with him. There was a fiery pulsing in her that urged her on, made her hold him tightly to her, her hips arching to meet his quickened thrusts. And when release came, washing over her in drowning waves, she knew nothing would ever be the same again.

Chapter Fifteen

The now-familiar sounds of camp being broken woke Bethany early the next morning. Clearing the sleep-haze from her drowsy eyes, she dragged herself from her cozy, warm blankets and stumbled toward the fire where a soot-blackened pot bubbled with strong coffee.

She looked forward to—and almost dreaded—seeing Trace again, and tried to look casually around the camp for him. He was nowhere in sight. Her fingers clenched the tin cup she held, and she sipped scalding, bitter coffee slowly as she tried to appear nonchalant. The memories of the night before were still as vivid as the aching soreness between her thighs. Where was Trace? she wondered. Had he meant any of the things he'd said? And would he want her again? She found it hard to think of anything else as she drained the last of her coffee and went to roll up her blankets and repack her saddlebags.

Bethany knew at once when Trace returned to camp, saw from the corner of her eyes as he casually paused by the fire to pour himself a cup of coffee. His gaze sought and found her, and she pretended not to notice, though she was tingling with a jumbled mixture of emotions. If she looked directly at him, she was certain her face would give everything away.

He looked more handsome than ever this morning. His thick, dark hair was wind-ruffled and he wasn't wearing his hat, though his gun belt was draped around his lean waist as usual, the knife tucked into his belt. His shirt hung open, and his skin was gleaming damply in the early morning light, as if he had just come from a swim. As Trace turned to speak to one of the Quechua bearers, Bethany dragged her gaze away from him. She had to concentrate on something else—anything else!

Her thoughts focused on Trace instead of the mundane task of breaking camp, however, and when Professor Brasfield spoke to her she answered automatically, not really even hearing him.

"That's nice," she murmured, her gaze shifting from her father's faintly startled expression to Trace and back. She flushed. "I'm sorry—what did you say, Papa?"

Professor Brasfield's eyebrows rose higher. "I said, Brody claims there are unfriendly natives just ahead of us, and that we may be in great danger."

"Oh." Bethany looked quickly toward Trace. "What does Tra—Mr. Taylor say?"

"He has not offered an opinion yet."

"I see." Bethany tossed her saddlebag over her shoulder and started toward her mule, glancing back to say, "I think we should wait until we hear his opinion before we worry."

"Perhaps you're right." Brasfield bent to lift his pack but his gaze was worried. "I only hope that the natives will not hinder our search for the lost city."

Bethany felt a flash of annoyance. Was that all he could think about? His precious discoveries? Couldn't he consider personal danger as important?

Or was archaeology the only thing of importance to him? Reading his daughter's irritated gaze correctly, Professor Brasfield added, "I only want us to be safe. We're so close now, so close. It'd be dreadful to have to turn back."

Apparently, her father was not the only one there who was concerned about the fate of the expedition.

Striding toward Trace, Brody's face reflected grim fear as he demanded, "What do you intend to do, Taylor?"

Shrugging, Trace leveled a dark gaze on him. "Do about what, Brody?"

"You know what! Those savages out there! Jivaros, or whatever they are—headhunters camped on the pampa ahead!"

"Not Jivaros," Trace replied coolly. "We're too far west for them. Maybe Campas. Or Aymaras."

Snarling, "I don't care who they are!" Brody took a quick step forward, then stopped short as Trace brought up his pistol in a smooth motion. He blanched. "Look, Taylor, what do you think you're doing?"

"Don't make angry noises unless you want me to react to them," Trace said shortly. "I don't see that there's anything to do now except wait. Hostile natives come with the territory, remember? Or did you think only Apaches resented trespassing?"

Not quite understanding his inference, Bethany looked from Trace to Brody. It was obvious that Bentworth's hired man knew what Trace was talking about; his face was creased into lines of anger and resentment.

"That was a long time ago!" Brody snapped. "This is a different country, a different situation."

"I'm not having any trouble remembering that. Maybe you need a reminder." Trace reholstered his pistol in an easy, graceful motion. "Just don't forget that you have an obligation to others besides yourself, Brody. If trouble comes, you'd better do your best to get *every*one out of it, not just yourself."

Glaring at him, Brody didn't say a word as he pivoted on his heel and stalked away. Trace's faintly amused glance slid from Brody to Bethany, and softened at her wide eyes.

"There's no guarantee there will be trouble, Miss Brasfield," he said quietly.

"And no guarantee there won't?" she quipped with a brave attempt at flippancy.

Trace grinned. "Maybe not. Whatever comes along, I'll be ready for it."

"I only hope the same can be said of the rest of us, Mr. Taylor," Bethany replied. Her gaze shifted to her father, who was frowning and shaking his head. His eyeglasses slid down his nose and balanced precariously on the tip until he gave them an impatient shove.

"See here, Taylor, I thought we were close to our goal! Are we to allow some sort of conflict to deter us?" he demanded testily. "I refuse to allow it!"

"Professor, as I just said, there's no guarantee there will be trouble. It would be foolish not to prepare for it, however." Trace's voice was firm, and his eyes narrowed slightly on Brasfields face. "I speak a bit of some of the Indian languages, and I intend to go ahead and find out if what Brody claims is true."

"And leave us here alone?" Brasfield rapped out.

"Not hardly." Trace waved one arm toward the Quechua bearers, Bentworth's men and the two Peruvian officers. "I think there are enough of you to survive for the short time I'll be gone. Just follow Santusa. He knows the path better than I do, I imagine. I'll be back."

Bethany wanted to plead with him not to go, but could not say a word. He didn't look at her again, but went to the Indian bearer he'd called Santusa and talked briefly with him in low tones. Then he was gone, fading into the dense jungle growth beyond the rocky path without a sound.

Bethany stifled a shiver of apprehension. The adventure had taken on a decidedly dangerous turn. Had it been only last night that she and Trace had stolen away to an Incan pool and made love? Now, danger lurked just beyond the camp in the dark shadows of the jungle. Perhaps, it had been there the night before. This time, she did shudder at the thought.

Following close on the heels of that thought came another, even more frightening thought—what if Trace never came back? What if Brody was right?

Bethany stared at the dark spot where Trace had gone into the jungle until a Quechua bearer put the reins to her mule in her hand and told her haltingly that they must move on. Slowly, as if in a dream, Bethany swung atop her mule and followed the small caravan led by Santusa. Trace would be all right. He had to be all right. She'd discovered that she loved him, and could not bear the thought of losing him.

Trace, stripped to the waist and wearing a light pair of llama skin boots, tread softly on the jungle path. Beads of sweat rolled over him, and occasionally he stopped to wipe his damp palms on his trousers. The jungle was steamy and humid. Tangled vines looped from trees that formed a ceiling sunlight could barely penetrate, and thickets were so dense as to require the use of his machete to follow the faintly visible path. Muffled mutters in the brush were evidence of ample jungle life; Trace was well aware that at any moment, he could find himself face to face with a wild puma or savage Indian. Neither one seemed particular about killing trespassers in the jungle.

Half stumbling over slippery rocks as he was forced to almost crawl along the path, Trace swore softly and wished his sturdy leather boots were more flexible. Those, at least, provided a degree of protection from snakes. The fer-de-lance was common to the area he was in now, and he knew how unpredictable and aggressive the small yellow vipers could be. But, he'd needed freedom of movement over the trail more than he needed protection, and had chosen thin llama skin boots instead of thick cowhide.

Finally climbing to a bald peak that jutted out of the thick jungle in a sudden, steep rise, Trace was able to see out over the area. Far below, he could see the tiny figures wending their way along the trail behind Santusa. Not far ahead of them lay a small, grassy plain hemmed in on three sides by high, jagged mountains, and on the other side by the raging river. It was the only level ground for miles, and he could see no evidence of hostile Indians camped upon it as Brody had said. It was the only way through. There was no other route to the lost city. In spite of no sign of hostiles, Trace felt an odd premonition of danger. He did not know why. Nothing indicated danger, yet some primitive instinct warned him of it. Then he shook his head. It would be foolish to turn back without more evidence of danger. They would go on with the expedition, but stay ready for trouble.

Damning snakes, Brody, and his past fatal expedition, Trace made his way back to the caravan after a slow, tortuous trek back through the jungle. He met them on the open plain just before they crossed over the river to reach the trail.

Bethany felt a rush of relief when Trace stepped out of the thick brush and paused on a rock ledge over the trail. Tilting back her head with one hand on the hat she wore to shade her face, Bethany looked up at Trace. The afternoon sun glinted from his bare chest as he called a greeting in a native dialect to Santusa, and was answered briefly.

Vaulting gracefully from the ledge to the ground a few feet below, Trace joined Santusa without even glancing at Bethany. Beside her, Brody muttered resentfully, "He acts like a cocky fool instead of a man who knows what the hell he's doin'! I'd like to know if we're about to get jumped on by those murderin' devils. . . ."

"Then why don't you ask him?" Bethany broke in coolly.

Flashing her a hard glance, Brody rode his mule ahead, reining it in beside Santusa and Trace. "Hey!" he snapped belligerently, "What'd you find out—or did you?"

Trace turned slowly. "Are you talking to me?"

"Who else would I be askin'?"

His dark eyes narrowed dangerously as Trace gazed at Brody for a long moment without speaking. "Look, Brody," he finally said, "I don't like your tone of voice, and I don't much like you. When I want you to know what I found out, I will make it my business to tell you."

Brody glanced back at his partner, then turned back to Trace with an ugly expression. His jaw jutted out at an angle, and his thick brows lowered over his eyes. "Damn you for a cocky bastard, Taylor! I've got as much right as . . ."

That was as far as he got before Trace moved in a swift motion, bringing his right arm up before Brody could dodge. His fist connected with the shorter man's jaw, sending his head snapping back, and he staggered several steps before hitting the ground with a bone-jarring thud.

Towering over him with his hands clenched, Trace said harshly, "You've got no more right than the rest of them, Brody! I'll tell all of you at the same time—not before."

Brody scooted back in a crablike motion, keeping his gaze warily on Trace. "No need to get so mad, Taylor," he said in a low mutter. "I just don't like the idea of havin' my head decoratin' a pole or Indian hut."

"Neither do I." Trace glanced from Brody to Reagan, who had stepped forward as soon as his partner hit the ground. "Do you have anything you want to say?"

Shaking his head, Reagan took a step back. "No. Not now. When I do, I'll let you know."

Eyeing the stocky, dark Reagan for a moment, Trace gave a short nod. "You do that."

Bethany didn't realize she'd been holding her breath until she released it at the aching prompt of air-starved lungs. For a brief moment she had witnessed a violence she had not thought might happen. It was as startling as it was vaguely frightening. She'd known Trace was capable of it; yet this evidence competed with the mental image she'd only recently formed of his tenderness and passion, confusing her.

As Trace turned away from Brody and Reagan, his dark gaze met hers, and he must have read her reaction in her eyes. He said nothing, but paused, one eyebrow lifted as if waiting for her to speak.

Bethany's heart was pounding loudly, and her throat was so dry she couldn't force out a single word. Mixed emotions pounded through her—could he be so savage at times and yet still be tender? It was bewildering, and when Trace said nothing, but walked past her to speak to her father, she leaned back against her mule.

Moving slowly, Bethany followed orders, heard Trace tell them that he'd seen nothing suspicious, but they were to exercise extreme caution. Instead of allaying her fears, his warning only served to make her more nervous. When they reached the edge of the steep ravine with the boiling river slicing through the deep gully, she couldn't hold back a gasp of dismay.

"How are we ever to cross that?" she demanded, half turning as she slid from her mule to face Trace. "It doesn't even have a rope bridge!"

"Those logs are the bridge," he said in a matter-of-fact tone that made her eyes widen.

Bethany turned to look at the slender logs bridging the deep chasm. Gaping holes yawned between the logs, and cut branches had been woven through the gaps in places. Slender reeds formed part of the bridge, swaying in the wind that billowed up from the rushing water far below. Fear turned to disbelief. "You must be kidding! Or insane, to think we could get across that!"

"It's the only way," Trace pointed out reasonably. "Do you want me to lead your mule across for you?"

"Do you honestly think a mule would cross that . . . that *thing* you're calling a bridge?" she demanded in a rising voice. Her legs trembled, and she shook her head. "I doubt it seriously!"

"The mule doesn't have a choice either." Trace met her startled gaze calmly.

"The inference being that I don't have a choice?" she snapped.

"Right."

Bethany couldn't help another fearful glance toward the spindly log bridge, and Trace smiled.

"Look, it won't be that bad," he said softly. "I'll do what I can to help you make it across."

Drawing in a deep breath to steady her nerves,

Bethany shook her head. "No. No, I'll walk across like everyone else."

Trace's smile broadened. "I knew you would."

"Did you?" she asked tartly. "Don't be so sure I'll make it!"

He grinned. "That bridge would not *dare* fall with you on it, Bethany Brasfield!"

"You're right!" She had to smile, but when' it came time for her turn to cross, she wished she felt as brave as she'd sounded. It was unnerving, with the wind rushing past and her legs shaking so badly, and she could feel the logs swaying beneath her. Trace had blindfolded her mule so it could not see, and she had been tempted to ask for a scarf over her eyes, too. *Don't look down!* she scolded herself as she forced one foot in front of the other. If only she could go just a few more steps. . . .

Terror gripped her just before she reached the other side. Both Bethany and her mule stood trembling on the tiny span across the river gorge, unable to go another step. She could hear Trace calling encouragement to her, could hear her father's reassuring voice, but it didn't make any difference. Her old fear of heights held her tightly in its grip and she couldn't force her feet to move an inch in any direction.

The wind whipped at her clothes and loosened her hair from its neat braid, and her fingers tightened around the mule's bridle as she stood frozen. For some reason, the sound of the river grew louder and louder, as if it was rushing up to sweep her away from the fragile bridge. Or maybe it was the blood rushing through her veins that she heard so loudly, pounding in her ears with the roar of a steam engine. Dimly, as if from miles away, she heard Trace calling to her through the roar in her ears.

"Bethany! Bethany, only a few more feet—you can

make it!"

"I can't . . ."

The words fell softly from her lips, and her terror was transferring to the mule. She could feel the animal's legs trembling, heard its frightened snort and muted braying. A wave of dizziness made her cling tightly to the mule, and she felt that at any moment, she would pitch over the side of the bridge and into infinity.

As she stood swaying, the mule shifted, one leg thrusting forward. The bridge quivered, and a shower of loose reeds fell to spin into the gorge.

"Bethany—take one more step," came a calm voice from close behind her that she vaguely recognized as belonging to Trace. "Just one more. It can't hurt."

Blindly, shaking her head with her hair whipping into her eyes, she moaned sickly, "I can't do it!"

"You have to! One step—*now,* dammit!"

Obeying the firm command reluctantly, Bethany took a step forward. The narrow log bridge swayed but did not fall away. It seemed to break her fear when she didn't plummet to the bottom of the gorge at once, and she took another hesitant step, then another, with Trace right behind her telling her to go one more step, one more step. Finally, she felt the steady footing of solid ground beneath her feet.

Almost sobbing, she leaped the last two steps, jerking the mule with her. It slid, a front hoof plunging through a gap between the logs. Braying in terror, the mule scrabbled wildly in thin air. "Help me!" Bethany screamed, her hands tightening on the leather bridle as the mule slid back. "Help me, Trace!"

"Let the mule go!" he shouted. "Let it go, or you'll go with it!"

"No!" Bethany flung herself forward, still holding tightly to the mule's bridle, and somehow the impetus helped the animal regain its footing and it scrambled to safety beside her. Bethany and the mule sagged weakly, both trembling with reaction and damp with perspiration.

Trace reached her in a series of angry steps and halfleaps, grabbing her by the arms and whirling her around to face him. "Dammit, why didn't you let it go? It's just a damn mule, and you could have been killed!"

Gasping for breath, Bethany mutely shook her head. She had no idea why she hadn't let go. She should have. Somehow she just hadn't been able to bear the thought of the mule sliding to its death.

"Little fool," Trace muttered in a harsh voice. His grip loosened slightly, and he let one hand drift from her arm down to her wrist, clasping it lightly in his fingers. "I think the mule has more sense than you do," he grumbled as she hid her face against his chest. "What would you have done if you'd gone over the edge with it?"

"But I didn't." Bethany's voice was muffled against his broad chest.

A faint smile tugged at one corner of his mouth. "No," he agreed, "you didn't. Not because you didn't try hard enough, though."

Shrugging, Bethany pushed at the light strands of hair in her eyes and managed a casual glance up at him. With her gaze locked on his, she murmured, "You aren't disappointed, are you?"

"Not so you can tell it." Trace was aware of the eyes of the others on them, and knew what they were probably thinking. With an effort, he let his hands fall away from her, and his tone was once more brisk. "Now that you've managed to delay us again, Miss Brasfield, I suggest we push on before it gets dark."

Startled by his sudden brusqueness, Bethany's eyes

widened before she understood and nodded. "Oh. Yes. Yes, Mr. Taylor, you're right."

She turned away from him and bent to the task of tending the gashes sliced into her mule's leg during its brush with death. But she watched Trace from the corner of her eyes, wondering how he could so efficiently hide his feelings for her. She couldn't hide hers. No matter how hard she tried, she just knew that everyone in the expedition was aware of how she felt about him, how she longed for his arms around her and his lips touching hers. . . . *I have to stop thinking about him like this!* she scolded herself in the next instant. It was insanity to be too distracted when on a mountain trail no wider than one of the mules.

And, she discovered a short time later, it was entirely too dangerous to let one's attention wander even for a brief instant. The trail grew more treacherous with each step. Bethany clung tightly to the saddle as the trail seemed to just fall away on one side. She could not look down or even ahead: to do so, would have been her downfall. Instead, she kept her gaze averted, looking at the rock wall looming on her left, depending upon the mule to step cautiously.

It was a quiet group that made their way on the trail spiraling around the mountain, rising higher and higher, until Bethany was certain the slight fog they encountered were clouds. Wisps of it clung damply to her face, hair, and clothes.

As it began to grow dark, the high mountain peaks hiding the sun from view, shadows wavered across the trail. Bethany suppressed a shiver and wondered if they would make it to a place to camp before it grew completely dark. Trace didn't seem worried, but then—he wouldn't want to alarm anyone, so he wouldn't let it show, either. Bethany worried her bottom lip with her teeth and tried to think about the fabled city of gold instead of the attendant dangers.

It helped. When they finally reached the edge of a flat expanse bordered by rock and trail on the one side and the dense jungle on the other, Trace called a halt.

"We'll camp here for the night," he said as he swung down from his mule. "Tomorrow, we should reach the city."

Professor Brasfield was beside himself with delight. "Tomorrow?" he exclaimed. "I had thought it would be much farther! Though I do feel as if I have climbed through most of Peru."

Sliding from her mule, Bethany stood on weak legs. She could not manage to move for several moments. The dizzying descent down the mountain by the narrow ribbon of rock had left her with little strength to contemplate the following day. Or to even think about that evening.

The Quechua bearers set about making camp, and Brody and Reagan took care of the pack animals as Trace scouted the area. Slanting rays of sun speared the top of the peaks and highlighted the grassy strip of land where they were, and Bethany rested her head against her mule and thought that she had rarely seen so lovely a sight. Even with the terrifying heights and frightening bridges, she was glad she had come, glad she had not yielded to Trace Taylor's obvious efforts to leave her behind.

Did he still feel that way? she wondered briefly, then decided that he couldn't possibly. Not after the last night together. Now, he had to be glad she was with him.

When Trace finally came to her later, after camp had been set up and a fire lit to cook their evening meal, he had a frown on his handsome face.

"What's the matter?" she couldn't help asking, and

he gave a shrug of his broad shoulders.

"Nothing I can put my finger on."

Leaning close to him, Bethany smiled as she drew the tip of her finger across his lowered brows. "Then why are you frowning?"

His eyes met hers, and a slow smile curled his mouth. "I don't know. No reason, I guess."

Scooting closer, she murmured, "Are you still angry at me for what I did earlier today?"

It was the closest she could come to out and out flirtation with him, and it was more than she'd ever dared. A tremor shook her at her temerity, and she wondered if she was becoming as brazen as the woman she'd seen with Trace in Huancayo.

Maybe she was, she thought in the next instant, because with him kneeling close to her, just the heat of his body so near made her breath shorten and her pulses quicken. She kept recalling the feel of his mouth against hers, and the touch of his hands on her, the soaring response of her own body to him, and it made her want to be alone with him again.

As if reading her mind, the corners of Trace's mouth kicked up in a wicked smile.

"Too bad we can't get rid of the rest of this group without them noticing," he said softly, and grinned at the quick intake of her breath. "I see that you've had the same thought."

"No . . . yes, I did," she admitted shyly, and dropped her gaze. A hot flush stained her cheeks with embarrassment. She couldn't just admit that she wanted him to make love to her again, not like that! But she was certain her longing for him to kiss her must be in her eyes. She felt so odd, half embarrassed by her need, and yet wanting too badly for him to hold her to deny it.

Well aware of casual and not so casual glances in

their direction, Trace managed to keep from reaching out for her. It was hard, much harder than he'd ever thought it would be to resist a woman.

But this was not just any woman, he reminded himself. This was Bethany Brasfield, a complicated mixture of shy, naive female and bold vixen. Her response to him the night before had been surprising. He'd not quite expected such a passionate nature to lie beneath her reserve; but it had delighted him as well as startled him. Trace found that he could not get her out of his mind even when he should be concentrating on other things.

Like now, when he should be posting guards around the camp and assigning times for duty, he was kneeling beside Bethany, fascinated by the play of firelight in her tawny hair, the soft color that was sometimes golden and sometimes just a warm brown. Odd, that with her light hair and fair complexion her eyelashes should be so dark—long silky spikes that hid the violet sheen of her eyes from his view at times.

Trace rose in a fluid motion, knowing that he had to redirect his train of thoughts.

"Don't wander far from camp tonight," he said, and added in answer to the swift question in her eyes, "I just like to be safe. You never can tell about night-feeding animals."

"Oh, like the jaguar we heard one night?"

"Yeah, like that." Trace hooked a hand on his gun belt and flashed her a reassuring smile. "This is the jungle, remember."

"I remember." Rising to her feet, Bethany met his gaze. There was an unspoken desire in his eyes that made her heart leap. Predatory lights glinted in the depths, and she felt the hot rise of response that made her yearn to lean close to him. She smothered the impulse with an effort, just as aware as Trace of the interested gazes of the others in their direction. "Good night, Mr. Taylor," she said aloud, and hoped her voice did not betray her longing.

It was hard for Bethany not to look at Trace too much that evening, and she could feel her father's questioning gaze on her as they sat together to eat. Finally, Brasfield cleared his throat.

"I note that Mr. Taylor seems to have forgotten his objections to your presence on the expedition, dear. Could it be that you've ended your hostilities?"

Flushing, Bethany kept her eyes on the tin plate in her lap. "It certainly makes things easier not to be constantly at one another's throats," she murmured after a moment. "I decided that it would be much better this way."

"Ah yes, of course," Brasfield agreed. He forked a bite of sweet potato into his mouth and chewed it slowly before he said, "Bethany, you do know that I trust your judgment. You've always been a level-headed girl, and I've never had occasion to complain. I hope that you don't embarrass me now."

She looked up in surprise, then felt a flash of anger. "I never knew you thought about me that much, Papa. Perhaps if you had bothered to talk to me once in a while, I would be aware that you trust my judgment."

"Do I detect a note of censure?"

"More than a note!" Bethany snapped. For some reason, her father's oblique reprimand stung, and brought to mind his years of benign neglect, of intense interest in his work and none in his daughter or her problems. Bethany recalled all too well how he had offhandedly dismissed her pain at Stephen Averill's defection, telling her that she was much better off without him. While that may have been true, she'd needed to hear more than those few cold words.

And now, when she had found a man who made her heart skip a beat and her emotions soar to new heights, he dared to criticize her!

Professor Brasfield peered at his daughter over his spectacles, and his bushy brows were lowered. "I *am* your father, I might remind you, and am only trying to. . . ."

"Oh, I've never forgotten that you are my father," she interrupted, "even when you've seemed to!" Her throat ached with unshed tears, and her chin tilted in an unconscious effort at keeping them back as she met Brasfield's astounded gaze. "While I appreciate the fact that you wish to keep me from harm, I wonder at your motives. You've not bothered before; as long as I didn't kick up too big a fuss or hinder your research, all was well. Now, you dare to tell me that you hope I don't embarrass you? I'm amazed that you've even remembered me at all!"

"Bethany! What has come over you? You've never been so rude, or so . . ."

"Truthful?" she supplied in a choked voice. The tin plate slid from her lap as she surged to her feet. Looking down at her father with tear-blurred eyes, Bethany said, "I know you haven't been deliberately cruel, Papa, but it hurts just the same. I . . . I . . . oh!"

Pressing a hand to her mouth, she fled blindly, leaving the professor to stare after her in dumbfounded amazement. A frown puckered his brows, and when his gaze shifted, he saw Trace Taylor staring at him. There was an iciness in the dark gaze that made Brasfield recoil, and he realized that perhaps his daughter was justified. He hadn't noticed her attraction to Taylor, or the guide's to her, until it was obviously too late. He'd been so caught up in the pursuit of golden dreams that he'd blinded himself to everything but his own selfish desires. Now, he felt a pang of sorrow that he had inadvertantly hurt Bethany through his selfishness.

The professor might have gone after her then, but Brody chose that moment to approach him about photographic equipment to be used when they reached the city, and Brasfield's attention was immediately diverted. It was left to Trace to find and comfort her.

Bethany had fled several yards back down the trail, until the campfires were only small, bright dots behind her. Luminous moonlight flooded the path, but she paused, not wanting to go too far. She was shivering with chill and anger when Trace found her.

"You don't ever dress for the climate," he observed in a mild tone that jerked her head around to glare at him. He met her gaze steadily. "And you won't change him, you know. It's a waste of time to try."

"I was not trying to change him!"

"Then why bother upsetting yourself like that? You're not going to get the answers you want." Trace raked a hand through his dark hair and smiled at her in the pale moonlight washing over them. "Bethany, you don't owe him or anyone else an explanation."

"I believe you're making a grave mistake," she said so coldly he arched an eyebrow. "I was not explaining anything at all! And I was not trying to defend myself, if you think that. I was only pointing out the reasons why I do not believe my father should take it upon himself to berate me. And I don't need you to try and comfort me! I know why you came after me . . ."

To her horror, tears welled up and threatened to spill onto her cheeks, and she turned quickly away. It was too late. Trace had seen them.

Putting a hand on her arm, he turned her gently back to face him. "I don't know why you feel you have to reject my clumsy attempt at offering you comfort, but if it makes you feel better, then I accomplished something after all."

A slight smile made her dimple flash briefly, but she couldn't look at him as she said in a small voice, "I don't know why I do some of the things I do, either. I just wish that . . . oh, I don't know what I wish!"

Folding her into his strong embrace, Trace said against her hair, "I can't even begin to understand, but I guess I don't have to. I'll just go on wanting to feel you close to me like this, no matter what."

It wasn't quite the response she'd wanted. Didn't *love* enter into it anywhere? On his side, anyway? Bethany didn't say anything, but kept her face buried in his shirt.

She wasn't surprised to feel his hands move beneath the tail of her blouse, sliding smoothly over her bare skin and making her shiver. When he placed his palm over the peak of her breast, kneading her flesh with soft, sensual motions, she moaned, and he wound his other hand in her hair to pull her head back, his mouth searing over her open lips. Time and place faded for both of them. Bethany could feel the taut urgency in him, in the hard press of his body against hers.

"Trace," she murmured when he briefly released her lips to trail a fiery path of kisses along the line of her throat, "someone might see us."

"I don't care," he growled roughly. "I'll shoot the first man who comes down that path." But he moved back with his arms still around her, taking her with him behind a high outcropping of rock.

A faint laugh quivered in the back of her throat, altering to a husky gasp when his mouth found the rapidly hardening peak of her breast and covered it.

Arching her back, she curled her fingers into the material of his shirt and clung weakly.

Impatiently shoving aside the edges of her blouse, Trace pulled it down around her waist. Moonlight bathed her ivory skin in a silvery glow, lent a mystical gleam to the soft, silky waves of hair flowing around her oval face.

"God," he muttered, sucking in a deep breath, his eyes lingering on her. "You're beautiful."

The simple words made her flush with pleasure, made her ache to have him as close to her as a man can get to a woman, and Bethany swayed even closer. Her fingers fumbled with the buttons of his shirt, and when she had it open, she slid her hands inside, feeling the taut ridges of his belly tighten at her touch.

It was a heady feeling to know she could make him react to her, to know that he felt something of the aching need she felt. When Trace drew an exploring finger lightly over the satiny curve of her breast, flicking gently at the taut rosette, Bethany reacted by boldly slipping her hand into the waistband of his cord trousers. He sucked in a sharp breath, freezing as she tugged his belt buckle free, then unbuttoned the top buttons of his pants.

A husky groan escaped him, and impatient with the delay and his own raging need, Trace's hand covered hers in an effort to help. With quick, deft motions, he removed his gun belt and dropped it to the ground, then unfastened the rest of his buttons. Without releasing her, he began to undo the buttons of Bethany's trousers, then lifted her in a smooth swing before placing her gently on the ground.

Thick clumps of grass cushioned her, and Bethany lay back, watching as Trace quickly shed his clothes. She had the choking thought that he looked like a pagan god, or like one of the powerful creations of Michelangelo or da Vinci. He was beautiful, with smooth flowing muscles and knotted bands ridging his stomach, taut, lean flanks and a proud male body.

He came to her, briefly blotting out the moonlight, then lying down beside her, his hands urgent and caressing as he peeled away her clothes. As the trousers slipped from her slender hips and over her thighs, Trace kissed every inch of her, ignoring her startled gasps, his mouth savoring the sweet taste of her honeyed skin.

Quivering, Bethany reached out for him and he came to her at last, covering her with his body, sliding between her eager thighs with a swift urgency that neither of them could deny a moment longer. In spite of his intention to delay the anticipation, Trace was too impatient. He slid inside her body in a smooth, hungry thrust that made her gasp and arch toward him, her heels digging into the spongy ground to give her leverage.

Holding him, her hands clutched at his back, her nails skidding over his skin in stinging rakes that only made him surge toward her more fiercely. Infused with the same driving urgency that he felt, Bethany could not stem the rising tide that coursed through her, could not slow the raging beat of her heart or slapping of blood through her veins as she met his quick, hard thrusts.

Release came in a hot, blinding flash of contracting muscles and pulsing flesh, and Bethany dimly heard someone cry out, then realized it was her. Trace's mouth quickly covered her lips, muffling her moan, his mouth hot.

Half sobbing, she felt her pulses gradually slow, felt the easing of her muscles and the damp, warm feel of his body resting atop hers. She began to shake with reaction, and his arms closed around her.

"This is crazy," Trace muttered, resting his forehead against hers. She felt his smile rather than saw it, and heard him sigh. "You make me do crazy things, woman."

"I suppose you think this is a regular nightly ritual for me?" she murmured in a faintly cranky voice, and he laughed softly.

"No, I know better than that." He rolled to the side, sliding his body from hers, and she felt a disappointing emptiness. "You were right," he said, taking her hand and kissing her fingertips. "Anyone could come along and find us here."

"Maybe they'd bring blankets and pillows with them, and we could stay the rest of the night like this," Bethany said in such a lazy voice that Trace laughed again.

"You're an insatiable wench."

"Trace?" she whispered after a moment, and his voice was sleepy when he answered "Umm-hmm?" She smiled, then said, "What will happen after we find the city?"

There was a brief pause, then he shifted in the tall, cushioning grasses, rolling to one side and propping up on his elbow to gaze down at her serious face. "Your father will explore what he wants, I guess, then do whatever it is archaeologists do. Why?"

"That's not what I meant."

"Ah." That one word held a wealth of comprehension. "I see. I guess that depends on how we both feel."

It was not a completely satisfactory reply, nor was it a completely unsatisfactory reply. But it was the best she felt she could hope for at the moment, so Bethany smiled and traced the outline of his dark brows with the tip of her finger.

"You're not really so fierce, you know," she said in

a low whisper. "I once had a little terrier that could bark more loudly than you."

His eyebrow winged upward. "Meaning?"

"Meaning, that when you bark and snap at me like you do sometimes, I'm not in the least impressed."

"Wait until I bite," he said, his dark head lowering to blot out the moon again. "That would impress a stone statue."

Bethany had no doubt that Trace Taylor could wring a response from a statue if he desired. As his mouth captured hers again, lingering, coaxing the embers of passion into roaring flames again, she ceased to think about the future. What mattered was now, was this unending need between them that sent them into each other's arms with careless abandon and fierce passion.

Chapter Sixteen

A stiff breeze sprang up and Bethany shivered, then wished she hadn't when Trace sat up and said it was time they returned to camp.

"Not that they haven't figured out what's going on by now," he muttered, "but we should at least keep up some sort of appearances."

Bethany dressed with clumsy, shaking hands, and Trace finally brushed aside her fingers and finished buttoning her blouse for her, his face patient and understanding in the cool wash of moonlight. When they were both fully dressed and he was wearing his gun strapped around his lean waist again, he knelt beside her and tilted her face up to his.

"We've got to be careful, you know. I don't trust Brody or Reagan not to make some sort of comment, and I'd have to kill them if they did."

"Trace!"

"I'm only half joking," he said grimly. "From now on, we'll have to use more self-control."

"That should be easy," Bethany muttered, "because I haven't used an ounce of it before now."

He laughed and pulled her close to him, his hand smoothing a tangled skein of her light hair from her eyes. "I can't say that I have either," he confessed.

"But we'd better begin. All right?"

"All right," she agreed with a sigh, and put one small hand on the back of his neck to pull his face to hers. "But a last kiss, first."

Trace obliged quite nicely, and when he pulled away they were both breathing a little faster. "This is going to be harder than I thought," he said, and put his arms around her to hold her close. Bethany snuggled into the hard angle of his chest and arms, then felt him stiffen.

She drew back to ask what was the matter, but he put a quick hand over her mouth.

"Don't say anything," he rasped, his breath whisking over her ear. "Be very quiet. . . ."

Her heart began to pound, and for a very different reason than Trace being so near. The rustling in the tall grasses beside the trail sounded ominous now, and she felt her muscles tense with expectation and her scalp tighten.

"Get up slowly," Trace whispered hoarsely, "and act like nothing is the matter. Walk casually and slowly with me. And *don't* look behind us."

In spite of his soft warning, Bethany could not resist a swift glance backward as they ambled slowly toward the camp again, and her blood grew cold as she saw the glint of moonlight on what appeared to be solid white masks peering at them from the bushes. It was a dead white, with no shine or return of color, and she couldn't imagine what it could be.

Trace's fingers bit deeply into her arm, and he half dragged her back with him, his strides long so that she had to trot to keep up with him.

"Slowly," he growled, and she shot him a quick glance.

"I could say the same thing to—"

"Not now. We're almost there. When I push you

forward, you go straight to your father. Stick with him, or with any man you can find who offers some protection."

Protection against what? she wanted to ask, but didn't dare. She did exactly as he said, and walked straight to her father, who was seated beside Brody and discussing the photographic equipment. As she sat down abruptly her father glanced up with a welcoming smile. It faded as he noted her pale face and wide, frightened eyes.

"My dear! Whatever is the matter?"

"I don't know," Bethany admitted helplessly. "I only know that Tra—Mr. Taylor told me to come to you and wait. He said something about protection, and there were white faces in the bushes by the trail, and now . . ."

Brody rose immediately, and disappeared into the shadows without speaking. Bethany exchanged worried glances with her father, and wondered what had occurred to upset the men.

Brasfield patted her hand awkwardly. "They're probably just exercising caution, dear. Try not to worry. Let's wait here for them, but to be on the safe side, why don't we put these pistols in our laps?"

Bethany had never heard her father even suggest touching a weapon, and her eyes grew wider as she mutely took the pistol he held out to her. It felt heavy and cold in her hands, and in spite of her fear, she couldn't help worrying about Trace, out there in the dark somewhere, doing God only knew what and risking his life.

A lump formed in her throat, and she tried to swallow. It was almost impossible. She could hear the screeches of birds in the dense foliage behind them, earsplitting at times, piercing the dark and making her shiver. A distant cough sounded almost human, but was closely followed by a snarl that sounded too vicious and predatory to belong to anything human.

"What was that?" she choked out, but her father didn't know any more than she did. They huddled together, pistols gripped tightly, waiting and watching. The Quechua bearers had melted into the shadows along with the others, and Bethany wondered if they'd been left alone to face whatever fate was out there.

Then she knew they hadn't, because she heard a hoarse shout nearby, then another, and a pistol fired. She could see the spurt of orange-red flame against the blackness but could not tell where it had come from. Was it someone from their camp?

Another shot fired, and a shrill cry echoed in the dark followed by a harsh curse. It sounded like Trace, and her heart dropped. Had he been shot? And what was going on? Who were the white-masked intruders?

"Get under this tarp," Brasfield instructed, and gave Bethany a push. "It's not much, but it's better than nothing."

"Papa! What about you? And what—?"

"Just stay there, and no matter what happens, what you hear, don't come out until one of us says it's all right," her father told her in the firmest voice she'd ever heard him use.

Cowering under the tarpaulin that had been spread as a makeshift shelter, Bethany shuddered as she listened to the sounds around her. A few more shots were fired, and she finally heard Trace's shout for the firing to cease. Heavy footsteps pounded on the ground, and then there was soft, blanketing silence. No birds screeched, no panthers coughed or snarled, no one shouted.

Several minutes passed before Bethany heard someone approaching, and she steeled herself. Gripping the pistol tightly in one hand, she drew back the hammer and waited.

Relief flooded through her when she heard Brody's voice instead of an unknown assailant, and she peeped from under the tarpaulin. Her relief quickly changed to alarm as she saw Trace bearing down on Brody with a furious scowl.

"Damn you, Brody! You may have just gotten us all killed with your heroics out there!"

"Hell, Taylor, I was just protectin' myself! I told you I ain't plannin' on havin' my head on a pole, and I ain't gonna take no chances!"

Bethany watched, appalled, as Trace advanced on Brody and shot out a fist. It connected with the shorter man's jaw and sent him sprawling backward. He recovered quickly, rolling to his feet, half crouched with an ugly expression on his face.

"You idiot," Trace was saying through clenched teeth, "those Indians were just checking us out! By shooting at them like a fool, you've eliminated any hope of passing through peacefully. We might as well turn back now and hope we make it out of here alive!"

"I'm gettin' sick and tired of you callin' me a fool and worse, Taylor," Brody growled. His hands were curled into fists and his stance was aggressive as he glared at him. "And I don't much like you hittin' me, neither!"

"Then do something about it or shut up," Trace returned coolly. "You should have known better than to go firing off your gun without knowing what you were doing." His mouth thinned into a harsh line. "Of course," he added softly and menacingly, "you've got a bad habit of doing just that."

"If you're talkin' about what happened in Texas years ago, I . . ."

"You know what I'm talking about. And I'd just as

soon you head back in the morning. I don't intend for you to get us all killed because you're quick with the trigger."

"Bentworth hired us to go the distance," Brody blustered with an uneasy glance toward the other men. "Me and Reagan, we plan on stayin'."

"Then you'd better not draw your pistol again without me saying it's all right," Trace snapped. "We're all liable to end up with our heads on a pole because of you."

Shifting from one foot to the other, Brody began to look more worried than mad, and Bethany drew in a deep breath. Perhaps the brief confrontation was over, but did Trace really think the natives might attack?

She had no chance to ask him before he was swinging around and stalking from the camp. Brody and Reagan exchanged glances, then walked in the opposite direction. Those watching remained quiet, as if afraid to speak. Only the professor dared say anything, and that was to mutter that he hoped this friction would not interfere with the expedition.

Bethany felt a wave of irritation at her father that lasted long after she had snuggled into her blankets and pulled them up around her ears. She wondered where Trace had gone, and if he was anywhere about. Surely he hadn't gone far, not with hostile natives nearby!

Trace had not gone far. He was perched atop a stone ledge overlooking the camp, his muscles tense with expectation and his nerves taut. Brody's precipitate action might have done more damage than they knew. Trace had been aware there was someone following them, but had not allowed any indication that he knew. He didn't intend to make the same mistake he'd made last time. The natives had probably been waiting to see what the white men would do. Now they had a pretty good idea, and Trace swore softly.

Did he dare risk another expedition? He'd meet with firm resistance from Brasfield if he suggested turning back, he knew that well enough. But if he pushed on and they all met with fatal consequences—Trace's mouth curled bitterly. If they all met their deaths, then it wouldn't matter about his reputation as a guide at all. But he did not intend to endanger Bethany Brasfield just to prove a point. There were moments—like this one—when he wished again she'd been left behind.

Frowning, Trace levered his lean body up from his crouch and started to return to camp; a faint glitter in the long grass caught his eye, and he paused. He leaped down from the high rock perch, landing lightly on the balls of his feet, and bent and picked up the glittering object. It was a broken knife. Not just any broken knife, but a polished blade that could only have been crafted by an expert artisan, not in the rough Andes. No native would carry this; it had belonged to a white man, and Trace wondered if it had been captured by the natives or left there by someone else.

His scowl deepened, and he pocketed the broken knife. There was no rust on it, so if it had been left by anyone other than a native, it had been recently. The discovery left him with a vaguely uneasy feeling.

Chapter Seventeen

Professor Brasfield almost danced with suppressed excitement. "I cannot believe that we are about to embark on the final leg of our journey! Success is close, I feel it!"

Trace, still disturbed by his finding of the knife, shook his head. "Don't get too excited," he growled. "We aren't there yet."

"But you said we should reach it before noon," Brasfield protested, and his spectacles slid to the end of his nose in his agitation.

"There's always a chance of something happening," Trace cautioned, and swung his narrowed gaze to Brody and Reagan. The two men looked disgruntled and sleepy, as he was sure he looked. During the night, most of their Quechua bearers had defected, slipped away into the shadows without a sound to leave the expedition behind. It wasn't exactly reassuring to know that they were too frightened to stay, but he couldn't say he blamed them. All he had to do now was act casual about it so as not to frighten the others.

It was not yet light, but he wanted to be on their way before the sun rose. He wanted plenty of daylight to find this damned, terraced city.

Bethany, looking cool and lovely in the firelight,

said softly to her father, "I'm certain we'll get there today, Papa. Try not to fret." Neither of them had mentioned the quarrel they'd had, or the sharp words. Though still a bit awkward with one another, the quarrel would be ignored.

Brasfield managed a smile. "Yes, yes, you're quite right, of course. I suppose I do sound rather like a sulky child at times, don't I?"

"At times. But this is your life's dream, so I think you're entitled to a little eagerness," Bethany replied. Her gaze shifted to Trace, looming dark and tense nearby. He certainly didn't seem in the best of moods this morning, and she wondered what had happened to make him so irritable with everyone.

There was no time to ask before Trace began snapping out orders for them all to shoulder packs they were sure they could carry, because he didn't intend to listen to any complaints.

"It'll be left behind if I hear one word about a pack being too heavy," he added, and his eyes flicked toward Bethany, making her stiffen.

"If you mean me," she couldn't help saying, "I assure you that I have no intentions of carrying something too heavy, or daring to complain."

"Good."

A wave of irritation washed over her, but Bethany did not voice it as she finished shoving the last item into her pack and hefted it to her shoulder. Common sense told her that Trace was not angry with her—she'd done nothing to incur his anger—yet a small insecure part of her wondered if she had somehow erred. Then she grew annoyed with the direction of her thoughts, and flashed Trace a dark glance.

Seeing it, Trace's mouth curled into a reluctant smile. She looked like a tawny feline when she glared at him like that, with her heavy-lashed eyes narrowed and smoky with emotion. She'd looked like that the night before when he'd taken her, and just the memory made his nerves tingle and his body tighten.

To cover his reaction, he growled, "Stay close, Miss Brasfield, and don't wander off."

"I have no intention of it," she returned coolly, wondering why he seemed to be searching for fault with her. When he gave a curt nod of his head and brushed past, she felt a twinge at the touch of his body against hers. It was not the most soothing of situations.

They started out on foot, with wisps of fog teasing faces and wreathing the landscape. Footsteps echoed eerily in the shrouded mist, and Bethany shivered at the damp air that penetrated her clothes. She was grateful for the light jacket she wore.

When the sun finally rose high enough to light the land beyond the peaks, it warmed the air with a muggy humidity that made Bethany remove her jacket and stuff it in her pack. Would the weather not stay the same for two consecutive hours? she wondered sourly. And how did Trace manage to look so composed when he carried such a heavy pack and wielded his sharp machete in a ceaseless swing to clear the path ahead of them?

Dense jungle growth matted the path with looping vines and thick branches, and small creatures made furtive noises as they scurried away. Insects swarmed in buzzing clouds around them, and there were muttered curses and the sounds of hands slapping exposed flesh as they trudged through the steamy jungle. Jagged spires of tree stumps jutted up from the forest floor, and she had to watch to keep from tripping over the fringes of skirted tree roots that belled out.

Bethany stifled a scream when she saw Trace slice

his machete in an unhurried motion, then saw a yellowish, coiling viper fly through the air, its triangular-shaped head cleanly separated from the writhing body.

"Fer-de-lance," Trace said unnecessarily, not even pausing in his stride.

Bethany shuddered and swallowed hard, flicking the still flipping body of the snake a shivering glance as she walked quickly past it.

Sunlight glistened from snowcapped peaks that rose far above even wisps of cloud, and jagged, surly crags of rock gleamed in colors from rose to deep blue. Thousands of feet below the path they now trudged the Vilcabamba River boiled in an unceasing rush of froth and foam. Patches of dark jungle covered the path at times, only to recede before claiming it again, and Bethany began to feel light-headed from the swift changes in temperature.

After what seemed like hours, but was in reality only a short time, they left the narrow path and turned sharply to enter the jungle again, stopping at a steep ravine.

"We cross here," Trace said, and pointed.

Bethany could feel his gaze shift to her, but she refused to allow her dismay to show on her face. It was the worst bridge—if it could be dignified with that name—that she had seen since arriving in Peru. Slender logs that looked half rotted were spliced together with vines where they did not reach the other side, forming a very shaky bridge of sorts. Moss furred the logs in places, and wind from the steep ravine yawning below brushed over her face with a chill whisper. A single misstep would be fatal.

Two of the native bearers who had accompanied them did not seem overly concerned, but took off their shoes and minced carefully across, gripping the logs with curling toes. Pale-faced beneath their swarthy complexions, the two Peruvian officers crossed in the same manner, their lips tightly compressed.

Swearing softly and wiping at beads of sweat on their brows, Brody and Reagan hesitated before doing the same. Trace watched them with a faintly sardonic smile, then turned to the professor and Bethany.

"Who's next?"

"I am," Brasfield said immediately. Disdaining dignity, he got down on all fours and proceeded to crawl like an infant across the dilapidated bridge, slowly, his brow furrowed into lines of determination.

Bethany chose to copy her father's method of crossing, and without glancing at Trace, took a deep breath and dropped to her knees. It took her longer, as she inched her way across, praying her hands would not slip on the slick, mossy logs. Wind tugged at her clothes and hair, and it blew in her eyes, thankfully masking a terrifying glimpse of rocky crags jutting up like teeth in the bottom of the ravine. Still she kept doggedly on, her teeth clenched tightly together to keep from chattering.

Upon reaching the other side, Bethany could not help but wonder how they would get back across if the logs fell. Any brisk gust of wind could sweep them away, it seemed.

As soon as Trace reached the other side, bringing up the rear as usual, they followed him along a barely discernible path into the jungle, then out again, treading along a rocky road that looked centuries old. To Bethany's groaning dismay, the path ended at what looked like an impassable wall. Her eyes widened as Trace reached up to grasp a rock and haul his lean body up, stepping from small ledge to even smaller ledge, working his way constantly up.

"Hey!" Brody shouted, scowling. "What the hell are you doing?"

"What's it look like?"

"I ain't no friggin' bird, Taylor," came the growling reply. "I can't fly."

No answer came back down, and in a moment Trace had disappeared from sight. Brody shifted uneasily and muttered something about having been given the slip. The others, too exhausted to protest for the moment, remained quiet.

As the minutes stretched past, Bethany began to wonder what had happened to Trace. Just when the tension drew out almost more than she could bear, she heard a light pelting of rocks skittering down from above, and saw Trace step out onto the ledge again.

"Catch, Brody," he called down, and a rope ladder shimmied toward them. Brody caught it easily, and gave it a sharp tug.

" 'Bout time," he grumbled, but there was a faint note of relief in his tone that made Bethany smile.

They all climbed the swaying rope ladder, skinning some knuckles in the process but without further injury, and joined Trace on the ledge. He offered no explanation, but led them through a deep chasm with rock walls that towered high above their heads. Their footsteps echoed loudly, and Bethany shivered.

It was so quiet. Only the sounds of their breathing and footsteps could be heard. No other sounds penetrated the rocky walls, and Bethany fancied she could almost hear the sunlight pouring down from the narrow slice of sky above them.

After passing through the rock walls and out into the open again, they all drew a collective breath of relief. A faint smile tugged at the corners of Trace's mouth, and his eyes sought and found Bethany's gaze.

"That wasn't so bad, was it?" he asked.

"Not if you're a goddam fool, I guess," Reagan snarled at him, and Trace's eyes shifted to the stocky man to linger for a long moment.

"Then you're in bad company, Reagan," he said at last. "See if you can keep up."

Nothing was said for some time as they followed Trace through the steamy jungle, and Santusa helped him hack a path through brush so thick no one could see more than a few feet ahead. From there, their progress grew even slower, and at several points, they were forced to drop to hands and knees to crawl painfully along mere slivers of rock ledge and up steeply sloping inclines. The heavy heat and humidity weighed on them, slowing them to a laborious pace as they climbed higher and higher.

Just when Bethany thought she could not go so much as an inch farther, Trace led them onto a surprisingly wide grassy area. "We'll rest here before we go the rest of the way," he said, and everyone dropped with sheer relief.

"How much farther?" Professor Brasfield asked when he could breathe again.

Hunkered down on his heels, his pack lying beside him, Trace raked a hand through his sweat-dampened hair and shrugged. "Not far at all. But it's even higher, so I thought we needed a breather before going on."

At the high altitude, Bethany found it difficult to draw a deep breath, and she felt slightly dizzy. Draped over her pack, she closed her eyes and lay as still as possible. The world seemed to shimmer with a palpable beat, like the whirring of giant wings, and she was grateful for a slight breeze that sprang up to stir tendrils of hair from her face.

"Here, drink this," Trace commanded, and she

opened her eyes to frown up at him.

"I'm not . . ."

"Drink it."

Obeying the inflexible command, she swallowed water from the leather pouch he held to her lips. It was almost hot from the heat, but at least it was wet. She sat quietly and allowed him to moisten her flushed face with a cloth damped from the same pouch.

"You'll be all right in a few minutes," he said, sitting back on his heels. His dark brows were drawn into a frown, and he tilted her face up with a finger under her chin, examining her closely. "Do you feel dizzy?"

Bethany wanted to nod, but knew that if she did, he would find a way to leave her behind. Slowly, she shook her head. "No," she whispered, "only a bit breathless from the climb."

He looked as if he might argue for a moment, then he accepted her reply without comment and stood up, handing the water pouch to her father. "Bathe her face again if she needs it. It's not much farther ahead, but it's higher up."

"It seems as if we should have reached the moon by now," Professor Brasfield observed with a weary smile, but the excitement in his eyes had not diminished.

When they started off again, shouldering their packs and heaving themselves to their feet, the small expedition was startled to see that they had been within a stone's throw of their destination.

Hundreds of stone terraces rose above them in a stair-step pattern, hundreds of feet long and nearly ten feet in height. Originally intended for crops, the terraces looked as if they could still support generous bounties of potatoes and beans, or tomatoes and peppers. Now, bamboo thickets and webs of tangled vines snaked over the stones, hiding them in places.

Brody gave a soft cry as they quietly walked closer, and bent to pick up a dully gleaming object from the ground at his feet.

"Look at this! By God, it's gold!"

Reagan immediately joined him, and the Peruvian officers crowded eagerly close. Professor Brasfield rushed to examine the object with shaking hands and in a quavering voice pronounced it a golden earplug.

"In excellent shape, too!"

Trace's eyes narrowed. For some reason, it seemed too easy. He didn't recall such objects lying so evidently on top of the ground the last time, but only after careful exploration. The golden medallion he'd brought back had been found in a burial area, and only by chance then.

Leaning against one of the intricately fitted stone walls, Bethany watched as the others suddenly scampered like monkeys around the terraces, eagerly tugging at loose stones and looking behind clumps of grass. They reminded her of children, and when her gaze shifted to Trace, she saw from his face that he was uneasy.

"What's the matter?" she asked, and he shrugged.

"I don't know. I don't like it."

"Is this"—she waved a hand to encompass the high stone terraces—"the city you spoke of? Somehow, it's not as I pictured it."

Shaking his head, he rested one hand on the butt of the pistol he wore. "Not yet. The city is just above these terraces. That's what's so damn strange."

"What do you mean?"

Trace gave an impatient shake of his head. "I mean, to find a gold earplug lying right out in the open is not exactly what I expected."

"Perhaps you're being too cautious," she said after a moment, and he shrugged again.

"Yeah. Maybe."

"But you don't think so."

His dark gaze moved to her face, and he smiled slightly. "No. I don't think so."

"Taylor!" Reagan yelled, and Trace tore his gaze from Bethany.

"Yeah?"

"Which way to the city?"

Trace hefted his machete in one hand, and moved to a thick clump of bamboo, wielding it in a rhythmic swing, the blade chunking through green spires as thick as a man's thumb. Leaves shimmied and fell with a swishing sound, and the rest of the men followed behind as Trace worked his way around an angled wall.

Bethany literally gasped as the foliage fell away to reveal a wall of the finest white granite. Her father was beside himself with glee, clapping his hands together and alternately pleading with them not to disturb anything and begging them to cut away more bamboo and vines.

Partially hidden in a veil of vegetation, a stone building lay slumbering in the neglect of centuries. Massive stones over six feet in height were fitted together so expertly that the thin blade of a knife could not be forced between the blocks.

"That huge block of granite must weigh at least fifteen tons!" Professor Brasfield breathed with near ecstasy. "No one will believe what we have found!"

"You did bring your new camera, I hope," Trace muttered dryly.

"Of course, of course! Oh, what wondrous sights we've found! I cannot adequately express my gratitude," Brasfield said as he dug busily into his pack for instruments with which to measure.

Trace shook his head when it appeared as if the professor had forgotten him already. Brasfield was absorbed in the careful insertion of a wooden peg into the ground, then the running of string from one peg to another, forming measured squares.

"He'll be this way until dark," Bethany commented when Trace glanced at her. "He won't remember us until then. Or unless he needs our help with something."

"You sound accepting."

She laughed, and pushed at damp strands of hair lying in her eyes. "Why shouldn't I be? This is, after all, why we came. This is the culmination of my father's most ardent dream."

Trace leaned against a towering stone wall. "Kinda sad, don't you think?"

Startled, she gazed at him with wide eyes. "What do you mean by that?"

He shrugged. "It's usually the pursuit of the dream that makes a man happy, not the ending of it."

"This doesn't have to be the ending. This is just the beginning for him. Even if the earplug is the only thing of monetary value we find here, Papa will be happy. Broken shards of pottery, just the exquisite stone buildings—all those will keep him contentedly digging for some time."

"And fame?" Trace asked with light mockery. "The credit he'll get for being the first archaeologist to record these ruins for posterity?"

Bethany's head tilted to one side, and she gazed at Trace in perplexed silence for a moment. Finally she said, "You don't like my father, do you?"

"Not much. I find broken pieces of pottery a poor substitute for flesh and blood, for a daughter's life."

"Then why did you continue with the expedition? If

you dislike him so much. . . ."

"I don't dislike his daughter," Trace said with soft meaning, and Bethany flushed. "And, anyway, I guess it's not that I don't like him, I just think his priorities are a little out of balance."

"We can't all be perfect, I suppose," Bethany said in a stiff voice that made Trace push away from the wall and cross the short distance between them.

"Look, Bethany Brasfield, I don't have to pretend to feel anything I don't want to feel, not even to keep from hurting your feelings. I'm sorry if you don't appreciate my honesty, but that's the way it is."

She looked up into his dark eyes, his frustrated gaze narrowing down at her, and thought she understood. "I see. And *your* priorities, Mr. Taylor—what are they, if you don't mind me asking?"

"To get us all back to Cuzco alive," he said promptly. His hand flashed out to curl around her wrist when she moved to turn away. "And especially *you*. I guess I've made you my top priority."

She searched his steady gaze. "Above clearing your name?" she couldn't help asking, then thought that she hadn't been fair. To her surprise, he grinned.

"Why are women never satisfied with *every*thing? I guess you need to hear that you mean more to me than anything else, so I'll agree."

Stung, she jerked her hand away. "Not if you don't mean it!"

"You'd never be satisfied with less."

"I'd never be satisfied with a lie!"

Whatever Trace might have said then was lost as Brody sauntered up, his beefy face cracked into a leering grin. "A lover's spat already? I thought you two lovebirds would be cozy as two—" That was as far as he got.

Trace turned in a peculiarly graceful motion, his

arm shooting out to grab Brody by his shirtfront and swing him in a wide circle. The needle-sharp tip of his knife was at Brody's throat when Bethany hadn't even seen him pull it, and she felt an odd tightening in her chest at the savage expression on Trace's face.

"Trace! No!" she screamed as the tip of the knife raked over Brody's skin and left a glistening trail of crimson. Brody choked out a weak moan, his eyes bulging from their sockets.

Deliberately, coldly, Trace let Brody feel the icy chill of death whisper over him before he took the knife away from the man's throat. His rage surprised even him, and Trace made a determined effort to control it.

"I don't want to ever hear you even say her name, Brody, do you think you can remember that?"

Mutely, terrified, Brody nodded, and Trace released his shirt to set the man back on his feet. "Next time, I won't be so gentle," Trace said as Brody swiftly backed away.

Bethany stared at him. "Why did you do that?" she asked in a hoarse whisper when Brody had fled. Trace's eyes were hooded and his expression unreadable.

"Brody is the kind of man who'll try to get away with anything, and if I let him there'll never be an end to it."

"But Trace—"

He slid her a cold look. "I know Brody, and I know what he's capable of, Bethany. Trust me on that."

Not understanding, Bethany gave a helpless shrug. No one else had seemed to notice the little drama just played out; everyone was intent on discovering gold, intent on his own pursuits. Even the Peruvian officers seemed to have forgotten their reason for being there; they eagerly sorted through the ruins while Professor Brasfield frantically called out warnings not to disturb things.

"Oh," Brasfield moaned plaintively, "I just know they will obliterate important relics!"

Reluctantly, Bethany murmured, "I guess I better help Papa. He can't be in but one place at a time, and I think it's frustrating him."

"Yes," Trace said with the slightest inflection of sarcasm, "go help your father. He needs you."

She hesitated, but Trace pivoted on his heel and strode away. An uneasy feeling enveloped Bethany. After the long weeks of struggle and exhaustion, there should be more to the final discovery than dissension. For the first time, she understood why Trace Taylor had been so reluctant to be their guide. There was a palpable feeling of doom that lay over the ancient city, as if the Incas had cursed those who dared intrude.

Shivering, Bethany dismissed such fanciful notions from her head and went to join her father.

Chapter Eighteen

Intricately cut stairways notched granite boulders, and jutted skyward in breathtaking rises to the tops of what had once been houses. Empty now, the dwellings boasted only thick vegetation and various wild creatures as inhabitants. Tiny garden plots adjoined many of the houses, evidence that the former occupants had been adept at wresting food from even the smallest area.

Conduits coursed from a bubbling spring above the city to a series of small basins and fountains in the main plaza that still provided a trickle of water in the weed-choked stone baths.

"Every modern convenience," Brasfield jested, his eyes glittering as he wandered the city taking notes on a thick pad of paper. He had Santusa following him with the camera, pausing to set it up and snap photographs at every conceivable angle.

"What's that, Professor?" Brody asked, and pointed to a building set apart from the others. "Does it look like it might hide gold?"

Brasfield flashed Brody an irritated glance, but walked toward the vine-covered structure. "I believe it's a temple of sorts," he murmured at last, running his hands over the tightly fitted granite blocks with reverence. He stood back and gazed at it with a critical eye. "Yes," he said in a decisive tone, "it is definitely a temple. It vaguely resembles the Temple of the Sun in Cuzco, don't you think, Bethany?"

She gave a shrug. "I did not go with you and Signore Bertolli, Papa."

"Ah yes, that's right."

Impatiently, Brody interrupted. "So this temple, isn't that where those Incas had a lot of golden gewgaws?"

"At times, I would presume they had *gewgaws* of a sort, Mr. Brody," Brasfield replied irritably. "The Incas would, however, have referred to them as ceremonial cups, staffs, statues, and so forth."

"Whatever. Come on, Reagan."

Brody and Reagan stalked around the imposing walls of the temple, hacking at vines with their machetes, their faces grim with purpose. Bethany could not help a glance in Trace's direction. He sat casually atop a large block of granite, his fedora pulled low over his eyes, his arms crossed negligently over his broad chest. She felt a wave of irritation that he could so easily disassociate himself from them.

"I suppose you have no intentions of helping with any of this," she said, and Trace shrugged.

"I've done my job in getting you here. All I have to do now is get you back. I don't dig."

Bethany glared at him. "I see! You don't mind if we do, however?"

Trace waved an expansive arm. "Help yourself. There seems to be enough dirt to keep you busy for a while."

Bethany wondered why he was being so stubborn. Was it because of their disagreement about her father? Surely, he could understand how she felt. Determinedly, she walked toward him, intending to ease the tension between them.

"Do you mind if I sketch you?" she asked, and saw a flash of surprise on his face before he quickly masked it.

"Why would you want to do that?"

Shrugging nonchalantly, Bethany said, "Oh, no reason. I just thought it might be nice to have a portrait of the man responsible for guiding us here. I'm certain Papa will insist upon having your photograph, but I'd like to put my own interpretation to your likeness."

Trace grinned. "This ought to be very interesting. Why do I have the feeling my likeness will have horns and cloven hoofs when you get through with it?"

"Guilty conscience," Bethany said promptly, and before he could change his mind, went to get the new set of chalks he'd given her. While she set the wooden box on a small rock and balanced a clean white pad of paper on her knees, she watched Trace fidget uncomfortably, and hid a smile. It was so unlike him to feel awkward, and for some reason, it endeared him even more to her.

"Sit still," she told him, "and stay in that patch of sunlight. I like the way it lights your face."

"I feel damned stupid," he growled, glaring at her from beneath the brim of his fedora.

"Take off your hat, please. Just lay it beside you. And it would be nice if you'd remove your gun. . . ."

"No." His tone was flat and final, and she gave in gracefully.

"Very well. Why don't you relax, now? Sit the way you're most comfortable."

She sketched quickly, doing one of him sitting stiffly and warily, his gaze boring into her almost challengingly. Then she flipped over the page and did another, capturing the lean, hard lines of his body in an almost indolent sprawl as he began to relax. Only his face did not seem to go with his posture, the expression still watchful and wary instead of casual.

Trace had never seemed so mercurial as now, when she was trying to put his likeness on paper with mere chalk and talent, and Bethany felt a moment's frustration as she drew yet another portrait that missed the mark in an indefinable way.

"Can't get the cloven hoofs right?" he asked her after a while, and she looked up with a smile.

"It's the horns. They're not pointed enough."

"Too bad. I don't suppose you're anywhere near through? I've sat here so long I'm beginning to feel an emotional attachment to this rock."

"Glad to see that you're capable of tender emotions," Bethany murmured, then to hide the sudden confusion that comment gave her, she smoothed out the chalked lines on the paper with her forefinger and gave a nod of her head. "All done."

Stretching lazily, Trace slid from the rock. "Do I get to see them?"

"If you like." She held out the pad, suddenly awkward and anxious at the same time. Trace took it, one dark brow lifting as he scanned the pages.

"All these of me, and not one that makes me look like a saint—or even a respectable human being," he said after a moment.

"Sorry. I was aiming for realism."

"Ah. In that case, I'd have to say that you're pretty good, Bethany Brasfield." He smiled, and his teasing tone altered subtly. "Do I really look like such a wicked rogue?"

"Only to those who know you," she whispered around the sudden lump in her throat. "Maybe it's the beard."

He rubbed a hand over the dark stubble on his jaw, and nodded. "Yeah. Without the beard, I'm the picture of pious respectability."

"I don't believe we will ever see that day!" Bethany said. "Now, you draw me." She handed him the pad of paper.

Grinning, Trace took a piece of chalk from her hand and began to sketch quickly. When he finished, he held it out to her and she burst into laughter. He'd drawn a stick figure of a woman with long hair and a huge bosom, wearing trousers and wielding a pitchfork.

"The devil's mate," he teased, and curved a hand under her chin when her smile faded. "Do you mind being my mate?"

"Not if you don't," she whispered back, hardly daring to hope that he meant it seriously.

Trace drew her up from the rock where she sat, taking the pad of paper from her hand and laying it aside, his eyes dark and intent. Sunlight gilded her face and made her hair gleam with golden lights, and her eyes were wide and hopeful. Recognizing the hope in them, he almost flinched away. He didn't know if he could give her all she expected. He didn't know if he was capable of it. A tender woman like Bethany deserved more than just a place in his bed; she deserved respectability, and that he couldn't give her. Not now. Maybe not ever.

"Bethany," he began when an excited shout halted him, and he half turned to see Brody racing toward them, hatless, his eyes glittering with excitement. Trace saw then the dully gleaming objects in his hands, some falling on the stone terraces as he rushed forward.

"Gold! Mounds of it! High as the ceiling. . . ."

Trace immediately dropped his hands from Bethany and strode toward Brody. "Before you go stuffing your pockets with it, Brody," he said evenly, "you'd better let the professor here record everything."

Brody swung toward Trace. "Record? Yeah, sure, Taylor. He can record it all. It don't matter none. There's enough gold in that damned room to buy all of Peru!"

Exuberant, gleeful, Brody led Brasfield and the others to the temple. Shreds of thick vines, some the width of a man's arm, hung in tatters where they'd been cut away from an arched entrance. It looked as if wooden doors had once graced the archway, but had disappeared with time. Slowly, they stepped into the high-ceilinged room. It looked remarkably clean, not as if it had sat in the darkness of the ages and waited to be discovered. Bethany, right behind her father, blinked her eyes.

White walls rose in serene silence; mounds of gold lay piled in chests and atop vicuña blankets. Statues, cups, tablets, urns, vases, figures of llamas and birds and men and women, were fashioned of bright gold, some crusted with jewels. It was a king's ransom, she thought, then recalled how the Spaniards had commanded a ransom for the Inca Atahualpa; a huge room had been filled with treasure, then filled again, and Pizarro, the Spanish conqueror, had then rewarded the king's subjects by garroting their ruler. It was an appalling note in history, but had effectively removed further resistance.

It gave her an uneasy feeling.

"Papa?" she murmured. "How would this have been hidden for so many years?"

But Professor Brasfield was beyond reason in his

intense excitement at making such a find. He knelt in near rhapsody before the gold, exclaiming over each piece, furiously scribbling notes in his pad. Brody and Reagan were still sorting through the treasure, and the Peruvian officers joined them.

"This may get out of hand," Trace said grimly, and Bethany turned to look at him. "This much gold is bound to cause trouble. Look at them. You can bet not a one of those men are thinking of the archaeological impact, but only of what that gold will buy for them."

It was true. Bethany could see it in the hard glitter of the men's eyes, and felt another twinge of uneasiness.

"What can we do? Papa is just as bad as they are, if for a different reason."

"We aren't going to do anything." Trace ignored her gasp of outrage as he pulled her to the door of the temple and shoved her outside. "Get out of here. Go find Santusa and tell him I need him, then go sit in a quiet corner for a while until I've got things straightened out."

"How does just one man expect to keep all the others in line without getting himself killed?" she turned and demanded, her hands resting on her hips and her expression wavering between anger and fear for him.

"Let me worry about that." Trace smiled at her muffled comment. "I think I can handle Brody and Reagan, and the Peruvian officers won't dare cross me. As for your father, he won't notice any of us if we don't trade too many shots. Now go on, Bethany."

She found Santusa with the other Quechua bearer, the only two who'd stayed with the expedition. The Indian listened gravely to her, then nodded.

"I will go to him at once," he said in a thickly accented voice. "And you may stay here with Artega. He will watch over you."

Left with no other option, Bethany did just that. She waited, listening to the shrill, piercing screeches of the birds in the jungle and the muted roars of animals, expecting at any moment to hear the thunder of shots. None sounded. It was extraordinarily quiet, and when she looked up to see Trace approaching with his loose, fluid stride, she felt an overwhelming sweep of relief.

"Trace!" She ran to meet him, and then saw the thin trickle of blood from one corner of his mouth. "You're hurt!"

"Not so's you can tell it," he muttered, but wiped at the blood with his sleeve.

"What happened? Is everything settled? How did you do it without having to fight?"

His dark eyes glistened with wry amusement, and he shook his head. "You're getting hardened when it comes to violence, Bethany. I guess only bullets impress you now." He dragged the back of his hand across his mouth again. "I did have to take on Reagan, but with Santusa as my well-armed guard, it didn't get any worse than that. Brody and Reagan aren't the kind of men who'll challenge a man, anyway. They prefer back-shooting to—never mind," he added at the dismay in her eyes. "They've agreed to list every single item before we pack them up to carry back with us, and that'll have to do."

"So it's all right now?"

"I wouldn't exactly say that. We still haven't made it back, and I don't trust those two for a minute." A rough sigh escaped him, and he shook his head. "I knew they'd be trouble."

Bethany could see what he meant. Bentworth's hired men were greedy and unscrupulous, and now that most of the Indian bearers had fled, they were all in a very precarious position. She shifted uneasily.

"Where's Papa?"

"Still counting and cackling." Trace raked a hand through his hair and his voice was impatient. "I don't think he ever noticed the fight, even when we almost fell on top of him. He's a man with a singularly focused mind, I'd say."

"He always has been."

Trace's eyes met hers. "And his daughter? Does she have the same kind of singular purpose?"

Her heart contracted, and she whispered, "Only when it means a great deal to her."

Something in Trace's hard, bright gaze softened, and a faint smile flickered at the corners of his mouth. "Good," was all he said.

Bethany walked with him to the wide, shallow basin in the middle of the vine-choked city, and washed the drying blood from his face with tender motions. An air of heavy silence lay around them, occasionally broken by the chatter of birds or scream of a panther in the encroaching jungle. Other than that, it was quiet.

"Kinda gloomy place, isn't it?" Trace said in a teasing tone meant to coax a smile from her.

Shivering, Bethany glanced around her. "Yes. I hadn't pictured it this way. Somehow, I thought the final refuge of kings would be more . . . hopeful, I guess."

"It probably was at one time." Trace dried his face on a square of cloth Bethany handed him, and tested his sore mouth with the tip of his tongue. "Well, you can't expect too much, I guess. And at least your father's content, and Bentworth will be happier than a rooster in a coop full of new hens."

She laughed at the image Trace's words provoked of Bentworth's reaction, her gaze resting on his handsome face for a long moment. Impulsively, thinking of Spencer Bentworth and the guarded hostility between the two men, she asked, "Trace, why do you and Bentworth work together if you hate each other?"

Her question caught him off guard, and Trace growled an oath before he thought. Then he said, "I've always heard a man should keep his friends close—and his enemies closer. Makes sense to me."

"That doesn't explain why you accepted his offer as a guide for our expedition."

"Bethany, I thought we'd already been through all this. I wanted to clear my name, and Bentworth gave me a chance to do it. That's all."

His eyes were narrowed at her, cold and dark and wary, and Bethany decided not to pursue it any longer. "Well, it certainly looks like you've succeeded," she said lightly.

"Then let's drop it for now, all right?"

She nodded. But the uneasiness stayed with her, in spite of the easy comradery and high spirits of the men that night, the laughing and joking with one another. They camped there in the city where kings had once lived, spreading out their supplies and trying to cook over low fires.

"Water just won't boil at this altitude," Trace said in disgust, then slanted Bethany a half smile. "I didn't want any dinner anyway."

Perched nearby, she managed a returning smile. "I'm not very hungry either." She glanced at her father, huddled over an oil lamp and scribbling furiously in his notes, his spectacles quivering on the tip of his nose. Bethany sighed softly. "Papa won't eat when he's like this. He'll be nothing but skin and bones before this is over."

"That's his choice," Trace said shortly, and her gaze swung back to him.

"I know that."

"Then don't get upset about it."

"Do I sound upset?" she snapped, and he looked at her with a lifted brow.

"No, you sound as happy as a dog with his tail caught in the door!" he shot back.

Bethany glared at him. "Maybe you don't know everything! Have you ever thought of that?"

"Plenty of times. I do know when to stop beating my head against a stone wall, though, and that seems to be something lacking in your extensive education."

"Meaning?" she demanded fiercely.

"Meaning, that if you haven't changed your father in the last twenty years, you're certainly not going to change him now. He won't ever pay any attention to anything but his work. That's the way he is. Make both of you happy by accepting it. He's probably as miserable with your efforts to change him as you are."

"That's all you know about it," Bethany said, but her voice held a tinge of uncertainty. Maybe Trace was right. None of her efforts to alter her father's habits had made an ounce of difference; she'd only become frustrated and irritated, and when—and if—he'd noticed, he'd not known quite what he had done to cause it. But pride and stubbornness would not allow her to give in easily, so her chin lifted slightly as she returned Trace's stare.

To her surprise, he seemed to soften. "It's hard for you, I know," Trace said, "and I guess I wouldn't want you to be any different." He smiled. "If you weren't so damned stubborn and hardheaded, you wouldn't be nearly as interesting."

"And you like interesting women?"

Dark eyes met hers, kindling with a flame she knew well by now. "I like *you,*" he said softly.

Bethany's heart skipped a beat. She wasn't at all surprised when Trace rose and held out a hand to her, flicking her engrossed father a glance as he said, "Want to take a walk with me?"

None of the others noticed as they left the center of the plaza and strolled along a high wall overlooking a sheer drop of several thousand feet. Oil lamps burned and flickered in the night, set out by Santusa and Artega for a small attempt at light. A few torches sputtered, but they shed light in small pools that didn't reach far.

Their footsteps echoed eerily on the stone steps leading from house to house, and a brisk wind blew over them. It seemed as if they were on top of the world.

"Standing here," Bethany whispered when they paused to lean out over a wall, "I feel almost like an ancient god or goddess looking down on the world."

Trace smiled, gazing at her face in the moonlight that filtered through high shreds of cloud. "You look like one."

She turned, leaning one arm atop the wall, her eyes studying his moon-shadowed face. She wanted so badly to ask what was ahead of them, what their future held, but she was afraid to hear his answer. If it wasn't what she wanted to hear, she would be crushed.

"I've improved from the wild-haired woman with a pitchfork in her hand, I take it?" she teased lightly, and he grinned at her.

"A little."

"Only a little?"

"Oh no, Bethany Brasfield," he said then, reaching out to pull her to him. "A lot."

His hands came down on her shoulders, drawing her even closer, as she'd somehow known he would when they'd left the camp together. Bending his dark head, his mouth slanted across her parted lips in a hungry kiss that made her legs tremble and her breath come in soft, panting gasps.

Sliding his tongue between the satiny lips that parted so eagerly for him, Trace plundered her mouth with greedy thrusts that wrested a throaty moan from her and made his body tighten. One hand slid from her shoulder to the small of her back, while his other cradled the back of her head to hold it still for his ravaging kiss. He wanted her. God, he wanted her even when he knew he needed to exercise more self-control. It was crazy, to always be wanting her like this, to want her so badly he allowed his desire to get the better of his common sense.

Bethany was a fever in his blood, a pounding need that he couldn't assuage without her lying beneath him, her soft skin bare to his touch. His body reminded him of his desire with an aching tautness that demanded relief.

"Let's go somewhere private," he growled after a few moments, and she could feel his arousal pressing against her as he held her tightly to him. She nodded wordlessly.

Trace led her down a series of steps and up some more, until they reached a huge, snow-white boulder set some distance away on a wide, grassy area almost overgrown with scrub and bamboo. It was remote and secluded, with a rock overhang at one side, and steps cut into the granite. A pool of water glimmered with dark shadows, reflecting only a faint glow from the moon.

For a moment Bethany hesitated, but when Trace took her by the hand and pulled her with him, not giving her the chance to hang back, she went willingly. There was an air of dense quiet that hung over the circle of terraced grass, an air that made her uneasy. Trace didn't seem to notice it or didn't care, so she tried to shake away the shadows of foreboding that filled her.

Then, when Trace pulled her to him in a swift, urgent motion, she couldn't think of anything but him, of his hard hot hands on her, and his mouth searing across her lips, her cheek, the arch of her throat and down to the soft valley between her breasts, bared now to the night wind as he impatiently pulled away her blouse. There was a driving sense of urgency in him, a restless, nameless emotion that was infectious, and Bethany burned with the same fires that ignited his blood.

Her hands were eager on him, unbuttoning his pants with clumsy haste, peeling them away to free his taut male body to her touch. She moaned when he guided her hand to him, curling her fingers around him, his breath coming fast and hard as she held him firmly.

"Bethany," he half groaned, then crushed his mouth over hers in a savage kiss that took away her breath. He kissed her until her senses reeled and her body quivered with need for him, until she arched her slender hips against his lean frame and felt his hot, solid heat against her stomach.

Lifting her in his arms, he swept her from her feet and put her gently on the ground, on the cushioning grass and tumble of discarded clothes. He slid up and over her body, his knees nudging her thighs apart, his head lowering so that his mouth could range hot and wet over her upturned face and trembling lips.

Bethany felt the coiling fire burning brightly deep in the pit of her stomach, felt the rush of heated blood flow like lava through her veins and seem to center in that one spot, aching for him to ease her need. When Trace's mouth covered the peak of one breast, sucking gently, his other hand cradling her other breast and rolling the taut rosette expertly between thumb and forefinger, she cried out.

Her hands clenched his smooth, broad shoulders in a convulsive movement, and her slim legs lifted to wrap around his waist, trying to bring him inside her. He remained elusively just out of reach, barely grazing her moist entrance, ignoring her frantic efforts to drag him closer.

Finally, when she thought she couldn't wait another moment, he muttered, "Are you as tired of waiting as I am?" and thrust forward, his body sliding inside the aching cradle of her hips and thighs. He rocked against her fiercely, thrusting again and again until she could feel the rising tension escalate almost to an unbearable pitch.

Release came first for Bethany; half sobbing, she felt the thundering roll sweep over her in a heated tide, felt her muscles contract in racking spasms, then felt the throbbing pulse of Trace's response to her body's velvet grip on his a moment later. He shuddered, then grew still.

Neither of them moved for a long moment as they lay in a damp haze of repletion. Trace did not withdraw from her, but remained imbedded deep within her, and Bethany's throat tightened with emotion. She loved him so deeply; just having him inside her made tears spring to her eyes. Did he feel it? Did he feel the same way? Or was it different for him?

Lifting his head at last, Trace rose to his elbows, one arm braced on each side of her, lying between her cradling thighs as he smiled down at her. "So much for my self-control," he said lightly. "I can't be near you without wanting this, Bethany."

Only this? she wanted to ask, but smiled back up at him and kissed his strong, square jaw.

"Your beard tickles," she whispered.

"Yeah. I guess I'll shave tomorrow. I look too much like a bandit, if your drawings are any indication."

"You *are* a bandit," she said, then added quickly when his lips curled in amusement, "You've stolen my heart, haven't you?"

He pushed back a stray thread of her hair, and looked at her without speaking for a long moment. An expression she couldn't read flickered briefly on his face, and she wished fretfully that there was more light. Had it been regret?

"I don't know," he said at last. "Have I?"

In an attempt to retain some self-respect, Bethany said more casually than she'd thought she could, "For tonight, anyway. After then—well, we'll just have to see what happens."

Trace dragged a finger over her lips, smearing moist trails from her mouth over his finger, then transferring it to his own mouth. "Umm. Not bad. Since I'm a thief of hearts tonight, why stop with just that? Let me have all of you, Bethany Brasfield, heart and mind and body and soul. . . ."

Bethany didn't bother to tell him he already possessed those things. She coiled her hands in his thick mane of dark hair and tilted back her head, closing her eyes as he began to move within her again, to take her to the point of forgetfulness and back. It was sweet torment; it was heady torture; it was her heart's desire well met to have him so close, holding her as if there was no tomorrow.

As far as she was concerned, there wasn't. There was only the here and now, and her and Trace, and that was all that mattered. She loved him. She loved him with every fiber of her being, and wanted only that he love her back. Nothing else existed.

Chapter Nineteen

Pacing restlessly, Trace felt the same prickle of hair on the back of his neck that he'd felt before. This wasn't the first time. He'd felt it only a few days ago, when he'd climbed to the top of a crest to look for hostiles. Now he felt it again, a feeling as if he were being watched.

A dark scowl knit his brows, and his expression was so fierce that Bethany thought twice about approaching him. He looked like a caged tiger, prowling back and forth by the east wall of the vine-wracked city. Finally, timidly, she crossed the plaza and stopped in front of him.

"It's a nice day," she said softly, hesitantly, and he swung his dark gaze toward her.

It's a good day to die echoed in his ears, and all of a sudden Trace was reminded of ten years before in Arizona, when he'd watched helplessly as his friend was ambushed and killed by Apaches. The memory still left a bitter taste in his mouth, still reminded him of his helplessness in the face of greater odds.

"Yeah. Great day," he said when it seemed as if Bethany expected some sort of response, and forced a smile. "What are you doing up here?"

"I just came to find you." She paused, gnawing at

her lower lip for a moment, then blurted out, "Trace, what is it? Is something the matter?"

He was tempted to tell her the truth, but knew he'd have a hard time explaining a gut feeling to anyone. So he shrugged. "No, everything's fine. I'm just tense, I guess, and ready to get away from here."

"We've only been here a few days. Papa should be able to finish some of his excavations soon. He said he'd have to come back with more equipment and trained personnel." A faint smile curved her mouth, and her violet eyes grew lighter. "It looks like you might be doing more of this, if you care for the work."

"I don't." Trace hadn't meant to make his reply so sharp, and saw from the look in her eyes that he'd hurt her feelings. "Look, I only agreed to guide this expedition because I needed the money," he said frankly. "I needed to clear my name, too, but the most important part was the money. Once Bentworth pays me, I won't have to come back."

"Does that mean you wouldn't, even as a favor for my father?"

Trace's laugh was brittle. "I don't think so. Nothing personal, I just happen to hate this place." He looked around him, feeling the same sense of foreboding that had kept him on edge for the past week.

Bethany glanced down at the wide ledge of the wall that contained the city on the very precipice of a mountainous peak. Her hand scraped across it idly, and she noticed with a vague sense of distraction that it seemed to shudder. It didn't occur to her then to worry about it. She glanced at Trace, at his restless figure pacing the smooth stones in measured strides, then looked away.

"So," she said carefully, "when we get back to Cuzco, I guess I won't see you anymore. I mean, Papa fully intends to come back here, and wants me to come with him, of course."

"Of course." Trace's tone was tinged with mocking irony that did not escape her notice. Her head flung up, and she met his dark gaze.

"He's my father!"

"Right. You owe him your life, not your right to live. There's a difference between the two."

"And I suppose if your father wanted you to help him, you'd just walk away?" she threw at him bitterly.

To her surprise, Trace laughed. "That, princess," he said softly, "is exactly what I had to do. You're barking up the wrong tree if you hoped to make a point with that little comeback."

Refusing to back down, Bethany pursued her point. "And just what did your father expect you to do that was so terrible—rob banks?"

She'd meant to be flippant, but saw from the suddenly savage expression on Trace's face that she had somehow missed. He crossed the distance between them in two long strides and grabbed her by the arms, jerking her close.

"In case you're interested in just how close you came to the truth," he growled, "maybe you'd like hearing how I found myself in Peru."

"Trace, I . . ."

"Oh no, sweetheart, you want to know everything, right? I intend to tell you, and then if I ever hear another word about it from you—" He stopped to suck in a deep breath, and his voice was softer when he said, "It doesn't really matter now, but it did then.

I was a kid, barely out of my teens, and my father made a comfortable living stealing from other men. He wanted me to join him. I was always fast with a gun, and he thought we'd make a great team." Trace's face twisted, and his eyes glittered. "My mother had died when I was real young, and I lived with her sister, my aunt. There was an argument between my father and my uncle, and before anyone could stop it, my uncle was dead."

Bethany couldn't move. The hard, cold look in his eyes held her still.

"I went with my father, not because I wanted to, but because I didn't know how not to. I didn't want any more trouble. So, when you asked me once if I had posters out on me, that was a pretty close guess. Yeah, there's probably some old posters out. The only way I could get away from my old man was to leave Texas and Arizona behind, leave the country behind. I ended up here, where no one asked any questions and no one cared who I was, where I'd come from, or what I'd done."

Silence fell between them, and Bethany felt the slight tremor of her legs. Trace still held her arms in his hard grip, his fingers digging into her soft skin.

"And your father?" she asked when the silence stretched out too long. "What happened to him?"

Releasing her, Trace shrugged. "I don't know. He went to prison. He's probably out by now. As far as I know, he's still robbing banks, running crooked games, turning a fast buck wherever he can. I never went back."

"Don't you ever wonder about him?"

"No."

His reply was flat, cold, noncommittal, and

Bethany wondered if he really meant it. How could a person not wonder about their father? Even a bad one? She didn't dare ask. There seemed to be nothing left to say.

Trace turned away from her and put both hands palms down on the flat, wide surface of the wall, staring out over the sheer drop without really seeing it. The tension of remaining in this city in the clouds was getting to him. He didn't like it. He didn't like Brody or Reagan, or even Brasfield. There was something just beyond his reach that nagged him, some little something that was wrong. He could feel it as vividly as he felt the hot sunshine pouring down on his head.

Standing awkwardly, Bethany started to turn away when she felt it—it was a slight quivering beneath her feet, the odd sensation of the ground shifting. Startled, she put out a hand to catch herself, but there was nothing to hold to. A distant rumble sounded, and when she glanced up with a puzzled expression, she saw trees and scrub shivering as if in a violent windstorm. It occurred to her that it could not be a storm because the sun was shining, and then Trace grabbed her.

"Get away from the wall!" he snapped in her ear, and swept her with him from the high terrace. Stone structures were quivering like jelly, and a hail of loose rock slid over the sides of buildings and bounced erratically on the ground.

"What is it?" she screamed, though she already knew. This wasn't the first earthquake she'd been in; far from it. Southern California had more than its share of them. This was just the first earth tremor she had experienced at such dizzying heights. Terrified, she barely heard Trace confirm her guess as he pulled her beneath the heavy overhang of a stone archway.

"We'll be killed here!" Bethany protested, but Trace held her fast.

"These archways have withstood centuries of earthquakes, so I think they'll last through another one," he said dryly. "It'll be the loose rocks that kill us."

Cowering with him, she turned her face to his broad chest and closed her eyes. She could feel the steady thud of his heart beneath her cheek, feel the reassuring rhythm of his lungs beneath her hand. He smelled faintly of tobacco and shaving soap, and she realized that he had, as he'd promised, shaved off his week's growth of beard.

It was over in a matter of minutes, then Trace was dragging her with him from their shelter. "Go pack your things," he said shortly, and she stared at him.

"Why?"

"We're getting out of here."

"But we're probably safer here than on the sides of the mountain," she protested, and he shook his head.

"I don't like it. Besides, landslides might cut off the only way out of here. Remember the hard time we had getting up here? Think about having to climb over loose rock on the way down."

"But leaving now would be dangerous! And, besides, my father hasn't finished—"

"He's finished for now." Trace's tone didn't invite any more argument. "By the time we get packed, the aftershocks will be over. Then we're getting out of here."

He didn't add that it was a good excuse to leave an area that was growing increasingly on his nerves. He didn't know how much more he could stand of Brody and Reagan parading around festooned with golden chains and even gloves of beaten gold. And he was growing increasingly irritated with Brasfield's singleminded obsession with his damned pottery instead of his daughter. Somehow, Bethany's hurt reminded him of his own, that long-ago pain at being just a convenience to his father. He hated it. And he hated watching it. He'd be glad when he could see the last of all of them. Except Bethany, and he didn't know yet what he was going to do about that.

"Hurry up," he said in a hard voice, "and tell your father and the others I want to see them."

"I still say we could have stayed longer, Mr. Taylor," Professor Brasfield murmured unhappily. They were down the steep mountain again, resting near the rope ladder that would swing over the side to lower them down. It would be hard with their loaded packs, but it was the only way back to the level stretch of ground and the trail.

"Maybe." Trace didn't look at him. He still had that damned funny feeling, and he didn't know why. After the earthquake, he'd thought maybe the feeling would go away. It hadn't. Odder still, there had been no aftershocks from the earthquake. Now he waited in tense expectation. His gaze shifted to the Peruvian officers, both of whom sat in quiet misery. One of them had been hit on the head with a rock during the tremor and the other had skinned his shins trying to escape a tumbling boulder. Neither was hurt bad, but they were both uncomfortable.

Only Brody and Reagan looked satisfied. Their packs were laden with gold, laden so heavily they could barely walk, but they refused to leave any of it behind. They walked so slowly and clumsily, it had taken much longer to get back down from the city than it had to go up.

Bethany looked quiet and strained, and the two Quechua bearers had impassive faces as usual. Trace wondered briefly what his own face looked like, and hoped it didn't betray his tense expectation.

It didn't. To Bethany, he resembled an expressionless statue, cold and remote. She sensed that there was something more the matter with him than he'd admit, but didn't know what it could be.

Trace paused when they reached the crest where the rope ladder waited, coiled in a heap where he'd left it. There was something different about the ladder. An indefinable difference, but it was there. Maybe it was in the way it was coiled, not neatly as he'd left it, but tossed in a careless heap on the rock. He knelt beside it for several minutes, as if it would yield a clue.

"Trace?" Bethany asked softly, and his head jerked up.

"Yeah?"

"There's something you're not telling us."

He gave an impatient motion of his hand. "Nothing that's definite. I just have this . . . this feeling, that's all."

Bethany was quiet, and a chill pranced along her spine. He looked serious, his eyes squinting at the rope, clenched fists resting on his bent knees.

"Is the rope rotten?" she ventured when he didn't

say anything else, and he shook his head.

"No. It's just—" He felt suddenly foolish. "It's just lying differently. Probably disturbed by an animal."

Brody's voice, impatient and irritable, drifted across the distance. "Let's get out of here, Taylor. I want to get back to the mules, and let them carry this heavy pack."

Trace flicked him a glance, and his mouth twisted. "As energetic as usual, I see. All right. Let's go."

It wasn't until they started down the rope ladder that Trace's premonition was proven right. Brody went first, his clumsy, turtlelike progress painfully slow. Then Reagan climbed down, and Bethany. The professor swayed on the rope ladder for a moment before finding his footing, then made a halfhearted joke as Bethany encouraged him. He was only halfway down when a shot rang out, startling him so that he lost his grip and fell backward, off-balanced by his pack. He plummeted ten feet to the ground and landed with a dull slap of his body against stone.

Screaming, "Papa!" Bethany ran toward him where he lay on his back gasping for breath, his face strangely pale. She barely heard the other shots or Trace's shout to take cover, could hear only her father's labored breathing. "Are you all right, Papa? Are you shot?"

"No . . . not shot. I think my leg is broken, though," the professor said through clenched teeth. "Silly of me to just let go of the ladder like that. . . ."

Frantically pulling at his clothes, Bethany saw the sickening angle of his leg and knew he was right. It was broken. Bullets whizzed overhead, thunking into dirt and smacking into rock, sending splinters spraying around her. She paid no attention to them, but attempted to drag her father to safety beneath a rocky overhang.

When strong brown hands slapped hers away and lifted the professor, Bethany was grateful to see Trace. His face was pulled into tight, angry lines, and he snapped at her to take cover before she was shot, but he carried Brasfield to safety.

She followed, and when the professor was laid gently on the ground, Trace shoved her roughly behind the same rock.

"Do you think you can stay here?" he rasped, and she nodded. "Then do it, dammit!"

He ran in a half crouch over the rock-littered ground, then dove behind another rock. Bethany could see him rise to aim his pistol, heard the sharp crack of it firing, and flinched at the orange-red flame spurting from the barrel.

"Who could be shooting at us?" the professor asked in a weak voice, and Bethany shook her head.

"I don't know, Papa. I guess natives."

"With rifles?"

Stunned by his whispered question, Bethany felt a sick lurch of her stomach. Native tribes would not use rifles, would they? What was it Trace had told her when he was trying to frighten her into remaining behind? "Arrows dipped in poison." Yes, that was it. Arrows and spears, and maybe dart guns, but not modern weaponry!

Who was shooting at them?

Brody answered that question. He crawled on his belly toward Trace, dragging his heavy pack with him, refusing to leave it even for a moment, even at the risk of his life.

Taking a flying leap, Brody bridged the distance between them and landed in a roll beside Trace. He looked up at him, his pale hair in his eyes and his face creased in a grimace. "What is it about you that invites ambushes, Taylor?" he grumbled, rolling to his knees.

Trace took careful aim and fired a shot at their attackers before replying, "It's the bad company I keep." He fired again, then asked, "Any idea who's shooting at us?"

"My guess is, it's another expedition." When Trace turned to look at him, Brody shrugged. "Bentworth was worried about it. He'd heard rumors, see, and so that's one reason he was so set on us coming along. Sort of as insurance."

"Yeah, well you're not being much help, if that's the case," Trace pointed out. He turned away, carefully aiming his pistol again, wishing his rifle was close. A handgun was not nearly as good as a carbine or rifle at a distance. The pistol bucked in his hand, and he heard a pained shout then smiled grimly. "Can you shoot off anything but your mouth?" he asked Brody without looking at him. "If you can, give it a try."

"You're a hard man, Taylor," Brody grumbled, but raised to his knees to peer over the rock. He laid his rifle atop it and waited for a good shot.

"Any idea whose expedition?" Trace asked a few minutes later, and Brody shook his head.

"Naw. All I know is that they're after the same thing we are. Looks like they decided to take it the easy way."

Taking careful aim, Trace fired and heard another yelp of pain. "Let's hope this ain't the easy way, Brody."

"Yeah. Guess you're right."

Trace paused to reload, flicking a glance toward the rock that sheltered Bethany. He couldn't see so much as a hair on her head, and nodded with satisfaction. She was keeping down like he'd told her. Too bad about her father. That was going to be a problem.

"Why is it that Bentworth's never close when trouble comes up?" Trace remarked to Brody as the bullets flew in a volley.

"He's been close before."

"Not for a long time. He seems to prefer taking a back seat these days."

Brody grimaced. "Gettin' old, I guess. Or cautious."

"Must be scared of dying and leaving behind all that money he's made," Trace said with a grunt. Brody didn't reply; but he didn't need to. Spencer Bentworth had turned his hand to several profitable endeavors since the time that Trace had first met him. It was common knowledge. Trace couldn't help but wonder if it had been made honestly or if the dapper Englishman had left the straight-and-narrow path he'd once suggested Trace follow.

"Where's Reagan?" Trace asked when there was a lull in the shooting.

"Caught on the other side of that rock. He's okay. And he's a decent shot."

"We don't need decent. We need good."

Shots still rang out, bullets *pinging* into rock walls and splattering sharp shards like rain. Trace felt a piece cut his cheek, but didn't stop to wipe the blood trickling into his eye. It didn't matter. Not now. He'd worry about it later.

The shooting stopped just as suddenly as it had begun, and it grew deathly quiet. Trace waited, his nerves taut and ready, his eyes narrowed.

"Think they've gone?" Brody muttered as he shoved more bullets into his rifle and snapped it shut with a metallic *snick*.

"For now, maybe. They'll wait and try to catch us at a place where we can't defend ourselves."

"Hell! What's worse than danglin' from a damn ladder?"

Trace looked at him quietly. "The ravine."

Brody didn't say anything. It was obvious from his drawn, pale face that he agreed.

When they reached the ravine and the log bridge, Trace saw that a landslide had made it extremely hazardous. As if they needed anything else to go wrong! He swore long and hard, and Bethany sat in tight-lipped silence. Her father was almost delirious, and even the coca leaves that Trace had insisted he chew had only a slight effect on him.

"I can't help it, Bethany," Trace came to her and said when she protested that her father was in no shape to try to negotiate the bridge. "It's either try or die."

Helplessly, she shook her head. "But how will we get him across?"

It was on the tip of Trace's tongue to say that they couldn't, but he knew she would protest. Besides, he didn't think he could leave him behind. He sat for a long moment, then said heavily, "I'll try to carry him."

Brody snorted. "You're crazy! Those bastards'll pick you off like a wooden duck, Taylor! And the old man, too. Don't you ever learn? Leave him here. We can come back for him when the shootin's over. . . ."

Bethany rounded on Brody furiously. "We will *not* leave my father behind! You can leave that pack here. That's probably what they want, anyway." She turned a beseeching gaze on Trace. "Isn't it? Don't you think that's what they want? Give them the gold! At least we'll escape with our lives!"

Brasfield moaned loudly. "No . . . not my artifacts! I won't go back without them . . . and my notes. Where are my notes and drawings? The photographs we took?"

Bethany didn't have the heart to tell him that the photographs as well as the camera had been left behind in their hasty flight. That could come later. And she could always sketch the city from memory.

When Trace's eyes slid toward Brody, the stocky man shook his head. "I ain't leavin' behind so much as one gold cup, Taylor. Forget it."

"I don't think it'd do any good anyway," Trace shot back with a shrug. "Now, let's get out of here."

Fashioning a sling from one of the blankets, Trace knotted it around the professor like a woolen cocoon. He gave one end to Santusa, and took the other end.

"Do you think we can get him across?" he asked in the Quechua language, and Santusa looked at him gravely.

"Not unless the gods smile kindly," he replied in

the same language.

"Well, we've got to give it a try," Trace muttered. "If I don't, she'll never believe I didn't want to leave him."

Pulling a knotted end of the blanket over his head and shoulders, Trace motioned for Santusa to do the same. The bearer did so without question.

"My notes, my notes," the professor moaned, and Bethany hastily scooped up a small leather packet.

"I have them, Papa. Don't worry. Now be as still as possible."

"Give him some more coca leaves," Trace said, and handed her several. "Let him chew them for a minute. I don't need him bouncing around once we crawl out on that damned log."

Bethany could not bear to glance at the rickety logs or the sheer fall into the ravine. She shuddered when Trace told her to go across right behind Brody.

"Reagan goes first, and he can cover the rest of us once he's across. Brody, you cover Reagan."

"Do you think they're still behind us?" Bethany asked with another shudder.

"I'd bet my last nickel on it." Trace gave the signal, and Reagan started across, this time dropping to his hands and knees as Bethany and her father had done the first time. Shots immediately rang out, and Artega and Brody shot back. Bethany wanted to scream from anxiety and fear, but kept her lips tightly pressed together. Screaming wouldn't do any good.

Brody made it across, though one of the bullets caught him across the back of his thigh, searing open a long track and bloodying his leg. Then Bethany went, her heart in her throat and her hands cold and clammy. She carried only her father's packet of notes with her, stuffed into a small case and dangling from her belt. She dared not look down, and, thankfully, no bullets came near as she crawled over the flimsy logs.

Weak with relief, she leaped the last two feet and landed in a spiny clump of brush, but rolled to her knees and stared back across. Trace and Santusa began their arduous journey, their awkward burden slung precariously between them. She could see her father's hand clutching the top of the blanket, could hear his muffled groans of pain. Her heart was beating fast, and she found herself murmuring prayers as they inched across at an agonizingly slow pace. The two Peruvian officers stood guard on the opposite bank, tense and ready, their weapons lifted.

Halfway across, a spate of bullets whizzed in a cross fire, and she saw Trace's hat spin from his head and float into the ravine. He slipped as a bullet snaked across his shoulder, then caught himself before he fell from the log. Brody and Reagan poured on more fire, until it seemed as if the world was nothing but hot lead and thunder.

Then, unbelievably, Bethany saw her father tumble from the blanket, saw the knotted ends separate and saw Trace's quick grab at him. They were only a few feet from the bank, now, only a few more feet to safety. Santusa grabbed at the professor, too, but managed to catch only the cuff of his shirtsleeve. It ripped away without slowing Brasfield's plummeting body.

Someone was screaming. She wasn't certain who it was; she could hear little but the fuzzy roar and pop of gunfire around her. Stumbling, Bethany surged from her knees to her feet and propelled forward, catching a glimpse of her father lying on a narrow rock ledge fifteen feet below the lip of the ravine. He was alive. He looked up at her with a dazed expression and grimaced.

"Papa!"

Trace reached her just before she scrambled over the edge of the ravine, jerking her backward and slamming her body to the ground. Her head snapped up, and she saw his lips moving but couldn't hear what he was saying. The buzz of gunfire still echoed in her ears. His face was drawn, and his eyes were bleak and cold as he gave her a slight shake. Bethany tried to avoid his holding hand as she twisted away, but he held her fast.

Snatches of what he was saying came to her.

". . . can't reach him yet . . . shooting . . . you'll be killed or . . . do what I can . . . may leave him for now. . . ."

"No!" she screamed, her body arching furiously away. "I won't leave him!"

There was a fizz and a pop, and her hearing returned in a rush. "You don't have much choice, Bethany," Trace said grimly. "We can't reach him right now, and if we try, we'll be just as dead as he will! Whoever's shooting at us means business!"

Panting, Bethany found a strength she didn't know she had. She pushed Trace back from her and surged to her feet, making it back to the edge of the ravine before he caught her. Grabbing her legs, Trace slammed her to the ground as a bullet snapped overhead, and his body landed atop hers.

"Damn you, you little idiot! What good will you do if you're dead, too?" he growled in her ear.

Lying flat on her stomach, Bethany had an excellent view of her father. He was sprawled like a broken doll on the rock ledge and looking up at her.

"Papa!"

He waved a feeble hand. "Go on!" he shouted. "I can't make it!" The effort to speak made him cough, and he covered his mouth with his fist. When his hand moved away, blood smeared it. "Bethany! Take my notes back. Tell them all about . . ." He broke into another spasm of coughing, then looked back up at her. "You must leave me!"

"No! No, I won't leave you, Papa!"

"Go . . . go on!" he managed to choke out before another coughing fit racked him. When his head lifted again, his lips were crimson. "Taylor—Trace—do what has to be done," he called in a quavering voice. "I'm done for—Save her!"

"Papa! Papa!" Her screams came from her stomach, tearing her insides apart, and she tried to wriggle from beneath Trace's heavy frame. "Let me go! Let me go, damn you, Trace Taylor!" she screamed, ignoring the bullets whining overhead and the soft curses of the men behind them.

Trace tried to pull her away, his voice in her ear. "He's right. It has to be this way, Bethany. He knows it. Didn't you hear him?"

She bit the hand he had curled over her wrist, and when he swore at her, drove her foot against his shin. "If you leave my father," she panted when he pinned her under his body again, glaring up at him, "I'll never forgive you!"

Another hail of bullets buzzed like angry bees in the air, and Trace ducked. He knew what he had to do, and he also knew she meant what she said. It couldn't be helped. He was having enough trouble dodging lead without having to wrestle Bethany. Clamping his lean thighs on each side of her struggling body, he lifted himself up and gazed down at her with reluctant sympathy. She stared back.

"Sorry, princess," he said softly, and clipped her on her chin with his clenched fist.

Lights exploded in front of her eyes, and Bethany could feel spinning velvet shadows claim her before there was nothing.

Chapter Twenty

San Diego, California—June 1890

"Señorita Brasfield?"

Bethany turned from her contemplation of the mountains rimming San Diego and gazed at the maid. "Yes?"

"You have a visitor."

"I'm not accepting visitors."

"That's what I told him, but he was quite insistent." The girl paused, then added, "This is a different gentleman from the others, señorita. He said to give you this."

Moving lethargically, Bethany held out her hand and gazed without interest at the small stone placed in it.

"I don't know what this is," she said after a moment, her voice indifferent. "And I don't want to see anyone."

A voice came from the door leading to the veranda. "Ah, have you given up all those who care about you, m'dear?"

Bethany recognized Spencer Bentworth, and stiffened. "I have not willingly given up anything. It was taken from me."

"Just so, just so. We all feel like that in the face of tragedy." Bentworth swept onto the veranda and motioned for the maid to leave. When she hesitated, Bethany sighed and nodded. "Excellent!" Bentworth said when the door had closed behind the girl. "You're making progress."

She held up the stone. "What is this?"

"A rock," Bentworth replied cheerfully. "I thought if I gave that dull-witted young lady something to bring to you, she might stop telling me you weren't receiving visitors. A brilliant notion, if I do say so myself."

"What do you want?" Bethany felt unutterably weary.

"Not much. Another chance, perhaps. Do you mind?" He indicated the cushioned lounge and she shook her head, watching as he sat down in it and folded one leg across his knee. "I'm afraid that I have a slight injury that necessitates my resting my leg," he apologized, his eyes still resting on her pale, drawn face. "A mismatched argument with a mule has left me a bit sore."

"Mr. Bentworth. . . ."

"Ah ah! Spencer, remember?"

Bethany smiled with an effort. "Spencer. I'm afraid that I don't feel very much like company now. Perhaps later in the week. . . ."

"M'dear, I fully realize that you have been quite undone by the recent events, and you have my fullest sympathies. However, I dislike seeing a lovely young woman hide herself away as you've done. Life must go on for those left behind, surely you know that."

Bethany's eyes flashed with more life than she'd shown in the past six months since her father's death. Deep violet sparks glittered coldly, and her voice was tight. "Perhaps, if I were as shallow as you, I might be able to recover more quickly! I'm not. Now, if you will be so good as to remove yourself from my veranda. . . ."

Bentworth did not move. He smiled at her, and his bushy gray brows lifted slightly. "Ah, I was wondering if you'd lost that lovely spark of spirit. I'm glad to see that you have not."

She stared at him with mutinous eyes. Couldn't he understand anything? Didn't he realize that she didn't *want* to feel anything? Nothing at all? To feel was to ache, and she'd had enough pain.

"Have you seen Mr. Taylor lately?" Bentworth asked then, and Bethany felt as if she had been slammed into a wall.

"No . . . of course I haven't," she managed to say with only a slight tremor in her voice. "And I don't expect to again."

"I see. You blame him for your father's death, as I understand it."

Bethany remained silent; only her eyes betrayed her rising hostility.

"It wasn't really his fault, you know. There are always choices in life, and Taylor did the best he could under the hazardous circumstances," Bentworth said.

"Odd, to hear you defending him," Bethany said tightly. "I thought you both hated one another."

"Oh, there's no love lost between us, that's true." Bentworth's teeth flashed briefly. "But I do recognize a valuable man when I see one."

"And Mr. Taylor is what you consider valuable?" Now her voice held a dangerous tautness to it, and Bentworth shifted uneasily on the cushions.

"I must admit to that," he answered after a moment. "I'm afraid he's the only guide capable of getting back to Vilcapampa."

"There were others with us," she reminded him. "Your two men—"

"Have sworn they will not attempt it again. That's what comes of my rewarding them so liberally." Bentworth's smile was rueful. "When they have spent all their money, I'm sure they'll be more agreeable, but I don't have that much time. Vilcapampa has incited a great deal of interest from other expeditions."

"So you're certain what we found was the lost city that you were seeking?" Bethany asked with reluctant interest.

"Reasonably so. Of course, that cannot be definitely established until we have photographs and detailed notes."

"I see." Her heart throbbed with renewed pain as she thought of the packet she'd saved, only to discover it was her own notes and sketches instead of her father's.

Poor Papa—he worked so hard, only to lose everything.

Bentworth coughed politely, and said when she looked up at him, "That is one of the reasons I came to see you, m'dear. I know how much it meant to Horatio, and to you, to have him receive credit for uncovering the city. However, without proper photographs and notes, the credit will—as it should—go to the next man to peel away the shrouds of the centuries."

"That is ridiculous!" Bethany glared at him. "My father died trying to bring back his notes, and he should receive credit for his efforts."

"Oh, he will. But you understand, that the next man to succeed in detailing history, will be credited with its finds. It's only fair. Failures are only footnotes in this business, I'm afraid."

"Footnotes!"

"A sad commentary for a dedicated, brilliant man like your father, I agree." Bentworth slanted her a shrewd look. "It doesn't have to be like that, you know."

Too incensed to pay strict attention, Bethany stalked to the walls enclosing the veranda and looked into the distance. Cloud banks floated over the rolling hills, somehow reminding her of the jagged teeth of the Andes, and for a moment she thought of Trace. She remembered the hard, brittle set of his face when she'd told him how she hated him, that he'd cost her father his life. He'd not denied it, not defended himself, just looked at her. Somehow, that faintly accusing glitter in his dark eyes still haunted her more than anything he could have said.

Maybe it wasn't Trace's fault her father had died, but he hadn't done enough to save him. If he'd only tried, only done a little more, then her father would still be with her, would be receiving credit for the years of hard work and dedication he'd poured into deciphering tablets and old manuscripts.

Almost absently, she lifted her hand to touch her jaw. The bruise was gone now, of course, but had lingered for weeks before finally fading. It had been a constant reminder of Trace's final betrayal. He hadn't liked her father, and he hadn't cared enough about her to try and keep him alive. She'd never forgive him. Never.

Dragging her attention back to Bentworth, she said, "It doesn't have to be like what? What did you mean by that?"

"You could claim those ruins in your father's name, you know." Bentworth watched her closely, saw her expression range from shock, to anger, then to a wary consideration.

"Impossible. I'm certain that another expedition has reached them by now."

"One probably would have, but there was an earthquake up there that destroyed any trace of a path, and with the rainy season and unwilling guides—well, no one has been able to find it."

"Didn't you want to send Mr. Taylor back?" She couldn't hide the note of bitterness in her voice.

"I wanted to very badly."

"Then?"

"He refused. No amount of money would sway him, nor any promises I could make." Bentworth's laugh was faintly malicious. "Not even bribery and blackmail helped."

Bethany didn't ask what kind of blackmail. She didn't want to know.

"Why are you telling me all this?"

Bentworth rose from the lounge, and a note of suppressed excitement quivered in his voice. His pale eyes glittered beneath his bushy brows as he said, "Because you can change his mind, m'dear. You can talk Taylor into going back."

Recoiling, she exclaimed, "Why would I want to do that!"

"Bethany, surely you recall an entire room filled with golden treasure, more than my mind can conceive. You *saw* it for yourself—can't you understand why?"

"I don't care about the gold. My father was killed! Do you think I really want to go back?" she demanded incredulously. Her fingers curled into her cotton skirts in a reflex action, and her body quivered with repressed emotion.

"Not for yourself, no. But for your father, to ensure his name in the annals of history? You could always realize his dream for him, Bethany. No one else would claim it in his name—you would."

"I'd have to be mad!"

"Yes. Or obsessed." Bentworth smiled. "Or maybe just determined to finish what he started."

Staring at him, Bethany felt her throat tighten. No, she couldn't even consider such an insane notion! Why, she would have to make that arduous, dangerous trek again, have to see Trace everyday, hear his husky voice mock her . . . no, she just couldn't do it.

Chapter Twenty-one

Lima, Peru—July 1890

Inhaling deeply to steady her pounding nerves, Bethany lifted her hand and rapped smartly on the heavy oak door. It was several moments before it swung open, and when it did, she was acutely disappointed to see a tall, blond man gaze at her inquiringly.

"Yes? May I help you?"

Floundering for words, she murmured, "Oh! I was looking for someone—a man—a guide, really, and . . ."

"Come in. He's not here right now, but he'll be back soon."

Opening the door wide, Gil Fortune shrewdly surmised that the young lady was most uncomfortable, and wondered if she had been involved with Trace. This was how they usually looked when they appeared on Trace's doorstep—embarrassed, half afraid, and hopeful. Or at least, that was how they'd looked before the last expedition. There had been a noticeable dearth of young ladies in his life since then, a fact Trace flatly refused to discuss.

"Please?" Gil prompted when Bethany hesitated

and looked as if she might flee at any moment.

Summoning her wavering courage, Bethany stepped into the room and stood awkwardly just in the doorway. "It's very good of you to allow me to wait," she said as Gil drew out a chair for her and she sank into it gratefully. She hadn't been certain her legs would continue to hold her up much longer.

She looked around the room. It was neat, airy, with a decidedly masculine feel to it. Leather couches promised a comfortable rest, and tall bookcases flanked a stone fireplace.

"No problem, Miss—?" Gil waited politely for her to supply a name, and was startled into silence when she did.

"Brasfield. Miss Brasfield." Bethany fidgeted with the strings of her velvet reticule. "I take it that Mr. Taylor has recently taken new lodgings," she said a moment later, almost desperately, searching for casual conversation. "I was misdirected at first."

Recovering his aplomb and mentally swearing, Gil said, "Yes, that's true." A faint smile curved his mouth, and his light blue eyes gleamed as he added, "Had a devil of a time talking him into it, though. Said he didn't give a da—darn about where he stayed, just as long as the roof didn't leak on him during the rainy season."

Actually, Trace had had a great deal more to say than that, but as he was almost totally indifferent to his surroundings most of the time, Gil had prevailed.

"You're his business partner, I presume, Mister—?"

"Sorry. Fortune. Gil Fortune. And no, not really his partner. I'm more of his scapegoat." He grinned. "I'm his accountant. I handle his money for him, pay his bills, see that his investments go smoothly, that sort of thing."

"I see."

I wonder if you do, Gil thought quickly, then said, "Of course, in the rainy season there's not much work, but that should change soon."

Bethany twisted the strings of her reticule. "Yes, I understand that."

She looked around with the expression of a trapped rabbit, and Gil wondered why she had come. He'd thought she was back in California. That's what Trace had told him, his voice almost savage when he said it, and Gil had known not to mention Miss Brasfield again. Now she was here, sitting as awkwardly as a goat on a fence, and looking as lovely as any woman had a right to be.

Her light brown hair was swept back from her face in a flattering wave, with tiny curls dangling in front of her dainty ears, and her wide amethyst eyes were shadowed by lashes so long they looked almost ridiculous. High cheekbones gave her face a fashionably exotic appearance, and her straight little nose and full, slightly quivering lips looked vulnerable and tempting. The elegant cut of her gown hugged her figure in enticing swells and curves, making a man long to explore the rich promises beneath the rust-colored moiré material. Oh yes, Trace Taylor was going to be very surprised when he got home, Gil decided with a malicious twinge of satisfaction.

It should be good for him. He'd brooded and growled for the past six months, and had not been fit company for man nor beast. No one could talk to him without risk of having their head snapped off, or at best, being lacerated with a mocking sarcasm that was as sharp as his machete. Yes, this should be very good for Trace.

"Tea?" Gil asked politely, and when she nodded with almost pitiful gratitude, he went to the small kitchen and lit the fire in the stove. The teapot rattled as he sat it on the burner, and he was shaking out some tea when he heard the front door open. Gil stepped to the doorway, and almost groaned.

Trace was home. And for the first time in six months, he had a woman with him. Dammit! Gil swore to himself, and forgot the teapot as he stepped back into the spacious sitting room.

Bethany felt a lump grow in her throat, and without realizing it, she surged to her feet. Her face was ashen, but her chin tilted up in proud indifference.

Stopping just inside the door, his arm still around the woman's waist and his hand resting familiarly on her hip, Trace saw Bethany immediately. Space narrowed to just her, to her pale, set face and faintly accusing gaze. He didn't move, didn't speak, but his eyes narrowed slightly.

"Excuse me, Mr. Taylor," Bethany said, and was proud of her steady voice. "I came to discuss business with you. If this is a bad time—as it seems to be—I can come back later."

Trace knew that if he let her leave, there would be no "later."

"Business?" he repeated finally, his slow, husky drawl so achingly familiar that Bethany had to grip her reticule tightly to keep from reaching out for him. "What kind of business?"

"As I just said, perhaps later would be . . ."

"Now's fine." Trace let his arm drop from the woman's waist and gave her a little push toward Gil. "Wait on me in the kitchen," he told her, and when she slid him a pouting, suspicious glance, he added, "This won't take long."

No, it certainly won't! Bethany agreed silently, and steeled herself. What had she expected? That Trace not meet other women? After all, she'd told him she hated him, that she never wanted to see him again, and that she blamed him for her father's death. How did she expect him to react?

Clearing her throat as Trace turned back to her with a narrowed gaze, Bethany said as pleasantly as possible, "I came here to present you with a proposition."

"Proposition?" Trace smiled coldly. "This sounds very interesting. Do go on."

"I wish to engage your services as a guide." Why did he have to be so endearingly handsome? So overpoweringly male? And why did she have to recall the feel of his mouth on hers, the touch of his hand on her in stirring caresses?

"Now, that surprises me, Miss Brasfield," Trace said as he crossed the room to the mantel and picked up a carved teak box. He removed a cigar from it, murmured a "Do you mind if I smoke?" without waiting for her reply, and scratched a match along the stones of the fireplace to light it.

"I imagine it does surprise you," Bethany said. "It also surprises me. I have a reason, however."

"Oh, I've no doubt of that. You always have reasons for what you do, even if they're not very good ones." His eyes briefly met hers over the glowing tip of his cigar, and thick smoke wafted lazily across the room.

Drawing in a deep breath, Bethany kept her gaze on his face. "I'm certain it seems that way. Perhaps if you keep that in mind, it won't startle you when I say that I want to go back."

"Back?"

"To Vilcapampa, or the lost city, or castles in the clouds or whatever you want to call it. But I want to go back and ensure that my father receives credit for what he did."

"Hardly worth it now, I'd think," Trace drawled. "He's dead and won't know about it."

His flat, brutal words took away her breath, and Bethany stared at him. Her hands trembled, and she wondered if he was being deliberately cruel or just casually so.

"But *I* know it!" she managed to say with only a trace of pain edging her voice. "And I intend for the world to know it."

Trace chewed on the end of his cigar and stared at her through the curls of smoke. "I take it you want me to guide you there."

"Yes."

"No."

She waited the span of several heartbeats. "No? Is that it? Just *no?*"

"Isn't that enough?"

"Not for me."

A faint smile kicked up the corners of his mouth. "You always were stubborn."

"I prefer determined."

"You don't always get what you want." Trace pulled the cigar from his mouth and tossed it into the fireplace. "No one goes up there during the rainy season."

"The rainy season is over."

He swung to face her, and his dark eyes glittered. "There are still bad bridges and high roads, you know. And there are no guarantees."

"I know that—now."

Sucking in a deep breath, he muttered, "That remains to be seen."

"Then you'll do it?"

"I'll think about it."

Fumbling in her reticule, Bethany drew out a slip of paper. "You'll find me here when you reach a decision." She handed it to him, and when his fingers brushed against hers she stifled a shiver. There was still the woman waiting on him in the kitchen. She could hear the shrill whistle of a tea kettle, and Gil Fortune's rumbling monologue.

Glancing down at the scrap of paper, Trace didn't say anything for a moment. He couldn't think of anything to say that wouldn't sound harsh or cruel. He wanted to tell her that he wouldn't risk being with her like that again, that he had no intention of going off on a month-long trek with her and keeping his hands to himself. He knew she expected that, but he'd be damned if he'd agree to it.

Trace lifted his head, and his voice was soft. "No promises, princess. Whatever happens, happens."

"I'm well aware of that, Mr. Taylor," she said in such a cool, collected voice that he felt like jerking her into his arms and showing her what he meant.

"And no regrets." His dark, liquid gaze bored into her like fire, and she nodded slowly.

"I'm certain that whatever happens, there will be no regrets this time." A faint, bitter smile curled her lips. "You see, I've learned a lot about self-control in the past six months."

"You have?" he mocked her, and for one, brief instant, debated on showing her how little self-control she really had. He decided against it. His pride wouldn't allow him to let her see how her accusations after Brasfield's death had mattered. "Then I won't have to worry about my reputation, will I?"

Her gaze swung deliberately toward the kitchen. "Not with *me,*" she said sweetly, and marched to the door. "I'll be expecting to hear from you," she said before she opened the door and left.

Trace glared after her, then crushed the slip of paper in his hands and tossed it on the floor.

"Tea, anyone?" Gil asked lightly, stepping into the room and looking around. "Oh. Your company left, I see."

"Yeah."

Behind Gil, the sultry brunette smiled. She advanced toward Trace with the swaying steps of a seductress, and put her hand on his arm.

"I thought she would never go, *amante.* Your friend, he made me brew tea so long, I began to think you wanted a cook instead of a companion."

Trace flicked her an impatient glance. "Actually, I don't think I want either right now, Rosa. Later," he said when she stiffened and her dark eyes flashed. "I have some business to tend to."

"Do you?" Gil asked when the girl had left with a last indignant glance at Trace. "Have business, I mean?"

Throwing himself on one of the leather sofas, Trace put a hand over his eyes. "Hell, I don't know. All I can think about right now is wringing her pretty little neck."

"All?" Gil echoed mischievously. "You're losing your touch, Trace."

Trace shot him a sardonic glance. "Try to think with your brain instead of your lower extremities, Gil. She tells me in no uncertain terms that she hates my guts, wishes I was dead, would like to see me castrated and hung out on a pole, and then six months later waltzes back into my life like nothing has happened. Am I supposed to fall happily in with her plans now? Huh-uh. I don't think so. If I agree to guide her back to that damned place, I want you to take me out and shoot me. Quick. No point in lingering like I did the last time."

Silence fell as they sat there. Neither of them spoke for a long time. As the shadows in the room deepened, Gil said, "What gun do you want me to use?"

Trace swore softly. "The Winchester."

"When do you think you'll leave?"

"As soon as we get supplies."

Gil smiled. "If you don't mind, I think I'll hold off shooting you until you get back. Then you might really need it."

"Sounds likely," Trace muttered, and thought again of Bethany and how good she'd looked. She'd lost weight, but it had only served to heighten her beauty, giving her interesting hollows in her face that hadn't been there before. Yeah, shooting would probably be just what he needed when he got back from an extended trek with her. *If* he got back reverberated in his mind, but he ignored it.

Bethany was wondering the same thing. Had she made yet another mistake? Staring out the windows of her hotel room without really seeing the snow-tipped Andes looming beyond, she considered returning home. It wasn't too late. Not yet. Not until they left, would it be too late.

A self-mocking smile curved her lips. She'd fallen in so eagerly with Spencer Bentworth's suggestion, as if she'd just been waiting for a reason to find Trace. If she was truly honest with herself, she supposed she'd have to admit that it hadn't really taken much urging to get her to leave California behind and return to Peru.

Restlessly, her nerves still quivering from seeing him again, Bethany turned away from the window. Just being near him had been a bittersweet agony for her. The familiar face that had haunted her dreams for the past six months had not changed much since last she'd seen him; become more caustic in a way, perhaps, more mocking. And she hadn't really been too surprised to find him with a woman. Not Trace.

She tore her thoughts from that direction, not allowing herself to wonder what he and the brunette were doing at that moment. Oddly, she was grateful that she'd seen him with the woman. It stiffened her resolve to avoid any more intimate contact with him. Now she could purge her soul and heart of Trace Taylor. She could do what she'd come back to do—see that the discovery of Vilcapampa was credited to her father, then leave. It would be much easier now; she wouldn't have this strange, empty feeling of not having ended her relationship with Trace.

Well, she decided firmly, when she left him this time, there would be none of her former ambivalence. This time, there would be no regrets. She had come to Peru to achieve two things—accredit Horatio Brasfield with his just due, and cleanse her mind of any lingering regrets concerning Trace Taylor.

It should, she thought caustically, be simple enough now. The lovely, sultry brunette he'd brought home with him had given her the strength she needed to resist him and the weakening memories she still held.

Yet when she idly shuffled through the drawings she had made in the ruins and saw the sketches of Trace, Bethany couldn't help but wonder if her resistance was strong enough. Her heart lurched painfully as she held up the one of him sitting atop the rock with one leg drawn up and his arm draped across it, his face a mixture of aggressiveness and vulnerability. The beard-shadow made him look piratical in a way, but his eyes gave him away. She'd done better than she had thought, Bethany mused with a raw pang.

Chapter Twenty-two

"Winter in the Andes," Trace growled irritably. "I must be crazy."

Bethany shot him a quick glance from beneath her lowered lashes. There had been little but taut silence between them since they had left Lima behind, climbing higher and higher into the mountains. Trace seemed to be making a concerted effort to avoid her. He spoke only when he had to give her directions.

They'd made the first leg of the journey like polite strangers. Now they were entering Cuzco, and memories assailed her of the last time they'd seen the city. Her throat tightened, and she peered from beneath the brim of her floppy hat in stony silence.

Rain drizzled in a fine mist, making the road slippery in places. Her mule stumbled, then caught its balance. She clung tightly to the horn of her saddle, determined not to end up in the street again. The memory of her introduction to Cuzco's slick, cobblestoned streets still rankled.

"Any objection to staying with Bertolli again?" Trace asked, and she shook her head.

She would welcome a diversion, someone to focus on besides Trace. It had been more difficult than she'd imagined it would be, being so near him and yet remaining distant. At night, when they'd camped with a host family at one of the *postes* scattered across the Andes, she had often felt his dark, brooding gaze on her, and wondered what he was thinking. Yes, Signore Bertolli would be a welcome distraction.

Bertolli, as last time, was a perfect host. He greeted them with smiling pleasure. *"Avanti, avanti!* It is good to see you again, my friends. Come in out of the wet. *Si accomodi, prego."*

Shivering from the cold rain and drenched to the skin, Bethany managed a smile. "It seems that I arrive on your doorstep looking like a beggar again, signore. I'll try not to make a habit of this."

Gallantly, Bertolli said, "You are always welcome here, *bella donna.* And you also, Signore Taylor."

Trace's smile was faintly mocking. "You don't seem very surprised to see us, I notice."

Bertolli grinned. "I had heard of your journey, you see. News travels fast in a country like Peru where there is so little else to distract one."

Not quite believing him, Trace shrugged. "I'd still be interested in hearing how you found out so quickly."

"Of course, of course, but shall we discuss it over *vino* after you are more comfortable?"

Bethany shifted uncomfortably. Why did Trace have to provoke even Signore Bertolli, who had offered them only friendship and hospitality? Did he have to inflict his sour mood on everyone else as well as her? She glared at him, but he didn't seem to notice.

And later, when they were comfortably dry and ensconced before a roaring fire in Bertolli's main *sala,* Bethany found Trace even more irritating. She pleated the soft cotton folds of her demure gown between her fingers, trying not to show her irritation at his scowling mood.

Rolling his glass of brandy between lean brown fingers and contemplating it with a serious expression, Trace asked without looking at the portly Italian, "Have you seen Spencer Bentworth lately?"

Bertolli shrugged. "Not since you were all here. You recall, after the . . . trouble."

Bethany winced involuntarily. Trace had brought her here after the disaster that had cost her father's life. He had left her in the care of Spencer Bentworth when she had lashed out at him, swearing she would never forgive him, telling him she hated him. Bentworth had accompanied her back to Lima and the port of Callao. Those days still remained a painful haze.

"Do you have a reason for asking?" Bertolli asked Trace in a remotely polite tone. "I sense a note of anger in your voice."

Trace flicked Bertolli a glance. "I don't know what it is, Bertolli, but something's going on that I can't figure out. There are too many loose ends, too many unanswered questions that keep hounding me." He leaned forward, fixing his dark gaze on the Italian merchant. "Who attacked us? No one seems to know. In six months, I haven't been able to find out one single clue as to who it was. That can mean several things, one of which is that the men who fired on us have powerful connections. You know as well as I do, that Spencer Bentworth has a great many connections. And now he sends Brasfield's daughter to me, presumably to talk me into refinding Vilcapampa. Why hasn't he found it himself by now? It's not as if there weren't plenty of men with us who could find it again."

Bertolli shrugged eloquently. "I understand that those men are not to be found. And the two men who were with you, Brody and Reagan, have gone back to America with a great deal of wealth and seemingly disappeared. Perhaps Bentworth has arranged matters to his satisfaction, and only desires to—" He paused delicately. "Only desires to narrow down the number of people who can find the lost treasure of the Incas."

"Do you really believe that?" Bethany demanded. "And if you do, why hasn't someone done something about it? Why, if Spencer was responsible for my father's death, then why would he send me back again?"

"What better way to coax young Lothario there into risking life and limb to go back?" Bertolli mocked, sliding Trace a slightly malicious grin.

Trace stood up and set his empty glass of brandy on the table next to his chair. "Money would have been a more efficient inducement," he said in a growling mutter that didn't fool Bertolli for a moment. "He wouldn't meet my price."

"Could it be that he did meet your price after all?" A faint smile curved Bertolli's lips under his mustache. "You are here, I note. And you are going back into the mountains to find Vilcapampa and Incan gold, something that truly surprises me."

A small muscle leaped in Trace's clenched jaw as he returned Bertolli's gaze. "But not for Bentworth."

"Ah! For this lovely young lady, then?" His smiling gaze shifted to Bethany. "Perhaps Bentworth is much more clever than I have ever given him credit for being, heh?"

Bethany squirmed uneasily in her chair, and wondered why Bertolli seemed intent upon focusing on her tense relationship with Trace. What could it possibly matter to him? Granted, Italians were rumored to be romantics at heart, and he might possibly want to see her and Trace mend the rift between them, but it seemed highly unlikely that he would risk his friendship with Trace to do so.

"Signore Bertolli," she murmured softly when it looked as if Trace was about to stalk from the *sala* in anger, "I think you are forgetting that most men such as

Bentworth put success above mere emotion. He would not think it very important that Trace and I become . . . friends . . . again."

"I never suggested he did." Bertolli smiled. "I merely pointed out that he would feel free to use you both to gain his own ends—that of risking extreme danger and possible death to recover treasure from the lost city of the kings." His smile broadened. "It seems to be working remarkably well."

"Not really," Bethany said with a snap. "I'm going back to ensure that my father receives credit for his hard work, and Mr. Taylor is the only man willing to take me there. It is that simple."

"Ah, things are never *that simple,* signorina. You will pardon me if I suspect Bentworth's outwardly benign motives, won't you?"

"Spencer Bentworth made it quite clear that he wanted the gold," Bethany said shortly. "He's not pretended any differently. I want something entirely different, however."

Signore Bertolli stood up and gave her a slight bow. "My apologies, signorina. Perhaps I have allowed my fondness for you both to affect my good judgment in holding my tongue. If I have offended you, I beg your apology many times over."

Mollified, Bethany nodded. "Of course. You understand, I hope, that my return to Peru has brought back many unpleasant memories, and I'm afraid I'm rather irritable."

Bethany glanced at Trace, but he remained stubbornly silent, his dark eyes resting speculatively on Bertolli. She felt another twinge of impatience with him. Couldn't he be polite and gracious enough to accept their host's apologies, for heaven's sake?

But Trace remained silent, his hooded gaze resting on the Italian merchant as if he had never seen him before.

No sign of what he was thinking showed on his face, and his manner was overly polite when he finally bid them both a good night and left the *sala* without a backward glance.

Compelled to smooth over Trace's rudeness, Bethany said, "It's been a strain on all of us these past months."

"I see. I understand perfectly, signorina." He took her hand between his own large palms. His penetrating gaze burned into her as Bertolli said, "I admired your papa very much. And I admire your determination to honor his name. If there is anything I can do. . . ."

"No, you've done too much already, Signore Bertolli." She managed a smile. "It is very gracious of you to offer your hospitality in the face of our rather prickly companionship. We will try not to impose too long. As soon as we have completed the necessary arrangements with the Peruvian officials, we shall be leaving."

"I will be more than happy to take care of that for you," Bertolli said immediately. "Please," he said with an uplifted hand when she started to protest, "it is the least I can do to make up for having been so rude this evening. I should have considered how my pitiful efforts to dissuade you from your purpose—and in the process see you and Signore Taylor reconciled—would be an imposition. You will allow me to take care of the details for you?"

She nodded. "I am in your debt."

"No, it is *I* who am in *your* debt," Bertolli assured her with another smile.

It was a comforting feeling, Bethany thought later as she slid between the cool sheets of the bed she'd been given, to know that a man as influential as Signore Bertolli was on their side. He'd hinted broadly that Bentworth was not. She lay back, propping her head up on fat pillows and gazing up at the canopy of the bed.

In spite of Spencer Bentworth's seeming perversity and outright avarice, she found it difficult to dislike him anymore. She didn't know why. It was obvious Trace disliked and distrusted him, but she couldn't feel the same and she didn't know why.

Trace had caustically remarked that women were usually taken in by smooth-talking men, and she had agreed with him immediately.

"Yes," she'd said shortly, "I certainly was taken in by *you!*"

That had had the effect of narrowing his eyes and making his mouth thin into a taut line, but he had not said it again. In fact, he had said very little on the entire trip, and she supposed she was grateful. There was an odd vacancy in her heart when she thought of him, as if a part of her had been removed. She was too vulnerable to the slightest sign of thawing from him, and did not dare risk casual conversation. Even open hostility was better than a softening of her heart. She had to protect herself from those buried emotions, lest they crop up and leave her open to his casual, careless seduction.

Bethany kept that in mind the next morning, when her heart lurched unexpectedly at the sight of Trace without his shirt, his smooth, gleaming muscles flexing as he stretched lazily. She should have thought to ask Martina or Signore Bertolli if anyone would be in the baths at that early hour, but somehow it hadn't occurred to her. And when she rounded the corner, intending to take a private bath, and saw him just pulling his pants around his lean waist, she jerked to a breathless halt.

His dark head, still wet from his bath, snapped up, and his eyes met hers. A faint, mocking smile curled his lips, and he made no attempt to button his trousers. He stood there gazing back at her.

Bethany tried not to notice how utterly virile he

looked standing there, his legs spread slightly apart and his hands moving to rest on his hips. The open edges of his pants didn't reveal his lower body, but still gaped enough that she could see—and remember the feel of—the hard bands of muscle on his taut belly. Her throat closed.

"I thought I was up early enough to beat the morning rush," Trace said after a moment. He saw the faint flush on her cheeks, and her deliberate attempts to keep her gaze on his face, and for some reason, that prompted him to sever her tightly held control. She'd been right when she'd told him she'd developed a great deal of resistance in the past six months, not once had she seemed inclined to renew their former intimacy. It had been just as well, because he hadn't been at all certain he wanted that either.

But now, with her standing awkwardly and staring at him as if she'd never seen him without his clothes, Trace was moved by a wicked impulse to shatter her restraint. Damn her for looking like a tarnished angel anyway, with her tempting curves and softly pouting mouth, the gleam of appreciation in her wide violet eyes that she hadn't been able to hide with her quickly lowered lashes.

Still not bothering to button his trousers, Trace bent and picked up his shirt with a lazy motion, then walked toward Bethany. He saw with a flash of satisfaction that she backed away a step, and that her eyes were even wider than before.

"The water's warm, princess," he said softly. "About the same temperature as the water in that Incan pool we swam in. Remember that?"

She nodded silently, wishing she could gracefully retreat. His voice lowered to a husky drawl.

"Of course, Bertolli has more modern conveniences, but we had more privacy."

Her throat clogged, and she felt a creeping warmth suffuse her neck and face. Why did he have to remind her of that night? It had been so wonderful, such a sweet memory until everything had gone wrong.

"I remember," she croaked when it seemed apparent that he expected her to say something. Why did he have to stand so close? She could almost hear his heartbeat, and could smell the fresh scent of soap clinging to his smooth brown skin. A drop of water slid from a slender thread of his hair to splash on her arm, and she shuddered. It should have sizzled. She felt so hot, burning up with a fever that pounded through her body and made her quiver with longing for him. And he knew it. She could see the awareness in his eyes, in the slightly mocking curl of his lips.

Her resolve stiffened, and her voice was coolly indifferent when she said, "I've learned not to swim with strangers since then."

The corners of his eyes crinkled in appreciation. "Have you? How dull your life has grown."

"But safe."

"Safety is for the very old and very young, not the rest of us."

"Please don't include me in that number," Bethany said stiffly. "I resent being lumped in a group."

"You resent a lot of things."

"Yes!" she flashed, jerking her head up to glare at him, "I certainly do!"

"So do I, princess," Trace said grimly, "so do I."

He walked past her, and Bethany stared after him. If only the time would pass quickly; if only she could complete what she'd set out to do and get back, get away from Trace Taylor and the havoc he wrought with her mind and heart.

Vilcapampa was only a few days away now, and then it would all be over. She would take photographs, make detailed notes, and bring back as many artifacts as was possible, all in the name of Horatio T. Brasfield. It would be a lasting tribute to her father. And with Bertolli's assistance, it would be done quickly.

But Trace had no intention of accepting help from the Italian merchant. Bethany was as perplexed as she was angry at him when he approached her in the dining room where she sat with her morning coffee.

"Why not?" she demanded when Trace coldly informed her that he would not allow Bertolli to intercede with the Peruvian officials. "It will expedite matters a great deal, considering that . . ."

"I don't give a damn for expediting matters," Trace broke in. "I intend to take care of it myself."

"Well, you're too late," Bethany said with a snap. "He has already taken care of it."

Trace's brows lowered over his eyes. "Did it occur to you to consult me first?"

"Why should it? You're just the guide, remember?"

"Fine. Then get there by yourself."

She stared at him in exasperation. "Trace, why are you being so stubborn? After all, it was your suggestion that we come here, wasn't it? Signore Bertolli is your friend, isn't he?"

For the first time since she had come back to Peru, Bethany saw the guarded expression fade from his eyes. He looked faintly puzzled. "I don't know," he admitted honestly. "I don't know why I feel the way I do. It's not Bertolli, I guess, it's just this feeling I have."

"What kind of feeling?"

"Like someone is always listening, waiting for us to get back to Vilcapampa. Bethany, there's something wrong, and I'm damned if I can figure out what it is."

"You don't think you're being overly cautious because of all the . . . the trouble we had last time?" Her voice broke slightly, but she kept her eyes on Trace.

"Maybe." He shrugged. "And maybe not. I usually trust my instincts. They've kept me alive a long time."

There was no way to argue with that, and Bethany didn't try. She rose from her chair and moved closer to him, her voice low.

"Are you trying to say that you don't trust Signore Bertolli?"

"No," Trace said with a sigh, "I'm trying to say that I don't trust *any*body."

"I see."

"I wish you did."

She shrugged. "It doesn't really matter if I do. What matters is that we are successful."

"And if we aren't?" His eyes burned into her pale face. "What then? What if we can't get there this time, if the trail is too covered with rubble or we meet more gunfire? What do you do then, without a cause to keep you going?"

Bethany recoiled from his dark gaze. "I don't need a cause. . . ."

"Sure you do. Before you decided that I was responsible for your father's death, you'd decided that you were responsible for his life. You arranged yours to fit in with his plans, whether it was what you wanted or not. Now, you're doing the same thing, only you're martyring yourself for a dead man. Interesting, but hardly healthy."

Furious, Bethany's hand flashed up to slap him, but he was too quick. He grabbed her wrist tightly, his fingers like steel bands around her delicate bones.

"I don't think I'd risk that, if I were you. I'm not the courtly gentleman I was when you first met me," he said mockingly, but the fury in his eyes was deadly serious. She took a deep breath and nodded.

"May I have my hand back, please?"

He released her wrist with a contemptuous shove,

then pivoted on his heel and stalked from the room. Bethany wondered wearily if the end would justify the means. She sank back into the cushioned chair and put a hand over her eyes.

Chapter Twenty-three

Cuzco was two days behind them. When they made camp at a familiar spot, Bethany tried not to look at Trace. He seemed to be of a similar mind.

Bethany recalled his taunting words reminding her of the "swim" they had shared, and couldn't help but wonder if he still recalled it as vividly as she did. The few Quechua bearers they'd brought with them from Cuzco had already rolled up in their blankets after tending to the mules, and only the Peruvian soldiers were still awake.

Frowning slightly, Bethany slid them a glance. They were not at all like the last officers who'd gone on the expedition, but looked villainous. There were three of them, and they wore the serge uniforms of soldiers, but not the official air of the military. Trace had disliked them on sight.

"They have the look of cutthroats," he said bluntly to Bethany. "I don't much like the idea of having to depend on one of them not to stick a knife in my back."

"I'm quite certain the Peruvian government would not be foolish enough to send bandits along to guard valuable gold and artifacts," Bethany shot back, and he shrugged.

"Suit yourself."

"I will."

"Just don't expect me to trust them any farther than I can see them. Or throw them."

"Believe me, Trace Taylor, I don't expect anything from you!"

On that note, they'd ridden out of Cuzco and into the Andes, with Trace giving Bethany a wide berth. And now that they were camped and Bethany was remembering things she didn't want to remember, she felt vaguely uneasy. It had to be the spot, so near the hot, bubbling springs where Trace had taken her that moonlit night, where they had . . .

She had to stop letting her thoughts drift in that direction! It was madness. It was dangerous. It was heartbreaking.

The tension was thick enough to slice with a knife, hanging over their heads as they sat in the shadows and watched the campfire flames flicker. Beyond the camp the jungle came alive for the night, with the coughing roar of a panther, and the shrill screeches of night birds. Bethany shuddered, remembering the huge cat she had seen the day before.

Trace had shot it just before it managed to finish off one of the mules, leaving raw weals across the frantically braying animal's haunches. The huge, powerful cat looked oddly pathetic lying lifelessly on the ground until Bethany had looked more closely and seen the wicked fangs still smeared with the mule's blood.

The poor mule trembled when Trace doctored the long scratches with antiseptic and some sort of salve, and he'd gentled him with soft, soothing words. Watching him, Bethany had wondered how he could be such an odd mixture of roughness and tenderness.

And in spite of her good intentions, she now recalled how gentle he'd been with her that first night, when he'd held her cradled in his arms and whispered sweet love-words in her ear, had been patient and not rushed her until she was ready. It was hard to reconcile that memory with the more recent memories she had of him, of his harsh, cold gaze and even harsher words, of his mocking comments to her slightest remark. No, the Trace she had known so briefly had disappeared.

Shivering at the chill of the wind, Bethany rose from in front of the fire and crossed to the small lean-to that had been erected for her use. It wasn't much, but it would serve to deflect some of the wind from her. It was still cold in the mountains. Rain had scoured the ridges for most of the day, and still threatened.

"Better pull down that flap," Trace advised when he saw Bethany duck into the small shelter. "It's going to get a lot colder before the night's out."

She paused, startled by his concern.

"Can't have you getting sick on me," he added with the familiar mocking smile, and her mouth tightened.

"No, that would be a dreadful inconvenience for you, wouldn't it?"

"Not as much as it would be for you." He leaned forward to light a cigar from the fire, keeping his eyes on her as she flounced inside the lean-to and dropped the flap. It didn't quite reach to the bottom, but left open a six-inch strip. He smiled grimly. Wonder if she knew that he could see pretty good through that tiny slit? Probably not, or she wouldn't be sitting there shrugging out of her pants so casually. He saw the brief flash of flannel, and shook his head. Ridiculous of her, to bring a nightie out into the jungle. Did she think it had changed any since the last time she'd passed this way? Common sense should have dictated that she leave such trappings of civilization at home, but it had been his experience that women rarely did such sensible things.

Most females seemed determined to wring a small bit of civilization out of the most desolate of wildernesses. He'd once thought Bethany was different. Now he revised that opinion.

Pulling on his cigar, Trace squinted against the curls of smoke and settled back on his heels to enjoy watching Bethany's bare legs. They were easily visible through the opening. Clean lines, ivory skin that felt like satin, well-turned ankles and slender thighs—he remembered those legs far too well for his own comfort. His interest heightened as the trousers she wore slid completely off and she curled her legs beneath her. Her tempting white bottom was as bare as the day she was born, cushioned by her feet.

Scowling, Trace flicked a glance toward the other men to see if they could see what he saw, but the bearers sat by their own campfire and the Peruvian soldiers were too far away, their blankets pulled over their heads for protection from the elements. The entertainment was for him alone, and his gaze shifted back to the lean-to.

What was she doing? Her bottom quivered as she shifted position atop her feet, half rising to her knees. He wished suddenly that he could see the rest of her, the firm ripe breasts of ivory and pink, a marvel of Creative ingenuity. It would take a saint to resist her, and Trace was not even close. His body ached, tightening to a point so uncomfortable that he had to adjust himself to accommodate the change.

There was a flushed heat in his groin, and his heart

sent blood slapping through his veins at an accelerated tempo. It hadn't been the first time he'd wanted her since he'd begun this cursed journey, but this was the strongest. The growing urge below his belt made even his throat ache with tension.

Yet he couldn't tear his eyes from her, could not make himself do the humane thing for his body's sake and get up and walk away. Bethany Brasfield had haunted his dreams for the past six months, and seeing her now—her slender, bare body so close—he could not deprive himself.

"God," Trace muttered through clenched teeth when she sat down on her blankets again, one leg drawn up beneath her. What the hell was she doing? Why didn't she put her clothes on, something on, *any*thing on, before he gave in to the frantic urges of his body? In spite of the cold night air and pressing dampness, he felt beads of sweat pop out on his forehead, and his mouth grew dry.

Trace tossed his cigar into the fire. His hands curled around a stick, and he tore his eyes from her to push it into the flames. When he looked back again, he groaned aloud.

Bethany was obviously washing herself. He could see the quick flash of a damp cloth as she dragged it over her legs and belly. There was an enticing glimpse of that sweet triangle between her creamy thighs, and that did it for him. He surged to his feet, his jaw tight, his teeth clamped together with determination. He had to get away from there.

But he'd gone no farther than three steps away from camp when a high-pitched scream rent the air. Whirling, he reached her lean-to in two leaps.

Bethany met him, her eyes wild, her long hair sliding around her bare shoulders and her nightgown clutched in front of her.

"S-s-nake!" she shrilled, pointing a finger and jabbering hysterically. "S-s-snake!"

Flipping back the canvas cover of her tiny shelter, Trace peered inside, one hand automatically going to the knife he carried on his belt. It took a moment for his eyes to adjust to the dim light provided by the campfire behind him, then he saw it. A long, coiling body as thick as a man's arm rippled in sinuous movements over Bethany's blankets, curving curiously around her small washbowl, burrowing under the trousers she'd discarded.

Anaconda. They looked more dangerous than they were, though only to man. The huge serpents could crush the life from a bird or small animal in minutes, then devour it with jaws that opened wide on tiny ligament hinges to swallow its prey whole. All in all, a very tidy way of eating, Trace thought, but he knew Bethany wouldn't understand any of that. Besides, she was still hopping about like a frenzied toad, the ridiculous flannel nightgown wrapped around her pale body without much success at hiding her attributes from prying eyes.

He scowled. No point in letting every man there see her like that.

"Shut up and put your clothes on!" he rasped, realizing that his body had not yet gotten the message that his brain had been trying to send it. "And do it quick!"

Shuddering and gasping, Bethany complied, sliding the gown over her head and twisting it around her slender hips. "Aren't you going to kill it?" she demanded breathlessly, staring at Trace as he studied the snake. "It tried to eat me!"

"It was trying to get warm, is my guess," Trace muttered. "I wonder what it's doing out on a bad night like this. I thought anacondas had better instincts."

Bethany glared at him. "Are you personally attached to that snake? Is he a pet of yours? Or a relative?"

Flashing her an amused glance, Trace shook his head. "No, not really."

"Then kill it!"

"Bloodthirsty little wench, aren't you?"

Her teeth were chattering, and Trace saw that she was truly terrified. He couldn't blame her. Anacondas did look dangerous, even if they weren't venomous.

"Here," he said in a conciliatory tone, "I'll take it away. It's only a little one."

"Little one! That slimy, slithery creature is at least eight feet long!"

"Maybe four. Some grow longer than thirty feet, you know," Trace said. "And it's not slimy. Kinda cool and dry to the touch, actually. Care to feel?"

She froze him with a glacial stare. "I do not."

"Guess I'll drag him out, then."

"An excellent notion, Mr. Taylor."

Bending, he pulled out the elegantly looping snake, grimacing when it immediately coiled around his arm. A thin tongue flicked out in lightning thrusts of warning, and he gripped it just behind the swaying head. He turned from the lean-to, and saw the Peruvian soldiers watching.

"Go back to sleep," he said in Spanish, not caring what they thought. "It's only a little grass snake."

One of the men laughed, and they went back to their blankets with barely a glance at Bethany. Apparently, Trace thought with a rush of gratitude, they had not seen Bethany prancing around in the altogether. He was glad. He didn't know if he felt like dealing with sexually excited soldiers when he still had his own urges to bring under control.

When Trace had disposed of the snake—which took some doing, as the creature kept wrapping its long body around him while he tried to walk, then hindered his efforts to pry it from his arms—he returned to the camp. Bethany still stood outside the canvas shelter, her lips almost blue with cold.

"What are you doing out here?"

"I'm not going back in there until you see if there's another snake in my blankets."

"Oh, for the love of—!"

Her violet gaze flashed mutinous sparks. "It might have a wife."

He grinned. "As amorous as that one was, it probably *was* the wife."

"Meaning?" she snapped.

"That it took me three tries to pry it loose."

"Did you kill it?"

He shook his head. "No need. I dropped it down a gully, and it'll find a warm hole to curl up in."

Teeth chattering, she muttered, "Great. Now I get to wait up all night to see if it prefers my soft blankets to a cold dirt hole."

"It won't. It's a lot quieter in the hole." He stepped forward to flip back the flap to her shelter, then knelt inside to investigate. "Empty as a preacher's purse," he announced cheerfully, and Bethany muttered something he couldn't quite hear. He bent her an inquiring gaze. "What was that?"

"I *said,* you and that snake have a lot in common."

"You're right," he said after a moment, and when she ducked into the lean-to beside him and pulled a blanket around her shivering body, he added, "We both want to get into your blankets."

Bethany's heart lurched. Startled, she met his dark, fiery gaze and knew what he meant. Why had she ever thought she would be able to forget him? Forget his touch, or the husky timbre of his voice? It was obvious she hadn't. Just a casual comment made her pulses surge with heated force, and her throat constrict so tightly she couldn't even get out an indignant retort.

Taking advantage of her unusual silence, Trace took one of her cold hands between his and began to rub it briskly. Her flesh was cold. Her lips were still bluish, and there was a pinched look to her face that made his eyes narrow.

"Are you all right?" he asked, and she jerked her hand free of his.

"How dare you!"

"How dare I what?"

"Say . . . say that you wanted in my blankets!"

"I do." Trace watched her face flush. "And what's more, you want me there," he added as she sputtered angrily. "Don't deny it."

"I'd rather have the snake!"

"That can be easily arranged."

Outraged just as much by his calm assumption that she wanted him as the fact that it was true, Bethany spit out a string of oaths she'd heard him use. He listened with polite attention, then corrected her.

"No, that's 'you sorry sack of shit,' not 'you sack of sorry . . ."

"Don't correct me!"

"Don't use the phrases if you can't use them right."

Her hand flashed out, but Trace had been half expecting it. He caught her arm easily, his swift, graceful motion carrying him forward, and he pinned her back to the ground with an economy of movements.

Tangled in her blankets and flannel nightgown, Bethany flopped uselessly. She could not pry her arm loose, or throw him from atop her. His heavy frame held her down.

She writhed and fought for several minutes, kicking her legs and hitting at him until she happened to glance up and see his calmly waiting expression. He was not even winded, merely amused. Her struggles ceased.

"Get up, please," she said when she could speak without gasping for breath. "You're very heavy."

"Not until you promise you won't get violent again."

"Oh, I promise," she said sweetly, and Trace laughed.

"I don't think I believe you."

She glared up at him. "You have more sympathy for a snake than you do me!"

"The snake was better tempered."

Trace's teasing amusement scraped a raw nerve in Bethany. How dare he behave as if nothing had happened? As if her father were still alive, and he had not left him behind to die? How dare he assume that she would just fall into his arms again simply because he finally said he wanted her? It was incomprehensible! It was reprehensible! It was devastating.

Before she stopped to think, Bethany flung out the worst insults she could think of using. "Bastard! Nameless outlaw! Son of an outlaw! *Murderer!*"

Trace's smile vanished. Sparks of fury ignited in his eyes, and his mouth thinned harshly. His soft drawl grew low and rough, sounding to Bethany like a panther's growl.

"I should have known better than to tell you anything. Women have never been known to fight fair, but I thought you were different."

It welled in her throat to say that she *was* different, that she hadn't meant to cruelly use what he'd once confided to her, but she had no chance.

Roughly, before she could speak, Trace's head lowered and his mouth burned across her parted lips, savagely, bruising her with his fierce kiss, dragging a moan from deep in her throat. His callused hands captured hers when she tried to push him away, pulling them over her head, his mouth still moving on hers with a determined ferocity that frightened her.

It was the first time Trace had ever frightened her to the point of mindless fear, of a raging desire to escape him. She wanted to call out for help, to scream for one of the bearers or soldiers, but she couldn't. His mouth smothered any sound she made, and he held her wrists in a steely grip that felt as if it was crushing her bones.

Bethany wanted to beg forgiveness, wanted to tell him she was sorry, but he forced her lips farther apart with his tongue, plundering her soft mouth with a demanding insistence that made her head swim. She couldn't breathe, couldn't think.

Transferring both her wrists to one hand, Trace raked his other palm down over her quivering body to the hem of her flannel gown. He shoved his hand up beneath the soft material, skimming her lush flesh, pausing to tease the velvet hollows and flat planes with his fingertips. His clever hands left a stinging trail of fire over her thighs as he pushed mercilessly upward, finding and plundering the rich tapestry of her shuddering body.

Bethany writhed helplessly. His mouth didn't leave her lips, but ravaged them until she was almost sobbing. Faint, muffled noises reached her ears, and she realized dimly that it was coming from her. Trace was relentless, and when he finally lifted his mouth from her bruised lips, it was only to sear a flaming path along the arched line of her throat.

Effortlessly sliding her gown up and off her body, keeping her still between the vise of his knees, Trace tossed it aside. He was consumed with need, consumed with a fierce hurt that could only be assuaged by proving to her that she wanted him as much as he did her. He had no intention of taking Bethany against her will. Oh no, she would plead with him for an end to the aching need inside her before he would satisfy either of them.

Still holding her wrists in one hand, Trace deliberately coaxed her taut pink nipples into rigid peaks. He rolled first one, then the other between his thumb and finger, then lowered his head to take it into his mouth, his teeth nibbling gently until she began to pant in soft, tortured little gasps for air. Her slender hips arched against him, and her legs tried to push him away.

"Please! Oh, Trace, please don't!"

Ignoring her, he continued until she was writhing in urgent thrusts, then he turned his attention to the wildly throbbing pulse in the hollow of her throat, lavishing kisses on her soft skin until he felt her tremble.

Bethany felt as if she were on fire. She couldn't think. Her body was betraying her, she knew that, but she almost welcomed it. Anything had to be better than the aching emptiness she'd lived with for the past six months, even this humiliating defeat. At least now she felt a pain of sorts, an agonizing screaming of her senses that was better than the dull absence of response.

But in spite of her body's treacherous yielding, she would not give in without a struggle. She still had her self-respect, her dignity, and she couldn't let Trace just ignore that. He had to respect her, had to see that she was more than just a warm, willing body. No, she wouldn't make it easy for him, though the outcome was inevitable.

Trace felt the surge of determination gathering in her tensed muscles, felt the renewed resistance. Shifting his lean body to throw one leg over her thighs, he lay to the side, his hands insultingly slow and encroaching as they touched her anywhere he chose.

Pride would not allow Bethany to plead with him again, and she kept her lips clamped shut. That seemed to challenge Trace, and he bent his head again, trying to force her mouth open with his tongue. When she kept it closed, he cradled her chin with one hand, his fingers wedging between her jaws to pry open her lips. Bethany took immediate advantage, feeling a fierce joy in being able to fight back. Her small white teeth clamped down on his thumb and held on as tightly as a terrier.

Swearing, Trace tried to pull it loose. It wouldn't budge, and he could feel her teeth dig in deeper. Tempted to swat her on the side of the face to startle her into letting go, he changed his mind. There was no point in degenerating into a man who struck women, though if there was ever one who deserved it, in his opinion, it was this one small termagent.

Finally, still swearing, he had to release her wrists to use his other hand to force open her jaws. He just barely escaped having his other thumb gnawed when she seized on fresh prey, and jerked it back just in time. Then Bethany took advantage of her free arms and began to yank at his hair, grabbing huge handfuls and tugging hard.

It took him several tries to capture her flailing arms again and successfully pin them over her head, and he was breathing hard and fast when he did. Surprisingly, all the arduous activity had not lessened his desire for her in the slightest. If anything, he was even more aroused by her determined struggles, the heaving of her soft body against him.

His heavy-lidded eyes lifted to hers, and Bethany grew very still. She saw in those dark pupils the banked fires that meant an end to his scorching seduction. Now, when he covered her lips with his mouth, she did not fight him. It would be useless.

The flaming search of his tongue lured a trembling response from her, and she closed her eyes. He kissed her until she moaned softly, low, in the back of her throat, and then his mouth left her aching lips to move lower. He slid his body down, pausing to circle the taut peaks of each breast with a flicking tongue, moving from one to the other until she moved restlessly beneath him.

Bethany didn't know quite when he released her wrists; she only dimly knew when he unbuttoned his pants and pulled off his shirt. Then he was as bare as she was, lying back over her shivering body, covering it with his lean, taut frame, warming her chilled flesh. Her arms curled around him, her fingers tangling in the thick, dark hair that grew down his nape to brush his shoulders. She could feel the hard insistence of him against her belly, feel the proud length of him nudging against her.

Stubbornly holding to the last shred of her pride, she would not reply when he growled, "Say it, Bethany—say you want me."

Her reply, her assent, was wordless. But no words

could have been as sweet as the opening of her body for him, the hot, satiny press of her thighs as they pulled him close into her embrace, the welcoming warmth of her steamy woman's body around his. And Trace accepted it; he knew she wanted him as badly as he wanted her.

Drawing in a deep, shuddering breath, he moved inside her with a sweet, fierce tempo that took them both to the heights of ecstasy, kept them floating on rolling waves of release that seemed to go on forever. It was a mind-shattering surrender to the inevitable, and almost humbling.

Chapter Twenty-four

Bethany woke first. She saw the pale gray glimmer of dawn beneath the lowered flap of the lean-to, and recalled with ruthless shame her capitulation. Yet, she could not find it in herself to be sorry.

Her head rolled slightly to one side to look at Trace, and she saw that his eyes were open. He stared at her for a long moment, not saying anything, his dark gaze drifting warily over her watchful face.

Outside the close warmth of the lean-to, men stirred, clanging tin coffeepots, voices a muted murmur. Trace's brow arched as he looked at Bethany, and she knew what he meant:

"They'll know that you . . . you stayed in here with me last night," she whispered, and he nodded.

"Yeah. Does it bother you?"

"A little," she admitted honestly. "Not that I care if they *know,* as much as I do that they'll say something."

Stretching lazily, his taut body reminding her of a lithe cat, Trace said, "None of them look that stupid."

Bethany suddenly remembered Brody, and the expression on his face when he'd made a comment and

Trace had put the tip of his knife against the man's throat. Her throat grew tight, and she wondered about the savage reactions simmering just beneath Trace's deceptively calm surface. He could be cat-quick in his responses, frightening her at times.

Even more frightening were her responses to his touch, to the stirring sensuality he summoned with just the brush of his hand over her body, or the caress of his lips against her too-willing mouth. She should be writhing with shame at this moment, thinking of ways to decapitate him or worse for forcing her body to yield, yet she wasn't. It was puzzling.

Trace Taylor had been inadvertently responsible for the death of her father. He'd coldly left Horatio Brasfield in a ravine to die, then expected her to be grateful when he'd gone back to retrieve the body. Those pain-hazed days came back to her with aching clarity now and then, and she would try to chase the memories away. Nothing had helped then, not Trace's silent acceptance of her curses, nor even Spencer Bentworth's insistence that everything possible had been done. It didn't matter. Horatio Brasfield was dead, and she'd never told him she was sorry for saying hateful things to him about how he'd ignored her.

Their last argument still haunted her. She wished that she'd been able to tell her father again that she loved him and that it didn't really matter how he'd ignored her all those years, but, of course, that was impossible. She carried the guilt with her, wrapped tidily in her determination to see him honored for his work.

And now she had compromised that determination by giving in to her body's aching need for Trace.

"Having second thoughts?" Trace asked softly, jerking her head around to stare at him with wide violet eyes.

"How did you know?"

"It's written all over you as clear as if someone took a paintbrush and wrote in big red letters—G-U-I-L-T-Y."

"Guilty?"

"Yeah." He shot her a narrowed glance. "Guilty of being human, I guess. You seem to prefer thinking you're not."

Stiffening, she curled her fingers into the blanket rubbing roughly against her bare body and snapped, "I am well aware of my human weaknesses, Trace Taylor! Lying here with you is an excellent indication of it!"

"Weakness? I thought maybe you were going to be smart enough to admit to emotion. My mistake."

"Not yours alone, apparently." She blinked back the unexpected sting of tears from her eyes. "I should have shot you before giving in last night."

Rubbing his chewed thumb, Trace muttered, "I didn't know you'd *given in.* I had the feeling you fought to the bitter end, princess, to spare yourself the scourging you seem so eager to suffer."

"You know what I mean." Her voice broke on the last word, and his glance was surprisingly tender.

"Ah, sweetheart, I think I know it far better than you do. I just wish you'd stop torturing yourself for something that wasn't your fault, wasn't my fault, wasn't anyone's fault. Sometimes, we just have no control over the way things turn out. Your father understood that."

Blinking rapidly to hold back the tears that threatened to spill onto her cheeks, Bethany whispered around the lump in her throat, "We had an argument not long before . . . before he died. I never told him I was sorry."

Trace was quiet for a moment, then said, "I didn't know. Now I understand why you feel so torn up with guilt." He reached out to skim a finger over her cheek, smearing her tears. "Somehow, I don't think your father held any grudges, princess. He wasn't that kind of man. He may not have been a very attentive father, but he certainly loved you. Only a fool would be too blind to see that."

Lifting teary lashes, Bethany stared at him with softly quivering lips that slowly stretched into a tremulous smile. "You're right, Trace. Why didn't I think of that?"

"Because you don't seem to have been thinking too clearly for the past few months. That's only natural."

The tension that had been with her for six months began to ease, and when Bethany recalled how her father had not mentioned their quarrel, nor been accusing, she knew that Trace was right. She'd been blaming herself for something her father had not concerned himself with, and in the process, had forced herself to stop feeling. If not for Trace and his determination to force her to feel something, even if it was hatred, she may have fumbled her way in her vacuum of emotion for years. She owed him more than he probably realized. Or that she was willing to admit yet.

"You're pretty special, Trace Taylor," she compromised by saying, and he shot her a wary glance.

"How do you mean that?"

Laughing at his suspicious gaze, she snuggled close to him beneath the rough blankets. One hand reached out to skim the taut angles and planes of his hard man's body, not erotically, but with genuine appreciation. Being male, however, his body didn't differentiate between appreciation and invitation, and responded immediately.

"I hope you know what you're doing," Trace growled. He caught her hand in his. "We may never leave this tent."

"Sounds good to me." Her tongue flicked out to wet the whorls of his ear beneath thick strands of his dark hair, and she felt him stiffen.

Lacing his fingers in the cup of her palms, twining them through hers and pulling her arms over her head, Trace rolled to lever his body over her accepting curves. He gazed down at her, faintly disbelieving, not quite certain of her. It was only when she arched into him with suggestive thrusts of her hips that he bent his head to kiss her.

Maybe, Bethany thought hazily as he took her with a fierce, sweet urgency that made her shudder, *everything will be all right, after all. . . .*

The rope ladder still dangled from the high cliff. It swayed with the wind, and Bethany winced from the memory of her father's fall. She had not had the nerve to glance into the ravine where Horatio Brasfield had died, but facing the rope ladder was inescapable.

Hunkered down on his heels and gazing narrowly up at the cliff, Trace gauged the reliability of the ladder. It was frayed in places. And it looked as if there had been another earthquake since he'd last been here. Loose rocks skittered underfoot, and boulders poised dangerously atop high crests.

He flicked a glance toward Bethany. She sat in stiff, pale silence, trying not to react. He smothered a curse. It had been difficult traversing the ravine. The former bridge was gone, but he'd known it would be. He'd been the one to send it careening into the gully to stop their pursuers.

Someone, however, had put up another. It didn't look as primitive as the first one, in fact, it looked as if someone had taken a great deal of care to build a sturdy replacement. Stone bollards held stout cables of *coya,* and the footing had been solid. Trace couldn't help but wonder who had gone to so much trouble, and why.

Bentworth, maybe? Possible. He'd said he'd tried to find Vilcapampa again, but had been unsuccessful. Of course he'd also tried to coax Trace into going back, but that had been useless. Until Bethany had returned. Trace gave a mental shrug. Hell, he should have known he'd never be able to refuse her anything when she turned her wide violet gaze on him, especially when it'd been obvious she thought he and Rosa were lovers. He'd almost enjoyed the flash of pain in her eyes; sort of a recompense for the months of aching need for her after she'd gone back to California.

Now here he was, squatting on the rock-strewn ground in the Andes again, endangering his life just to make her happy. He had to be crazy. It was a fool's errand, anyway. Bentworth would take the credit for finding the city in the end. He just wanted someone to do the dangerous part for him.

A slight frown knit his brows. He wondered who had taken Brasfield's packet of notes, and the bulky pack laden with gold and silver artifacts. He'd tossed them to Brasfield before being forced to abandon him for a while, and when he'd gone back to attempt rescuing him, they were gone. Brasfield was dead by then, a bullet hole in the middle of his forehead. It had been a blessing of sorts, Trace had decided, to die quickly instead of lingering. At the angle where the professor had lain on the ledge, it had probably been a ricocheting bullet.

The irony of being held responsible for the ambush had not escape Trace. Bethany blamed him for her father's death in much the same way as he blamed Brody and Reagan for Rick Scanlon's death years before. Somehow, it gave him a better understanding of both sides of the issue.

But none of that mattered now. What mattered now was figuring out if it was safe enough to climb up the rock face, or if it was too risky for Bethany.

Rubbing his jaw with one hand, Trace estimated the time it would take to fashion a new rope ladder, and decided against it. It was about to start raining again, and he didn't want to be caught up on a high crest when the wind started blowing hard.

Rising to his feet in an easy motion, Trace caught hold of the bottom rung of the rope ladder and gave it a yank. It held. He put one foot on the rope and climbed hand over hand up the side of the cliff. It was maybe twenty-five feet high, not that steep, but not anything a man would want to try to jump, either.

When he reached the top, he turned and motioned for the others to follow. He remained crouched down by the ladder, making certain it remained secured to the huge boulders tethering it, watching as Bethany shouldered her pack and began to climb. She came up more slowly than Trace, but did not falter.

Behind her came the two Quechua bearers, then the three soldiers. They were outfitted light this time. Trace had no intentions of lingering in the ruins any longer than it took to satisfy Bethany. One of the bearers carried the bulky camera, a smaller, more portable version of the last camera they'd brought. The photographs may not be the best quality, but they'd serve to prove that they'd been there.

Catching Bethany's arm as she reached the top, Trace hauled her over and onto the patch of level ground. She looked at him mutely, but her mouth was thinned into a line of satisfaction that made him smile.

"Not bad, princess. Now step back so I can help the others up."

When they pushed on, climbing the steep precipices with toes and fingernails, Trace swearing as he tried to find the original trail that had been covered by a landslide, it began to rain. Torrents fell on them, almost blinding them. It filled eyes, nose, and mouth, until scarves had to be brought up to cover noses and lips. Breathing was difficult but they dared not linger on the steep slope for fear of a landslide or mudslide. That would be fatal. Rocks, mud, and trees would come slushing down the slope with all the force of a freight train, carrying away anything—or anyone—in the way.

After several false starts, Trace discovered the faintest suggestion of a path. It looked to have been little used in quite some time, maybe even since the Incas. Haphazard stones dotted it erratically, indicating that at one time, at least, it had been some sort of road. It wound through the jungle, and the heat and humidity was oppressive in the extreme. It had stopped raining, and steam rose from their clothes now.

Dense tropical jungle teemed with murmurs of wildlife, and Bethany kept as close to Trace as possible. She didn't recall any of this, and when she said so to Trace, he slid her an amused glance.

"We didn't come this way. The other way's blocked by an avalanche. Probably from an earthquake."

"Oh." She swatted irritably at a thick cloud of

buzzing insects droning doggedly just in front of her face. "I don't like this. Are you certain this is the right way?"

"Don't worry, princess, I think we're headed in the right direction. And if nothing else, I can at least get us back down the mountain."

She accepted his reply with a nod. She had few qualms about his ability to keep her safe, in spite of the ominous roars and shrill screeches that surrounded them as they trudged through overhanging trees that allowed in only erratic rays of sunlight.

Gigantic tree ferns sprouted along the path, festooned with orchids on trunks and the spreading branches. Bamboo thrust spindly leaves upward, and tiny clusters of raindrops clung from the tips of leaves. A ray of sun shot a finger of gauzy light down to make the rain drops glow like pearls, some of them sparkling like diamonds along the stems.

"What's that?" Bethany gasped out when a nearby screech rent the air. Her fingers clutched tightly at Trace's arm.

"Sounds like a howler monkey. They're noisy little devils, and thieves to boot. They must not appreciate our being here." He kept his machete out and ready, hacking at foliage, expecting snakes. Brief glimpses of gaudy-feathered parrots decorated the trees, some beating the air with their wings as the intruders passed beneath their lofty perches.

The recent rain made the jungle glisten, and drops still plunked down to spatter on them as they trudged through the thick brush. Another screech erupted in the quiet, and Bethany swallowed a scream. Trace put out an arm to stop her.

"Look. Up there. See?"

Half expecting to find a huge snake ready to drop

down and crush the life from her, Bethany levied a fearful gaze upward. Her eyes widened. Large birds with scarlet, blue, and yellow feathers gazed serenely back at her. "Trace! They're beautiful! What are they?"

"Scarlet macaws. Damn loud birds, if you ask me. Not nearly as entertaining as a parrot."

Bethany had some experience with parrots. She'd found them to be singularly ill-tempered and prone to shouting vulgar remarks. But she didn't intend to tell Trace that, so she just nodded. The trek through the dense jungle with Trace turned out to be informative. He showed her things she hadn't known existed, pointing out exotic animals such as sloths, kinkajous, and even a newly hatched butterfly with a distinctive 88 marking on its back. She was quite content to see only the less dangerous of creatures, though Trace told her he could find her more lethal ones if she liked.

"I appreciate your thoughtfulness, but no thank you!" she said with a shudder, and he laughed.

"There's something for you to sketch, princess," he said a few minutes later, and pointed to a tiny harmless-looking frog perched in the thin cup of a delicate, apricot-colored mushroom.

"Oh! What a beautiful creature," she breathed softly, and stepped forward as if she was going to pick it up.

"I wouldn't do that," Trace said, putting out a hand to stop her. "That's a poison-arrow frog."

"A what?"

He grinned. "Poison-arrow frog. Indians coat their blow darts and spear points with a secretion from them."

Bethany looked at it uncertainly. The frog looked

back at her with solemn innocence, unblinking, its large dark eyes seeming to radiate friendliness. A brilliant scarlet back made it look as if someone had brushed it with a thick coat of paint, leaving legs and belly a deep green.

"Oh," she said after a moment, not quite certain she should believe him. "Somehow, I thought they would look more . . . ugly."

"Danger doesn't necessarily advertise with warts and whistles," Trace said dryly. "Sometimes it's the prettiest flowers that have the deadliest poison."

By the time they stepped out of the dense jungle and approached a riverbank, Bethany thought she had never seen so many varieties of animals. Trace seemed to know where to look for them, and could point out a well-camouflaged bird where she saw only leafy ferns or palm branches.

"Here's where we cross," Trace said, dragging her attention to the spindly bridge spanning a froth of rapids. He eyed her quickly when she stifled a gasp, then glanced at the Peruvian soldiers. None of them looked happy. He couldn't blame them.

This bridge—if it could be dignified with such a title—was the worst yet. It was actually some roughly hewn logs slammed over the yawning gaps between crusty boulders jutting up out of the foaming whirl of water. Rotting vines laced them together so casually, that huge empty spaces entertained spewing geysers of river.

And to make it worse, the raging waters of the river churned only a few feet below the bridge. A fine mist coated the slender logs that were slick and covered with moss. Anyone losing their balance would plunge to their death in the icy rapids.

"Who goes first?" Trace asked, sliding his glance

from the soldiers to the Quechua bearers. Shrugging, one of the Indians slipped off his sandals and stepped out onto the precarious span, inching his way across by gripping with his toes. The other followed suit, and Trace began to yank off his boots.

Fortunately, they all made it across without mishap, though Bethany was terrified that at any moment she would slip and never be seen again. She looked back at the logs and wondered how long they would be there. The rapids were growing higher and higher, threatening to sweep them away. One more good rain would do it.

More jungle waited on the opposite riverbank, but in a few minutes they reached the bottom slope of a mountain that wasn't too littered with loose rock. Grumbling and muttering oaths, the soldiers followed as Trace led the way up, climbing several thousand feet. The stolid, quiet Indian bearers brought up the rear.

On her hands and knees, digging into the loose soil and hard rock as best she could, Bethany could barely breathe for the heat and humidity. It pressed down heavily as she crawled up the face of the steep slope with grim determination. How could anyone have ever lived in the ruins, she couldn't help wondering, or built them? It seemed impossible, yet she had seen them with her own eyes.

When they reached a flat, grassy area and Trace called a halt, Bethany flopped down on the ground under a shady overhang with relief. She decided that she was never going to move again, and when Trace knelt beside her, told him so. His dark brow lifted slightly.

"You probably don't remember, especially as we got here a different way, but it's not that much farther," he said with a slight smile. Sweat beaded his forehead, and his shirt stuck damply to his broad back. There had been an anxious time earlier when he wasn't certain he was going in the right direction, and he'd been relieved to recognize this small, grassy area below the ruins.

Bethany opened a disbelieving eye and stared at him. "I don't believe you," she said flatly. "We have to be at the top of the world by now. We can't go any farther."

Lowering his tired, aching body to the ground beside her, Trace said softly, "Giving up?"

Her chin tilted stubbornly. "Not for long. Just for a week or two."

He laughed, softly, then said, "Look, princess, I'm going to scout out the trail ahead and make certain it's not covered with rocks like the last one was. You wait here and rest."

"Agreed." Her eyes drifted shut again, and she vaguely heard him tell her the others were staying to keep an eye on her. Exhausted, she slipped into a light doze.

When she woke, she saw that the soldiers were lying in another square of shade not far away, and the Quechua bearers were squatting close by, alert and watchful.

"It's a good thing for the soldiers that the Indians aren't as lazy as they are," she muttered as she sat up. Her mouth was dry, and her throat ached with the scratchy roughness of thirst. She lifted her water pouch and drank from it, grimacing at the hot, musty taste of the water. It was quiet, with the sun beating down and nothing stirring.

Bethany eyed the fringe of jungle just beyond, and gave a slight sigh. She had to attend her private needs, and knew she couldn't wait on Trace to return. Awkwardly, she approached the Quechua bearers. Neither of them spoke any English at all, and her Spanish was apparently not the same rough dialect they spoke. Still, she did her best to make herself understood, and when they bobbed their heads, she gave them a satisfied smile. They smiled back uncertainly.

Remembering the time she'd gotten lost, Bethany had no intentions of wandering far into the jungle anyway. Just far enough for some privacy would do.

When she had gone only a few yards into the jungle, she chose a private area to relieve herself and did so quickly. It wouldn't do to irritate Trace by not being there when he returned. Matters were going too well between them. There had been an absence of the friction that had existed since her return to Peru, and she had no desire to cause any more.

As she was leaving the fringe of jungle, Bethany heard the soft, musical patter of water. Curious, she slid her scarf from around her neck and tied it to a bush to mark her way, then cautiously sought the source of the water.

Only a few yards from where her scarf hung, a waterfall cascaded from high above, forming a small pool in the rocks below, the water crystal clear and cool and inviting. Bethany was enchanted. Where had it come from? And here it was, hidden in the jungle away from admiring eyes, a source of fresh cold water that would taste much better than the hot, stale water in her pouch.

She bent and drank deeply, then splashed her face and throat with it, recalling with a smile the last time she had done so and Trace's leering remarks at her wet blouse. Well, it should dry quickly enough once she stepped back out into the searing heat. And he need never know.

Bethany found her scarf and untied it, looping it back around her neck. She felt quite proud of herself for having accomplished the small feat of securing privacy and a fresh drink of water, and was tempted to point out the pool to the Quechua bearers before she recalled her tortured attempts at communication earlier. No, best to let them find their own water, she decided as she curled up beneath the rocky overhang again. She'd be content to wait on Trace to return.

By the time Trace returned, Bethany was doubled over with nausea. She was chilled and shaking, her teeth chattering as if she was in the midst of a blizzard while the sun beat down with a vengeance.

"Dammit!" Trace growled roughly to cover his anxiety. "What did you do? Eat? Drink?"

"Nothing!" she gasped out, writhing, barely aware of the interested faces of the Indian bearers. One of them said something to Trace in his own language, and Trace turned back to her.

"You went into the jungle. Did anything sting you? A small caterpillar, maybe?" He pushed up the sleeves of her shirt and scanned her arms, but there was nothing to see.

Bethany was finding it difficult to focus on Trace. She could hear his voice, see his scowling face, but it seemed to recede with the waves of pain racking her.

"No," she murmured, "nothing stung me."

"Did you eat anything? Pick up a frog, maybe? Anything like that?"

Her head rolled back and forth on the grass, and shock waves of thudding reaction reverberated in her skull. "No, nothing to eat. Picked up . . . nothing."

"Dammit, Bethany, you had to do something to cause this!" His hands curled tightly around her wrists, and he could feel the escalating of her pulse. "Did you drink anything? Water?"

"Water," she moaned, remembering her cool drink at the cascading falls, "only a little water. . . ."

Trace strung together some ripe oaths, none of them complimentary to her, and began rapping out orders in their native language to the Quechua bearers. Within a few minutes, he had some hot water simmering, and a healthy amount of brandy poured into a hot cup.

"Drink this," he ordered, holding her head up on his arm. "All of it. It should help."

Shivering uncontrollably, Bethany spilled more than she got down, and Trace patiently poured more between her chattering lips. He poured, mopped up the mess, and poured more, until he was satisfied that she had swallowed enough to do her some good.

By the time the Quechuas were able to get some hot soup made, Bethany was vomiting. She was too dizzy to stand, and he had to carry her to a private clump of bushes when diarrhea struck. Moaning in embarrassment and acute distress, Bethany was forced to submit to Trace's gentle—if growling—ministrations. He nursed her as tenderly as any mother would have done, wrapping blankets around her to warm her when the chills became unbearable, then holding her head over a basin when the nausea overtook her.

Ranging between extreme pain from her cramping body, and regret that she was causing Trace so much trouble, Bethany alternated bitter self-recriminations with cries of pain. It was enough to try the patience of a saint, which Trace was not. But still, he would not leave her side even at the worst of the illness, and kept her as clean as he could considering the unrefined nature of her illness.

When she finally drifted into an uneasy sleep, aided by a brew of coca leaves and hot tea, Trace rested his head on the arms he lay across his drawn-up knees. It was almost dark. They'd have to stay here. Bethany couldn't be moved, not yet, anyway. Mountain sickness took a couple of days to run its course, usually. If the patient did not become dehydrated, there was normally no lasting aftereffects. But up here in the mountains, he had no medicine to keep her from becoming dehydrated, and her body was throwing off fluids more quickly than he could get them down her.

He built a fire near her and lay down on his blankets with a grunt of disgust. She never listened to him. Hadn't he told her before not to drink cold water at this high altitude? And she'd thought he was just making up something to irritate her. A grim smile slanted his mouth. At least now she wouldn't doubt his advice anymore. Maybe.

In the morning, he would go into the jungle and look for the tree whose bark he'd use to make into a foul-tasting brew that would ease her diarrhea. *Garcinia punctata* was the botanical name, and its shavings should work in a matter of hours. But until then, he had to wait through the night and hope for the best.

Rolling up into his blankets, Trace fell asleep. He didn't wake until he heard Bethany moaning and thrashing about in her blankets, and he got up quickly.

"It's all right, princess," he muttered raspily. "I'm here."

"Trace?"

"I'm right here, sweetheart." He leaned over to touch her on the cheek with one hand, poking at the fire with the other to make it blaze up. The light flickered over her, and he could see that her clothes and blankets were damp. He stuck the tin cup over the flames and poured in a liberal amount of brandy, then turned back to tuck some dry blankets around her shivering body. In spite of the sweat oozing from her pores, she was still cold, and her skin was clammy to the touch. His brows knit in helpless frustration as he held her hand.

Lifting her lashes with difficulty, Bethany looked up to see Trace scowling down at her. A sob caught in the back of her throat. He was angry with her. And she was dying. She knew she was dying. She was afraid of *not* dying. If death did not release her from this undignified purging of her body, from the racking cramps that made her muscles ache, she would go mad. Yet she didn't really want to die. She wanted Trace not to be angry with her, not to scowl so fiercely at her.

"Trace? Trace, I'm sorry I didn't listen," she managed to force out between chattering lips. "Do you hate me?"

"Not yet. But the night's not over. Rest. Don't try to talk. You'll need your strength."

"But . . ." A long shudder tore through her, and her muscles felt as if they'd shredded from the effort. "But I have to tell you something before . . . before I die."

A faint smile twitched his lips, but Trace knew that she wouldn't understand if he laughed. Gravely, he asked, "What dark confession do you have to make?"

Winged lashes drifted shut, then opened with an effort, and her shadowed violet eyes fastened on his face. "I love you."

There. It was out. She'd told him she loved him, and now it didn't really matter if he loved her back or not. She was going to die. She'd never know.

Her hand fluttered helplessly toward him and he caught it. He held it between his broad, callused palms, staring down at her with a ragged mixture of emotions that threatened to tear him apart.

And then, unbidden, came the thought that she would probably be embarrassed when she recovered from her illness and discovered that she'd confessed love for him. A wave of amused tenderness made him turn her small-boned hand over in his and gently, lovingly, kiss each slender finger.

"That's quite a confession," he said when it was obvious she expected some sort of reply. "Are you sure?"

She nodded, then winced at the pain that action wrought in her head. "Quite sure."

Not quite knowing what to say back to her, Trace bent and kissed the tip of her straight little nose. "I think your tea is ready," he said awkwardly, and she sighed and closed her eyes. He suddenly felt irritated. What was he supposed to say back? That he loved her? Hell, he wasn't sure he did. He *was* sure he wanted her, that he wanted her badly enough to risk his life for her on a stupid mission of recognition for a dead man he hadn't particularly liked, but he wasn't certain that qualified as love.

Love had always been an elusive emotion, a word used too often in novels and casual conversation. He'd heard a lot of definitions, but had yet to find one that suited him. When he did, he'd use it. Until then, he intended to do as he'd always done—avoid the word like the plague.

By the time Bethany's tea was ready, she'd slipped back into an uneasy sleep. Trace decided not to wake her. Rest was just as important as the fluids, and he could give her a double dose when she woke again.

He sat cross-legged on his blankets, his eyes heavy

with the need to sleep, but his mind was too active to allow it. Dammit, why had she had to use that word? Things had been fine without it. Now they'd be complicated. Now she would expect him to return her offering; once it had been said aloud, there was no going back.

Softly muttering an oath, Trace hoped she wouldn't remember saying it.

Chapter Twenty-five

It was the first day she felt like doing more than dying. Bethany squinted up at the sky surrounding her little overhang of rock, and tentatively tested her arms and legs by stretching them. So far, so good. No riveting pains that threatened to tear her in two.

The incapacitating symptoms of her illness had necessitated the removal of her shirt and trousers, and she wore her flannel nightgown. It was bunched up in an uncomfortable knot around her hips, and Bethany squirmed beneath the blankets in an effort to slide it back down around her legs. Whatever the foul-tasting stuff was that Trace had forced—literally—down her throat, it worked.

A faint sense of embarrassment enveloped her when she remembered struggling against him, insisting that he allow her to die in peace. Trace had grimly persisted in his efforts, and only his superior strength had succeeded. Logic had failed disastrously.

That vague feeling of embarrassment still lingered when he came to kneel beside her, his eyes briefly examining her face and noting her healthier color.

"I think I'm supposed to say thank you for saving my life," Bethany murmured, not quite able to meet his dark eyes, plucking nervously at her blankets with her fingers.

"All in the line of duty, ma'am," he drawled, his mouth kicking up in a smile when she avoided his gaze.

Clearing her throat, Bethany asked softly, "Would it be a dreadful inconvenience if I were to ask for a bath soon?"

Thunderstruck by the suggestion, Trace snapped, "Have you lost your mind? Do you want to go through something almost as bad as this again?"

"No, but I feel so dirty and unwashed. . . ." Her voice trailed into silence, and her fingers twiddled tiny balls of wool from the blanket. She could feel Trace's eyes on her, almost feel his frown, and when she dared a glance up at him, saw something in his eyes. What was it? Exasperation? Anger? It was gone as quickly as it had been, and his eyes were once more just speculative.

"I'll think of something," he said at last. "I know how you probably feel. Just give me a little while to come up with an idea."

She smiled. "I don't think I'm going to be running any races soon, anyway, so that sounds good to me."

Trace folded up one of his blankets and put it behind her back, propping her up against the granite wall of the overhang.

"At least you chose a fairly level spot to get sick," he said when he'd finished. "It would have been hell trying to take care of you on that slope back there."

"Wouldn't it? Wasn't I thoughtful?"

"Extremely." He took one of her hands in his, and fixed his gaze on her face. "Bethany, I want you to try very hard not to do anything like this again. You scared the Indians silly. They thought you were going to die."

"Weren't *you* scared I would?" she couldn't keep from asking.

"I knew you wouldn't take the easy way out. You're

too stubborn." His grip tightened on her hand. "As far as I'm concerned, this incident is forgotten, all right? Just don't try a repeat of it, and I'll never mention it again."

Bethany nodded, and was grateful that her head did not feel as if it was about to drop from her neck into her lap. She would never take good health for granted again, she decided when Trace gave her hand a final squeeze and said he'd be back, then left.

Watching as he strode across the grassy meadow toward the Quechua bearers, Bethany had the inescapable feeling that she'd forgotten something. It lingered just out of reach, a fragment of something that she'd thought important but that she couldn't recall now. Ah well, she'd think of it sooner or later. Now she wanted to concentrate on regaining her strength. There were still the ruins to see, to detail and photograph and record as much as possible.

True to his word, Trace managed to rig up a bath of sorts for Bethany, though it would never have passed inspection in civilization. The Quechua bearers had heated water laboriously, then hauled it in to Bethany in several pots. There was one for her feet, one for her torso, one for her face. And a blanket had been strung up from the rocky overhang for privacy. Not exactly the best, but it did nicely to get her clean.

They spent three days on the small plain, then started out again for the ruins. The soldiers had grown impatient, and Trace didn't intend to worry Bethany, but he'd almost had to shoot one of them when the man demanded they leave her behind. It had been an ugly scene, and if not for Trace's quickness with a gun and his accurate warning shot, the man might have drawn a rifle on him.

An uneasy truce existed as they climbed the final slope to the brooding ruins atop the mountain peak. Trace was aware that the soldiers had searched for it on their own, but had also known how easy it was to miss the telltale signs. Highland natives lived side by side with ruins for years, and because of the thick vegetation and encroaching jungle, never knew they were there. Stone terraces could be missed, and entire buildings sat shrouded in vines and bamboo for centuries.

As it was, he had to backtrack several times to find the right path—even after he'd already scouted for it—due to recent landslides. Rubble covered a lot of the ground, shifting underfoot, making it hazardous to climb at times. Trace kept a close eye on Bethany to ensure that she wasn't too weak to make it.

When they finally reached the stone terraces that she recalled, Bethany was breathless and had to sit down for a moment.

One of the soldiers eyed her closely. "If she's too weak to keep up," he said in Spanish to Trace, "perhaps she should be left behind."

Trace's voice was deceptively casual. "Oh, I don't think so." He turned to face the man, a swarthy, bearded fellow with a nasty scar on one side of his face. "She's the reason we're all here. If she stays behind—so do the rest of us."

In the face of his congenial refusal, the man obviously felt compelled to try again. "But señor, surely you agree that she is slowing us down."

This time, there was no mistaking the menace in his tone when Trace said, "Maybe you didn't understand—*you* may not make it to the ruins, but she'll be there. Is that clear enough for you?"

A bright red suffused his face, and the soldier nodded as he turned away. He went back to stand beside his compadrés, including the man Trace had drawn on, his face ugly.

Bethany had followed their conversation, and her eyes were anxious when she looked at Trace. "Should I fear for my life?"

"Not from them. I've been keeping an eye on them, and I'll go on keeping an eye on them."

"But you're only one man, and . . ."

Irritably, Trace broke in, "Look, do you have to keep reminding me of that every time there's trouble? Why do you think I'm so damn tired all the time? I have to sleep in five-minute shifts."

"I only meant . . ."

"I know what you meant. Sorry. I'm just touchy lately." He raked a hand through his hair and tugged his hat back on. "Ready?"

The ruins were almost as Bethany remembered them. Vines choked the walls, having grown back almost as quickly as they had been hacked away. There were few traces of their former expedition, but Bethany's throat clogged as she recalled her father's ecstatic glee at finding the ruins.

Remembering her father left her with renewed determination instead of sadness, and she walked across the baked stones of the plaza toward the Temple of the Sun. The smooth granite spear Trace had called the Hitching Post of the Sun cast a long shadow, and Bethany edged around the weeded walls of the temple, with her hands rubbing over the granite left centuries before by expert craftsmen.

Awe creased the faces of the soldiers, and it took them several minutes to force themselves forward from the center of the city. There was an air of abandonment instead of decay that pervaded the city; few buildings had crumbled with time. Only the swift-growing vegetation altered its appearance.

Trace joined Bethany in her search for the temple

door, and when they found it, he was forced to hack away the loops of thick vines once more covering it. It didn't take as long this time as last, and in a few minutes they ducked into the white-walled room.

As her eyes adjusted to the dim, hazy light, Bethany caught her breath. The room was completely empty.

"It doesn't make sense, Trace!" Bethany argued. "Where did it all go? And when? We took only a very small portion of that gold, and you know it!"

"Hey, easy, princess," Trace drawled. "I'm on your side, remember?"

Fuming, Bethany snapped, "I'm glad *some*one is!"

He grinned. "Look, calm down. I know you're upset about the missing artifacts, but not half as upset as those ugly soldiers out there. Did you see the one with the scar? I thought he was going to cry, he was so disappointed."

Bethany smiled in spite of the gnawing sense of failure she felt. "All right. And I guess all this doesn't really matter when it comes down to it. I mean, Spencer was the one truly counting on the gold, while the archaeological society wants to record everything else. At least that can still be done."

"But not by you."

"No," Bethany agreed with a faint smile, "not by me. It will take months of painstaking measuring and careful digging to uncover the secrets of this city. Why didn't I remember how large it was?"

Swinging his long body down from the shelf of granite where he'd been perched, Trace muttered, "It looks bigger without all that gold cluttering it up."

She smiled gleefully. "So! It bothers you, too, doesn't it?"

Grinning, he admitted, "Yeah, I guess it does. Makes

a man wonder just who found this place and removed all that gold."

"Not a trace of it, not so much as one tiny earplug," Bethany said with a sigh. She heard Trace's soft curse, and turned her gaze to him inquiringly. He'd stopped in the middle of his long-legged stride and whirled around to face her.

"That damned earplug!"

"What?"

"You know, that heavy chunk of gold the Incas used to wear in their earlobes. Remember, we found one below when we first got here with your father, and I said then that it was damned odd that it should just be lying out there like that."

"Yes, but . . ."

"Don't you see? Someone has been using this place to *store* priceless antiquities, Bethany! The Incas didn't leave behind mounds of treasure, those cups and statues and even gloves—they would have taken it with them. To them, the gold and silver was sacred—Sweat of the Sun and Tears of the Moon, they called it. No, someone has been using this place to hide stuff stolen from other ruins."

"Ridiculous," Bethany scoffed. "How would they get it here? Why, look how long it took and how much trouble we had getting here!"

"Obviously, someone knows a much more efficient route," Trace said dryly. His dark eyes glittered with excitement. "That would explain a lot of things, Bethany, like why I always had this feeling we were being watched, and why we were ambushed once we'd left here."

"But if someone wanted to kill us, wouldn't they have come in here and done it while we were camped here?"

"Maybe. And maybe not. Maybe they didn't think we could find this city in the first place. Remember, I had a lot of trouble this time. It was as if someone went to great lengths to disguise the road. Dynamite would have the same effect as a landslide or earthquake, you know."

Frowning, Bethany said slowly, "I don't know. It still seems like a lot of trouble to go to when all they had to do was move their stolen goods."

Trace grabbed her by the hands. "They may have tried. That may be why the earplug was lying out in the open. What we saw, Bethany, may be just a small part of it all."

"Why hide it at all? Why not just display it in a museum, or sell it outright?"

"And risk the Peruvian government stepping in? While there are still corrupt officials, a find like what we saw would involve a lot of people. It would be a big risk to get rid of it all at once. A little at the time, now that would be a lot easier." Releasing her hands, he raked his fingers through his hair and began pacing the stone floor.

Bethany abruptly sat down on a stone bench and stared at him. It came to her that her father had not died in the pursuit of a dream, but because of someone's greed. It left her with a growing anger. And a growing sense of danger.

"Trace," she said suddenly, "I think we need to leave here as soon as possible."

His dark gaze swung to her, and he nodded slowly. "I think you're right, princess."

Morning came in a blast of sunlight and no rain. It was a welcome relief from the gray days before, and Trace took advantage of it to explore the slopes leading down from the stone city. He knew that the ancient Incas had most often buried their dead in caves, and had found some himself a long time before. The mummies in the wet highlands would be too damp to be well preserved, but the dry coastal region had provided some excellently preserved mummies and their attendant artifacts. Why not look for the caves?

Leaving Bethany still asleep in her blankets, Trace slipped quietly from the city and down the slopes. No one saw him go. The soldiers had huddled together in a vacant building, and the Quechuas had managed to drift away to a remote spot of the city. Just as well. He didn't want anyone to see him.

Of course, local Indians who found the caves would have already looted them of treasure, but that wasn't what he was looking for, anyway. It wasn't long before Trace was successful in his hunt.

Cool, dank air greeted him as he stepped cautiously into a cave in the mountainside. When he was certain no wild animal had holed up inside, he lifted the lantern he'd brought and began searching for signs of occupation. A scrap of cloth caught his eye, and he knelt on the damp floor of the cave and began scooping up handfuls of dirt.

Covered by time and drifting debris, a cloth-wrapped mummy in the traditional kneeling position with legs drawn up and bound tightly, grinned up at him. It was so rotten, however, that when he reached out to touch it, the bones crumbled to chunks of dust.

"Damn wet climate," Trace muttered, and sorted through the dirt in search of anything valuable. Only a few shards of pottery and the crumbling bones of a large dog remained. Obviously, not a royal burial.

Several caves later, Trace was streaming with sweat and knowing Bethany would be wondering where he was. So would the soldiers. One more, and then he would go back up and admit defeat. He didn't know why, but he'd thought that just maybe, the burial caves would hold a link to the city.

When Trace stumbled into the next cave, he found what he'd been looking for. Piles of neatly stacked golden plate and silver objects lined newly carved shelves of stone. It fit in with his theory well enough, and his mouth curled with grim satisfaction. It explained a lot.

When he turned toward a thick, black hole yawning at the end of the spiraling tunnel, something alien caught his eyes and he paused. He bent and picked it up, frowning down at the mundane square of leather in his hand. Comprehension scoured his brain, and Trace swore softly.

Tucking it into his shirt, he continued his exploration of the cave. Farther back, he found what he was looking for. A jumble of rock with raw, charred edges had been swept to one side. Black powder scorched the ceiling, and a dot of light glittered at the far end of the dark tunnel. An unopened crate of dynamite sat against the tunnel wall.

"Eureka!" he mocked, lifting the flickering lantern high as he walked forward. He went deeper and deeper into the cave, noting that the rock floor sloped sharply upward. By the time he reached the far point of light, sweat streamed down his face and soaked his shirt.

Stepping through the small opening and out into the bright sunlight, Trace saw that he was on the terraces just below the city atop the mountain. His mouth curled into a smile. Now he knew how it had all happened.

"Well, I'm glad you've figured it out," Bethany said irritably, "because I haven't the faintest notion what you're talking about."

"The earplug."

"Damn the earplug!" she snapped, glaring at him. "Why are you so obsessed with that wretched earplug?"

"Because it shouldn't have been lying out in the open like it was," Trace explained patiently. "We were all so excited about finding the rest of the gold, that we didn't pay any attention to the significance of the earplug."

Almost bursting with irritation and impatience, Bethany tried to keep her voice calm. "All right. I concede the importance of the earplug. What does it have to do with the rest of the stuff?"

"Nothing, really," he began, then grinned when she groaned with exasperation. "It could have been a vase, or a statue of a llama, or even a silver tooth cap. What *is* important, is that it was left out on the terraces while the rest of the stuff was stacked neatly inside the temple. Remember the alpaca rugs? Those should have rotted years ago if left by the Incas. They didn't. They were fairly recent."

"So?"

"So, it should have been obvious that someone in a hurry didn't pay any attention to one small piece of gold as they tried to hide a much larger portion of treasure."

"Obvious to who?" Bethany muttered. She pushed back a strand of light hair from her eyes. "But you didn't find any treasure in the cave."

He hesitated, then lied, "No, I didn't."

"Doesn't that ruin your theory?"

"No, it strengthens it. Look, someone apparently knew that we were coming here. So, after seeing that we could find the city, that we were very close to it even after trying to frighten us away, they decided the best option is to hide it for a while. After all, we're not a full-fledged expedition, and can't take it *all* back. And, anyway, if we take too much, it's easy enough to ambush us on the trail."

"But what if we'd stayed a long time?" Bethany asked.

"Simple—arrange a small earthquake with some dynamite, and watch us leave in a hurry!"

Bethany's jaw dropped. "But who—?"

"That, princess," he said grimly, "is what I mean to find out. Someone's been causing my bad luck since the last expedition I brought up here, and I think I know who it is."

"You mean—?"

"Bentworth."

She frowned. "Oh, Trace, are you sure?"

"No, but I mean to make sure. Sucking in a deep breath, he held out a small, leather-bound notebook. "You might want to look at this. But I warn you—it's not going to be easy to read."

Her hand trembled as she reached out for it. She'd already recognized her father's journal, the one he'd always been scribbling in. It brought him back to her with painful clarity.

"Have—" She had to clear her throat. "Have you read this?"

"Yes."

Bethany sat back down on the stone bench at one side of the abandoned building, and turned so that the sunlight streaming in through a window overlooking the Urubamba River Valley would light the pages. The ink had faded in the months since it had been written, but it was still legible. The pages crackled as she flipped them over and found a portion that did not detail sizes and shapes of buildings and the arrangements of artifacts.

Most unusual findings here. Am truly excited. It's a dream come true for me.

Another entry, dated several days later:

We must leave today. Earthquake has made staying a danger. Just as well. Need intricate instruments to continue. Camera faulty. Thank God for Bethany and her talent.

She looked up at Trace with swimming eyes, then read on.

Am hurt. May not make it. Will depend on Bethany to continue with project. . . .

"When did he write this?" she looked up to ask, and Trace shrugged. She read on, wiping at the tears gathering in the corners of her eyes.

Sent you on, my darling daughter—I will not make it out of here in spite of Taylor's assurance that he will return for me. Am grateful for pack he threw me, so that I may write this last farewell to you. I love you, Bethany, in spite of my seeming indifference to your needs. I rejoice that you will survive. . . . Can hardly hold the pen, but must put down my last thoughts. . . .

A familiar voice—perhaps I am saved, after all! The bullets have flown so thick and fast that I've lost count of time. Others have retreated, heard Taylor call that he would come back for me, to hold on. But now, I hear rescue, and see above me the face of my savior. Odd, that it should be Be—

The page was torn, and it was the last entry. Bethany looked back up at Trace with streaming eyes.

"Bentworth?"

"Stands to reason, doesn't it?"

She closed the journal. "Yes, I suppose it does." Then her brow puckered in a frown. "No, it doesn't."

"What do you mean?"

"Why would he go to all the trouble to coax me into getting back up here if he already knew where it was? It would be a total waste of time, as well as money. And to do all this, hire all these men—" She waved a hand toward the bearers and soldiers outside. "Just more witnesses to his crime, I would think."

Trace's gaze swung slowly to the Peruvian soldiers in the sunlight outside, and his brow furrowed. She was right. Bentworth wouldn't have done all that just to cover his tracks. Damn! He'd let his hatred for the man drown out his common sense. He'd wanted it to be Bentworth so badly, that he had overlooked the obvious. It had suddenly taken on a much more dangerous note.

"Come on, Bethany," he said, reaching and pulling her up by the arm. "'We're getting out of here."

Chapter Twenty-six

"Not so fast," the scar-faced soldier said with a leer when they stepped outside.

Trace's hand dropped to the pistol at his side, but he paused when he saw the drawn rifle pointed at his chest. He swore softly. Why hadn't he thought this out more clearly? And the soldier was obviously enjoying himself. Dammit!

"Por favor señor, you will give me your little pistol for safekeeping, heh?"

Stone-faced, Trace allowed the swarthy man to take his pistol from the holster. He could feel Bethany quivering beside him, and his jaw clenched.

"Now, your knife, please," the man said in that polite, mocking voice that made Trace's eyes narrow. The knife slid from his belt, and the soldier indicated that he should lift his hands and place them behind his head. As he did so, reluctantly, Trace kept his eyes on the soldier.

"What do you intend to do with us? I don't think anyone could be paying you enough to risk hanging. . . ."

"Ah, there is no risk of that, señor." Yellow teeth flashed briefly. "Not for me, at any rate."

Trace had no choice but to do what he said when

the man pointed his rifle toward another building and told them to go there. He hoped Bethany would keep her wits about her, and not try anything foolish, or go into hysterics as some women were prone to do. Of course, he'd yet to see her in hysterics, but if there was ever a wrong time to do it, it would be now.

Jabbing the muzzle of the rifle into Trace's back with particular relish, the soldier marched them both to the small, squat building with no windows. A small patch of sunlight glistened on the floor and picked out the woven blankets lying in a tumbled heap against one wall. There was nothing else.

"Wait inside, if you please," he said, still polite, his voice grating on Trace's nerves. Bethany almost ran inside, obviously seeking refuge from the soldier.

Half turning, Trace entertained the brief idea of trying to unarm the man, but the other two were right behind him, rifles resting casually across their forearms, but easily lethal. Frustration burned in him as Trace was forced to duck his head to enter the building. The grating squeak of a door shut out the rectangle of light and left them in total darkness. He tried the door, but it was solid and sturdy, and he swore softly when he heard the heavy *thunk* of a bar being lowered across it.

Bethany's voice was remarkably calm, considering the circumstances. "So what do we do now?"

"I don't see that we have many options," Trace growled. "Turn into toadstools, I guess."

"Or corpses?" The suggestion of hysteria that he'd been dreading edged her voice.

Reaching out in the pitch-dark, his hand brushed over her and he said quickly when she yelped, "It's me. Give me your hand." Her fingers slid into his palm. "Now, give me your lips, Bethany."

"Trace, this is no time for—!"

"Kiss me, dammit! Who knows when we'll get another chance?"

It wasn't just because he wanted to kiss her that he insisted, it was to keep her from becoming hysterical and losing her ability to react. He could tell her first-hand what happened when one lost their ability to think clearly. Hadn't he allowed his hatred for Bentworth to cloud his judgment? Now they were in a mess because of it.

Yielding, Bethany leaned into him, burying her face in his shirt, feeling his hands tangle in her hair to draw her head back for his kiss. His mouth found hers easily, sought the velvety sweetness that never failed to arouse him, then lingered. He could feel her cold lips warm beneath his; she drew in a shaky breath when he briefly released them, and he smoothed back a tickling strand of hair that brushed against her cheek.

"That wasn't so bad, was it?" he murmured, and he felt her shake her head.

"Trace, what are we going to do?" she asked again, an edge of desperation to her voice, and his arms curved around her.

"Make love."

"What!"

"Can you think of anything better to do in the dark?"

"You must be out of your mind! In here?"

"Why not? I don't think anyone's going to bother us for a while." He smiled in the dark. "And if they do, just think how surprised they'll be to find out we don't scare that easily."

A gurgle of laughter threaded her words as she said, "I am now convinced that you must be either completely mad, or a genius."

His hands smoothed over her hips, then up to cup her breasts. He didn't need light; he'd memorized every little hollow and plane of her body, the soft ivory curves that had haunted his thoughts for months.

"We'll vote on it later," he muttered against the rich tapestry of her throat, his lips finding and nurturing the small, fluttering pulse there.

Bethany shivered as he unbuttoned her blouse, felt his hands whisper over her body in a slow, heated caress, then felt him peel the garment from her shoulders and toss it away. It was insanity to agree to this; it was utter madness of a kind she had never before experienced.

Yet there was a heightened urgency to their passion that lent a fine-tuned excitement to the act. Trace's hands were swift and certain, his mouth hot and searing across her body, eliciting response from her in shuddering ripples of desire. And when she tore at his clothes, popping some of the buttons in her haste, he helped her.

Darkness shrouded their nudity, but loving memory provided all the details that the shadows hid. Bethany did not have to see his lean, flat belly or the band of muscles riding it, did not have to see the sinewy flow of skin and bone and tissue to admire the taut perfection of him. She could feel it beneath her fingertips.

Fully aroused just by the skim of her satiny skin under his searching hands, Trace stripped her with fiery haste, then pulled her up and hard against him. Her full breasts pressed against his chest with teasing enticement, and the gentle swell of her hips beneath his palm made him groan.

Though there were blankets on the floor, he didn't want to use them. Instead, he turned her, reaching out with one hand to find and brace himself against the smooth stone wall. With Bethany between his hard body and the wall, Trace bent slightly and lifted her, then slid her down in a smooth, slow motion that took her breath away. He could hear it, hear her quickly indrawn gasp as he thrust forward and put himself inside her in a surging jab of heated desire.

Bethany clasped her hands behind his neck, feeling the abrasive rub of the cold stone at her back, and the searing thrust of Trace's body inside her. Her muscles contracted in an involuntary movement, and she squirmed in a sinuous twist of her hips and legs as she tried to keep up with the increasing tempo of his rhythmic motions.

Release was simultaneous, explosive, shattering. Trace held her tightly, his hands splayed beneath her hips and cradling soft flesh, his fingers digging into her thighs as he gave a last, fierce thrust.

Half sobbing, Bethany cried out, the sound echoing in their dark prison, and Trace quickly covered her lips with his mouth. When he released them at last, he could barely stand. His muscles were so relaxed that all he wanted to do was lie down on the floor and stay there.

They pulled apart slowly, and he slid her down his body again to set her firmly on the floor.

It was Trace who retrieved their discarded clothes, Trace who decided what belonged to who. And it was Trace who exchanged the shirt he'd given her for her own. In the inky blackness, he managed to find the blankets he'd seen, and spread them on the cold floor.

Bethany sank down gratefully, not caring if the woven squares were alive with all sorts of creatures.

She could not remain standing a moment longer, and it had ceased to matter about minor inconveniences. Trace had been right. It had been just what they needed to relax them. She felt as if she could handle anything now—as long as it wasn't too soon. At the moment, she was far too drowsy to do more than sit on the blanket with her head on Trace's shoulder and smile.

The hours passed in a haze. Without light, there was no way of marking time. It had ceased to exist. The gnawing uncertainty of their future weighed heavily.

Bethany laid her head back against the stone wall. Was this what death was like, perhaps? A total absence of sight or sound or sensation? Not if she believed what she'd been taught from childhood. Yet, she couldn't help but think that perhaps it wouldn't be too bad. If this was the worst that could happen, then it might be bearable.

"Thinking gloomy thoughts?" Trace asked when she stirred restlessly, and she nodded before recalling he couldn't see her.

"Yes. What are you thinking about?"

"Something to eat."

"If that isn't just like a man—!"

"I'm willing to bet it's better than what you were thinking about," he countered, and she shrugged.

"All right. You win that point."

"It's about time." Stretching, Trace brought one leg up and draped his arm across his knee. "If it's not Bentworth, it's got to be somebody, you know," he said after a moment. "Someone your father knew, someone whose name begins with a B."

"I can't imagine who that would be."

"Can't you?" Trace lapsed into silence. "Who do you think would benefit from your father's death?" he asked after a moment. "Anyone?"

Startled, she said, "No, only me. And I don't really benefit. Oh, there's the house and probably a small annuity that will run out in a few years, but other than that, my father had nothing of value. His treasure was in his work."

Trace's boots scraped across the floor, sounding quite loud in the darkness. "That's not much help."

Detecting something in his voice that she might not have noticed if they'd been anywhere but locked in a small, dark building, Bethany asked, "You know something, don't you?"

"Let's just say—I have my suspicions."

"Tell me."

"No point in it now. I certainly don't feel like arguing with you over a hunch, and that's all this is. I'll tell you more when I know more," he added in an effort to forestall her next question.

"That may be too late—or never," she grumbled.

"Might be," he agreed, and she wished she hadn't said that.

By the time they heard the bar rattling on the door, they were braced for whatever came. Trace rose slowly to his feet, not wanting to be sitting down for it.

The door swung slowly open after an agonizingly long rattle of metal against wood, then the groaning protest of the bar being drawn back and the squeal of hinges. As light brightened the interior of the small building, they flinched from it, their eyes splintering with pain.

What had seemed like blinding sunlight at first was only hazy light from a gray day. The soldier confronting them blocked out most of it, thankfully, and it took a few moments for their aching eyes to adjust.

"Out!" he barked in Spanish. "And hurry!"

Bethany grabbed her father's journal instinctively, and stepped out into the city. She breathed deeply of sweet, cool air, and turned her face to the wind. It smelled fresh, smelled of rain, and she was suddenly glad to be alive. If she could only stay that way . . . .

Their hands were bound behind them and they were pushed forward, marched across the city and down the stone steps that led to the temple. It began to rain, slashing down in drenching torrents, rivulets cascading over ancient stones. The soldier prodded them on, swearing softly under his breath at the miserable weather.

Trace shook his head. "You're not going to try to walk out of here anytime soon, are you?" he asked the soldier behind them. "It's dangerous enough when the weather is dry."

Shadows wavered, and the man's voice was filled with bravado. "Our *jefe* can find his way in any weather."

"Good. I hope he's got a patron saint who likes fools."

The rifle jabbed into his back, making Trace stumble. His mouth tightened grimly. A feeling of heightened danger made his body taut. He wondered what these men had in mind, and just how they figured into the grand scheme of things. Did they intend to just push them over the edge of a cliff and be done with it?

Bethany tried to keep from sliding on the slick surface of mud and stone, her gaze shifting to the soldier. He'd taken her father's journal from her, and held it carelessly under his arm, heedless of the wet weather that would ruin the pages. It was Brasfield's last words to the world, his final tribute to his daughter, and she didn't want it to be lost.

"Please," she murmured as they picked their way down the stone steps, "be careful with that journal!"

The soldier ignored her.

When they had crossed the main plaza and the temple loomed just ahead, he ordered them to halt. Trace peered through the rain. He could see faint sprays of light coming from the open doorway. The soldier called out a greeting, and then they stepped through the stone portal and into the temple.

Oil lamps shed pools of light over the walls and ceiling and brightened the interior. Vicuña and alpaca rugs had been spread on the floor, and a massive gold medallion hung on the wall behind a low chair, reflecting splinters of light from the lamps in glittering rays.

Several lamps were at the far end of the room, and a man was seated in the low chair, the light behind him and his face in shadow. Bethany, wet and shivering with cold and fear, strained to pierce the hazy shadows, to see the face of the man who was obviously the leader. Somehow, it didn't look like the scar-faced soldier who'd turned on them.

It wasn't.

"Ah, signorina," came the low, pleasant voice, "how nice to see you again, if under somewhat strained circumstances."

A swell of hope sent her forward several steps, and her voice was relieved. "Signore Bertolli! Oh, you can't imagine how glad I am to see that it's you! Why, these men have been absolutely awful to us, and we have so much to tell you . . ."

Trace's voice snapped her head around. "Shut up,"

he said in a low growl. "Can't you see that he's enjoying himself?"

Still not quite willing to believe what her eyes and ears indicated was true, Bethany shook her head. "Trace, it is Signore Bertolli. . . ."

"I know who it is," Trace shot back at her, his eyes dark and glittering in the dim light. "I just didn't know soon enough."

Bethany's head swung back around to gaze at the portly Italian merchant, who rose from the low chair and stepped down into a pool of lamplight. His face was benignly pleasant and courteous, and a faint smile curved his lips beneath his luxurious mustache.

"I'm honored that I was able to deceive a man as clever as you're reported to be, Signore Taylor," Bertolli said in a satisfied purr. "It is quite a feather in my cap."

Trace's mouth curled into a mocking smile. "Isn't it? I always wondered how you were able to afford such a luxurious home, but just didn't put two and two together until recently."

"Ah, well, we all make mistakes," Bertolli replied smoothly. "Hopefully, however, they are not fatal ones, as yours seems to be."

"Hopefully." Trace met his gaze steadily. "You'll excuse me if I don't tell you how clever you are, won't you? I have an aversion to thieves."

"So I hear." Bertolli's mouth twisted beneath his dark mustache. "There has been much gossip about you, signore. I wonder how much of it is true?"

"Probably all of it."

Bertolli's gaze slid to Bethany when she made a strangled sound and stepped forward. "I am sorry to include you in this tragedy, signorina, but you will recall that I did my best to discourage you from coming.

I even had my stout 'soldiers' attempt to keep you from harm's way. Alas, you did not cooperate at all."

"None of this makes any sense at all!" Bethany forced out between chattering lips. "Why are you doing this?"

Shrugging with Gallic eloquency, Bertolli went forward and took her by one arm to lead her close to a brass brazier filled with glowing embers. "Warm yourself, and I will tell you a little tale, heh?" His hand gently pushed her down to kneel beside the warm brazier, and he smoothed back wet strands of her hair that coiled around her face in thick ropes. She shuddered away from his touch.

Turning to Trace, Bertolli said, "I am sorry I cannot offer you the same hospitality, signore, but you are too dangerous a man to allow any comforts. I am certain you understand."

"Not really." Trace shrugged, and his wet, dark hair dripped onto the floor as he narrowed his eyes at the Italian. "The convoluted workings of the criminal mind has always eluded me, I'm afraid. I've found that most thieves are rather common little men with bloated egos."

Bertolli's eyes glittered with malice. "Ah, you should know, *giusto?*"

Trace stiffened, but his voice was calm. "I should know better than anyone."

"Your father, he was not a very good thief, as I understand it."

"Obviously not," Trace returned dryly. "If he had been, he would not have gone to prison."

"And your good friend and mine, Signore Bentworth, he was responsible for putting him there, *giusto?* Ah, how fickle is the nature of man! You were so certain all this time that Bentworth had devious schemes at work, and I found it quite amusing to foster such notions. Of course, he was not clever enough to see through my ploys, either, so you should not feel badly."

"I don't. Disgusted, maybe; sickened by your greed and avarice, but not bad."

Bertolli laughed. *"Buono!"* His hand dropped to rest atop Bethany's bent head, and she cowered away from him. He looked down at her. "Ah, you are quite disillusioned by me, are you not? I understand. It is a very difficult thing, to have one's hopes dashed. I would have spared you that, if at all possible, but you insisted upon listening to Signore Bentworth and your handsome lover. Too bad. Now you are here, and I have little choice in your fate."

Staring dully into the glowing coals nestled inside the brazier, Bethany felt her throat tighten. Why had she ever thought Bertolli a gentleman? It had been a thin veneer of respectability and courtesy to hide evil, and she had not even suspected.

"You don't have to kill her," she heard Trace say to Bertolli. "Let her go."

"And risk losing my profitable little business? You must be mad to suggest such a thing, signore!"

"Who's going to listen to her? Everyone knows she left Peru after her father died, half mad with grief. And it's common knowledge that she blamed me and everyone else for his death. People will listen politely, then dismiss any accusations she may have."

"Ah, quite gallant of you to try, but obviously less than successful. I have no intention of arousing the least suspicion. It has taken me years to carry out this grand scheme, and I am not going to risk it for anyone, not even this lovely flower of femininity." He drew a finger along the curve of Bethany's cheek and she shuddered again, making him smile.

"How will you explain our deaths?" Trace persisted. "I don't think another fatal expedition will go uninvestigated or unremarked. Bentworth will want to find out what happened to us."

"An unfortunate accident will be arranged. By the time they find your poor bodies, I will be far distant. This spot remained remote and undiscovered for so long, but now has become entirely too frequented. I have found another place to hide my cache." Bertolli smiled widely. "I must admit that Incan artifacts are quite in demand."

Lifting her head, Bethany murmured, "You said that you appreciated art, Signore Bertolli. You said that you did not want to see it lost."

"Oh, and I meant every word of that! I appreciate the fine gold and silver statues and jugs, and I most assuredly do not want to see them lost. They are far too valuable, and few collectors buy them only to melt them down."

"But . . . but your collection!" Bethany blurted out in bewilderment. "You even have some sort of booby-trap . . ."

"Ah, thieves can never trust other thieves, signorina, surely you must know that."

Stunned, Bethany shook her head. She looked at Trace, standing furiously taut, his body radiating energy and danger. Little wonder Bertolli chose to stand well away from him, with an armed guard close at hand. Trace's expression was murderous, and his voice was a low, menacing growl.

"Bertolli, you're as good as dead and you know it. The government will be on your trail before you can sell off all your stolen loot. You can't get away with it for much longer."

"A pitiful attempt at frightening me into fleeing," the Italian said in amusement. "There are always new finds to keep me well-supplied. I only sell a few at a time, nothing to stir up undue interest or alarm. Besides—I am well aware of the government's investigation. Who do you think is helping them?"

"Bentworth."

"Of course. And also myself. How do you think I know where all the soldiers are going to be, and when there is to be a raid on one of the agents who deal in my goods?" He laughed richly. "You amuse me, signore. All this time you have blamed poor Bentworth, even for the ambush of your first expedition as well as the last, and . . ."

Bethany's head snapped up. "*You* were responsible for shooting at us?"

Bertolli shrugged. "I admit it. It was unfortunate that you found the city again at all, but too many valuable items were removed, and your poor papa, he had every intention of returning. I could not allow it, of course. It is so much trouble to find new, undiscovered ruins that are intact enough to hold my little collections."

"But how did you get here? Did you follow us all the way?"

"I have my methods," Bertolli said obliquely, then turned to Trace. "I am not a completely uncivilized man, signore. You will both be drugged before you meet with your fatal accident. Murder is abhorrent to me, but alas, quite necessary at times."

"You mean like when Brasfield recognized you at the ravine?" Trace grated, and Bertolli shrugged.

"Unfortunate, that. I had no idea he was lying in the ravine. When he saw me, I had to shoot him. It was a kindness of sorts, however, because he would have died soon anyway. I saw the blood on his lips, and knew he was bleeding inside." Bertolli's gaze shifted to Bethany. She was staring at him in horror, her wide violet eyes darkening to a stormy purple and her mouth twisting.

"You shot my father? But I thought—" Her gaze darted to Trace, who was staring at her with knowing eyes. He had known that her father died from a bullet wound, yet had let her go on thinking that he'd been responsible. Why?

Trace answered her unvoiced question. "He was just as dead. It didn't matter how he'd died. And, besides, I thought maybe a bullet had ricocheted and hit him. It didn't occur to me that it had been deliberate murder."

Bertolli's voice was a sneer. "Ah, you are such a noble man, signore! You will endure all for love, heh?"

A white-hot rage swelled up in Bethany, and her gaze swung to the Italian. He was looking at Trace, his lips twisted in such a sneering leer that she felt like killing him. With her hands still tied behind her back, she could do nothing, but she had to release the pounding fury that seared her to the core. She surged to her feet, her knees inadvertently knocking over the brass brazier filled with glowing coals in the process.

Turning, Bertolli chided, "Now, look what you have done to my rugs, signorin—"

A howling cry burst from her throat as Bethany flung herself at the portly Italian, catching him by surprise, the force of her body sending him backward into Trace and knocking them both down. Bethany landed on top of Bertolli, and immediately seized the opportunity to vent her pain and rage on him. Her strong teeth clamped down on his wrist as he struggled to get to his feet, eliciting pained cries.

He swore at her in Italian, and snapped out an order for the guard to remove her from him at once. The man shifted his rifle to his left hand and reached down to pick Bethany from Bertolli's portly frame.

That was a mistake.

Trace, still lying on his back on the hard stone floor, waited until the soldier was bent over, then kicked up with a foot, catching the man on his jaw and snapping his head back. A deep grunt signaled success, and Trace rolled to his feet. With his hands tied, he was limited in what he could do, but he intended to inflict as much damage as possible before he was taken down or more men arrived.

His booted foot crashed down on the fallen soldier's nose and sent the bone driving back into his skull. The man went limp, and Trace turned his attention to Bethany.

She still had her teeth sunk into Bertolli's wrist in spite of the Italian's frantic efforts to yank her head away by her hair. Tears streamed down her face at the pain, and it was only when Bertolli lifted a fist to slam into her head that she knew she was doomed.

Surprisingly, the blow did not fall.

Trace pivoted from the fallen soldier to Bertolli, his foot lashing out again, catching the Italian just beneath his chin and slapping his head back. Another kick destroyed his Adam's apple and Bertolli began to choke.

"Get up!" Trace snapped at Bethany. "Hurry! Let's get out of here."

"But our hands are tied," she said as she got clumsily to her feet, averting her eyes from Bertolli's retching, gurgling struggle.

"We'll worry about that later," Trace shot at her with a scowl. "Come on !

"My father's journal!" Bethany protested when she saw it lying on the stone floor. "I have to take it with me."

"Dammit, forget the goddam journal!" Trace growled so furiously Bethany scuttled out the door and into the driving rain without a backward glance.

Off-balanced by their bound hands, they skidded and slipped over the slick stones as they ran across them, expecting to hear a shout at any moment, or feel a bullet in their back. Fortunately, the miserable weather seemed to keep the other two soldiers huddled inside one of the stone buildings. No one tried to stop them as they flew down the steep terraces.

"Where are we going?" Bethany asked when they paused in the towering shelter of a stone archway. Rain glistened on her upturned face, plastering her pale hair to her head in dark ropes. Silvery drops clung to her eyelashes as she blinked up at him with desperate hope, and Trace drew in a deep breath.

There wasn't much daylight left. It would be suicide to try getting back down the mountain in the dark and with their hands tied. Yet he didn't see another option.

Then his searching gaze fell on the hidden cleft in one of the terraces, and he remembered the cave. It would be the first place Bertolli's soldiers would look, but it was their only hope.

"This way," he said, and darted out into the pounding rain again, almost falling before he managed to reach the dark entrance to the cave.

Bethany stepped inside with him, and wrinkled her nose at the musty smell. She was shivering with cold and terror, and stepped closer to Trace as if for protection. He looked down at her, his features shiny with rain, his mouth taut with tension.

"Do you think we'll make it, Trace?" she dared ask, and he shrugged.

"We'll give it a damn good try, princess."

They turned and made their way cautiously down the steep, dark tunnel.

Chapter Twenty-seven

"Be quiet," Trace warned softly, nudging her with his shoulder to stop her. Bethany paused just behind him. A faint wavering light danced not far ahead, and she felt a rush of relief.

"The end of the tunnel?" she whispered, and he nodded.

"Yeah, but you can bet Bertolli didn't come up here by himself. He's probably got men in the cave with his stolen treasure."

"You didn't tell me there was treasure here," Bethany muttered irritably, and felt Trace's shrug of impatience.

"I wasn't sure you wouldn't insist on claiming it in your father's name. We didn't have time for that. Now we sure don't."

There was a moment of damp, tense silence, then she whispered, "So what do we do now?"

"Try to get past those men down there before someone comes behind us to tell them we escaped and their boss is dead."

It seemed impossible. Especially with their hands still tied behind them.

Bethany shifted position and a rock rolled from beneath her foot, clattering loudly down the slope toward the cave. She froze, waiting, but no one seemed to notice. She could hear the muted laughter, the low rumble of male voices just beyond, and shivered.

"Sorry," she murmured, and Trace nodded.

"Be careful. Here, I'm going to turn around, and I want you to see if you can untie the knots in this rope with your teeth."

"With my *teeth?"* she echoed doubtfully.

"Since biting seems to be one of your favorite methods of warfare, I thought you'd welcome this chance," Trace mocked as he turned around and bent slightly from the waist.

Bethany sighed and bent to worry the foul-tasting rope with her teeth. It frayed slowly, and her back began to ache from remaining in a bent position, but finally she was able to tease it loose. She stood and sucked in a deep breath, then bent again to pull it the last small bit.

Jerking his arms apart, Trace finished the task for her, then turned her around and deftly undid her ropes.

"Now all we have to do is get a gun, and we're on our way," he muttered as he tossed aside the ropes.

"What do you think happened to the Indians who were with us?" Bethany asked as they knelt in the shadows and studied the rocky, winding tunnel. "Were they in Bertolli's pay, too?"

Trace frowned. "I don't think so. They're probably dead by now. Or ran when they figured out what was going on."

Bethany shuddered. "Bertolli is pretty ruthless, isn't he?"

"Was ruthless," Trace said softly, then added, "Yeah, I guess he was. I don't know why I never knew it."

"He was very good at hiding it." She paused. "Trace? Why do you think he came up here in the mountains? Didn't he have men who would do what he told them?"

"It's always good business to check up on your employees, I'm told," Trace mocked. "But none of that matters right now. Right now, we need to figure out a way to get out of here before they start looking for us."

Shifting his lean body along the rock wall, Trace went several feet down the tunnel before pausing. He could see shadows of men moving, could hear them more distinctly, and swore to himself. There looked to be at least ten or twelve of them. What could he do against that many? And without even the smallest weapon?

He pressed back against the wall and studied them for a few minutes. The men were packing gold into boxes and bags for removal. It was obvious that Bertolli had definitely decided not to risk anyone else coming to the city, and had given orders to remove the treasure to another, safer, spot.

A feeling of frustration swept over him. What could he do? He had to get Bethany out of there. Trace's hands clenched, and he darted a gaze around the dark tunnel. Then he saw the crate a few feet ahead, the crate he had seen on his first exploration. It held sticks of dynamite in it, tightly sealed to prevent dampness. Hope surged through him and he smiled grimly. Maybe there was a way out of this after all.

"This will never work," Bethany moaned, her hands trembling as she withdrew the matches Trace had given her. "They're wet!"

"There ought to be one or two that isn't. That's why I carry them in that leather case. It's waterproofed. Try to see what you can find, while I try to get the crate open."

It took several minutes to pry open the lid of the crate without being too noisy, and Trace began to sweat with the effort. One loud noise, and it would bring men up from the cave to investigate. How long before those in the city above noticed that the prisoners had escaped? Time was their enemy right now, slipping past with inexorable certainty and bringing them closer to being discovered.

Finally, prying open the lid just enough to slide his hand inside, he was able to bring out several sticks of dynamite, scraping his hand raw in the process but succeeding.

"Here," he returned to Bethany and said, "I got it. Now we have to figure out where it will do the best."

"Don't we need more than that?" she asked doubtfully.

"I don't think so. We're not trying to blow up the world, only a tunnel. And a few men."

The blunt remark made her throat tighten. She was about to kill someone. It had never occurred to her that she would do such a thing. But then, before today it had never occurred to her that she would ever be crouching in a cave, wet, shaking, and in fear for her life.

"Tell me what I have to do," she said after a moment, and he smiled down at her.

"Kiss me."

"What?"

"Why do you always say that when I ask for a kiss?" Trace teased. "Don't you like kissing me?"

"It's your timing that I don't like," she retorted, but smiled when she rose slightly to kiss him full on the lips. "Is that satisfactory?" she asked when she drew back, her breath coming a bit faster.

Trace nodded. "It will do until we have more time."

"I blush from your effusive compliments," Bethany muttered, but she was smiling.

"All right," Trace said, moving forward, "let's see what we can do, princess."

She crawled behind him, her nerves stretched to the breaking point, her heart pounding so fiercely she wondered why no one else could hear it. Below in the cave, she saw the men walking around, some crouching beside a fire and some packing gold and silver artifacts in wooden crates. It was obvious they didn't suspect anyone was watching.

Edging forward, Trace motioned for her to join him, and she did so with trembling legs. Her wet clothes didn't help the chills shaking her, nor did the ripples of fear that pranced along her spine with gleeful pricks.

Positioning himself, Trace said tersely, "Light a match for me," and Bethany tried to comply.

It took several attempts before she found one that was still dry enough to flare into flame, and she applied it quickly to the fuse dangling from the thick stick of lethal explosive. Hauling back his arm, Trace let fly with the dynamite and sent it arcing into the air. It landed several feet from his intended goal, and he swore softly, then held out another stick for her to light.

"Another one?" she murmured shakily, holding the match to the fuse. As soon as it caught, she shook out the thin match before it burned her fingers. "Trace—aren't you going to throw it?" she demanded in a hoarse tone when he still held the stick.

"In a minute. I'm going to let it burn down a bit, first. I want to wait until it's just the right time. . . ."

"You're going to blow us up!" she grated, and he shook his head. "Yes, you are—throw it!"

"Quit nagging at me! You'll see what I'm going to do in just a minute."

The first stick had clattered to a pile of rocks some distance from the men, and had attracted the attention of one of them. Rising from his warm spot by the fire, he went over to investigate the source of the noise.

Before he could do more than yell a warning, the stick of dynamite exploded with a shattering blast, tossing the man backward and sending up a shower of heavy rocks. The walls of the cave shuddered with the force of the explosion and rained huge chunks of rock from the ceiling.

Deafened by the noise, Bethany could dimly hear the shouts of men, some wounded, some alarmed, then flicked a glance to Trace. The fuse to the stick he held had burned dangerously low.

"Trace . . . !" Her voice was urgent, and he sliced her an impatient glance.

"In just a minute."

"Oh, God," she moaned, and closed her eyes.

Trace's muscles tensed. Some of the unharmed men were starting warily up the slope of the tunnel, guns drawn. He waited until they were closer, then tossed the dynamite. It landed in the middle of them, and they scattered with hoarse shouts.

The explosion rocked the cave a second time. Bethany's eyes snapped open, and her stomach lurched when she saw the carnage. Sickened, she hid her face in Trace's shirtsleeve and moaned.

"We don't have time for that now," he growled at her, pulling her to her feet and dragging her with them. "Bring the matches. And the extra dynamite."

She did as he said without speaking, snatching up the sticks of explosive and struggling to keep up with his long, half-leaping strides. Trace paused to pull a pistol from one of the dead men's hands and stuck it in his belt, then stopped at the next one to take another weapon. He gave it to her.

"Stick it in your pants," he snapped when she stared at him helplessly. "It may come in handy."

Bethany didn't bother to tell him she had no idea how to fire a gun. Now wasn't the time.

More men crouched behind rocks and crates on the floor of the cave, and when Trace and Bethany came into view around the bend of the tunnel, they began firing. She squealed with alarm, and barely felt Trace's quick shove.

Landing behind an outthrusting of rock, she watched as he aimed his weapon and fired, then leaped to lie beside her. To her amazement, he grinned.

"Now, this is more like it! I don't mind fighting when I've got a gun and I can see what I'm shooting at."

"I don't think you're mentally balanced," she said in a faint voice, but he was no longer listening to her. He'd rolled to his belly and was firing over the rock again, his dark gaze intent.

"Light another stick of dynamite," he told her a few minutes later.

Trembling, she struck another match and it caught on the first try. She held the small flame to the long, dangling fuse.

"It's lit," she said, and Trace stopped shooting to

roll to his back and take it from her hand.

A bullet suddenly smacked into the rocks behind them, and Bethany screamed. They were being fired on from the tunnel now, as well as the cave. They were caught in a dangerous cross fire.

"Trace!" she screamed. "What are we going to do?"

"Blow them to hell!" he snarled, ducking a bullet. Rising to his knees, he drew his arm back, but a bullet caught him, spinning him around and sending the dynamite flying from his hand.

"Trace! Trace! Oh, God, Trace. . . ." She crawled to his side and gasped at the blood squirting from his shoulder. "You're shot!"

Grimacing, Trace muttered, "Always the obvious with you, isn't it? Find the dynamite, sweetheart, or we're going to be splattered all over this tunnel. . . ."

Frantically, she felt for the stick of dynamite as Trace attempted to cover her actions with a hail of bullets directed at the tunnel.

"Hurry," he growled in a pained gasp. "I'm almost out of bullets in both guns. . . ."

She found the dynamite and curled her hands around it in a reflex action, jerking to face the tunnel. "What do I do?" she asked, not knowing where to aim.

"Throw it!"

"Where?"

"Jesus, *any*where! Just throw the goddam dynamite!"

When she still hesitated, Trace lunged forward and grabbed it from her, groaning with the effort as he threw it as hard as he could. It landed with a soft clatter, and they heard frightened squeals.

Then, when nothing happened, they heard a triumphant shout, and one of the soldiers who had come with them from Cuzco called down a laughing taunt.

"You have chosen a wet stick, it seems, señor!"

A rushing sweep of despair made Bethany groan, and she heard Trace's soft, pained curse. The grinning soldier was in sight now, his eyes glittering maliciously.

"You have killed our *jefe,*" he said, and motioned his companions forward with a jerk of his arm. "You will die for that. Your death will not be pleasant, even though I am not sorry they are dead. Now, the gold can be used by those who have worked the hardest for it, right, *amigos?*" he half turned to ask, and the men behind him laughed.

Bethany's eyes widened. There were several men with him, and as he approached, the soldier in front began to tell Trace what he intended in great detail, and what he would do with his woman once Trace was dead. A shudder cut through her, but she refused to answer when the soldier asked if she did not have any pleas.

He shrugged, and stepped around a huge rock in the way. "Very well, señorita, but we shall see how long it takes you to beg for . . ."

A thundering explosion ripped through the air, sending the soldier flying, ripping him to pieces. Blood and rocks flew everywhere, and Bethany screamed again and again. She finally stopped in a choking gasp, and dared to look closely. Not a man was left standing, and dust settled in a thick haze, reminding her of a shroud.

"Must have had a longer fuse than I thought," Trace observed calmly. "I'll have to watch that."

Her head turned slowly, and she stared at him for a long moment. His shoulder was bleeding profusely, blood oozing out and dribbling down his arm, staining his shirt. The smell of blood and death was almost overpowering, mixing with the sharp, acrid tang of the explosive. Rocks still pattered noisily down, rolling along the winding tunnel, smashing onto the stacks of golden treasure in the cave.

Trace frowned at her pale, set expression, at shadows in the pansy eyes that looked like bruises in her face. "Are you all right?"

Collapsing against him with a sob, Bethany squeezed her eyes shut. She was near the end of her strength. It wouldn't take much to have her in hysterics, and Trace knew it. Grimacing against the pain the slightest movement gave him, he pushed her to a sitting position.

"Look, we have to get out of here," he said. "We don't have much time to cry right now. Sorry."

Sniffling, she wiped her running eyes and nose on her shirttail with an inelegant motion, then nodded. "All right. I'm ready."

"Good. I'm not sure how many men are left alive. No one seems to be hanging around. Guess they don't want to have sticks of dynamite tossed at them. Let's grab some more, and some more ammunition, then get out of here."

"Where are we going?" she asked when they stumbled warily out of the cave and back into the driving rain.

"Cuzco sounds good."

Her glance was skeptical. "In your condition?"

"I won't be in this condition long. You're going to get the bullet out for me when we find a place for the night."

"I've never done anything like that!"

"Now's as good a time as any to learn. Besides, you don't have much choice. If you don't get it out, I'm liable to die, then what will you do?"

Bethany's gaze moved from his torn, bleeding shoulder to his face. It was already gray beneath his normally dark tint, and she knew he was right. Gulping, she nodded. "I'll do the best I can."

"I knew you would." His arm draped around her shoulder and he leaned heavily on her. "Let's find someplace quick. I don't think I'm going to last much longer if we don't."

Terrified that she would lose him, Bethany tried to hold him up as they made their way down slick, muddy slopes that threatened to shift and sweep them along in a tide of mud and brush. When they'd gone just a mile or two, the ground began to shake under them, a vague, ominous rumbling that made the trees quiver and limbs sway in a frenzied motion. Raindrops almost obscured the ground in places, bouncing from the dancing earth in erratic waves.

"Earthquake," Trace said in a painful growl. "Just what we need."

Bethany felt as if they were about to be pitched head-first down the steep slopes of the mountain, falling one end over the other to the bottom amid a jumble of huge rocks and tons of mud. The shaking grew stronger, and she could hear the screeches of birds and barking coughs of jaguars in the rain-wet trees around them.

"What'll we do?"

"Duck," he said, pulling her with him, ignoring the stabbing pain in his shoulder as a shower of rocks came bouncing down the slope. Flying debris from the rocks cut their faces, but caused no major damage as it cascaded past in a race to the bottom of the slope.

"Too bad we can't get to the bottom that fast,"

Bethany observed a bit breathlessly when that danger was past. The ground felt unstable beneath her feet, and she waited in a sort of daze for a yawning chasm to open up and swallow her completely.

"We can," Trace said through pain-clenched lips. "I just don't think it'd be too healthy."

"Probably not."

"Come on. Let's see how far we can get before the aftershocks hit."

But the path that Trace had seen earlier was gone, scoured from the mountainside by the avalanche of rocks loosened by the earthquake. He paused for a moment, feeling definitely unsteady on his feet, trying to think past the pounding pain invading his body.

"Guess we'll just have to find another way out of here," he said around the thick waves of pain. Rain molded his dark hair to his skull, and his eyes looked bright with fever.

Bethany swallowed hard. "Are we lost?"

"Not us. We're right here. It's the road that's lost," Trace muttered with an attempt at a smile. "Don't worry, princess. I'll find the way down. We can always just roll the rest of the way."

Somehow, Bethany found it hard to smile. She looked around at the inhospitable mountain, and the dense, green forest stretching greedily around the slopes. If only the rain would stop! Fear knifed through her, fear that they would not reach safety after all, and that no one would ever find their bodies.

Aftershocks rumbled beneath them, rolling like ocean swells, and they managed to stay on their feet until they ended.

"What will we do?" she asked Trace when they'd stopped, and he straightened, his lips white, deep grooves etched in his face as he met her gaze.

"Tonight, we're going to find a place to sleep. Then we'll worry about getting back."

They searched for something reasonably dry and protected, but with the day quickly fading into enveloping shadows of night, the outlook was bleak.

"This'll have to do," Trace muttered finally, crawling under a rocky overhang that kept out some of the rain but not all. "I can't go any farther."

Shivering and wet, Bethany crawled in beside him. They had nothing but a few matches, drenched sticks of dynamite, a knife, and four loaded pistols. No food, no water, no blankets. It promised to be a long, hard trip back to Cuzco.

The night stretched endlessly. It was too dark to try to get the bullet out, and Bethany did the best she could to keep him warm by putting her body in front of his and snuggling close. Shared body heat was better than nothing. She could feel his faint shivers, and the increasing warmth of his flesh against hers. He was growing feverish. The bullet had to come out!

With Trace barely clinging to consciousness, she lay through the long night listening to the roars of jaguars, and imagining that every rustle in the thick undergrowth was a deadly snake or ferocious-looking iguana. She tried not to surrender to terror or tears, but it was hard. If Trace died, she wouldn't survive out in the jungle.

But if Trace died, she told herself, she didn't want to survive.

"Drink this." Bethany forced a cup of hot water to his lips and made him drink. His ridiculously long eyelashes blinked in surprise.

"Water?" he croaked. "What kind of pain-killer is

that to give a man?"

"It's all we have," she said grimly, "and it's not for pain. It's to keep you alive."

"How'd you get it hot?"

"A fire." She gestured to low flames flickering beneath the overhang. "It was hard finding any dry wood."

He looked up at her with a faint smile. "I bet. But you did."

"Sort of." She shrugged when he looked at her. "I'm burning my pantalets," she said primly. "It was the driest thing I could find, and I wrapped it around some wood. It seems to be working."

Trace laughed weakly. "What are you going to do when you run out of drawers?"

She looked out from under the rocky cleft. "It stopped raining during the night. Maybe it'll dry out a little." Reluctantly dragging her gaze back to him, she noted that his face was flushed with fever, and that his skin was dry to the touch. "Trace. We have to get that bullet out."

"Yeah."

"I don't know how. You'll have to tell me."

He nodded. "I know. It might help if you can find some coca leaves. That'll kill the pain enough so I won't pass out."

"I have no idea what coca leaves look like in the wild. Do they grow on trees? Bushes? I've only seen the ones you had in that pouch."

Grimacing against the pain throbbing in his shoulder," Trace looked out from under the rock. Thick foliage thrust toward the sky, and he saw the large, shiny leaves of *drip tips* draping down, the vinelike *liana,* and spreading fans of palm leaves. There had to be some coca plants growing in this high, moist forest in which it thrived.

"It's a shrub," he told Bethany, "and bushy. The leaves are roughly oval, maybe two, three inches long. Strip a few branches and bring them back. We'll squeeze the juice from them over my wound. It'll numb it for a while and slow the bleeding."

Faintly skeptical—after all, she'd heard rumors of the coca leaf's ill effects—Bethany asked, "Are you sure?"

Exasperated, Trace muttered, "I'm too tired to argue about it if I wasn't. Take one of the pistols with you, just in case. And a knife to notch the trees so you can find your way back."

It took quite a while to find the shrub he'd described to her, but when she did, Bethany stripped it of as many leaves as she could carry. Removing a bullet from the body of a conscious man promised to be a long, drawn-out ordeal, and she didn't want him fainting in the middle of it.

In spite of her earlier skepticism, Bethany was grateful she had found the coca leaves. Under Trace's direction, she prepared a paste of them and smeared them on his wound. It slowed the bleeding, and numbed the raw, oozing flesh so that she could probe with her fingers for the bullet.

Fortunately, the bullet had not struck a bone, and was only lodged firmly in the muscle, but it was still more than enough to leave Bethany drenched with perspiration. A wave of relief washed over her when she got it out.

Beads of sweat dotted the beard stubble above Trace's upper lip, and his face was drawn as he lay on the cold rock shelf. "Good job, princess," he croaked when she sat back on her heels with the bullet in her palm. Then he closed his eyes.

Bethany washed her hands again with some of the hot water, and tore the last square of her cotton drawers into strips to use as a bandage for his wound. He didn't open his eyes while she wrapped it with quick, clumsy motions, and she wondered if he'd fainted.

As if sensing her uncertainty, he opened one eye and managed a slight smile. "Never thought I'd wear lace drawers," he murmured, and Bethany laughed with relief.

"You certainly didn't seem like that sort of man when I first met you, Mr. Taylor. I'm appalled."

His eyes closed again, but his smile remained. "So am I."

While Trace slept, Bethany gathered more wood. She did not dare wander far from their camp, keeping the high rock in sight. She'd almost gotten lost finding the coca leaves, and didn't want another scare.

She came back and stacked the dry wood beneath the overhang, then drank some more warm water, trying to ignore her hunger pains. At least she had water. And at least Trace was alive. Very little else mattered at the moment.

Drawing up her knees as she sat by the fire, Bethany crossed her arms over them and rested her forehead against her wrists. She was so tired, and it seemed as if she had never known what it was like not to be.

Closing her eyes, she fell asleep.

Chapter Twenty-eight

"I will *not* eat live ants!" Bethany snapped.

Trace eyed her mutinous face. "I thought you were hungry."

"Not *that* hungry."

"They're nice and crunchy. Some people consider live ants a delicacy."

"I'm not one of them."

His dark eyebrow lifted slightly. "Then I suppose that means you won't try iguana eggs or grubworms, either."

She glared at him. "Not on your life!"

Shifting slightly on the pallet of gathered ferns and huge leaves Bethany had made, Trace winced against the pain his movement caused. "How good are you at hunting and fishing?"

"Better than I'll be at gathering live ants or iguana eggs!" she shot back.

But when Trace handed her one of the pistols and told her to conserve ammunition, Bethany looked at it with a doubtful frown. Maybe the time had come to tell him she had never fired a weapon. Then the thought of eating live ants or juicy grubworms inspired her to at least attempt shooting a meal.

It might not be too bad, she consoled herself as she

walked cautiously through the thick jungle, pausing every few feet to notch a tree as Trace had told her to do. Maybe she could shoot something that wouldn't look at her with reproachful eyes.

In the end, they had to fill their growling stomachs with a variety of wild nuts and berries Bethany gathered.

"It's hard to believe you couldn't find a single bird to shoot," Trace grumbled as he downed the last fistful of wild nuts. "And half of those berries you brought back are poisonous."

"At least you can tell which half," she replied. "I had no idea. And as for shooting something once I found it, I might as well tell you that my talents are limited on that score."

"Great." Trace's mouth quirked up in a small smile. "I had a feeling you were more talk than show."

Bethany shrugged. She didn't care what he said. He was at least well enough to talk to her, to banter with her, even if he did tire easily. And maybe in a few days, he'd be well enough to lead them out of the jungle and back to Cuzco.

She slid him a speculative glance. He'd lost weight in the two days they'd been camped under the rock cleft. Deep shadows etched his face, and his eyes had faint rings under them. At least his color was better, more normal now, and his wound had stopped bleeding and begun to heal. Pink, healthy flesh had formed around the hole she'd probed to get the bullet out. It probably needed stitches, but she had no needle or thread.

"What's for dessert?" Trace drawled, snagging her wandering attention.

She made a face at him. "Not a thing for you. You do nothing but complain. I'm quite put out with you."

He laughed softly. "Then I suppose sex is out of the question?"

Startled, Bethany shot him a quick look. "It'd kill you!"

"Maybe you overestimate your abilities," Trace said, reaching out to grab her hand. "Humor a dying man. This may be the last chance we have . . ."

"You've used that line before," Bethany said sternly. "Can't you think of anything new?"

"Didn't it work the last time?"

"Well—yes."

"Then why tamper with success?" Pulling her slowly toward him, Trace felt the growing evidence of his desire, and wondered briefly if it wouldn't kill him to do what his body was urging. He was still weak. But he'd done nothing but lie on a leafy pallet for two days, and the sight of Bethany with her light brown hair tumbling around her oval face, and her blouse gaping open where the buttons were missing, was almost more than he could stand. Maybe it was better to die from sex than a fever. Come to think of it, what better way was there?

"Come on, Bethany," he coaxed in his soft drawl when she still resisted. "I'll let you do all the work, if you want."

She laughed, throatily, flushing when she saw the fires of desire burning in his dark eyes. "You're too thoughtful. Are you sure you want to relinquish that privilege?"

His hand smoothed under her blouse and up over the firm thrust of her breasts, caressing gently. "I could be talked into it," he murmured, shifting slightly to lie flat on his back.

Caught between her own need and her fear for him, she still hesitated, and Trace swept his hand down the curve of her ribcage to her hips, urging her closer to him. His other arm lifted, and his hand fumbled with the few remaining buttons of her blouse, tearing two off in his impatience, ignoring her soft cry of protest.

Then the blouse was gone, peeled away from her body and tossed carelessly aside, and Trace's hands cupped her breasts in his warm palms.

"Trace! You're going to start your wound bleeding," she said in a final effort to appeal to his better judgement, but he was past caring. Silently determined, he curved his hands around her to bring her body slowly down, to brush her tightening nipples over his mouth. Bethany gasped. The abrasive scrape of his beard was stimulating, it rasped over her quivering flesh with enticing sweetness; and when his warm, wet mouth closed hotly over the taut peak, she closed her eyes and yielded.

Lavishing her breasts with attention, Trace's head went from one to the other, and his hand tugged at her trousers. Lifting herself, she shrugged out of them, gasping when he pulled too hard at her nipple, then moving closer. She eased down beside him, her head tilted back, the large leaves beneath them cushioning her bare knees, her body half across his torso.

Trace wore only his pants, and those were unbuttoned for convenience. She'd given him a sponge bath the day before with a wad of damp leaves, but at the time, he'd not felt like more than a comment or two about it. He'd recovered a lot in twenty-four hours, she thought hazily.

As the banked fires in her rose to a hotter and hotter pitch, making her ache with need for him, Bethany drew away to slide his pants down his legs. She could see the hard ridge of his arousal outlined beneath the material, but when she paused, he said in a husky voice, "Don't stop now, princess," and she smiled.

With the pants gone, Bethany straddled his lean body, her thighs nestled on each side of his hips. The smooth flex of his chest muscles knotted briefly as he reached for her again, and Bethany quickly leaned forward. As his hand captured the throbbing peak of her breast, she slid slowly down, gasping a little at the entry of him into her body.

Staring up at her through narrowed eyes, Trace felt a surge of response flow through him at the sight of her bare breasts, the miracle of pink and ivory flesh that could make him think of little else but kissing them. His hand looked so brown against her pale skin, almost a profanity of hardness against such a lush, satiny body. Her eyes were glistening with a dewy violet sheen, dazed with a passion that he shared, and he could see the quick, throbbing beat of her pulse just beneath skin that looked almost translucent in places.

He could feel her slender thighs quivering where they clasped his hips, could feel the velvety moist heat of her around his rigid body. It was agonizing pleasure, and his hands moved to clasp her hips, ignoring the pain in his shoulder as he guided her rocking motion.

Bethany could feel the gathering heat of her release, felt Trace's quickening thrusts into her, and then it happened so swiftly that she cried out in shock and pleasure, her wordless moans filling the air. Racking convulsions made her body's muscles clutch fiercely around him, and Trace joined her with an explosive rush, his mouth tightening as he felt his burning release.

Sagging over him, Bethany buried her face in the angle of his neck and uninjured shoulder, breathing raggedly. Her breasts flattened against his chest, and she could feel the erotic scrape of his chest hair over her sensitive nipples. For a moment she just lay there, then lifted her face with a worried frown to see if he was in pain.

He wasn't. Instead, a hot gleam shone in his eyes, and he was getting hard within her again. Bethany stared at him with wide eyes, not quite certain it was possible. Always before, there had been a pause: now he seemed determined to do it again.

"Are you trying to kill yourself?" she asked, but when he held her fast atop him, his big body pounding into her again and again, anxiety whirled into a pinwheel of rising sensation. Shuddering under the impact of his upward thrusts, Bethany felt completely out of control. Nothing mattered but that barely attainable goal, the soaring that would lead to a blinding, mind-jarring release.

And after, when they were limp and spent, and Bethany lay across him again, her heart pounding so fiercely she could feel her entire body vibrate, Trace gently pushed back the damp strands of hair from her forehead and smiled at her.

"I think you were right," he whispered.

Her head lifted. "What do you mean?"

"I think it's killed me . . ."

Bethany stared at him as his eyes closed and he gave a long shudder. Then his head rolled limply to one side.

"Trace! Oh, you idiot, you idiot, I told you it would!"

When Trace regained consciousness, he looked up at her with a sheepish smile. "I'm not normally a man prone to fainting," he said. "Maybe I underestimated your abilities, after all."

She glared at him. "Do you always have to be so

. . . so *male?* Can't you forget stubborn pride and ego and be satisfied with only proving yourself once? "

He had the grace to look slightly ashamed. "I guess I got carried away."

Bethany sniffed. "I guess you did."

"How long have I been asleep?" he asked, shifting to look out from under their rock. "And what's that funny smell?"

"Almost twenty-four hours. But you don't have any fever now, and you needed the rest." Her mouth tightened. "*I* needed the rest. Here. Eat this."

She pushed a pile of something shredded toward him. It was on a large leaf, and it looked brown and crispy. He eyed it dubiously. "What is it? And what's that funny smell?"

"Just eat it. It's good for you."

He looked at her suspiciously. "Aren't you going to eat any?"

"I've already eaten some." She made a motion of crossing her heart with one hand. "Honest. Now eat."

"I'm not sure eating this is wise when you're mad at me and I can't tell what the hell it is," Trace muttered, but he gingerly picked up some of the shreds and put them into his mouth. He chewed slowly, a frown creasing his brow. "It tastes vaguely familiar—what is it?"

"Eat it all, then I'll tell you." Bethany watched as he reluctantly ate it all. Her mouth curved into a triumphant smile, and she leaned forward. "Monkey."

Trace stared at her. "Monkey?"

She nodded smugly. "I shot it."

The beginning of a smile tugged at his mouth, and he cleared his throat. "I'm proud of you. Who skinned it?"

Bethany made a face. "That was the hard part. It took me awhile to figure out what to do, and then I

. . . well, I did the best I could. Nuts and berries aren't the best diet for a convalescing man."

Trace glanced at the tiny pile of shredded meat left on a large leaf close to the fire. "It must have been a very *small* monkey, judging by the amount of meat you got from it," he said, and she sighed.

"It was. I really didn't mean to kill it," she added in a rush of honesty.

Trace's brows lifted. "Monkeys usually die when you skin them and cook them," he mused, "unless, of course, you thought of another way to do it."

She flushed. "Actually, I was shooting at a bird, but the monkey fell out of the tree instead, and I guess the fall killed it. I didn't see any marks on it, and no bullet wounds, so when it didn't move and began to grow stiff . . ."

Trace made a faint sound in the back of his throat, and she finished in a rush, "And I didn't really skin it, either. I just, uh, roasted it whole, and cut off the meat when it was done."

"Ingenius," he muttered, and closed his eyes again. "That explains the funny smell. I feel sick."

A long silence stretched out, then Bethany said in a soft, pathetic voice, "I just couldn't bring myself to cut it up while it still looked so . . . so cute. Once it was cooked, it looked different."

"I imagine so," he said with his eyes still closed.

"Well," she snapped crossly, "I did the best I could!"

His eyes opened, and he smiled at her. "I know you did. And I really am proud of you." He shut his eyes again, and said, "Just don't feed me any more meat. I think nuts and berries are enough."

"I think you're right," she agreed with relief.

It took two more days for Trace to gather enough strength to move from under their rocky shelter.

Bethany spent that time with domestic chores like washing out their clothes. Trace felt a pang of regret when the washed garments were dry and they put them on again. He'd felt like Adam to her Eve, but had not dared risk another bout of lovemaking. There was no way he intended to admit to any weakness, but he realized how much blood he'd lost, and how weak he was. He just didn't want her to know.

On the morning of their fifth day in hiding, he rose from his leafy pallet and stretched, wincing slightly at the puckering pain of his wound. Bethany looked up at him.

"Today?" she asked, and he nodded.

It didn't take much to get ready. They carried the few weapons they'd brought from the cave, and the small leather pouch with the few remaining matches and a handful of coca leaves. The dynamite was useless, but Trace brought along a couple of sticks anyway.

"Never can tell when even damp sticks might come in handy," he drawled.

They left the overhang and trudged through the jungle. The sky was fairly clear. No rain pounded down to make them miserable, but the humidity was fierce. Swarms of insects buzzed in front of their faces, irritating them.

Bethany felt an intense wave of relief when they left the overpowering dankness and humidity of the jungle and were out in the open again. They finally paused to rest at the top of a steep slope.

Panting a little from her exertions, Bethany slid Trace a close glance. He was breathing hard, and his face was a little paler than usual.

"How do you feel?" she asked, and was startled by his quick, dark frown.

"I feel fine. I'm not dying, just not as ready to

climb mountains as usual."

"Oh." She paused uncertainly. She hadn't thought he might be sensitive about his weakness. The prickly male ego again. "Well, I'm tired. Do you mind if we rest a little while before we go on?"

"If it isn't too long," he agreed. He rested his hands on his knees and gazed out over the sloping mountain and the valley below. The Urubamba or Apurimac River should be somewhere. He didn't see it, just dry gorges and high mountain peaks wreathed in clouds.

A condor lazily rode a wind current, its wing span stretching to almost twelve feet. Though he knew that the gigantic birds were not normally aggressive, they certainly looked fierce, with curved beaks and sharp talons, and with it examining him at close range, he felt suddenly uneasy. Then the bird shifted direction, and soared away on another wind current, as graceful as a dancer. Trace watched it with growing envy.

Finally he stirred. "Ready?" he asked Bethany, and saw with appreciation the smooth roll of her hips as she rose from the rock, and the steadiness of her stride. She wasn't tired. She just didn't want him to know she knew *he* was. A faint, rueful smile curved his mouth. Neither of them was fooling the other for a moment. But he didn't have any intention of exposing her small fiction. It probably made her feel good to think she was fooling him. And it made him feel good to know she cared enough to try.

"Ready," she said, then added, "but I'm still tired."

"Yeah. We'll stop again soon."

Small rocks skittered from beneath their feet, bouncing erratically down the mountainside as they stepped carefully around large boulders and rocks. The wind blew around them with increasing chill, and as they walked on, it began to snow, tiny flakes that fell irregularly.

"Snow?" Bethany said incredulously. "We were just in incredible heat, and now . . ."

"It snows at these heights. We've come from a vally out onto some slopes, down, and then back up again." Trace shrugged. "Another few thousand feet, and the weather will be different."

He was right. When they reached the next valley, the sun beat down relentlessly. Bethany's blouse was drenched again, not with rain or snow, but perspiration. And she was worried about Trace. He kept on, stoically, refusing to admit to weakness or pain, but she knew his wound bothered him. She saw his occasional flinch, the surreptitious touch of his hand to his shoulder. She also knew better than to mention it.

"Where are we?" she asked him when they stopped to rest again. "Are we close to the river?"

Trace hesitated. He didn't want to tell her that he'd lost his bearings. He didn't see anything familiar, not a single landmark. Hell, he couldn't even find the Urubamba River, and it and its tributaries ran through most of the central length of Peru!

"Not yet," he said finally.

Nodding, Bethany drew one leg up, resting the sole of her boot on the rock where she was perched. It was a most unladylike posture, but she felt strangely free of any sort of convention. Why shouldn't she? She wore trousers like a man, and that hadn't made her feel any less a woman. She'd traveled through dangerous mountain reaches and steaming valleys, waged warfare, and even scavenged the jungle for food, and she didn't feel any less a woman. Of course, such radical thinking would shock the staid matrons of San Diego but that was too bad. She didn't think she would ever live her life in someone else's shadow again.

Her gaze drifted to Trace. Not even his. If he

should decide that he wanted her—and she hoped fervently that he did—she would not do as she once might have done. No, she would demand her rights as a person, as a helpmate, not a poor, pitiful creature without even the right to vote on her own future. She admired the toughness in Trace, his quiet strength. She would insist that he respect it in her.

"Let's go," Trace said a short time later, and they rose from their resting places to walk in comfortable companionship down the mountain.

Chapter Twenty-nine

"What is it?" Bethany whispered, her body tense with anxiety. Another rustling sounded in the dense underbrush, and Trace shook his head.

"I'm not sure. Maybe a big cat. Or a tapir."

She felt a chill. "What's a tapir?"

Trace thought a moment, peering through the leafy veil that hid them from sight. "Kinda like a short elephant with an abbreviated trunk. About the size of a large goat, I guess, only fat."

"Is it dangerous?"

"Just to plant life."

Squinting, Trace felt the hair on the back of his neck begin to prickle. *Oh, damn, not again!* he thought with a groan. His premonitions were too far in advance, leaving him on edge for days before finally proving true.

"Come on," he said to Bethany, rising from behind the thick plants and pulling her with him. "We need to move on."

She followed obediently, her nerves too shredded to ask any questions. Besides, she wasn't certain she wanted to know the answers.

"I see the river below," Trace told her when they paused atop a crest. He pointed, and she looked to see the tiny silver ribbon winding its way through rocky gorges. A high waterfall dropped from a shelf of rock and fell a thousand feet into the river, and Bethany was so impressed by the view, she didn't hear the note of relief in his voice.

"The Urubamba?"

He nodded. "Yeah. Once we make our way down, it's not far to Cuzco. And we're sure to pass some huts or villages before then."

Her gaze swung to his face. His mouth was thinned into a taut line, and she wondered if his wound was bothering him still. He'd toasted and chewed some of the coca leaves the day before, explaining to her that it was only to ease his discomfort. That had alerted her to the fact that he was not healing quickly, and even when he spit out the leaves after a short time, she was uneasy. It would do her no good to ask. She knew that.

"Maybe we can get a doctor to look at your wound once we get to a village," she said casually, and added when he looked at her, "just to make certain it's healing properly. I wouldn't want to have crippled you with my butchery."

A faint smile crooked his mouth. "Yeah. Maybe you're right. I might end up like that monkey you fed me."

"You might," she agreed with a wide smile. "I wouldn't leave anything to chance."

"Not where you're concerned, Bethany Brasfield!"

No villages came into view any time soon. And it began to rain again, a steady, ceaseless rain that kept up even as they traversed the descending trail. The zig-zagging path was already treacherous, and the rain made it more so. Gray wisps of cloud wreathed the mountain, and they couldn't see down into the steep gorge below.

But when they finally reached the bottom of the path, they were back in a hot, tropical jungle. Steam wafted up from the valley floor, looking almost like fog, and they had to inch their way forward because of a trail so narrow it would not have accommodated a small animal easily. Trace led her over jagged rocks, and around the slick faces of cliffs, muttering curses under his breath, praying his strength would hold out.

It was when they entered a dense jungle thicket, that his instincts surfaced again.

"Stop here," he murmured to Bethany, putting out a hand. She halted immediately. Birds screeched loudly, then it grew ominously quiet.

Bethany's nerves crawled. She could almost hear her hair grow, and the blood in her ears sounded as loud as thunder.

"Campa Indians," Trace said a few moments later, and pointed to a marking on a tree.

"Hostile?" she whispered, and he nodded.

"Very. Poison arrows; very aggressive in defending their territory. Be careful, and stay close by me."

It was an unnecessary warning. She had no intention of leaving his side for a moment. Leeches could get no closer than she intended to stay. They walked silently, their steps sounding too loud in the unusual stillness.

The *scree scree* of birds was distant, not close by, and Trace wondered if the Campas were watching them. They could be, and waiting to decide if these intruders were suitable for killing.

His gaze flicked to the river nearby. If they could get to the river, cross it without being seen, maybe they could escape. It was certainly worth a try.

"This way," he murmured a few moments later, and nudged her toward the steep decline of the river.

Bethany shuddered. Not another bridge crossing! Dear God, but she had come to dread them so since being in this wretched country of extremes!

As they stepped from the dense protection of the trees and ferns and onto an open trail, a shower of arrows rained down from apparently nowhere. Bethany screamed, and Trace grabbed her by the hand and began running, half dragging her when she stumbled.

Bethany looked back and gasped with terror. Naked brown men were running after them, faces contorted with triumph and hate, some fitting arrows to bows as they ran. The jungle seemed to be alive with them, scores, and they were gaining on the two white trespassers. . . .

"Trace!" she screamed, but he didn't pause to look. He knew well enough what he'd see. He had no hope of shooting his way out. There were too many of them. Their only option was flight.

More arrows fell, thankfully missing, and strange, high shouts filled the air.

"Run!" Trace snapped when Bethany fell, jerking her arm from his grasp. He stopped to pick her up and give her a rough shove forward. "Those arrows have poison on them, and all it would take is one . . ."

He didn't finish the sentence. He didn't have to. She stumbled forward again, side aching with her efforts, her breath coming in heaving gasps. Her legs felt strangely boneless, and her stomach throbbed and her throat was dry. She was half sobbing, and her legs began to grow heavier and heavier as she forced herself on.

Down the rocky trail, half-sliding in loose rock and dirt, falling in clumps of spiky brush, getting up to go on, she pushed forward, vaguely aware of Trace just ahead of her, his hand reaching back to urge her with him time and again.

Finally they reached the edge of the steep river gorge, and this time, instead of a fragile, swaying bridge, waited a stone span that looked remarkably sturdy.

"Thank God!" she gasped out, relief flooding her. "A decent bridge!"

"Too bad," Trace muttered as he pulled her forward with him.

"What do you mean?"

"If we can get across easily, princess, so can *they.*" A jerk of his head indicated the naked, pursuing savages, with bows and arrows and spears.

That hadn't occurred to her. "What are we going . . ."

"No time to talk. Just run."

Bethany didn't look down, but skimmed across the bridge with a speed she didn't know she could muster. When they reached the other side, Trace gave her a rough shove up the small incline and told her to keep going.

"What are you going to do?" she screamed when he paused and knelt down by the broad stone bollards. "Trace!"

"Dammit, Bethany, don't stop to chat—get out of here!"

He was pulling the dynamite from his belt, scraping it against a rock with quick motions.

"But it's wet," Bethany protested. "You said it was useless. . . ."

Whirling, he glared at her. "I've got too damned much to worry about without you hanging over my back and nagging at me! Will you just get out of here? Run, head west. *Go!*"

Tears stung her eyes, but Bethany did as he told her. She stumbled along the trail with scalding eyes, hearing the shouts of the pursuing savages grow closer and closer. They were almost at the bridge now, and would swarm over it and kill her and Trace. Trace. Why didn't he run? He'd have a chance, maybe, if he would.

But Trace was busily placing the three sticks of dynamite in a wedge of stone near the carved bollards. One stick would have been enough to incapacitate the bridge, but he wasn't at all certain that the dynamite would work, anyway. Well, he didn't have anything to lose by trying.

As the Campas started across the bridge, Trace lit the fuses. One of them immediately fizzled out, and he relit it with patiently steady hands. An arrow whizzed overhead, clattering harmlessly to the ground but close enough to make him swear softly. He couldn't get rattled. He had to light the fuses, and he had to get them short enough. He'd already sawed one end off on a sharp rock, but that was the stick that sputtered uselessly. He relit it a third time, acutely aware of the men halfway across the bridge. This time, it stayed lit, and he leaped backward, scrambling up into the rocks. If it didn't ignite, then maybe a bullet would do the trick.

An arrow whistled by his head, parting his hair but not even scratching his scalp, and Trace pulled his pistol. Might as well try to pick off as many as he could before the ammunition ran out and the savages got across the bridge. If the dynamite was too damp to explode, then maybe they'd be satisfied with just killing him. Maybe they'd forget about the fleeing girl. Aiming carefully, he squeezed the trigger.

A thundering explosion rent the air, flinging Trace backward in a hailstorm of rocks and debris. For a split second he wondered what had happened, then knew that the dynamite must have ignited. Maybe he shouldn't have used it all. . . .

Black shadows swirled around him, and he slowly realized that he'd been hurt. He could feel no pain, but a crushing weight felt as if it perched on his chest. Something warm trickled down the side of his face, and he could feel a warm dampness spreading beneath him.

A groan that he dimly recognized as his own whispered into the air. Men usually lost control of their bladders when they died. That must mean he was dead. Or dying. God, he hoped Bethany made it to safety. They'd been close, so close, maybe someone in a remote *poste* or village would find her and help her . . . Bethany, with the light brown hair and soft violet eyes . . . he loved her. It hit him with more force than the dynamite had done. He loved her, and he'd never told her so. Now it was too late.

Wings of darkness brushed over him, then briefly lifted again, and he saw her anxious face, the perfect pale oval peering down at him, her voice sobbing.

"Trace, oh, Trace—! You're hurt . . . blood everywhere . . . I have to get you out of here!"

Annoyed because she was still there when he'd told her to run, Trace rasped, "Don't you *ever* listen to me?" then surrendered to the comforting shadows.

Sobbing, Bethany ran her hands over his body, shuddering at the blood on his face, chest, and in a pool beneath him. He'd lost so much blood, so much, and he would die out here without swift medical attention. This wasn't a bullet in the shoulder. She couldn't help him now. He needed much more help than she could give him. . . .

Tilting back her head, she gave an anguished cry that seemed to echo through the river gorge and back, repeating over and over to haunt her. Then she wiped the tears from her face on the hem of her ragged blouse, and began to lift Trace. She would carry him, if need be, but she would not sit idly by and watch him die without at least trying.

It was a nightmare of an ordeal. Bethany could barely lift Trace. He was a big man, and his inert frame was even heavier when he was unconscious. Still, she was determined. She fashioned a crude litter from hastily woven tree branches and managed to drag him a short distance before it came apart. Patiently, desperately, she rewove the broken branches, tearing strips of her shirt to tie them together, then dragged him some more before she had to repeat the process.

At times, she broke down and sobbed at the thin trail of blood they were leaving behind. He'd be dead before too much longer. No one could live after losing that much blood and suffering the injuries he must have suffered. He still hadn't woken, but he was breathing. At least he was alive, and as long as he was alive, she would keep going.

But it was hard. At one point, Bethany broke down and began sobbing exhaustedly. Trace was going to die; she knew it, and there was nothing she could do to save him. Burying her face in the cup of her palms, she sobbed until her shoulders shook painfully, until her throat was dry and her stomach was heaving. She cried until there were no tears left, until she was spent and exhausted and left with no option but to go on.

Gritting her teeth, Bethany heaved herself up from the ground and began pulling Trace behind her again, her feet slipping on the steep mountain trail, but her dry eyes glittering with grim determination.

That was how Bentworth found her.

They took her by surprise. She rounded a bend, carefully keeping Trace's litter against the inside wall, and saw a line of men approaching. Her heart thudded painfully in her chest, and she thought for a moment that it was the savages again before she recognized the man striding purposefully in front.

"Spencer," she whispered in a sort of croak. "Spencer Bentworth!" Tears flowed freely from eyes she'd thought devoid of any more, and she stood still until he reached her.

"My, my, I *thought* perhaps you had been the cause of that noisy explosion we heard, m'dear," Bentworth said in a light voice. His blue gaze flicked to Trace lying still and pale on the litter. "Looks like you've had a spot of trouble."

"Just a spot." She indicated Trace with a wave of her hand. "He's lost a great deal of blood. Did you by any chance bring a doctor with you?"

"Not by chance, m'dear—by design. I'm familiar with Taylor's work, and knew *some*one would need a physician when we—are you unwell, m'dear?" he ended with a frown, but Bethany didn't hear the last few words.

Silently, she slipped into an unconscious heap on the mountain path before he could catch her, her body dropping beside Trace. Bentworth shook his head.

"Bloody impolite of her to fall asleep in the middle of a conversation," he said with a wry smile, and motioned for one of the bearers to join him. "Get the doctor, my lad. I think he's going to be kept busy for a little while."

While he waited for the physician to complete his examination of the two unconscious patients, Spencer Bentworth lit his carved pipe and rearranged his jaunty hat atop his graying head. Deuced good fortune to find them. If not for the explosion reverberating through the mountains, he might have gone in another direction entirely. His gaze flicked to Bethany.

Her lovely oval face was serene in slumber, her long lashes hiding her eyes. She'd endured a great deal. He'd heard the story from the two bearers who had managed to escape Bertolli; the simple *mestizos* had made their way back to Cuzco and the authorities, and he had been informed of what had happened.

The past two weeks had been spent searching for them in the trackless jungle, a hopeless task at best. Now, by a miracle, he'd found them. And it looked as if one of them would live, anyway. His brow furrowed.

Trace Taylor had lived through a lot worse, but he'd lost a lot of blood, and there was the matter of a festering bullet wound in his shoulder. Bentworth wondered if he'd pull through. He hoped so—for Bethany's sake. It would be too cruel if she lost him, too.

"I think he's going to make it," the physician said, and drew the clean sheet back up over Trace's frame. "A little worse for wear, perhaps, but alive."

Bethany sagged with relief. They were back in Cuzco after a harrowing journey down from the mountains, and staying in a wing of the house Spencer Bentworth had rented. She flashed Bentworth a look of gratitude, and he smiled.

"Don't give me any credit for his survival, m'dear," he said. "His strong constitution saved him. And stubbornness. And probably your efforts, too. He'd not have lived if you hadn't dragged him so far."

"Almost killing him in the process," she murmured with another glance at Trace's thin face. He'd been unconscious for days, tossing and turning, muttering in his fevered state. "That litter was abominable."

Bentworth shrugged. "I imagine the dynamite didn't do him a lot of good, either. Whatever possessed him to use so much, I wonder?"

"It had gotten wet. We weren't sure it was any good." She smiled slightly. "It looks like it was."

"I should say so," Bentworth remarked dryly. He studied Bethany for a long moment, the pristine line of her profile and the shadow of her lashes winging across one cheek. She was much more composed than when he'd first met her; the hardships she'd endured had strengthened her instead of destroyed her. Upon first seeing her again in Lima, he had thought she would never endure. Yet she had; she had not just endured, she had *triumphed*. What a wonderful epitaph that would make for her adventure, Bentworth thought with a sigh.

He motioned for Bethany to join him, and they left the room where Trace was sleeping.

"What are your plans now, m'dear?" he asked, and watched her ivory skin suffuse with a faint shade of pink.

"I . . . I don't quite know," Bethany admitted after

a few moments. "I suppose I'll go back to California eventually."

"Alone?"

His soft question jerked her head up, and Bethany's wide eyes met his for a brief moment. Then she looked away, turning to walk to the window and gaze out at the snowcapped peaks ringing the city.

"That's quite possible," she said after a moment. "But I think you know that better than I do."

Bentworth joined her by the window. "Perhaps I do. It might help if you were to understand a few things, however. If you're already aware of these things, feel free to ask me to stop. Do you mind?"

Bethany turned to look at him, her arms crossing over her chest and her palms cupping her elbows. "No, I think I need to hear what you may say."

A faint smile curled his lips, and Bentworth nodded. "I agree. You see, ten years ago, Trace Taylor and I met at the opposite ends of rifles. It was not, as you may guess, a very friendly introduction. He and his father had just robbed a bank and gotten away with quite a bit of money. As an employee of the Pinkerton Detective Agency, I had been assigned the task of asking him to cease and desist from such activities. Naturally, I met with resistance."

She smiled. "Naturally."

"Actually," Bentworth continued, his gaze resting on her face, "it was Ted Taylor who resisted most. We had been led a merry chase through the hot buttes of Arizona and to the most fascinating spot I had ever seen. Aztec ruins, they were, which sparked my interest in archaeology. But I digress—when I and my posse caught up with Taylor and his gang, there were only four of them left. The others had been shot or captured by then. So there we were, shooting at each other from behind rocks, waiting to see who had the most ammunition.

"It might have ended much differently if not for the Apaches. They attacked, and myself and my posse were caught in a cross fire. Trace Taylor was responsible for getting us all out of there and away from the Apaches, but in so doing his friend was killed. The man's name was Scanlon, and Brody and Reagan—bounty hunters at the time—abandoned him to the Apaches. There were so many of them, and there was so little we could do." His mouth twisted with regret. "Unfortunately, Trace did not see it the same way. He would have risked all to save Scanlon, see. And I had my hands full with that murderous Ted Taylor, trying to keep him from getting away." Bentworth shrugged. "Well, as you may guess, when I took Ted Taylor back to stand trial, I had to make a decision about Trace."

There was a long moment of silence, then Bethany asked in a soft voice, "Did he escape?"

"In a way." Bentworth shook his head. "I was sworn to carry out justice, but I felt compelled to repay Trace for rescuing us when he could have just left us to the Apache. I deliberately allowed him to run, and—as I suggested he might with his father in jail—he left the territories and bank robbing behind. I've always prided myself on being a fairly good judge of character in a man, though I am fooled on occasion, and I respected Trace. That did not mean that I would not shoot him if he turned back to robbing banks, however. For a while, I didn't hear anything about him, and assumed he'd settled down somewhere." A rueful smile curved his mouth. "Then I left the Pinkerton Agency and came to Peru to find ruins and riches, and here he was! The only white guide willing to look for them. I hired him, and as you already know, that first expedition failed badly. Not his fault, I know now, but disastrous, at any rate."

"Bertolli?"

Bentworth nodded. "Obviously, the wily Italian had been robbing ruins for years, selling most of the artifacts for his own profit, and showing just enough to the Peruvian government to keep them happy. And keep certain officials well-paid. I feel like ten different kinds of a bloody fool for not figuring it out sooner, but one can't be perfect, I suppose."

"So what happens to Trace now? Or when he gets well? Can he go back to the United States?" Bethany waited tensely for his answer.

"I imagine, in light of recent developments, that there will be no problem," Bentworth said with an enigmatic smile that made Bethany's eyes narrow. "It will be entirely up to him. You must understand, however, that he may still be too bitter to return. After all, his life of crime was not really his choice, but forced upon him by his father."

"He could have stopped at any time," Bethany began, then halted. She realized how difficult it would have been for Trace. Hadn't it been almost impossible for her to do what she wanted to do in life, instead of what her father had wanted her to do?

"He must be allowed to make his own choices, m'dear," Bentworth said softly. "Just provide him with the right reasons."

She looked at Bentworth, and her mouth was set in a resolute line. "I intend to do my best."

Chapter Thirty

Trace was irritable. His shoulder hurt. His back hurt where a huge chunk of flying rock had lacerated it, and one of his ribs had been broken, and it hurt the most. The fool doctor insisted that nothing could be done for a broken rib but binding and bedrest, and Trace hated the inactivity he was forced to endure.

Even Bethany couldn't cheer him lately. He wanted to do more than look at her, but his body throbbed with protest if he so much as lifted an arm to touch her. He'd been told how she'd dragged him down the mountainside on a litter of tree branches, and he wanted to tell her how proud he was of her, but the words stuck in his throat.

The sharp memory of his discovery that he loved her kept him from saying much of anything. It wouldn't be fair to her to love her. She'd never want to stay in Peru, and he couldn't go back to the United States. Maybe not ever. A helpless rage consumed him when he thought about it, and he steered his mind from that direction.

"What are you reading?" he asked, not realizing how growling his tone was. Bethany looked up in surprise.

"You're awake," she stated calmly, and shut her

book. "Blackstone's Treatises."

He blinked. "What?"

"The book I'm reading. Blackstone's Treatises. It's a book about law. Quite interesting."

Trace shifted, and the muscles on his bare chest flexed smoothly. He was totally nude beneath the sheets except for his bandages, and he kept the covering around his waist. "If you say so. It sounds pretty dull to me."

Laughing, Bethany rose from her chair by the window and went to his bedside. He looked much too big for the narrow bed, and much too restless to be lying there.

"The doctor said that you may be able to get up soon. If you don't toss and turn too much and reopen your stitches." She put a cool hand on his brow, and smiled when he glared at her. "I've heard that a complaining patient is usually well on their way to recovery," she observed, "which means that you should be well by tomorrow."

Trace grunted irritably. "I hate lying in bed. And I hate the food you've been shoving down my throat. And come to think of it, I don't much like the doctor, either."

Bethany's lips twitched with amusement. "Why is it that the biggest, most fierce man becomes a petulant child when faced with convalescence?" she wondered aloud, and saw his mouth tighten. "If a jaguar ate your arm off clean to the elbow, you wouldn't do more than offer a protest or two, but just put you flat on your back in a bed, and you'd think the world was ending."

His hand flashed out to grab her by the wrist. "I'll stop complaining if you'll get in the bed with me," he said with a tempting smile. He patted the sheets invitingly, and she disengaged her wrist from his grip.

"Remember the last time you made that offer?"

Trace shrugged, and winced against the pain that motion caused him. "It'd be worth it. At least this time, we're in a safe place. And we don't have to walk a hundred miles to get back to civilization."

"Is that supposed to convince me to fall into bed with you?" she asked. "Sorry. You'll have to do better. I have no intentions of being the cause of your relapse. Doctor Mendoza would be most upset."

Trace growled something uncomplimentary about Doctor Mendoza, then scraped his hand across his beard-stubbled jaw. "Then if you're not going to get into bed with me, at least find someone who can give me a shave."

"I believe I can manage that," Bethany said, and went to the washstand in the corner. She came back with a razor and soap, some towels and a bowl of water. "Do you like your towels heated?"

He eyed her narrowly. "I like my throat uncut. Isn't there a barber around?"

"You insult me. I used to shave Papa all the time, and I never cut him. Too badly," she added with a mischievous smile. "I'll go heat the towels for you."

When she returned, she leaned over him with an efficient manner and carefully placed hot towels over his face to soften his beard. After they cooled, she removed them and began to lather his cheeks and jaw with a stiff bristle brush and soap. Trace's dubious gaze gradually altered to one of admiration. He watched her face, the expression of intense concentration and the way she held her tongue between her teeth as she worked. Just the tip showed, small and pink and inviting, and he closed his eyes. He didn't need to be thinking along those lines, he reminded himself. Not seriously. Not now.

But when he opened his eyes again, Bethany was leaning over him with the razor in her hand, bringing it down in clean, smooth swipes. His gaze was level with her breasts straining against the polished cotton of her pale blue gown, and he couldn't help his immediate physical reaction. If he looked closely, he could see the darker outline of her nipples through the thin material, the small buds that tipped the peak of her breasts with sweet perfection.

Beads of sweat popped out on his forehead as he recalled the honeyed texture of her skin, the luscious taste of those ivory and pink marvels, and Trace clenched his hands into fists. This promised to be the worst shave he'd ever gotten.

By the time Bethany finished shaving the beard from his face and stepped back to admire her handiwork, the evidence of Trace's arousal was lifting the sheets. He met her startled gaze evenly.

"A man can't help some things," he said. "Do you expect an apology?"

She shook her head mutely, and her hands trembled as she quickly gathered the shaving things and took them away. She wanted him so badly it made her ache, yet she knew it was too soon. If only he'd get well, if only he'd indicate what he wanted from her—besides *that*. That was only his body's desires, not the desires of the heart, of the soul. She had to have more than that, and even if she never saw him again, she wouldn't settle for less.

Once upon a time, she had thought she could settle for less, and Stephen Averill had shattered her life. Never again, not even if she lost Trace, would she take less than all from a man.

"So," she managed to say calmly when she'd put

away the shaving things and come back to his bedside, "do you think you're capable of rising? To *walk,* I mean," she added with a hot flush when he smiled mockingly and slanted a wicked glance at his bedsheets.

"You're a sweet temptation, princess," he said with a sigh, and nodded. "Yeah. Send Santusa in for our daily stroll along the bedroom walls."

Bethany fled gratefully. She wished that Trace would say something to let her know where they stood. As much as she hated it, she would be bold enough to ask him, if he didn't speak soon. A woman could only stand so much suspense before breaking!

Tightly, struggling to retain her composure, Bethany said, "So, that's what you want."

Trace shook his head, his dark brows lowering over his eyes. "No. Not what I want. What has to be."

She couldn't keep the bitterness from showing. "I never thought you'd take the coward's way out, Trace Taylor!"

A small muscle leaped in his jaw, but Trace didn't allow any other reaction to show on his face. "I'm sorry you feel that way."

Whirling to face him, Bethany said in a gasping, tortured voice, *"Sorry!* That's too human an emotion for you to claim now!" In spite of her resolve, hot tears welled in her eyes, and she dashed them away with the back of her hand. Her throat was aching horribly, and she wanted to run from the room and not look back. Well, she'd made her choice and so had he.

All or nothing, she'd told herself. Now she knew that nothing was her future as far as Trace was concerned. He did not intend to leave Peru, and he did not ask her to stay with him. He'd not mentioned love, or even caring, and he stood as still as a stone watching her weep, no emotion showing on his handsome face.

Gathering her composure and dignity with a supreme effort, Bethany turned back to him and stuck out her hand. "Well, I must say that it's been a memorable experience, Trace. I won't forget you."

Reaction finally showed on his features, and he looked faintly surprised, then amused as he took her small hand in his large one. "I hope not," he said in the husky drawl that made her heart ache. "I know I'll never forget you, Bethany Brasfield."

She clung to those words in the days that followed, holding them as a talisman against the pain of leaving. A small hope that he might change his mind faded when she boarded a steamer in Callao and left the coast of Peru behind. He had not changed his mind, nor had he accompanied her back to Lima. Spencer Bentworth had done so, gallantly claiming he had been on his way to the harbor city to meet a boat.

"I shall be most happy to be your escort, m'dear," he'd said; and had waved a farewell to her from the docks.

Turning her face to the salty wind pressing against it, Bethany tried not to think of Trace. There was a great deal to be done upon her return to San Diego. Bentworth had secured a grant in her father's name, guaranteeing funds to explore archaeological ruins. The Horatio T. Brasfield grant would finance future explorations. Though Brasfield would not have his name recorded as having discovered the legendary city of Vilcapampa, he would be written in the journals as having succeeded in a smaller way.

Journals . . . Bethany glanced down at the leather-bound journal in her hands. Bentworth had given it to her. Though too ruined by rain to be of much use as proof that Horatio Brasfield had rediscovered Vilcapampa, it was precious to Bethany, as Bentworth had known it would be.

A man had brought it in from the ruins, he'd said with rising excitement, and could possibly lead them back. They would find the city again in spite of the earthquakes that had destroyed all signs of the roads leading to it. And he would bring back the treasure Bertolli had not been able to hide . . .

Bethany didn't want to hear any more about gold or silver, or statues or urns, or Sweat of the Sun or Tears of the Moon. She wanted to go home. She wanted to live a quiet life alone. She fully intended to go back to the university at San Diego and take classes in art. This time, she would allow nothing or no one to stop her dream.

But as she stood determinedly at the rail of the steamer chugging up the South American coastline, Bethany could not help the sweeping feeling of loneliness that engulfed her. Was half a loaf better than none? she thought with a lingering shudder. Should she have pleaded with Trace to allow her to stay?

White-tipped waves slapped against the sides of the steamer, and Bethany knew that she could never have been happy on the fringes of his life. It would have destroyed them both in the end. There had to be complete commitment between them.

And now she had her art, had busy plans for her future that would keep her from thinking of Trace Taylor . . .

Chapter Thirty-one

San Diego, California, October, 1890

Another October. Had it been only a year before, that she had stood here on the veranda and stared out over the rolling California hills, dreaming about the excitement and adventure of a trip to Peru? It seemed a lifetime ago.

Bethany paced restlessly across the stone tiles. She had been home a month; not as she had been the last time, a blank, emotionless puppet still shocked from her father's death. This time, she was filled with determination. She had already enrolled in art classes at the university, and as a concession to her unusual circumstances, the professor had allowed her to begin immediately instead of waiting for the next semester.

A faint smile curved her mouth. He'd been delighted to see her back again, saying that she could add so much to the course. She had shown him a portfolio of sketches she had done on the voyage back from Peru, and he'd been pleased and amazed.

"You make these things come alive with your chalks, Miss Brasfield!" he told her, shaking his head. "I feel as if I could almost touch these ancient stone walls and feel the moss and vines covering them . . .

and this one—this man looks so dangerous, I feel a chill!"

Bethany had forgotten about her sketches of Trace. She had yielded to despair late one night on the moonlit deck and drawn him as she remembered him most, with a mocking smile and glittering lights in his eyes. She very quietly removed that sketch from her portfolio after the professor had remarked upon it.

There was no sense in yearning for the unattainable. It had never worked for her before.

Leaning her palms against the wide stone wall around the veranda, Bethany watched the warm California winds blow across the hills. Bright splashes of color dotted the hills with alluring beauty, and she decided to take her paints and canvas out to try and capture the elusive beauty of the changing foliage the next day.

As night fell slowly over the hills and she could see the lights sprinkling below, Bethany remained on the veranda. Her only retainer, a young Mexican girl, had already gone home for the day, leaving a meal in the kitchen and a lamp burning in the sitting room. She was all alone, and had never felt it so keenly.

A swollen moon rose in the sky, suspended in soft glow, shedding pale light on the veranda. The wind had grown cool, and her thin cotton gown was not warm enough. She shivered, and crossed her arms over her chest.

"Don't you *ever* dress for the climate?" came a deep, mocking drawl from behind her, and Bethany turned slowly.

Her heart lurched, and her breath caught in her throat—a tall shadow darkened the open door, silhouetted by the light from the house. It pushed away from the doorframe and approached her with the easy, graceful stride that she remembered so well—too well.

"I dress appropriately on occasion," she managed to say past the growing lump in her throat.

"Liar," he said softly, reaching her, his face only half-shadowed now by the light behind him. Dark eyes stared down into her face. "I can think of only one time that you dressed appropriately."

"And when was that?" She couldn't touch him, couldn't let him touch her. She'd be lost if she did . . .

"In the jungle, when you washed our clothes."

She frowned. "But we weren't wearing anythi—" Jerking to a halt, she flushed with the memory.

He laughed huskily. "Right, princess. And you were never dressed better in your life."

"Trace, I don't think this is wise," she said wretchedly as he reached out to pull her close. Bringing her hands up between them, she would not look up at his face, but kept her balled fists as a barrier between their bodies.

"Don't you?" He bent to kiss the top of her head, her forehead, the straight line of her nose.

"No."

"Why not?" Hot kisses drifted from her cheek to her ear and then below to her neck, making her shiver.

"Because . . ." She gulped in a steadying breath of air. "Because it will only start things all over again."

"Good." His mouth worried the scooped neck of her gown until it slid aside and he could taste the smooth texture of the skin covering her delicate collarbones. When his lips shifted to that erratically pulsing hollow, then nudged below within tasting distance of the valley between her breasts; Bethany shuddered and strained away from him.

"Trace!"

His mouth swooped upward to capture her lips then, taking her by surprise, his tongue flirting with hers in a breathtaking duel.

"I'm glad you haven't forgotten my name," he said several minutes later, holding her weak, trembling body so close to his she could feel the heat of his arousal. "I wasn't sure at first."

"What did you expect?" she muttered against his broad chest, damning her betraying body. This must be how good women went bad—they had a man to lead them. Only Trace wasn't just leading her, he was pulling her along at a swift pace.

Tilting back her head, she met his gaze at last. "The last time I saw you, you were not inclined to see *me*. If I remember correctly, there was some garbled speech about not wanting to end it, but you had to, and so forth."

Trace slid her a hangdog look. "Yeah. Well, I've been counting on your forgiving nature to forget that."

"I may be forgiving, but I am *not* stupid!" she snapped.

"Ah, princess, I've never thought for a moment that you were," he said softly. "I have been, but you've been a lot smarter than me."

Her eyes narrowed suspiciously. "What do you mean by that?"

He shrugged, and in the faint light spilling onto the veranda from the opened door, Bethany could see the shadows in his eyes. "Just that I shouldn't have let it matter to me about unfinished business. I should have been ready to damn everything and take the consequences, even if it meant having you for only a little while."

Pulling away from him, she walked to the lounge at

one side of the veranda and sat down abruptly.

"You're making my head ache, Trace," she said so plaintively that he crossed to her immediately. "What are you talking about?"

Taking her hands between his, he knelt down in front of her, his dark eyes fastening on her face. "Bethany, sweetheart mine—I didn't want to risk having you for just a little while, and I knew—or thought I knew—that I couldn't come back to the United States."

"And now that's changed?"

"Now that's changed. I'm here, and I intend to stay. I gave my business to Gil." He paused, then said in a rough voice, "Bentworth told me my father died not long ago. He was killed in another robbery."

Bethany gave a sympathetic murmur. "Trace, I'm sorry."

His mouth twisted. "Too bad I can't feel that way. He'd only been out of prison for a month."

"He was your father! In spite of what he did, don't you feel anything?"

"Yeah. Regret, I guess," he admitted after a long beat of silence. "It shouldn't have been that way. I used to try and—aw hell, that doesn't matter now. He's dead. He was gut shot and took a few days to die. During those days, when he knew he was dying, he wrote out a paper and asked that it be given to Bentworth. My father took full blame for all the robberies we did, and asked that I be pardoned. Of course, that's not really enough to matter to the justice system, but Bentworth seems to think that his influence *is*. He's promised to get me a job with the Pinkerton Agency and erase my dubious past if that's what I want."

"Is it?" She held her breath.

"I'm not sure I want to run around the country chasing after guys who are doing what I used to do, but there are other positions available. And it's honest work."

"I'm glad for you, Trace. I hope you're very happy now, and can make a new life for yourself."

His voice tightened. "That's what I intend to do. Look, Bethany, I'm not real good with these kind of words, but I've done a lot of thinking on the ship up here. And I know I made a mistake. I was willing to die for love, but not willing to live for love."

She swallowed hard. "And now?"

Grinning, he said huskily, "I've grown selfish. I want you even if it's only for ten minutes. I know you love me, and . . ."

She stiffened. "I've never told you that!"

He laughed. "Oh yes, you have." When she stared at him skeptically, he said, "When you had mountain sickness, and were generally too repulsive to be around, you told me you loved me. I didn't know what to say, especially as you thought you were dying, and you never mentioned it again, so I didn't either."

Closing her eyes, Bethany shook her head. "And you're going to take the word of a hallucinating woman?"

His warm fingers gripped her chin. "If you'll take the word of a stubborn man." Her eyes snapped open to stare at him. "Bethany Brasfield, I think I've wanted you ever since you fell over those boxes in the warehouse and told me to go to the devil when I laughed. I just didn't recognize it. I didn't know, see, and wasn't certain what the definition of love was."

"And now you think you know?" she whispered, her heart beginning to drum a rolling thunder.

"No." He kissed her gently. "Now, I *know* I know

what the definition of love is . . ."

She stared at him. It might be the closest she came to hearing it at all. Maybe he couldn't say it. Maybe it was one of those phrases that would not be heard from him. And she did love him, and maybe she should take what he could offer.

Surrendering at last, Bethany put her arms around his neck and kissed him back long and sweet.

"Trace?" she murmured when their lips parted and she could breathe again.

"Umm hmm?"

"Are you . . . are you completely healed now?"

Instead of answering, he put one arm beneath her legs and the other behind her back and lifted her from the lounge. Striding toward the door, he growled, "Which way is your bedroom?"

She pointed, and he stalked down the unlit hallway with the surefootedness of a cat. Kicking her bedroom door open wide, he crossed the room to her bed and lowered her to the mattress. It gave beneath her weight, and she felt it dip as he knelt beside her.

Bethany could see the moonlight streaming through the windows and highlighting his face, his features sharp with desire as he began undressing her. When their clothes lay in an indistinguishable tangle on the floor and they wore only the silvery light of the moon, Bethany took his face between her palms. She searched his handsome features for a clue, wondering if he just *wanted* her, or if he loved her. He still hadn't said. He'd come after her, and she knew he wanted to be with her, but she yearned to have it all.

As if sensing her slight withdrawal, Trace curbed his urgency, forcing himself to go slow.

He kissed her on the mouth, then her cheek, then seared a trail of kisses down to the throbbing peak of her breast, his tongue making wet circles around the taut nub. Bethany's fingers tangled in his dark hair and her back arched, and he shifted to lie across her, his body nudging insistently close.

When she opened for him, gladly, half sobbing with love and desire, he eased himself inside, slowly at first, then with a surging rhythm that swept them both along on fierce heights. The gripping convulsions of her body urged him closer and closer to release, but he held back until he felt her shivering approach, then met her in a long, shuddering embrace.

Holding him tightly, feeling his hard man's body cradled within hers, Bethany murmured, "I guess you're healed, all right."

Trace laughed, and lifted his dark head to stare down at her upturned face. "I love you, Bethany."

She grew still beneath him, and sudden tears welled in her eyes. He'd said it. He loved her. And he would stay; now, she knew it. Trace had come home, come home to her, and no matter what else happened in the world, they would have each other.

"I love you, too, Trace Taylor!"

Dear Readers:

I hope you've enjoyed Trace and Bethany's story. Peru seemed like a perfect setting for two such characters, and provided a great deal of diversity for their travels.

The lost city of Vilcapampa is real; it was the final refuge of Manco Inca in those dark days when the Spaniards came and conquered and destroyed a people surprisingly advanced for their time.

On July 24, 1911, Hiram Bingham, an American explorer, discovered the lost city that has come to be known as Machu Picchu. The stone city towers over the Urubamba River valley about a hundred miles from Cuzco. Authorities argued for some time that Machu Picchu—so named for the mountain peak nearby—was the lost city of Vilcapampa, but it is now generally believed to have been a garrison for soldiers.

Hidden in the jungles and on high mountain peaks in Peru are more cities, some unfound mysteries, some already discovered and plundered by robbers—white man and Indian alike. Shrouded by clouds and forgotten by time, those cities of a conquered people remain a tantalizing goal for intrepid adventurers. . . .

If you enjoyed Trace and Bethany's story, please let me know. Write to me in care of Zebra Books, 475 Park Avenue South, New York, New York 10016.

Best wishes to all of you—

Virginia Brown

THE TIMELESS PASSION OF HISTORICAL ROMANCES

FOREVER AND BEYOND (3115, $4.95)
by Penelope Neri

Newly divorced and badly in need of a change, Kelly Michaels traveled to Arizona to forget her troubles and put her life in order again. But instead of letting go of her past, Kelly was haunted by visions of a raven-haired Indian warrior who drove her troubles away with long, lingering kisses and powerful embraces. Kelly knew this was no phantom, and he was calling her back to another time, to a place where they would find a chance to love again.

To the proud Commanche warrior White Wolf, it seemed that a hundred years had passed since the spirit of his wife had taken flight to another world. But now, the spirits had granted him the power to reclaim her from the world of tomorrow, and White Wolf vowed to hold her in his arms again, to bring her back to the place where their love would last forever.

TIGER ROSE (3116, $4.95)
by Sonya T. Pelton

Promised in wedlock to a British aristocrat, sheltered Daniella Rose Wingate accompanied the elegant stranger down the aisle, determined to forget the swashbuckling adventurer who had kissed her in the woodland grove and awakened her maidenly passions. The South Carolina beauty never imagined that underneath her bridegroom's wig and elegant clothing, Lord Steven Landaker was none other than her own piratical Sebastian—known as The Tiger! She vowed never to forgive the deception—until she found herself his captive on the high seas, lost in the passionate embrace of the golden-eyed captor and lover.

MONTANA MOONFIRE (3263, $4.95)
by Carol Finch

Chicago debutante had no choice: she had to marry the stuffy Hubert Carrington Frazier II, the mate her socially ambitious mother had chosen for her. Yet when the ceremony was about to begin, the suntanned, towering preacher swung her over his shoulder, dumped her in his wagon and headed West! She felt degraded by this ordeal, until the "preacher" silenced her protests with a scorching kiss.

Dru Sullivan owed his wealth and very life to his mining partner Caleb Flemming, so he could hardly refuse when the oldtimer asked him to rescue his citified daughter and bring her home to Montana. Dru dreaded having to cater to some prissy city miss—until he found himself completely alone with the violet-eyed beauty. One kiss convinced the rugged rancher not to deny Tori the wedding-night bliss that he was sure she would never forget!

Available wherever paperbacks are sold, or order direct from the Publisher. Send cover price plus 50¢ per copy for mailing and handling to Zebra Books, Dept. 3466, 475 Park Avenue South, New York, N.Y. 10016. Residents of New York, New Jersey and Pennsylvania must include sales tax. DO NOT SEND CASH.